Book 2 of the Cordell Dynasty

The Hondo Kid

SUNDOWNERS
a division of
Treble Heart Books
1284 Overlook Dr.
Sierra Vista, AZ 85635-5512

Published and Printed in the U.S.A.

ISBN: 1-932695-45-1

Other Books by Dusty Rhodes

Man Hunter

Shiloh

Jedidiah Boone

Death Rides a Pale Horse

Shooter

Vengeance is Mine

Longhorn: Book I (series)

Longhorn
Book II

The Hondo Kid

by

Dusty Rhodes

Sundowners
A
Division of

Treble Heart Books

PART I

CHAPTER I

The Making of a Man

That first shovelful of dirt falling into the shallow grave on top of his parents made him sick to his stomach.

He didn't even have a blanket to wrap them in. All he could do was lay them side by side on the stone cold ground at the bottom of the single shallow grave and cover their faces with his blood-soaked shirt.

Fourteen-year-old Cody Cordell stood beside the grave with the shovel in hand. He stared through tear-drenched eyes at the mutilated bodies of his ma and pa and felt as if his heart was being ripped from his chest.

But he had it to do.

Somewhere between the first shovelful and the last, Cody Cordell became a man, a man full of bitterness and hatred, a man convinced that life was unfair and that only the strong survive in this world, a man who had made up his mind that whatever it took, he would be a survivor.

When the heart-wrenching task was finished he sat down beside the fresh mound of dirt. He was exhausted. Not only physically, for he hadn't slept a wink since he'd discovered the bodies, but he felt completely drained, shattered, abandoned.

It happened two days before. He was off in the woods several miles from the house hunting turkey when he saw the smoke. The thick black plume billowed and climbed toward the blue sky. He knew something was wrong.

He dropped the gobbler and lit out as fast as his legs could carry him. He was too late. By the time he got to the house it was nothing but a roaring ball of flames.

He screamed at the top of his lungs for his ma and pa. The only answer he heard was the loud crackling of hungry flames as they boiled higher and higher. He ran as close as the heat would allow. He raced around the house, then back again, screaming frantically, searching for a way to get inside to save his parents. Then he saw his pa.

He was tied to the split rail fence of the empty corral. Arrows were buried deep into his chest. It looked like the killers had used him for target practice.

Where his pa's sandy hair should have been there was nothing but a bloody skull. His stomach laid cut open and his intestines stretched across the dusty yard.

Cody fell to his knees and emptied his stomach at the gory sight. Wave after wave of vomit racked his body until there was nothing left inside him.

He struggled to his feet and stumbled crazily to the watering trough. He ducked his head into the ash-covered water and held it there for a long time.

He found his ma lying on the other side of what was left of the barn, and wished he hadn't.

What he saw, no fourteen year old should ever see. He

couldn't bear to look. He stripped off his shirt and covered as much of his ma's naked body as he could.

After the burying was done Cody spent two whole days carving the letters into boards ripped from the side of the barn. He lashed them together with some wire and drove them into the ground at the head of the single grave.

He went back for the turkey he had killed and cooked it over an open fire and lived on that while he worked on the crosses.

Grief and barely controlled panic tore at his heart and boiled just below the surface of his mind, threatening to explode. He moved about in a dazed awareness, his mind a mass of tangled, confused thoughts. He was having trouble sorting things out, deciding what to do next.

He was tired, so tired. He curled into a fetal position beside the mound of fresh dirt and stared up at a pale blue sky for a long while. Finally, exhaustion took control of his body and he slept.

Cody awoke. It was coming day. He had slept the night away. He sat up and crossed his legs, leaned his elbows on his knees and stared off into eternity for a good long time.

His mind swirled in a jumbled maze of thoughts: he had no home, no family, no money, nothing. What would he do? Where would he go? How would he live? Who could he turn to for help? He was alone, the last one left of his family. His ma and pa were dead, most likely his big brother was dead, too, since they hadn't heard from him for over a year. These and a thousand other questions went unanswered in his young and confused mind.

Finally, he tried to blink reality into focus. He let his slow gaze survey his surroundings. The Indians took everything, and what they hadn't taken they destroyed. The two Cordell horses, two mules, and even Sadie, their milk cow was gone. They killed

Collie, Cody's dog. Cody buried him near Ma and Pa, since he was like part of the family and all.

All he had left were the clothes on his back, a pocketknife and his pa's double-barreled shotgun with four shells. It was ten miles to the Johnson place, their nearest neighbor, and another ten to the isolated Hondo Trading Post down on the Hondo River. In the other direction it was forty miles to San Antonio, the nearest town.

One thing for sure, he couldn't stay here. The Indians might come back. What good would four shotgun shells do against a pack of murdering savages? No, there was nothing or no one left for him here. He had to move on to somewhere, but where?

Deciding, he pushed to his feet. He would walk to the Johnson place. Mr. Johnson was a good man and would know what to do. Besides, he hadn't seen Sarah Johnson in a long while. A picture of her flashed into his mind and stayed there for a time.

Having made up his mind, Cody rummaged around what was left of the barn and found an empty fruit jar with a rusty lid. He washed it in the water trough and tied a length of wire around the neck so he could carry his makeshift canteen over his shoulder.

After he drew a fresh bucket of water from the dug well, he filled the fruit jar, drank its contents, and refilled it. It would be a long, hot walk through the desert country between their house and the Johnson place.

He stuffed what was left of the cooked turkey, which wasn't much, into a pocket of his bib overalls and retied one of his Brogan work shoes. He draped the wire holding his jar of water over a bare shoulder. He was shirtless, since he had used his shirt to cover his ma and pa's faces during the burying. Taking one more look around and deciding he hadn't forgotten anything, he picked up his shotgun and patted his right front pocket that contained his four shells.

He struck out.

Walking half the morning away he figured he was near halfway to the Johnson home. The March sun was blazing. It cooked into the sandy soil of the desert countryside and made life near unbearable for man or beast.

Gnarly mesquite bushes, thorny cactus, yucca plants and groves of stunted cedar clung to sandy terrain or the rock-strewn low hills that hugged both sides of the road.

Up ahead he saw a group of large vultures circling low beyond a line of hills. They floated on wide wings in an ever-descending spiral. Something was dead up ahead. As he drew closer he could see that desert scavengers feasting on something just off the road. He couldn't tell what it was because they completely covered their victim.

The huge birds would hop in, tear loose a bloody bit of flesh with their razor-sharp beaks, and retreat a safe distance to devour their meal.

Thirty yards away a second group huddled around something else. The ugly birds sat near their prey, waiting patiently. As Cody approached he saw some of the more aggressive scavengers hop close to the object of their attention, and then quickly retreat. Cody left the road and walked closer. Suddenly he was able to make out the object of their interest.

It was a man's head.

The chilling sight brought Cody to a standstill. As he looked closer he saw the head was still attached to a body. It twisted sharply each time one of the vultures got close. The man was *alive*.

Cody switched ends with his shotgun and ran among the vultures, swinging his weapon wildly, chasing them away from the helpless man. They opened their beaks wide, squawking at him before spreading their wings and lifting into the air.

Cody turned his attention to the man attached to the head that protruded from the sand. He dropped to his knees beside the man, a Mexican. His dark, sunburned face was heavily bearded. Sweat-caked sand mixed among his whiskers. His dry, cracked lips were badly swollen and oozing blood. But it was the man's eyes that captured Cody's attention. Both of his eyelids had been split. His dark, unseeing eyes stared off into space with a blank expression. The man was blind.

"Can you talk?" Cody asked.

The Mexican struggled to reply, but nothing came out. Cody quickly took his jar of water and unscrewed the rusty lid. He poured a few drops onto his fingers and gently wet the man's cracked lips. The Mexican opened his mouth, silently begging for more. Cody cupped a hand underneath the open mouth and poured a small trickle inside.

Replacing the lid, he set it aside and used his hands to begin scooping sand away from the man's throat. Although the sandy soil was mostly loose, small pebbles and hard clumps tore and ripped at his fingers. Cody's searching gaze of the surrounding area revealed nothing that would help, no broken limbs, no sticks, nothing.

Handful by handful he clawed deeper and deeper, scooping and raking the sandy soil away from the Mexican's body. Cody's fingertips were soon bloody and raw. Still he kept digging. It took a while.

Finally he was able to free first one arm, then another. The man was so weak he was unable to even lift his arms. Cody had to lift them from the hole. But he refused to give up. He kept digging.

The sun was unmerciful. From time to time Cody forced himself to stop long enough to sip the precious water from his jar. Each time he poured a little into the Mexican's mouth.

The jar was half empty by mid-afternoon when he finally got the hole deep enough to pull one leg free. In minutes the second leg was free. Now he faced the enormous task of pulling the man from the hole. He tugged and pulled. Sweat poured off him. Finally, with great effort that sapped his last ounce of energy, he dragged the man from his sandy grave.

Cody felt completely exhausted. He collapsed on his back beside the Mexican. For several minutes he lay there, breathing hard, his eyes closed, giving his body time to recover.

Pushing himself to a sitting position, he stared at the fellow he had rescued. An average size fellow for a Mexican, he wore typical Mexican peasant clothes, the kind Cody saw on the few trips to San Antonio he had made with his pa. Dried blood was mixed into his whiskered face. His eyelids had been slit. Cody had heard stories that Comanche often did that to their victims before they staked them naked in the sun or buried them alive with only their head above the sand.

Cody reached for his jar of water and felt concern when he saw only a small amount remaining. Still, he knew the Mexican needed it worse than he did. He unscrewed the lid and lifted the man's head. He slowly poured the remaining water into the Mexican's mouth, being careful not to spill even a single drop of the precious liquid.

When the last drop was gone the Mexican licked his dry lips with a swollen tongue and tried to mouth a word. Only a raspy mumble came out that Cody couldn't understand.

It dawned on him that both of them needed to find shade. He swung a searching gaze around. A nearby scrub cedar's welcoming shadow offered the best hope. It was some thirty yards away.

Pushing himself to his knees, he lifted the Mexican's arm and tried to pull him to a sitting position. It was no use; the man was too weak to sit up.

Cody climbed to his feet, took the man's wrists and tried to drag him along the ground. In Cody's weakened condition it was hard and slow work. Each time he tugged, the man moved only a few inches. It took a while, and when he finally had the Mexican lying in the shade under the cedar tree, Cody collapsed, completely drained of energy.

Something touched him awake. Cody jerked his eyes open. It was dark. He was shocked that he had been asleep. The desert air cooled off, once darkness set in. Cody shivered and cast a look at the Mexican. His mouth was moving. Cody leaned closer. A hoarse, raspy, whispered word reached his hearing.

"Wa...ter."

"I don't have any water left, we drank it all."

The man shook his head weakly.

"Wa...ter, east."

Cody wrinkled his forehead, not understanding what the man was trying to tell him.

"Are you saying you know where there is water?"

The Mexican bobbed his head up and down once.

"How far is it to the water?"

The man held out two fingers.

"Are you saying there's water two miles east?" Cody pressed.

Again the Mexican nodded.

"Okay," Cody said, threading the wire sling attached to his fruit jar canteen with an arm and pushing to his feet. "I'll be back as quick as I can."

Cody lifted his gaze to the sky, determined his position, and headed east. The moon was full and bright. Stars twinkled in a sea of dark gray sky. His thoughts returned to all the nights he had sat on the front porch with his ma and pa, gazing up at those same stars. How different things were then.

He hurried his steps, trotting a while and then slowing to a fast walk. *Reckon who the Mexican fellow is? Don't rightly know if he will live or not, but I've got to try my best to save him.*

Cody's throat was dry and parched. His tongue felt like sand. He couldn't even make spit. He knew if he didn't find water soon, both he and the Mexican were done for.

His steps led him down into a deep arroyo. Suddenly he saw a blackish-blue ribbon snaking through the desert. His heart leaped inside him. It was the river.

He broke into a jogging run. Reaching the river's edge, he dropped to his knees and plunged his head into the cool water. It felt wonderful. He lifted his head, shook it like his dog used to do, and then lowered his lips and drank his fill.

He rinsed the fruit jar and filled it, then screwed the lid on tight and pushed to his feet. Scrambling back up the low bank, he retraced his steps back to where he left the Mexican.

Cody held the jar for the man as he drank the life-saving liquid. When the man finally had enough, Cody replaced the lid. Having satisfied their thirst, they slept.

The morning sun woke Cody. He glanced quickly over at his Mexican friend. Movement told Cody the man was awake.

"How you feeling?"

"Better," the man replied, his voice sounding clearer and stronger. "We go."

"Go? Go where?" Cody inquired.

"My place, back to the river."

"Can you walk? I shore can't drag you that far."

"I walk," the man said, struggling to get to his feet.

Cody rose and helped him up. The man was obviously still very weak and staggered when he reached his feet. Cody wrapped the man's arm around his own shoulders. The first few steps were wobbly, but as they walked, he seemed to get stronger with each step. They took their time. The sun rose halfway to noon high when they reached the river. They both drank long from the refreshing water.

"This Hondo River," the blind Mexican said.

"Now which way?" Cody asked.

"Follow the river upstream."

With Cody leading the blind man, they complied. Traveling quickly got harder. Huge rocks rose from the riverbank and lifted into the sky. Cody and the man were forced to weave among the rocks to find a trail.

"Find a small stream that runs to the river between large rocks. Go up stream," the man told him.

Rounding a sharp bend in the river, they came upon a small stream running from between two giant rocks. The opening appeared only large enough for one man at a time to squeeze through. The opening became a passageway. They waded the knee-deep water upstream. They gained no more than thirty yards when Cody noticed an opening in the side of the cliff face. It was a cave.

The Mexican trailed his fingertips along the surface of the rock. His hand reached the opening.

"This my home," the Mexican said as he kneed onto the small bank fronting the entrance to his cave.

"Well, I'll be," Cody exclaimed, surprised at the cave.

Once inside, it became clear to Cody the Mexican was no recent arrival. Rocks were piled in a circle to form a fire pit in the center of the spacious cave. A large iron kettle hung from a metal tripod over the ashes of a long-dead fire. A blackened coffee pot sat on two flat rocks nearby. Several wooden crates were stacked along one wall. A wooden workbench sat fitted against the other wall. A bedroll lay not far from the fire pit. A pile of firewood lay stacked neatly near the back of the cave. Cody was impressed.

"All the comforts of home," he said, looking around.

"I'll build a fire and put on some coffee," Cody told his friend.

Cody went to the woodpile and returned with an armload of wood. In minutes he had a fire going. He took the coffee pot and went to the small stream in front of the cave, rinsed it out and filled it with water.

"Coffee is in the wooden crate near wall."

Cody worked his way through three of the crates before he found the coffee, but in the process he found several cans of beans, a slab of salt pork and a hunting knife. He dumped a handful of the dark coffee into the coffee pot and hung it over the fire. Finding a blackened frying pan, he sliced several pieces of salt pork into it and sat the pan over the fire.

He sat down beside the fire cross-legged and fixed his gaze on the flickering flames.

Life shore takes some twists and turns. Reckon it won't hurt to stay with this fellow a couple of days before I head on to the Johnson's. Don't know what's gonna happen to him after I leave, him being blind and all.

The coffee was boiling. Cody discovered two tin cups while searching for the coffee and poured them both a cup, handing one to the Mexican.

The man held his cup with both hands and blew away the steam. His eyes stared blankly at the flames for several minutes before he spoke. "I am called El Diablo ," he said softly. "In my language it means the devil. My papa was a gunsmith. I learned the trade from him. When I was small boy, banditos kill my mama and papa. I learned to use a pistol, become *pistolero*. Kill bad men that kill my mama and papa.

"For many years I became famous in my country as the fastest *pistolero* in all Mexico. I killed many men. *Federales* offer ten thousand pesos for my head. Many try to kill me. A bullet hit me in elbow, making my arm stiff. If I stay in Mexico they will kill me. So I come to your country two years ago. I find this cave. Safe here.

"Three days ago I take my donkey, go to the trading post. Comanche kill the donkey. Bury me in sand. Painted faced one cut my eyes with a knife. Leave me to die. I owe you my life."

Cody was amazed. The man was a gunfighter. Now he understood why he lived in the cave.

"Why are you in desert?" the Mexican asked.

Cody told his story. It took a while. When the telling was over he felt drained, sad. But for this man, he was alone now.

"Where do your friends live? The Johnson's?"

Cody explained their place was five miles northeast. For a long moment the man sat with his head lowered. A sad look swept over his face.

"Comanche killed your friends, *señor*. Burned the house. They are all dead. I found them four days ago."

News the Johnson's had been murdered hit Cody hard. His first thought was of Sarah and what she must have suffered at the hands of the savages. He slammed his eyes shut and lifted his head upward. His face hardened. A large lump crawled up the back of his throat and lodged there.

"You will stay with me," the Mexican offered.

"I'm obliged."

CHAPTER II

The Making of a Gunfighter

Since his new friend could no longer see, it fell upon Cody to provide food. Deer, antelope, mountain goats and turkey were plentiful. The Mexican gave Cody his Henry rifle since he could no longer use it. Cody was a good hunter and kept them well supplied.

Cody discovered that his friend had several weapons, both rifles and gun rigs. Over supper a few nights after his arrival, Cody asked El Diablo about them.

"Could you teach me to use the pistol?"

His friend thought on the question a while before answering. "*Si*, if that what you want."

"That's what I want," Cody replied, setting his jaw.

"Look in small wooden box," El Diablo told him. "You will find a gun belt and holster."

Cody found the gun rig and brought it back to the fire. He looked closely at it. It looked weird. The holster was attached to the gun belt at an angle. He had never seen anything like it. The silver-colored gun had a bone handle.

"It is a Colt .44. There is no better. I make the Holster myself. It fits in the middle of the belly. Much faster than on the hip.

"You must get use to how it feels in your hand. Keep in your hand day and night, sleep with it. Never put down. It must become part of you like the hand. I will tell you when you are ready to go to next step."

Cody did as his new friend instructed. He carried the unloaded weapon with him everywhere he went. After a while he didn't even notice it in his hand. It was as much a part of him as his fingers.

One day Cody was looking at some of his friend's tools and discovered a hacksaw. He asked El Diablo if he had ever shortened the barrel of a shotgun.

"*Si,* many times. Why do you ask?"

"I have my pa's double barrel shotgun and I was thinking about shortening the barrel, but I don't know how."

"Let me feel the gun."

Cody's blind friend took the shotgun and moved his hand slowly over it, exploring every inch with his fingers. He trailed fingers along the barrel and then back again. His hand reached a point about twelve inches forward of the wooden handhold.

"You cut here," the former gunsmith said.

Cody worked for the rest of the day before he finally had the barrel off.

"Got it," he said excitedly. "It looks funny."

Cody decided to also saw the handle off short and drill a hole for a rawhide thong to make it easier to carry. The weapon looked scary.

For the next month, the only time the Walker Colt was out of Cody's hand was when he was actually firing his rifle to hunt their food or to do the chores. He slept with it and ate with the weapon in his hand.

They sipped their morning coffee. "How does the gun feel in you hand, Señor Cody?"

"I don't even notice it's in my hand anymore. It feels natural, like it's a part of me, just like my own hand."

"Then you ready for next step. Strap the holster and gun belt around you and place the unloaded gun in your holster."

Cody did as his friend instructed.

"Now slowly draw it from your holster. Do not worry about fast. That will come later. As it comes out, let your thumb pull back hammer. This must become part of same motion as drawing. Practice over and over until I tell you stop."

All day Cody practiced, and the next and the next. Every day, all day, he continued the motion as El Diablo instructed. After two weeks he began to think his friend had forgotten about the instructions he gave him.

"Am I supposed to continue practicing drawing and cocking the gun?" he asked one morning.

"Si."

El Diablo had been doing his own practicing, not with a weapon, but familiarizing himself with his surroundings. All day, every day, he walked around the cave, touching, feeling, and counting the number of steps between each area of the cave. He could now move about almost as if he still had his sight.

After a solid month of practice drawing and cocking the weapon, even Cody was surprised how easy and natural it felt.

"Now you work on speed," the Mexican told him one morning. "You learn to catch flies."

Cody thought he hadn't heard his friend right.

"Catch flies?"

"Si, look around this cave. You see flies?"

"Well, yeah, lots of them."

"You catch one, señor. Tell me when you learn."

Cody felt foolish, but he started trying to catch a fly. He tried everything he could think of, but each time the fly simply eluded him. He waited until he found one on a rock near the campfire. He eased his hand close, but when he reached out to snatch the fly it lifted from the rock and easily avoided Cody's cupped hand.

Obviously El Diablo became aware of Cody's frustration at not being able to catch a small fly.

"The fly is quicker than a *hombre*. So...you must be smarter than the fly. Watch how it lifts off. You will see that it does it the same way every time. When you reach to catch it, allow for its speed."

It took three days before Cody figured out what his friend meant. He let out a loud yell when he caught his first one.

"I did it!" he yelled. "I caught one!"

"It is good," El Diablo told him. "Keep trying until you can catch them each time."

Another week passed before Cody could catch most every fly he tried for. He bragged to his friend of his success.

"That is very good. Now catch them in flight."

That sounded impossible to Cody, but he was determined to do what the Mexican suggested. After a few days Cody learned the lesson his friend was trying to teach him. He learned to anticipate the fly's action and adjust for it.

"A man is same. Learn what he is going to do before he does it and use that against him.

"Now you practice drawing your gun and thumbing back the hammer as fast as you can, as it comes out of holster, point gun in front of you. Replace and do again. Keep practicing that until I tell you stop."

Except when he was hunting or doing the few chores that needed done, he spent every waking moment practicing.

He practiced standing in what El Diablo called a *gunfighter stance,* with his feet spread apart, knees slightly bent, his hand hovering only a hair's breath from the butt of his weapon.

Suddenly his hand swept the Colt from its holster. His thumb pulled back the hammer even as his hand swung in a sideways arc to point directly in front of him.

Cody could tell that his speed was improving with each passing day. His goal was to make each draw faster than the one before.

Two whole months passed. Cody now drew the Colt, swept back the hammer, and trained on an imaginary foe faster than the blink of the eye.

"Now you learn to hit what you shoot at," his friend told him. "I want you go into the hills. Find a deep arroyo a few miles away. We do not want to attract anyone to our cave."

Cody did as his instructor told him. He filled his gun belt with shells from a full box and put an extra handful in the pocket of his overalls. El Diablo gave him a worn serape to wear, since Cody didn't even have a shirt. He pulled the cover over his head and adjusted it. He liked it; it hung below his waist and hid the pistol rig he wore. He scooped up his Henry rifle and struck out.

He left their hideout at daylight and walked for two hours before finding what he was looking for. A deep canyon, maybe fifty feet deep, wound between two lines of mountains that crowded both sides of the canyon. Cody figured between the canyon and the mountains they would muffle most of the sound from his shooting.

Cody spent all day in the canyon practicing. By the end of the day he felt he had improved quite a lot, but knew he had a long way to go. He arrived back at their cave just before sundown.

Each night Cody and El Diablo spent several hours talking about the finer points of gun fighting.

"What I tell you now, most never live long enough to learn. With practice anyone can learn to draw fast. But gun fighting is more than drawing fast and shooting straight.

"There are things that will give you an edge and help you stay alive. I want you learn them and practice until they become as natural as breathing.

"First, Señor Cody, you pick a time and place to fight. If daytime, keep your back to sun. If night, keep lights at your back. Light in your eyes will get you killed. Second, never bluff. Bluffing is for poker games, not gun fighting. If there is no way out of a fight, only thing left is to kill him before he kills you. Third, and last for tonight, watch a the hombre's face, not his hand. His face tells you when he is going to draw."

"What do you mean? What do I look for?"

"You will know. Sometimes a squint, sometimes lowering the eyebrows, sometimes gritted teeth or clenched jaw, but you will know."

Cody spent most of every day practicing. He could tell he was getting faster and a better shot with each passing day. Each night his Mexican friend went over and over the things he had learned during his years as a gun fighter.

The last antelope Cody shot was about gone. They needed food. He strapped on his pistol and stuck his head through the opening in his serape. "I'm going to find us some meat this morning," he told his Mexican friend.

"Si," Walk softly."

Cody smiled. His friend always said that every time Cody left the cave. He picked up his Henry rifle and stepped from the cave entrance down into the small stream. He decided to go east today into the mountains. Maybe he'd get lucky and bag them a deer.

He walked half the morning away before finding a good spot. He sat down against a large cedar tree on a hillside overlooking a small pool of water. There was a chilly wind coming in from the north and Cody was thankful for the serape.

An hour passed, then two, before he spotted a nice buck approaching the watering hole. Slowly he eased his rifle up and thumbed back the hammer. The buck was cautious as it soft-footed nearer the water, stopping every few steps to cast a long look around for any signs of danger. Cody waited.

When the deer reached the water it took another look around before dipping its head to take a drink. Cody shot him. The buck leaped straight up in the air and hit the ground running full out. Cody levered another shell and followed the wounded deer. It had been a good shot and he knew the buck wouldn't run far.

Sure enough, he found the animal in some thick bushes no more than a couple hundred yards away. He field-dressed the deer with his knife, draped it across his shoulders and headed back to the cave.

It was mid-afternoon when he crossed the river and started upstream toward the cave. Rounding a bend, he stopped dead in his tracks. Three horses were tied to a bush in a small clearing beside the river. One was a beautiful black and white pinto, the other two were paints. They were Indian ponies.

Cody laid the deer behind some large rocks and jacked a shell into his rifle. He moved cautiously among the rocks, making his way toward the cave. His heart pounded in his chest. His hands made sweat on the rifle. He licked dry lips.

He reached the small stream that fronted their cave and waded cautiously upstream. He felt sweat on his forehead as he eased between the tall rocks forming the channel for the stream. His heart was in his throat as he inched along with his back against the rock.

From inside the cave he heard laughter, strange laughter, Indian laughter. He held his breath and chanced a quick look around the edge of the cave. Three Indians were prowling among the boxes.

Then he saw his friend lying near the far wall. El Diablo didn't move. His throat had been cut. The sight gave birth to anger. It boiled up his throat and flushed his face.

He climbed up the low bank and stepped into the cave. One of the Indians jerked his head around and stared full into Cody's face. He shot him in the chest. The impact of the .44 slug lifted the Indian off his feet and slammed him against the far wall. No sooner had Cody pulled the trigger before he levered another round.

One of the two remaining Indians rushed at Cody with a knife in his hand and a wild look on his evil face. The heavy slug from the Henry rifle struck the Indian in the very center of his chest and he went down. Cody levered another shell.

The last Indian stood motionless. He held a tomahawk in his hand. For a moment they stood facing one another, neither moving. The Indian in front of him represented everything Cody hated. This savage could well be the very one who did the evil things to his ma and pa. Cody gritted his teeth with unbridled hatred and pulled the trigger.

He rushed to his friend and knelt beside him. El Diablo lay dead. The murdering dogs had killed a helpless blind man. He shook his head at the senselessness of it all. Why did they have to kill him? He couldn't hurt them, he was blind!

CHAPTER III
Long Road to Nowhere

After disposing of the three Indian bodies, Cody buried El Diablo the following day in a small clearing not far from his cave. He felt he had to leave the sanctuary of the cave for the same reason he had to leave their farm, the memories hurt too much to stay. But this time he was leaving a very different man from the one who arrived.

Among his friend's belongs Cody found a packsaddle. He loaded it on one of the three Indian horses and made several trips from the cave carrying things he would need and stowed them.

He brought along all the ammunition, two extra gun rigs, his sawed off shotgun, and the Henry rifle. He brought his friend's bedroll and two extra blankets along with all the trail supplies he could carry. Taking one last look at the place that had been his home for the better part of a year, he mounted the beautiful black and white pinto and heeled it south. The pinto was a high-stepping spirited horse that pranced sideways against a tight rein. Cody figured him to be a runner. His new pack horse and the extra horse trailed along behind on lead lines.

He decided to ride to San Antonio and try to sell the extra horse for enough money to keep him going until he could find a job.

It was just before sundown when Cody reined up at the combination livery and blacksmith shop on the outskirts of San Antonio. A large fellow wearing a leather apron and a face full of whiskers doused a red-hot horseshoe in a tub of water and fixed a long stare at him. Cody slid off the pinto and tied the reins of his three horses to the corral fence.

"Where'd you get the Indian ponies, boy?"

"They killed my friend, I killed them, didn't figure they had use for 'em anymore."

The hostler pursed his lips with something akin to a smile and dug a plug of tobacco from his pocket. He gnawed off a piece and returned the plug to his pocket. "Nope, I reckon not. What's your name, kid?"

Cody thought on the question before answering. *Might be best I not use my real name since I just told him I killed three Indians.* "Hondo, the Hondo Kid."

The hostler offered a full-fledged grin at Cody's answer.

"Well, Kid, what can I do for you?"

"You got a saddle?"

"I got saddles, but judging from the looks of you, I doubt you got money to buy one."

"What'cha give me for the paint?'

The liveryman's gaze swung to the horse and took its measure. He walked over to the extra Indian pony, felt a front leg, lifted a hoof and looked at it, then pried open the paint's top lip to judge its age.

"I've got a good used saddle I'd trade you and give you fifteen dollars to boot."

"Show me the saddle," Cody said, knowing the horse was worth more than that.

Together they walked inside. Several saddles hung along an inside wall suspended from a rafter by a rope. The hostler patted a black saddle that was obviously well worn. A matching black bridle hung on the saddle horn. Cody looked the saddle and bridle over carefully. He liked it.

"Now there's a saddle that still has many-a-mile left in it. And, like I said, against my better judgment I'll give you fifteen dollars to boot."

"Make it twenty-five and you've got a deal,"

"Can't do'er, Kid, that paint ain't worth that much."

"Then I'll go down the street, I reckon there's other liveries in town."

Cody turned and walked back toward his horses. He began untying the reins before the liveryman stopped him.

"Okay, okay, you drive a hard bargain, Kid. Twenty-five it is, but I won't make a penny on this deal, I can tell you for shore."

Cody smiled a satisfying smile to himself. The liveryman took a small, snap pouch from his pocket and counted the money into Cody's outstretched hand.

"What'cha charge me to stall my horses for the night?" Cody asked.

"A dollar."

"That include me sleeping in your hayloft?" he asked as he handed the man a dollar.

The liveryman just shook his head and walked away. Over his shoulder he called back, "Yeah, Kid, I reckon so."

Cody led his two horses to an empty stall. He took down his new saddle and bridle and slung them across the slat rails separating the stalls. Then he took time to rub the horses' noses before closing the gate to the stall.

It was good dark as Cody walked slowly along the wooden

boardwalk. He had never been in San Antonio after dark. On those few occasions when he accompanied his pa to town, it was always in the daytime and they headed back toward home before dark.

Most of the stores were already closed and the street appeared mostly deserted. A cur scrambled from under the boardwalk and yipped at his heels, barking loudly.

Up ahead a yellowish light escaped through a saloon's open doors, painting a square across the boardwalk. He hurried on by. Loud music from a piano blared out the open doors.

As he passed the saloon a woman came walking out the door. Her sudden laughter jerked his head around. She had long blond hair hanging over her shoulders and what looked to him like a painted face. The dress she wore was short at both ends. It showed more woman than he had ever seen. She looked like five pounds of woman stuffed into a three pound sack. He turned quickly to walk away.

"Well darlin', if you ain't a sight," she called after him.

Cody stopped and turned around.

"You, you talking to me?"

"You see anybody else on the street?"

Cody unintentionally glanced quickly around the street before slowly shaking his head.

"You just come in off the farm, Kid?" she asked, sarcastically.

Cody realized she was making fun of him. It hurt. He just nodded his head and turned and walked away.

"You got any money, Kid?" she called after him.

He kept walking.

The café was a small one tucked between two large businesses. The businesses were closed, the café open. Cody opened the door and walked inside. Three tables with straw-bottomed chairs were all empty. He pulled out a chair and sat down.

A lady who had been eating too well, too often, wearing a dirty apron came from the kitchen wiping her hands on a dishrag. She picked up a blackened coffee pot and a white mug and waddled toward his table.

"Just fixin' to close, but I'll dish you up something if'n you're hungry," she said as she poured the cup full of black coffee.

"Yeah, whatever you got will do."

"Got beef stew and cornbread."

"Sounds good," Cody said, blowing steam from his coffee and chancing a small sip.

As the woman went to spoon up his supper, Cody sipped his coffee and thought about the saloon girl's chiding comments.

When he thought about it, she was probably right, he most likely did *look a sight*. His bib overalls were worn to a frazzle with holes in both knees; he had worn nothing else for almost a year. He didn't have a shirt, just the faded serape that hung over his head and down past his hips. His work shoes were run-over and had holes in both soles. He was bareheaded and his corn shuck-colored hair hung below his shoulders.

What he wore hadn't mattered living in the cave with El Diablo. His blind friend hadn't been able to see him anyway, but he could see how town folk might think he had 'just come in off the farm.' He made up his mind then and there. *Come mornin I'll buy myself some new clothes.*

Cody ate his stew and cornbread hurriedly, knowing the woman was waiting to close. It was good, almost as good his ma used to make. He wanted another bowlful but figured she might charge him double. He scraped the bowl and swallowed the last of his coffee and wiped his mouth on the edge of his serape.

"How much I owe?" he asked.

"Fifty cents."

He paid her and pushed out the door. He looked up and down the street, then headed for the livery. He walked slowly along the boardwalk. It was early and he was in no particular hurry.

Some feeling of another's presence caused him to twist a look over his shoulder. On the boardwalk behind him, some twenty yards away, a large dog with short, golden hair seemed to be following him. Cody thought little of it and continued on toward the livery.

The liveryman was gone for the day. Cody climbed the ladder and felt the Colt that rested in his belly holster before settling down on a pile of loose hay.

Natural night sounds from below filtered up through the floorboards of the loft: a horse snorted, another munched on a mouthful of hay and faint sounds of piano music from the saloon drifted on a light breeze. In minutes he fell asleep.

His inner sense woke him and told him it was coming day. Faint tinges of graying light filtered through the wide cracks in the walls of the loft and chased away the darkness. Cody climbed to his feet, stretched his big frame, and combed through his long hair with his fingers. Down below he heard footsteps.

"Get outta here!" the voice of the liveryman from below shouted. "I got enough stray dogs hanging around and shore don't need another."

Cody climbed down the ladder.

The liveryman and the big golden dog Cody had seen the night before were in a standoff. The dog stood glaring at the liveryman with his teeth bared. The hostler grabbed a long leather rein from a wooden peg and doubled it in his hand. He took a step toward the dog. The dog didn't move. Instead, a low rumbling growl came from deep inside him. The hair on the dog's neck stood up and his top lip lifted to reveal long, razor-sharp fangs.

"What'd he do?" Cody asked.

The liveryman crooked a look at Cody.

"This your dog?"

"No, just wondering what he had done."

"He ain't *done* nothin', just don't want him hanging around."

Cody walked cautiously toward the dog with his hand out. The dog stood his ground. Its dark, wolf-like eyes fixed upon Cody and his teeth still bared.

"Better watch yourself, Kid. That dog could take your arm off."

Cody ignored the man and moved closer, speaking to the animal in a soft, soothing voice. The dog lowered his lip and stepped backward a step, his eyes never leaving Cody.

"Good dog," Cody said in a soft voice. "You don't want to hurt me do you, boy?"

Cody's hand was only inches from the dog. His gaze locked with the dog's. His hand touched the dog's head, rubbing it gently, scratching its ear, patting it softly.

"Well, I'll be a monkey's Uncle," the hostler said. "You shore got a way about you, Kid."

"Used to have a dog named Collie," Cody said. "Reckon I got me another one now."

"Well, you're welcome to him and good riddance."

"Obliged for the night in the hayloft," Cody said. "I'll be riding on."

He walked back and saddled his pinto and strapped the packsaddle on his other paint horse. The golden-haired dog stood nearby watching. Cody threaded a foot in the stirrup and swung into the saddle. As he walked his horses from the livery the hostler looked up from the anvil with a hammer in his hand.

"Tell me something, boy. Is your name really the Hondo Kid?"

"It is now."

He rode up the dusty, rutted street leading his packhorse. The golden-haired dog trotted along behind him. His black saddle felt good. In the east a streak of early sunlight mantled the horizon. *Things are looking up,* Cody thought.

An hour later, Cody walked out of the San Antonio Mercantile wearing new pants, shirt, boots, and hat. He still wore the faded serape that El Diablo had given him; he couldn't bear to part with it. Besides, it hid the Colt .44 in the belly holster.

He fingered the two dollars and fifty cents he had left in his pocket. He had one more stop he wanted to make and led his two horses back down the street to the barbershop he had passed earlier.

"Morning, young fellow," the bald-headed barber greeted as Cody walked in.

"Morning. Need a haircut."

Cody hung his new black hat on the rack and took a seat in the barber chair.

"You want it long or short?"

"Little long, about my shoulders, I reckon."

"You from around here?"

"Hereabouts. Looking for a job. You heard of anybody hiring?"

"Can't say I have. What kind of work you do?"

"Anything that keeps my belly full."

"With the war going on and all, nobody's got two nickels to rub together, let alone money to hire help. Yes, sir, times are hard."

When the barber finished, Cody looked at himself in the mirror behind the barber chair. He hardly recognized the man staring back at him.

"How much?"

"Fifty cents."

Cody paid him and walked out to his horses. The dog lay nearby. Cody toed a stirrup and settled in the saddle. He reined his pinto and packhorse up the street, taking the north road out of town. The golden-haired dog trotted along behind. *Yes, sir, things are shore looking up.*

CHAPTER IV
The Making of a Reputation

San Marcos, Texas was a dusty little town about fifty miles northeast of San Antonio where the El Camino Real crossed the spring-fed San Marcos River. Cody reined up at the edge of town just after dusky-dark and let his slow gaze take it in.

It wasn't much of a town. Only a single narrow street ran its length. The street was guarded by low, slat-board buildings along both sides. He saw a livery, a general store, a ladies dress shop, and of course, a saloon. He reckoned every town with a dozen folks or more had to have a saloon. Some ways off behind the businesses, smoke trailed upward from chimneys of a couple dozen houses.

He gigged his pinto and walked his horses down the street. It seemed the only place open was the saloon. *Maybe I can get a bite to eat,* he thought, and reined up at the hitching rail out front. Two other horses stood tied. Judging from the horse droppings, they had been there a while. His new dog lay down near Cody's horses.

He opened the door and stepped inside. The sour smell of stale air, sour whiskey, and cigarette smoke greeted him. A long board stretched between two upturned barrels served as a bar. A short bartender with a dirty white apron about his middle leaned on the bar. Two small tables with ladder-back chairs filled out the room. Two hard-looking men sat at one of them. They all turned their gaze on Cody as he walked in.

Near the back, a pot-bellied stove provided the heat. A black pan of something with a spicy aroma simmered on top of the stove. Cody walked to the bar facing the bartender.

"Got anything to eat in that pot?" he asked.

"Hot tamales and beans. Bowls are there on the end of the bar. Help yourself."

Cody picked up a bowl and spoon and walked to the stove. He spooned a bowlful and pulled out a chair at the empty table. The two men were still eyeing him.

"Where you from, boy?" one of the men asked.

Cody flicked a glance at the man who asked the question. He was tall and skinny. His face was pockmarked and stretched tight over high cheekbones. He wore a black hat with silver Conchos on the hatband. He also wore a tied-down gun on his right leg.

His partner was a heavy fellow with a full beard and mustache. He, too, wore a gun cinched tight around his ample middle. A half-empty bottle sat in the center of their table and each man held a glass of whiskey in his hand.

"Down the road a piece," Cody replied, lifting a spoonful of beans to his mouth.

"Where you headed?"

"Yonder," Cody said, nodding his head northward.

"Where'd you get that pinto you rode in on?"

Cody waited a long minute before he answered.

"Why you askin'?"

"Cause I use to have one just like it. Somebody stole it. Mind if I step out and take a closer look at him?"

"Yeah, I do," Cody replied, taking another spoon of beans.

"Well, neighbor, you might as well get use to it cause I'm gonna look that pinto over. I got a feeling that's my horse."

Both men pushed from their chairs and walked to the front door. They opened it and stepped outside. Cody laid down his spoon and rose. He glanced at the bartender. The man hadn't moved a muscle. Cody stepped outside.

As the two men approached the pinto a low growl erupted from Cody's dog's throat. The dog rose to its feet and bared his teeth and growled again.

"Don't touch my horse, mister," Cody said, flipping his serape back over his shoulder with his left hand, exposing the Colt in his belly holster.

"Whoa, looky here, Mort, the kid's got a big ole gun. We got us a ring-tailed twister here. What'cha gonna do, kid, you gonna tangle with both of us? We'll kill you where you stand."

Both men squared around, their hands hanging just above the guns on their hips. An evil smirk spread across the skinny fellow's face.

Cody's hand rose to hover near the bone handle of his own weapon. He figured the talker would draw first and locked his unblinking stare on the man's face. He waited.

Just like El Diablo had said, the tall man's eyes squinted an instant before his hand dipped to grasp his weapon. Faster than the eye could follow, Cody's hand drew and fired. The heavy slug drilled the tall man in the very center of his forehead before he could get his sidearm up level. His shot went straight down into the dirt in front of his boot.

Cody's Colt didn't stop even for a split second. His thumb swept back the hammer even as the nose swung toward the man's fat partner. The bearded man was slow. His gun just clearing leather when Cody's bullet pumped into his chest. The man stumbled backward, but his weapon continued to rise. Cody shot him again.

This time the man tumbled over backwards, his shot sailed upward as he fell.

Cody's sixth sense warned of someone behind him. He whirled and swung his Colt in the same motion. The bartender stood just outside the doorway.

"Don't shoot!" the man pleaded, throwing his hands up. He backed away, stumbling as he did.

Cody eased the hammer off. Gray smoke curled upward from the nose of his gun and licked at his hand like a serpent. He thumbed shells from his gun belt and reloaded his Colt before returning it to his holster. The bartender came back through the door shaking his head; his eyes were big as saucers and his mouth hung open.

"Who are you, boy?" the bartender asked excitedly. "I've seen some fast guns in my time, but I never seen anything like I just seen. That ain't like nothing human. What's your name?"

"The Hondo Kid,"

He untied the dead men's two horses and loosed their lariat ropes from their saddles. Then he dropped a loop over the heads of each of their two mounts and gathered the lead line to his own packhorse.

"Come on, dog."

The bartender stood and watched him ride out of town on the pinto leading three horses, until the darkness swallowed him from sight.

Cody sold the two horses and saddles in Austin, Texas two days later for a hundred dollars. One of the saddlebags matched his own saddle, so he kept it. He found two boxes of .44 cartridges in the saddlebags and kept them as well.

He inquired about a job every place he could think of in

Austin, but met with the same answer; nobody's hiring, nobody's got money. That he couldn't find work didn't bother him much, because he had a hankering to see the country anyway, so he moved on.

Cody rode into the fairly robust city of Waco, Texas in February of 1865. Waco lay situated on the west bank of the wide Brazos River, about half a mile from it. He checked into the Cattlemen Hotel and stowed his gear in the small, upstairs room overlooking the main street.

After stalling his two horses in a large livery at the edge of town, he asked the hostler if he knew of anyone in the area who might be hiring.

"Might try the Brazos River Ranch out north of town a few miles," he said. "You'll find it in the horseshoe bend of the river. Seems I remember somebody saying they were looking for a man or two."

Cody nodded his thanks. "I'm obliged."

Leaving the livery, he went looking for a café. He found the Brazos Café and stepped inside where he was greeted by a pretty lady with a pot of coffee in her hand and four empty tables. He judged her to be nearing twenty or so.

"Morning to you, cowboy."

"Mornin', ma'am."

"You're late for breakfast and early for supper. What'll you have?" she said with a smile as she poured him a cup of coffee.

"Reckon a piece of that apple pie over there and coffee would be good."

"Baked the pie myself this morning. You from around here? Don't recall seeing you before."

"No, ma'am, I'm from Hondo, Texas."

"Don't guess I know where that is."

"It ain't really a town or nothing, just a little trading post on the Hondo River."

"I see. What are you doing in our fair city?"

"Looking for work. The fellow down at the livery said he heard the Brazos River Ranch might be hiring."

"Is that right? I happen to know the foreman of the Brazos ranch. Del Horton's his name. He's a good man."

"Think I'll ride out tomorrow and see if they're hiring."

"Well, if you get on I hope you'll stop back in when you're in town."

"Obliged, ma'am, I'll do that."

Cody spent the afternoon walking around town and looking at the various shops. He bought himself another change of clothes and a sheepskin coat. It was getting pretty late that night when he returned to the Brazos Café for supper. Secretly he hoped to get to talk to the pretty lady again; she was the only friendly person he had met during his travels.

The café was busy and he came close to turning around and leaving, but the pretty lady spotted him before he could make his exit and motioned for him to occupy a table which had just been vacated.

She leaned close and said softly, "Glad you came back," she said on her way to deliver two plates full of food to an older couple nearby. "I'll be right back."

Cody felt awkward, somehow out of place. He looked around the room. Besides the well-dressed older couple, two men in business suits occupied another table. A fellow who looked like a well-to-do rancher sat at a table with two other men.

The pretty lady returned with a coffee cup and coffee pot and poured him a cup.

"What can I get you for supper?"

"What'cha got?"

She leaned close. "Try the fried chicken plate. It's good."

"Then that's what I'll have."

She smiled. He liked the way she smiled.

She was right. The fried chicken, mashed potatoes, and green beans with a hot roll and honey was maybe the best supper he'd ever ate, except for what his ma use to cook, of course.

By the time he finished eating, the other customers had left. The café was about to close.

"Don't reckon you'd have any chicken bones left back there that I could feed my dog?"

"Sure do," the lady said. "And you're welcome to them."

She sacked up a batch of bones and handed them to him. He paid for his supper and left. He decided to walk down to the nearby livery and check on his horses and feed the dog.

There was a lantern burning in the aisle of the livery. His pinto and paint recognized him and nickered as he walked up to their stall. He patted them and rubbed their noses and forked some hay into their stall from a nearby hay cradle. The golden dog lay just outside the stall. Cody emptied half the bones for him and put the sack with the remaining bones in his packsaddle for later. Having satisfied himself that his horses and dog were well cared for, he headed back toward the hotel.

Loud music and drunken laughter spilled from a saloon between him and the hotel. A wad of drunken cowboys stood sharing a bottle on the boardwalk out front of the saloon. Cody was about to walk across the street to avoid them when he saw the pretty lady from the café approaching on the boardwalk from the other direction.

She obviously saw the cowboys and had the same idea Cody did. She stepped off the boardwalk to cross the street. The cowboys saw her and said something Cody couldn't hear. One cowboy separated from the others and staggered into the street to intercept her.

"Hey, Lady!" he shouted. "Where you going? We won't bite."

The pretty lady ignored the remarks and sped up to get past him. The drunken cowboy took two staggering steps and grabbed her by the arm. She tried to tear her arm loose from his grasp, but he held on tightly.

Cody saw what was happening and hurried his steps.

"Turn me loose!" she demanded and slapped the man's cheek.

The cowboy swung a backhand blow that landed on her right ear, sending her reeling. She landed in the dusty street flat of her back.

Cody arrived just after the blow was struck. His gun was in his hand. He swung it with all the anger that welled up in him. The heavy weapon's barrel struck the cowboy squarely in the mouth. The crunch of bone sounded. Blood, teeth, and part of the man's upper lip flew through the dimly lit darkness. The cowboy crumpled into the dirt, out cold.

Two of his companions rushed off the boardwalk into the street toward Cody. He saw their movement and swung the nose of his Colt in their direction.

"Hold it right there!" Cody shouted, firing a warning shot into the air, then lowering the nose of his gun in the mens' direction.

"The next shot will be about belly high. You saw what happened, same as me. Your partner shouldn't have hit her."

The men stopped in their tracks at the shot and Cody's words. They raised their hands and backed up a step or two.

"We'll drop it, but Hugo won't," the fellow in front said. "You better hope he's dead, mister, cause if he ain't, he'll come looking for you."

"I won't be hard to find," Cody told him, still palming his Colt, but backing over to where the lady was trying to sit up.

He reached his spare hand. She took it. He lifted her to her feet.

"Are you gonna be all right?" he asked.

"Yes, I'll be fine. I've never been hit before and it just stunned me."

"Where do you live? I'll see you home."

"I live with my folks. It's only a couple of blocks that way," she said, pointing with a nod of her head down the street.

The cowboys still stood in a huddle in front of the saloon as Cody and the lady walked slowly down the middle of the street a ways before mounting the boardwalk.

"Thanks for coming to my rescue," she said, still holding a hand to her cheek. "I don't even know your name."

"Most folks just call me the Hondo Kid."

"It's nice meeting you. I'm Ellen Richardson. Mind me asking how old you are?"

"I'm fifteen."

"You seem much older."

At that minute he felt much older and wished he were. He guessed her to be pushing twenty.

"Well, this is where I live. Thanks for walking me home," she said, pausing for a moment before leaning over and kissing him on the cheek.

Cody stood there as she turned and hurried into the house. Except for his mother, he had never been kissed by anyone before.

The cowboys had removed their companion from the street and left when Cody passed the saloon on his way to the hotel. He climbed the stairs to his room and went inside, locking the door behind him. Removing his clothes and tucking his Colt under his pillow, he crawled beneath the worn blanket.

For a long while he lay there in the darkness of his room, remembering that kiss. He knew it didn't mean anything to her; after all, in her eyes he was just a kid. It was nothing more than a way to show her gratitude for coming to her rescue. Still in all, it sure felt good. With that thought in mind he dozed off to sleep.

Morning sun crept through faded curtains and inched its way across the room onto Cody's bed. Light from it shocked him awake. He bolted upright to a sitting position. For an instant he was back home on the farm. Pa would be upset with him for oversleeping.

Then, his mind returning to reality, a sad feeling swept over him. A feeling of loneliness overwhelmed him. First his brother was killed in the war, then his parents were murdered by the Comanche, then Sarah Johnson, then El Diablo was killed, the only friend he ever had. He was alone. Everybody needed somebody. He couldn't name a single person who cared whether Cody lived or died. That feeling tugged at his mind.

The pretty lady's kiss came to his thoughts. He lifted a finger to trail it along his cheek before swinging his feet to touch the braided oval rug on the floor.

He rose, washed his face and hands, made use of the slop-jar underneath the bed and dressed. Gathering his gear, he took another look around the room before leaving and going downstairs.

As he walked toward the livery he was tempted to stop in the café for breakfast, but then admitted to himself the *real* reason wasn't breakfast at all. He granted himself a look as he passed, but walked on.

Just like the hostler said, he found the Brazos River Ranch about eight miles north of Waco in the big bend of the Brazos River. It was prime land of a thousand acres or so surrounded on three sides by the river. Buffalo grass grew thick and hock-high to his pinto. Herds of fat longhorns grazed contentedly as he rode past.

A carved plank hanging from a pole on top of two uprights identified it. Cody walked his pinto and packhorse under the sign and continued up the worn trail toward the slat-sided house on a gentle rise.

A dirt-roofed bunkhouse, a cook house with smoke rising from a rusty stovepipe, a large barn and a rail corral sat apart from the house a ways. He saw a couple of herds of longhorns grazing peacefully off in the distance. Two cowboys were unloading a wagon of feed that was backed into the wide aisle of the barn. Cody reined up. The men climbed down off the wagon and walked near.

"Looking for Del Horton," Cody said.

"You found him, son. What can I do for you?"

The man was a tall, wide-shouldered fellow. His face was well weathered with pale eyes and a square-set jaw. Cody judged him as a no-nonsense type who even looked what Cody thought a foreman ought to look like.

"Folks call me the Hondo Kid. Reckon 'cause I'm from Hondo, Texas. Fellow in town told me you might be hiring. I'm needing a job. I'll give you an honest day's work for a day's pay."

For a long moment the foreman didn't respond. His slow gaze looked Cody over from head to toe and then back again. When he spoke his voice was hard.

"You wouldn't happen to be the fellow who pistol-whipped Hugo in town last night would you?"

Cody locked gazes with the foreman.

"I hit a fellow who struck a lady and laid her out in the street, if that's what you mean."

The foreman darted a quick look at his companion standing beside him.

"Is he telling it straight?" he asked the other man.

"I...I didn't see what happened, boss. I was in the saloon minding my own business."

The foreman's gaze swung back to Cody.

"How old are you, boy?"

"I'm fifteen, but I've worked hard all my life. I ain't afraid of work."

"Jim, you finish unloading that wagon. Kid, tie your horses there and come with me."

Cody tied his horses and followed the foreman's long steps

to the bunkhouse. He pushed open the heavy door and strode over to a bunk where the cowboy called Hugo lay. His lower face was wrapped in bandages with a length running over the top of his head to hold the bandages in place.

Recognition showed in the man's eyes when he looked up and saw Cody. He sat upright and fixed a stare filled with hatred straight at Cody.

"Is this the fellow who pistol-whipped you last night?" the foreman asked.

Hugo tore his glare away from Cody and looked at his foreman.

"Yeah, that's him," he mumbled through swollen lips.

"Tell me again how it happened."

"It's it's hard for me to talk, boss," the man stalled.

"Try real hard."

"Well, like we told you last night, I was just talking to this woman and this fellow butted in. We had words. Before I knew what was happening he just drew down on me and pistol-whipped me."

"As I recall, *we* didn't tell me that story, *you* did. I'll ask around. For your sake, it better be the way you say it was. I don't hold with hitting a woman. A man who would do that won't work for me. If you are lying, you best pack your gear and fork a saddle before I get back."

Hugo swung his hate-filled stare on Cody. The foreman turned and walked from the room. Cody followed.

"Wait here," the man told Cody after they got outside.

The foreman walked to the barn and emerged on his horse. Cody watched as he disappeared over the horizon. Cody sat down on a bench outside the bunkhouse to wait. From what he could see it looked to be a good ranch. The main house was nothing fancy, but it looked what he imagined home ought to look like.

The door to the bunkhouse opened. Hugo emerged carrying his bedroll and saddlebags. He stopped short when he spotted Cody and glared angrily.

"This ain't over, boy!" he mumbled through busted, swollen lips, "Not by a long shot."

He stalked away, headed for the barn. In moments he galloped from the barn, lashing his horse with the long reins.

Cody waited. It took a half hour before foreman Horton's big chestnut gelding crested the hill and short-loped to the bunkhouse. He reined up, stepped to the ground, and started toward the door. It was obvious he had a mad on.

"He's gone."

The foreman stopped short. He stared at the toes of his boots for a long minute.

"It's just as well I reckon. He lied to me. Won't put up with a man who lies to me. Looks like I'm one man short, Kid. The job's yours if you want it."

"I want it. What about my dog?"

"Don't see a problem with the dog as long as he don't cause one. I'll say a word to Swede, our cook. I'm sure he can give your dog some scraps. Job pays forty a month and found. Stow your gear in the bunkhouse. I'll get you started come morning."

"Yes, sir. I'm obliged."

Cody took his horses to the barn and unsaddled them. He found a currycomb and brush, groomed both horses and then turned them into the corral. The feed cradle was already full of hay. He found a tack room to store his trail supplies and extra weapons.

The man who worked with the foreman earlier was backing another wagonload of feed into the barn. He got it positioned near a large feed room and jumped to the ground.

"Did you get the job?" he asked.

"Yep. Seems Mr. Horton talked to some of the hands and they told him the straight story."

"Did he fire Hugo?"

"Reckon he quit. The boss told him if he was lying he might as well fork a saddle. He did."

"Good riddance. He was a troublemaker anyway. But if I was you I'd watch my back."

"Intend to."

"Name's Lefty Hobart," he said, sticking out a hand.

"Hondo Kid, pleased to meet you. Let me help you unload that wagon."

"I'd be obliged."

Working together, they had the heavy sacks of feed stacked neatly in the feed room in no time. When finished, they were both wet with sweat. They walked outside and sat down with their backs against the barn. Cody's golden-haired dog trotted over and lay down beside his master.

"Good looking dog. What's its name?"

"I just call him dog."

"Reckon that's as good a name as any. Shore a pretty pinto you ride. Don't suppose you call him horse?"

That brought a rare grin from Cody. "Haven't had him long. No time to name him yet."

"Heard a fellow telling about some big general that named his horse Cincinnati. Might be a good name."

"Reckon it's as good as any."

"You'll like it here," Lefty told him. "We've got a good bunch of hands. The food is good and they treat a man fair."

Cody said, "Can't ask for more than that."

"How many hands they got?"

"Eight now, talk is we'll be taking a small herd down to New Orleans in a couple of months."

"Reckon who the boss will pick to do the drive?"

"Most likely anybody who wants to go and some that don't. Most of us have made the trip before and ain't particularly anxious to make it again."

"How come?"

"Lots of woods between here and there. We spend half of our time chasing strays back to the herd and looking for the ones we can't find. Cattle thieves steal you blind."

"Hope I get to go."

"I'd say there's a better'n even chance. You seem like a nice enough fellow, but let me clue you in on something. The boss will most likely give you the worst jobs he can find for a while to see if you're gonna last. Once you've proved yourself, things will get better."

"Obliged for the warning."

"Who owns the ranch?"

"Fellow named Nate Swenson. He ain't around much. He's got another ranch down in south Texas he stays at most of the time. Del pretty much runs things around here."

"How many head do they have?"

"Somewhere around two thousand head of steers. They don't sell their heifers."

The sun disappeared, burying itself somewhere beyond the horizon, leaving behind a golden legacy splashed across the western sky. Dusky-dark set in.

The cowboys began to straggle in and see to their horses. They unsaddled, fed them, and brushed them down while they were eating, and then turned them into the corral. Each one introduced themselves, shook hands with Cody and welcomed him to the ranch. Lots of good-natured joking made the Brazos Ranch seem like a happy place. Cody yearned for the time when he would be accepted and could feel a part of the crew. He needed to feel like he belonged to something.

As darkness swallowed light, a bell rang announcing supper. The cowboys ambled up to the cook shack, washed up at the wash bench and went inside. Cody and Lefty walked up to the cook shack together.

The cook was a short, heavyset fellow. He had a thin mustache and yellowish hair cut short. He had a permanent smile revealing two gold teeth.

"What's the cook's name?" Cody asked Lefty.

"Don't reckon I ever heard him called anything but Swede," Lefty said. "Course I've only been here two years."

Cody quickly discovered he agreed with Lefty's opinion of the food, it was good. Del Horton joined the crew for supper. It was clear from the laughter and good-natured joking the crew liked the foreman.

"Hope you men have met our new hand," Del said. "This is the Hondo Kid. He'll be working with us. Reckon you've all heard what happened. Hugo's gone. I won't have a man working for the Brazos that would hit a woman or lie to me. Hope we're clear on that."

"He's been trouble ever since he's been here anyway," one of the men spoke up. "Good riddance, I say."

All the men nodded agreement.

After supper they broke out the checkerboard. Cody learned the game was a regular evening event. He watched a while and then turned in.

It was still dark when the bell rang announcing breakfast. Cody was enjoying his scrambled eggs and bacon, fried potatoes and hot biscuits when Del Horton sat down across the table and ruined it all.

"Want you to get a wheelbarrow and scoop shovel and clean out the outhouse this morning. Wheel it down to Swede's garden and pile it up. When you finish that, start on the horse stalls in the barn."

Lefty warned him what to expect so it came as no surprise. He just cut a grin around a mouthful of biscuit.

"Yes, sir."

The foreman looked surprised Cody didn't complain about his work assignment, but said nothing.

Cody worked the day away. The dog lay nearby, watching his adopted master. Just after sundown the other hands rode in, tended to their horses, and went to supper. Cody kept at it. When it got too dark to see, he lit a lantern and continued to shovel the manure out of the stalls. He was about to finish the last stall when Del walked up.

"How come you didn't show up for supper?"

"This is the last stall, I wanted to finish up."

"I didn't mean you had to finish 'em all today."

"I know, boss, but when I start something I like to finish it."

The foreman looked at him for a couple of minutes.

"You'll do, Kid. Now wash up and go eat. I told Swede to save you some supper and give his table scraps to your dog. Tomorrow I want you and Lefty to take a couple of wagons into town and get two more loads of feed."

"Yes, sir."

Cody and Lefty backed their wagons up to the loading dock of the Coleman's Mercantile and Feed store at mid-morning. Smiling, Mr. Coleman walked out to meet them. "Morning, boys."

"Mornin', Mr. Coleman," Lefty replied. "Say howdy to the Hondo Kid. He just hired on out at the ranch."

"The Hondo Kid, huh? Where you from, Kid?"

"Hondo, Texas, that's why they call me that."

"Makes sense," the storekeeper said. "Need more feed, Lefty?"

"Yep, need two loads."

"Let me get my two-wheeler and I'll bring it out to you."

"There's two of us, Mr. Coleman," Lefty told him. "Me and the Kid can handle it. You got other stuff to do."

"Well, I am pretty busy, but don't mind helping you boys. You know where the feed is, help yourself."

With Lefty wheeling it out and Cody loading the wagons, they had both wagons loaded in short order.

"We've got a little time," Lefty said. "Let's mosey over and have a beer before we head back to the ranch."

"We left before breakfast this morning, how about you come with me over to the café and let's eat a bite. I'm buying. Then I'll go with you to have your beer."

"Say you're buying?"

"You heard right."

"Then what are we waiting for?"

They walked to the Brazos café and stepped inside. Ellen saw them and flung a wide smile at Cody as she hurried to meet them.

"I've been wondering about you. Did you get the job at the Brazos?"

"Yes, ma'am. Matter of fact, we're in town to pick up two loads of feed for the ranch. This is Lefty Hobart, one of the hands at the ranch. Lefty, this pretty lady is Ellen Richardson."

"Nice to meet you, Lefty," she said, smiling and shaking his hand.

"It's a real pleasure to make your acquaintance," Lefty said, obviously enjoying holding her hand.

"You fellows have a seat and I'll bring you some coffee. How about a slice of apple pie? It's fresh baked."

"Sounds good," Cody said.

As they scraped out chairs and folded into them, Lefty leaned close and whispered.

"You do get around, Kid. I think I'll stick real close to you."

Ellen brought coffee and poured them a cup.

"Remember that man we had the trouble with the other night?" she asked.

"Yeah."

"He's been telling all over town that you got him fired from the Brazos Ranch. He's bragging what he's going to do the next time he sees you."

"He's nothing but a windbag."

"I just don't want you to get hurt on my account."

"Don't worry about it. He's not gonna do anything 'cept talk."

"We've got hot roast beef open-faced sandwiches for the lunch special," Ellen told them.

"Sounds good to me."

"Me too," Lefty agreed.

After she left to fix their lunch, all Lefty wanted to talk about was Ellen.

"She shore is pretty," he said, his long gaze following her all the way into the kitchen.

"She's a nice lady," Cody agreed.

Their lunch came and they talked as they ate. Ellen came over to their table and visited between customers. After their meal they sipped coffee and visited some more.

"When do you think you will be back in town?" Ellen asked Cody.

"Don't know. I hear talk about a cattle drive down to New Orleans before long. I'm hoping I get to go along."

"Hope you can come to see me again before you go."

"We're gonna go have a beer before we head back," he told her, as they stood to their feet.

Cody paid for their meal and left Ellen a generous tip.

She shook Lefty's hand and gave Cody a warm hug. He was kinda embarrassed, but it sure felt good. She was the only lady that had ever hugged him except for his ma.

They walked down the street to the Double-Deuce saloon

and pushed through the batwing doors. Cody's quick look showed him two local businessmen types sitting at a table and another table occupied by four hard-looking men. One of them was Hugo, the one he had the run-in with. His face was still swathed in bandages.

"There sits trouble," Lefty said softly.

Cody was tempted to turn around and leave. But on second thought, he decided it might look like he was running from the bully if he did. Cody and Lefty walked to the mahogany bar. A long mirror on the back wall ran the entire length on the bar.

"Two beers," Lefty told the bartender.

Cody was watching Hugo's reflection in the big mirror. He saw the bully say something to his three companions and then push from his chair. Cody noticed the troublemaker lift his sidearm and settle it gently back into the holster.

"You!" Hugo shouted. "Turn around and face me like a man."

Cody turned. As he did, he flipped the serape back over a shoulder revealing his bone-handled Colt in the belly holster. He saw the big man's look drop to the pistol and his eyes widen as he fixed a long gaze on it. A surprised expression washed across his face.

"You blindsided me the other night and broke my nose. No man pistol whips Hugo Hix and lives to tell about it. I'm gonna kill you!"

Cody nailed the man with an unblinking stare and waited. He didn't have to wait long. Hugo's hand dipped to the butt of his gun and pulled it out with a jerky motion. He was slow, way too slow.

The bully's weapon swung up near level when Cody's Colt suddenly appeared in his hand as if by magic and struck like a thunderbolt. It belched fire and hot lead. One, two, three times his gun fired. Cody's slugs nailed Hugo chest center one after the other, all in the space of two heartbeats, each shot slammed him a step backwards. The man was dead before his body hit the floor.

Cody swung a look at Hugo's companions. They sat stone cold still with shocked expressions on their faces. It didn't seem they were in a mood to take up the fight. Cody ejected the spent cartridge and thumbed in a fresh one before returning his gun to its holster.

"Reckon somebody best go get the marshal," he said.

The bartender hurried around the bar and out the door. In minutes, a big man with a Walker Colt in his hand entered. His quick, searching glance swept the room and settled on Hugo.

The dead man lay sprawled on his back on the plank floor in a growing puddle of blood. His unfired weapon still clutched in lifeless fingers.

Cody and Lefty leaned with their backs to the bar, sipping their beers.

"Who killed him?" the marshal asked.

"I did."

"What's your name, son?"

"They call me the Hondo Kid."

"Uh-huh, I'm Henry Bell. I'm the marshal here in Waco. You the one who worked this fellow over out in front of the saloon a couple of nights ago?"

"Yes, sir. He hit Miss Ellen from the café and knocked her down. I did what any man would do."

"Miss Ellen is a friend of mine. She told me how it happened."

"Did you see what happened here, Sam?" the marshal asked the bartender who stood nearby.

"Yep, the big fellow claimed the kid pistol whipped him and he was gonna kill him for it. The kid never said a word. The dead fellow drew first, sure as shootin', but the kid was too fast for him. Never in all my born days seen anybody that fast with a gun. He's one tough knot that's for sure and certain."

The marshal looked around the room.

"Anybody see it different?"

Everybody shook their heads.

"That's the way it was, Henry," one of the businessmen agreed. "It was self-defense, pure and simple."

"Then I reckon you're in the clear this time, Kid. I hear you're working out at the Lazy J?"

"Yes, sir."

"Well, hope you don't plan on visiting town real often, get my meaning? We got a peaceful town and I mean to keep it that way."

CHAPTER V

Riding for the Brand

News of the shooting in town spread like wildfire. By breakfast the next morning every hand on the Brazos knew. It was the topic of every conversation.

Cody and Lefty sat at the table eating flap-jacks swimming in honey when Del Horton walked in. The foreman poured himself a cup of coffee and sat down across the table from Cody. For a long moment you could have heard a pin drop. Del sipped his coffee and stared at his cup with his head down. When he lifted his gaze it settled on the kid.

"Hear you were involved in a shooting in town yesterday."

"Yes, sir."

"I'd like to hear your side of it."

"Me and Lefty stopped in the saloon for a beer before we headed back with the load of feed. Hugo Hix was there. He called me out. Said he was gonna kill me. He drew on me and I killed him."

"That the way you saw it, Lefty?"

"That's the straight of it, boss."

"If that's the way it came down you got a right to defend yourself, but the big boss don't want word getting around that we hire gun slicks. That's bad for business."

"I understand, Mr. Horton."

"Then that's the end of it as far as I'm concerned."

"Much obliged."

From that moment, Cody sensed a new respect from the other hands on the ranch. Whether it was because he had killed a man none of them liked, or because the boss cleared him of any wrongdoing, or out of respect for his ability with a gun, clearly he had been accepted as one of the boys.

He quickly fell into the daily routine of ranch work. He liked working with cattle, paid attention and worked hard. As the weeks passed, Cody couldn't help but notice the foreman gave him more and more responsibility.

"We'll be taking a small herd down to New Orleans in a week or so," the foreman told him over breakfast. "I want you to pick a couple of the boys this morning and cut out about five hundred of the older steers. Bunch them over on the north pasture."

"Yes, sir."

"You and the boys keep them circled so they don't get a hankering to rejoin the other herd."

"I'll take Lefty and Slim Wagner if that's okay with you?"

"They'll be fine. I'll ride out this afternoon and look over the herd."

When the other hands arrived for breakfast, Cody called Lefty and Slim over to his table.

"boss wants the three of us to cut out five hundred head of the older stock and bunch 'em over on the north pasture."

"Sounds like we're getting ready for a drive," Slim said.

"Yep, heading them down to New Orleans in a few days," Cody told him.

"How many hands is he taking on the drive?"

"Don't know, he didn't say."

"You going?"

"Hope so. I've never been on a trail drive, much less to New Orleans."

Lefty spoke up. "I don't care a hoot about New Orleans, too many folks for my liking."

"How many trail drives have you fellows been on?"

"Just one for me," Slim said. "That was enough. You think we got it rough here on the ranch, just you wait until the drive. Its long days and short nights and trouble behind every tree."

"What kind of trouble?"

"Last time we took a herd down, we had folks stealing our cattle right out from under our noses. One fellow created a diversion while two more jaspers cut out several head and made off with them before we even knew what was happening."

"Yeah, but those dark-eyed French ladies make a man forget the trouble of getting there," Lefty said, grinning from ear-to-ear. "Wait until you see them, Kid. They make a man think he done died and woke up in heaven."

"We best finish breakfast and fork a saddle," Cody told them. "Or we'll be looking for another job."

The day was mostly used up before Cody, Lefty and Slim had the five hundred head of older cattle grazing peacefully in the valley of the north pasture. Cody sat his saddle with his leg crooked around the saddle horn. His black and white pinto, which he now called Cincinnati, munched lazily on the lush green grass. His dog lapped cool water from the small stream that threaded through the valley.

"You sure we got five hundred head?" Slim asked as he walked his horse near.

"Yep, counted them three times to make sure," Cody told him.

"Where'd Lefty get off to?"

"He felt the calling and headed for the bushes, most likely asleep by now."

"Better not be, I see the boss riding over the hill yonder."

They watched Del Horton as he trotted his big buckskin toward them. Cody liked the foreman. He was a fair man. Cody figured the man knew about all there was to know about raising cattle.

Maybe if I keep my eyes and ears open I can learn the cattle business. It just might come in handy someday.

"Looks like you boys got 'em settled down," the foreman said, reining up beside Cody and Slim. You sure you got five hundred?"

"Yes, sir, counted them three times."

"Thought Lefty was with you?"

"He is. He's over yonder in the bushes."

"Well, one of you stay with the herd until midnight. Somebody can ride out and relieve him. We need to keep 'em bunched until the drive."

"I'll stay," Cody volunteered. "Slim or Lefty can relieve me after a while."

"Suit yourself. Work it out however you think best. You boys done a good job. I'll see you back at the ranch."

"Much obliged, boss," Cody said.

Del reined his buckskin around and rode away. Cody and Slim watched him until he topped the hill and disappeared. Lefty walked his horse up beside them.

"Was that the boss I saw riding over the hill?"

"Yep," Cody told him. "He said for you and Slim to come for supper. I'll stay with the herd. One of you can come and relieve me about midnight."

"Want me to bring you something?" Lefty asked.

"Might bring me a biscuit or two if Swede's got an extra."

"You got it, partner."

Cody yawned, stretched, and watched his friends ride away. *Feels good to be part of something.*

The drive pulled out on a crisp morning in mid-April of 1865. Del Horton led the way. Cody and Lefty rode swing on the left side, with Slim and Grady Wilson on the right side.

Josh Clymer and Juan, the only Mexican on the Brazos Ranch, rode drag and doubled as wrangler for the small remuda of extra horses. Swede drove the chuck wagon and brought up the rear.

Del left only two hands behind to care for the ranch while they were gone.

Cody stood in his stirrups. His slow gaze swept the long, thin line of longhorns that stretched near a quarter-mile, and felt excitement and pride swell his chest.

They headed southeast. Del had told them it was about four hundred miles to New Orleans. He said it would take them a month.

Late in the afternoon of their first day out, they passed within sight of the abandoned Fort Parker.

"The fort was named in honor of Cynthia Parker," Lefty told Cody, as they walked their horses alongside the longhorns.

"Never heard of her."

"You never heard of Cynthia Parker?" Lefty asked, sounding surprised. "Why she's might near as famous in these parts as Sam Houston. She's a white girl that was captured during an Indian raid back in 'thirty-six. She ended up marrying a Comanche chief. She's the mother of Quanah Parker, surely you've heard of him?"

"Nope, can't say as I have."

"Son, your education is seriously lacking. Quanah Parker is about the most famous Comanche chief there is, I reckon."

"What's he famous for, killing white folks?"

"Well, yeah, I reckon so. He's still at war with the whites and they say he's never lost a battle. The Army has a whole passel of men out looking for him."

"Not much of a way to get *famous,* to my way of thinking. The Comanche killed my folks. I ever meet up with this Parker fellow, I'll kill him myself and save the army the trouble."

It was a tired bunch of cowboys who sat in front of the campfire that night and ate their stew and biscuits by firelight. Del sat down beside Cody and sipped a cup of coffee.

Cody asked, "How far you figure we come today?"

"Best part of fifteen miles, I reckon. We ought to hit the Trinity River day after tomorrow. You ever been to Louisiana?"

"No, sir. Truth is, I never been much of anywhere. Got me a hankerin' to see some country."

"Well, you'll see some on this drive for sure. The Cajuns are a strange sort, but they pay a good price for beef."

"Why are they called Cajuns?"

"They're part French, part Indian, and a mixture of everything in between. Their language is like something you never heard before. You'll see what I mean after we get there. Just watch yourself, they're right handy with knives."

The herd settled down for the night. Slim and Grady took the first shift riding night herd around the cattle's bedding ground. Their job was to ride a circle around the animals to keep them settled down. Cody and Lefty would relieve them at midnight when the longhorns would get to their feet, mill about a while, and then settle back down until daylight.

Cody fell into the daily routine of the drive. They crossed the Trinity, Neches, and Angelina Rivers, as well as numerous smaller streams, all without major incidents. Two weeks after the drive began they crossed into Louisiana.

Shortly after crossing the state line, the country quickly began to change. Huge trees, with limbs heavy with moss, grew thick and slowed the drive. Keeping the cattle in line became a major problem. The cowboys used coiled lariats to beat the stubborn longhorns back into line.

The herd broke out of heavy woods into a valley where the only vegetation was long-stemmed grass growing belly high to his pinto. A half-mile in front they faced a thick pine grove hugging a low-rising line of hills. Waiting at the edge of the pine grove were at least a dozen horsemen.

Cody didn't like their looks. Just as a precaution, he lifted the double-barrel shotgun hanging from his saddle horn and retrieved a handful of shells from his saddlebags. He threaded his left wrist through the rawhide loop and thumbed two shells into the weapon, closed it with a flick of his wrist, and slipped the rest of the shells into his pocket. Next he slipped the snub-nosed shotgun underneath his serape and gigged his pinto up alongside Lefty.

"That bunch up yonder looks like trouble to me," Cody told his friend. "Let's ride upside Del and see what they want."

On the other side of the line of cattle, Slim and Grady had the same idea and were riding up to join the foreman. Cody reined up beside his boss and swung a look at the riders.

They were a tough-looking bunch. Cold. Hard. They sat their saddles, staring stone-faced at the approaching Brazos River cowboys.

The obvious leader sat atop a midnight-black horse. The animal was a high-spirited, long-legged mount that pranced in place, held by a tight rein in the rider's hand. Looked like a runner to Cody.

The rider was a tall, thin fellow with sun-toughened hide stretched tight over high cheekbones. His face was long. His jaw jutted forward under thin lips. He wore a floppy black hat pulled low. His long black duster hung to his boot tops. His unwavering gaze fixed squarely upon Del Horton.

"You there," he hollered in a raspy voice. "I'll have a word with you."

"You got something to say, say it," the foreman replied.

"Name's Cyrus Barclay. I'm the chief inspector for New Orleans. These are my deputies. We got orders to inspect every herd coming into these parts."

"I suppose you got papers showing them orders?"

"Don't need to see no papers. You got my word on it."

"'Fraid that ain't good enough. I've brought herds down every year and never had them inspected before."

"They just passed a new law."

As the man spoke, Cody thumbed back both hammers of the shotgun concealed underneath his serape.

The leader of the thieves reined his black horse to a stop no more than twenty feet in front of the Brazos River riders. His men reined up behind him. He fixed a hard stare at Del Horton.

"Let's stop playing ring-around-the-rosie. We're taking the herd. You and your boys can ride away or die where you stand, makes no difference to me."

Cody flipped the serape over his shoulder with his right hand, revealing the double-barreled shotgun he pointed directly at the leader. He feathered the front trigger. The blast of double-aught pellets struck the outlaw square in the chest and lifted him out of his saddle. He did a back flip over the back of his horse.

Before the sound of the blast faded, Cody swung the nose of the shotgun and triggered another shot. Two more riders left their saddles with arms flailing and died on the way to the ground.

Even as the second shotgun blast sounded, Cody's right hand drew and thumbed back the hammer of his Colt. An outlaw to his right started bringing his pistol level for a shot. Cody shot him in the face. The man's head flew backward. A gurgled half-scream erupted from his throat as his body twisted out of the saddle.

Del and the other Brazos River riders joined the fight. Out of the corner of his eye, Cody saw Grady Wilson grab his shoulder and slump in the saddle. A large bearded outlaw swung his gun for another target. Cody shot him. The man's weapon spun out of his hand, flying through the air. As the wounded man fell, his boot caught in a stirrup. The outlaw's frightened horse wheeled and bolted away, dragging the rider along the ground.

As suddenly as the fight began, it ended. Only five outlaws remained in their saddles. The rest of their companions in crime were either dead or dying. Those left alive wheeled their mounts and galloped away leaning low in their saddles.

Cody quickly holstered his Colt and jerked his Henry rifle from the saddle boot. He levered a shell and settled the front sight on a fleeing outlaws back. He squeezed the trigger. Forty yards away, the outlaw arched his back and spun from his saddle.

Before the body hit the ground, Cody levered a shell and found another target. He took a deep breath and let it out slow before triggering the shot. His target almost made it to the trees before the slug plowed into his back. He slumped forward and slid out of his saddle. The three remaining outlaws disappeared into the pine thicket.

Cody swung a look around. Grady Wilson clung to his saddle horn, bleeding badly. Del and Lefty rushed to Grady's aid and helped him gently to the ground.

Riderless horses trotted about trailing their reins. Men lay dead or dying. The entire battle lasted only a few minutes.

Cody walked over and knelt beside Grady. "Is he gonna be all right?"

"It's a shoulder wound," Del said. "Looks like the bullet passed through right underneath his collar bone. He'll be laid up for a while, but he'll be okay. We'll get him to a doctor as soon as we get to New Orleans. That was some kind of shooting, Kid. If it hadn't been for your quick action, things might have turned out different."

"He beats all I ever seen," Slim spoke up. "The kid's a one-man army. I never seen anything like it." The others gathered around all nodded heads in agreement. Cody said nothing.

CHAPTER VI

Sow The Wind—Reap The Whirlwind

Cody's first impression of New Orleans was disappointing. The Brazos River cowboys had talked excitedly for a month about all the big city offered.

"Liquor, lovely ladies and lucky gambling tables," they bragged.

Cody saw only a dirty city with loose women standing on every street corner. He was ready to leave thirty minutes after he got there.

The city was abuzz with news that the war was over. The newspaper splashed the headline across the front page shouting General Lee surrendered on April nineth at a place called Appomattox.

The doctor patched up Grady's shoulder and put his arm in a sling. Their herd milled safely in the cattle pens and Del had his money from the cattle buyer. The Brazos River crew gathered in the hotel dining room to collect their wages.

"I'm adding a fifty dollar bonus for each of you boys," Del told them. "If you hadn't sided me back there we would have likely lost the herd. I'm obliged."

He paid everyone off and most of them headed for the nearest saloon to celebrate. Cody sat alone at a table sipping coffee.

"Ain't you gonna celebrate?" Del asked, walking over with his cup of coffee and pulling out a chair.

"Naw, I'll leave the celebrating to the rest of the boys. Most of them will be flat broke and nursing a hangover before morning."

"Yeah, this bunch around here is good at taking your money. Kid, I wanna tell you again how much I appreciate what you did. Hadn't been for you, we'd of lost our herd for sure."

"A fellow oughta ride for the brand. Just doing my job."

"Well, I want you to know you got a job at the Brazos River Ranch as long as you want it. Can I buy your supper?"

"If you're of a mind, I'd be obliged."

They talked. They ate. They talked some more.

"I usually don't ask a man about his past. I figure his past is just that, his past, and it's where it ought to stay. I judge a man by what he does after he hires on. But in your case, I can't help wondering how you got so good with those guns in such a short time."

Cody told the foreman his story, at least everything except his real name; he still wasn't sure about revealing that.

It took a while. Del listened intently. When it was over he sat silently with his head down for a spell before he spoke.

"Sometimes life ain't fair, son. Sounds like you've been dealt a bum hand. But it also sounds like you took the worst life threw at you and made the best of it. To my way of thinking, that's the sign of a *real* man.

"You're almighty good with them guns, Kid, maybe the best I ever seen. News like that is gonna travel fast and far. Men are gonna hear about you, bad men, men willing to risk their life so they can brag they were faster with a gun than the Hondo Kid. They're gonna come looking for you. Are you ready for that?"

Cody took a deep breath and let it out slowly. He stared at his coffee cup.

"I ain't trying to build no reputation."

"I believe that. But try or not, it's yours and it will hang around your neck like a millstone for the rest of your life. You may be young but you pull a mighty fast gun."

A silence passed as Cody thought about the foreman's words.

The Brazos River cowboys left New Orleans at mid-morning the following day, most of them with hangover heads and empty pockets, just like Cody had predicted. They had plenty of time to reflect on their poor judgment on the long ride back to Waco.

The next few weeks were busy ones on the ranch. Their spring calf crop was a good one and required constant attention until they were weaned. Del continued to give Cody more and more responsibility. It was clear the hands on the ranch liked him and didn't resent the foreman putting Cody in charge when the foreman had to be gone.

A month after returning from New Orleans, Cody asked permission to ride into town on Saturday.

"If it's all right, me and Lefty would like to ride into town today. We'll be back before first light on Monday?"

"I see no problem with that," the foreman said. "Enjoy your time off."

After breakfast they saddled their horses. As they tightened their cinch straps, Cody's dog scampered back and forth, seemingly sensing they were saddling up for a ride.

"You stay here this time, big fellow," Cody said softly to his dog. The golden-haired dog whined, turned and lay down.

Cody and Lefty booted their stirrups and headed to town. They reined up in front of the Brazos Café just before noontime and tied their horses to the hitching rail.

"Let's get a bite to eat," Cody suggested.

"Fine by me. Give us a chance to look at that pretty lady again. What was her name?"

"Ellen, Ellen Richardson."

"Yeah, pretty as she is, how could I forget?"

They opened the door and stepped inside. The little café looked packed. Ellen rushed from the kitchen with several plates of food in her arms for waiting customers. She spotted Cody and Lefty and flashed them a wide smile.

Cody spotted the marshal sitting alone at a table. The lawman saw him and motioned them over.

"You boys are welcome to join me if'n you're of a mind."

"We'd be obliged, Marshal," Cody said. "This is my friend from the Brazos ranch, Lefty Hobart."

"Pleased to meet you, Lefty. Hope you boys ain't planning on staying in town long."

"No, just a couple of days," Cody said. "Why?"

"There's a fellow in town been asking around about you. Looks like a gun slick. I had a word with him, but weren't nothing I could do until he causes trouble. Like I told you before, Kid, I don't want no trouble in my town."

"What's this fellow's name?"

"Said his name was Pike. Billy Pike. Tough looking kid, maybe pushing twenty. I looked through my fliers but didn't have anything on him."

"Don't know anybody by that name. Don't know why he'd be asking about me."

"I figure he's heard you're a fast gun and wants to try you."

"I ain't looking for trouble, Marshal."

"But trouble has a way of finding you, don't it, Kid?"

"Yeah, seems so."

Ellen came by their table and greeted them with a smile.

"I was afraid you decided our fair little town wasn't to your liking and moved on."

"No, just been busy. We took a bunch of longhorns down to New Orleans and just got back a few weeks ago," Cody said. "You remember my friend, Lefty?"

"Of course, glad both of you stopped in. Want some lunch? As I recall you like fried chicken?"

"Sure do. I'll have that."

"Me too," Lefty told her, offering his biggest smile.

"Coming right up. I'll be right back with coffee."

"Say you took a drive to New Orleans?"

"Yes sir," Cody replied.

"What'd you think of it?"

"Didn't like it."

"Me neither. I was there a few years back. Didn't take me long to get my can full of that place. Where'd you say you're from?"

"Hondo, Texas. About thirty miles or so west of San Antonio. It ain't really a town, just a trading post."

"Uh-huh," the marshal murmured as he rose. "Well, I best be moseying along. You boys take care now."

Ellen brought their food. Their plates were piled high with fried chicken, mashed potatoes covered with gravy, corn on the cob and hot rolls with honey.

"And I thought old Swede fed good," Lefty said, picking up his fork and digging into his lunch. "This may take a while."

It did.

When they finally cleaned their plates, Ellen found time to return.

"How about a piece of fresh apple pie?"

"Thanks, but I'm about to pop now," Cody told her. "That shore was good, Miss Ellen."

"Sorry I've been so busy I haven't had time to visit. Are you staying in town a while?"

"Just tonight, I reckon. We promised Del we'd be back to the ranch by first light Monday morning."

"Then you'll be in town tomorrow?"

"Yes, ma'am, I expect so."

"Then I hope you will stop to see me again while you're in town."

She rushed back into the kitchen. Lefty fixed a long stare at Cody.

"What is it about a gunman that draws women like a fly to a cow patty?"

"Naw, she's just a nice lady. Come on, I'll let you buy me a beer."

Cody left money for their meal on the table with a generous tip. They walked down the street to the Double-Deuce Saloon. They pushed through the bat-wing doors and bellied up to the bar. The bartender Cody remembered as Sam arrived and wiped the bar in front of them.

"What'll it be?"

"Two beers," Lefty told him.

The bartender eyed Cody with a long look as he set their beers in front of them.

"Ain't you that kid who shot the fellow in here a while back? Call yourself the Hondo Kid?"

"I reckon,"

"That fellow over yonder's been asking about you," the barkeep said, motioning with a nod of his head.

Cody turned to look. The man the marshal had described earlier sat alone at a table near the back. He had a hard stare fixed square on Cody. He stood when their gazes met.

Like the marshal said, the man looked to be straddling twenty. He was a bit shorter than Cody, clean-shaven with shoulder-length black hair. He wore a black, bib-buttoned shirt and dark pants and matching black hat with a Concho hatband. A pearl-handled Colt rested in a cutaway, slim-jim holster, a gunfighter rig.

He walked over to stand near the far end of the bar and swung a look at Cody.

"You the one they call the Hondo Kid?"

"Who's asking"?

"Name's Billy Pike. You might have heard of me."

"Nope, can't say I have."

"I heard you were pretty slick with a gun. Don't see one. Reckon I heard wrong."

"Reckon so."

The sound of boots pounding hurriedly on the boardwalk outside and the squeak of the batwing doors behind him caused Cody to crook a look. The marshal hurried into the saloon carrying a short-barrel shotgun in the crook of his arm. He walked slowly to stop a dozen feet from the bar.

"Listen to me, both of you," the marshal Bell said, his voice rising. "I've done told both of you there would be no trouble in my town."

"Like I told you, Marshal," Cody said. "I ain't looking for trouble."

The gun fighter ignored the marshal. His glaring flat stare remained fixed on Cody.

"They say you hide your gun under that serape. Lift it up and let's take a look."

"Done told you, mister, I don't want trouble."

"I come a long way to try you. I ain't leavin' till it's done."

"Pike!" the marshal bellowed. "Gonna tell you something. You pull iron on this boy and he's gonna kill you, straight up. But even if you was to win, you lose. If you kill him, I'll see you hang for murder. If you make a move on me, I'll kill you where you stand. Ain't working out exactly the way you planned, is it?

"You got a losing situation whichever way it goes. The only way out is to fork your horse and make tracks outta town."

A silence passed as the two gunmen stood staring at one another. Cody saw a wild, glazed look in Pike's eyes and he knew the reputation craving gunfighter wasn't about to back down.

"No!" Pike shouted. "I come here to kill him and that's what I'm gonna do, law or no law! Now lift that thing up and let's see if you're as fast as they're saying."

Seeing there was no way out of it, Cody took a long, deep breath and let it out slowly before he flipped the edge of his serape over his right shoulder with his left hand, revealing his holstered Colt. His right hand settled a hair's breath from the bone handle. His cold stare locked on the gun fighter's eyes. A few heartbeats passed.

Suddenly Cody saw it. Pike's eyes squinted. He was about to draw.

Pike's hand suddenly came up filled with the pearl-handled Colt. He was young and fast and determined to earn a reputation at the Hondo Kid's expense. He was faster than any Cody had faced. But not fast enough. Cody's first shot hit him dead center of his forehead before he got his Colt up level enough to take aim. His shot ploughed into the wooden floor in front of his boots.

Pike flew backwards. The back of his head exploded like a ripe watermelon. Blood sprayed out in a crimson shower. The gunfighter was dead before his body tumbled to the wooden floor with a loud thud. His boots jerked just once in false life before falling deathly still.

"Crazy fool!" the marshal spat out the words. "His kind ain't got the sense God gave a goose. Folks won't even remember his name a week after we put him in the ground."

Cody calmly ejected the spent cartridge and thumbed in a fresh one from his gun belt.

"I'm sorry, Marshal. I tried to talk him out of it."

"I know, Kid. It weren't your fault. He drew first. It was self-defense, pure and simple. He come here looking for a fight with you and he got it, it just didn't turn out like he thought. The thing is, he's just the first in a long line that will be coming for you."

Cody glanced over at Lefty. His friend was still standing at the bar in wide-eyed wonder, slowly shaking his head.

"Am I free to go, Marshal?"

"Don't see why not."

Cody headed for the front door. The large crowd gathering around the front door of the saloon and along the boardwalk melted aside as he approached. They seemed to want to get a look at the young gunfighter everybody was talking about, but not too close a look. Lefty fell into step behind Cody. They walked across the street to where their horses were tied.

"Let's stable our horses and get us a room at the hotel," Cody said. "I'd like to get away from this crowd for a while."

They led their horses down the street to the livery. The hostler was a grizzly old fellow who wore bib overalls and a floppy hat. His face was covered with a long, gray beard that failed to completely hide the deep wrinkles and weathered skin. He greeted them with a crackly, high-pitched voice.

"You young fellows just getting into town? Too bad you missed all the excitement. A gunfighter they call the Hondo Kid just killed another fellow up at the saloon. They say he's faster'n scat. Shore wish I had been there to see it."

"You don't say," Lefty said, flicking a sideways glance at his companion.

Cody paid little attention to the old man and led Cincinnati into an empty stall. All the time they were unsaddling their horses, the old hostler kept up a steady, detailed account of gunfights he had supposedly witnessed over the years.

"Word is this Hondo Kid might be faster than any of 'em," the liveryman continued, even as Cody and Lefty walked out.

"Word spreads faster than a prairie fire," Lefty commented as he sidled close alongside Cody as they made their way toward the hotel.

"Yep," Cody replied, not in a talking mood.

They pushed through the front door of the hotel and walked up to the counter. A skinny, sickly-looking man with a baldhead and thick glasses widened his eyes when he looked up and saw them.

"You're the gunfighter," the clerk said excitedly. You're the one that killed that fellow over in the saloon."

"We need two rooms," Cody said, ignoring the man's comments.

"I didn't see it myself, but everybody's talking about it. They're calling you the fastest gun in Texas. Most excitement we've had in Waco in a long time. Wait until I tell folks you're staying right here. Right here in our hotel."

"Just as soon you didn't," Cody said. "You got two rooms or not?"

"Got eight rooms, all of 'em empty, take your pick."

"Give us two facing the street."

"You bet. Right proud to have you," the man said, handing them two keys. "You will be in rooms one and two, our finest rooms, at the top of the stairs."

Cody picked up the keys and handed one to Lefty as they headed toward the stairs.

"Did you hear what he said, partner? He said folks are calling you the fastest gun in Texas. Ain't that something? I never do see you draw. One second your gun is in the holster; the next it's in your hand. Beats anything I ever seen."

They topped the stairs and found their rooms.

"Wake me up about five o'clock," Cody told his friend. "We'll go eat a bite."

Cody opened the door to his room and stepped inside, closing the door behind him and propping a chair underneath the doorknob. He hung his hat on the bedpost and flopped down on the bed.

He swallowed a tight knot in his throat and drew a long breath and then let it out in a sigh of relief. *I just killed another man. Could I have talked him out of it?* He lay there staring up at the ceiling, running the fight over and over in his mind. *Where will it all end?*

CHAPTER VII

Everybody Needs A Friend

A loud knocking on the door to Cody's hotel room woke him from a fitful sleep. He swung his feet to the floor and made his way to the door.

"Lefty," he called out. "Is that you?"

"Yeah, it's me. You ready to go eat supper?"

Cody removed the chair from under the doorknob and swung the door open.

"Yep, let me wash up and I'll be ready."

He walked over to the dresser and poured water from the blue and white pitcher into the matching wash bowl, washed his face and hands and dried them on the towel hanging nearby. He threaded fingers through his long, wheat-colored hair and clamped his John B. in place.

They made their way down the stairs and out the front door. Evening sun crowned the western horizon. The fiery-red ball fought hard for survival, but inevitably lost the battle and was slowly swallowed up by the distant hills.

Cody and Lefty walked along the boardwalk. The men

stepped aside for two older ladies approaching along the boardwalk and touched thumb and fingers to their hat brim in greeting. The women offered a nod and a thin smile in return.

"Don't know about you, but I'm hungry," Lefty said, as they approached the café. "We ain't et since lunchtime."

"You'd eat a dozen times a day if you could."

Ellen spotted them and broke a wide smile across her pretty face as they opened the door and stepped into the small café. "Have a seat. I'll pour you boys some coffee,"

They made their way to a table and folded into the chairs. Cody gave the room the once-over with a quick glance while Ellen poured them coffee. Only two other people were there. Cody could tell by their clothes they weren't local cowboys. He studied them over the rim of his coffee cup.

One was a small, sickly looking fellow who wore a black bowler hat. Clearly he was the less impressive of the two.

The other looked what Cody pictured a gambler would look like. He was somewhere close to thirty, Cody judged, and what most folks would call handsome. His black hair lay slicked back and his face looked clean-shaven. He wore a dark broadcloth suit and starched collar white shirt with a matching string tie. His brocade vest sported a raised pattern in gold thread. A gold chain was attached to a vest button and disappeared into a watch pocket. He wore a tied-down, hand-tooled, black holster cradling a pearl-handled Colt. The man puffed on a long, thin cigar and had a flat, squinty-eyed stare that worked its way slowly over Cody.

"I was beginning to think you weren't coming tonight after what happened today. I worried all afternoon about you," Ellen said. "Were you hurt?"

"No, ma'am, I'm fine."

"I swear it makes no sense to me. All this killing just to see who can kill the other the quickest."

"I didn't ask for a fight. I tried to talk him out of it."

"That's what the marshal said, too. I'm just glad you weren't hurt."

Wanting to change the subject, Cody asked, "What'cha got good for supper?"

"Got some nice, fresh-cut beef steaks."

"Sounds good to me, what about you, Lefty?"

"Just what I had in mind."

Ellen hurried away to prepare their meals.

"You the one they call the Hondo Kid?" the gambler-looking man asked in a deep baritone voice.

Cody swung a look in the man's direction.

"Some call me that."

"Just rode into town and heard about the shooting. Heard you put down Billy Pike."

Cody didn't answer. He just sipped his coffee and stared long at his cup.

"I saw Billy take on the Hobbs brothers down in Abilene. He killed both of them before they got off a shot. He was quick, but I reckon you must be quicker."

Still Cody didn't reply.

The door opened and Marshal Bell walked in. His glance slid quickly over Cody and Lefty and settled on the two newcomers. He paused; his long gaze took their measure, and then walked over to stand close to the newcomers' table.

"I'm Marshal Henry Bell. I don't know this fellow," the marshal said, glancing briefly in the skinny man's direction before fixing a look on the fancy-dressed man, "but you're Vance Longley. What brings you to Waco?"

The one called Longley locked gazes with the marshal and took time to draw a deep inhale from his cigar before replying.

"Just passing through, Marshal. Any law against that?"

"No, but let me make it simple so even you can understand it, we don't want your kind in Waco. I'd suggest you finish your meal and move on."

"That's not very hospitable, Marshal."

"Longley, I ain't in a very hospitable mood. We just had one gunfight today. We don't want another. If you're still in Waco come sunup, I'm gonna lock you up and that's a truth you can write down. You got my word on it."

"On what charge? I ain't broken no law."

"Spittin' in the street, breathing our air, take your pick. Just see you ain't in Waco come sunup."

With that said, the marshal turned and walked to Cody's table, pulled out a chair and sat.

"Reckon I'll have a cup over here, Miss Ellen."

The two newcomers rose from their table, paid for their meal and left without saying a word. The marshal watched them closely until the door closed behind them.

"Who was that fellow, Marshal?" Lefty asked, as Ellen poured them coffee.

"Vance Longley is a known man far and wide. They say he's the fastest gun alive. I've never actually seen him in action, but word is he's killed more'n twenty men in straight-up gunfights. One thing for sure, anywhere he goes there's gun trouble."

"You don't reckon he's here because of me, do you, Marshal?" Cody asked.

"More'n likely, Kid. More'n likely. He might have been on Billy Pike's trail, but now that you put Billy down, chances are he'll be gunning for you. Gunfighters like him chase a reputation like a dog chases a rabbit. They don't like competition. They get real jealous when they hear somebody's rumored to be fast with a gun."

"Do you think he'll leave town like you told him to?" Ellen Richardson asked, worry clearly showing on her face.

"Hope so, Miss Ellen, but I doubt it. Men like Longley ain't used to taking orders from anybody."

"Who's the man with him?" Lefty asked.

"Never seen him before, but I'd say he's Longley's back-up. Most gunfighters have someone they can depend on to tilt the odds in their favor."

"You mean he's a back shooter?"

"I wouldn't be surprised, but only if Longley thinks the outcome might be in question."

"So," Cody interjected. "What am I supposed to do? Do I fight him or what?"

"I'd suggest you remember you got business elsewhere," the marshal suggested.

Cody stared at his coffee cup for a minute, clearly considering the marshal's words.

"You mean run. I'm sorry, Mr. Bell, but I can't do that. I've never taken backwater and I ain't gonna start now. It just ain't in me. Besides, if he's the kind of man you say, he'd follow me wherever I went. I don't fancy having to look over my shoulder the rest of my life."

"Sorry to hear you say that, Kid, but I ain't surprised. I had you pegged as someone who didn't have run in him. You gotta find a life you can live with.

"Well, if he's still here at sun-up, I'll do what I said I was gonna do, or die trying."

Marshal Bell swallowed the rest of his coffee and pushed up from his chair.

"Better make my rounds, I reckon. Watch your back, Kid. I've sorta taken a liking to you."

"I'll be watching his back, marshal," Lefty said. "Don't worry about that."

After the marshal left, Miss Ellen poured herself a cup of coffee and sat down. "Marshal Bell is a good man. Maybe this fellow will leave town,"

"Maybe so," Cody replied. "Maybe not."

"Then you will be in town tomorrow?"

"Planning on it. Why?"

"We're having a pie supper at the church tomorrow night. I was hoping both of you would come."

"Don't see why not," Cody told her. "Never been to one. What do they do?"

"It's a lot of fun and it's for a good cause. We're trying to raise money to put a steeple on the church. All the ladies of the church bake a pie and bring it. The pies are auctioned off. The person who buys the pie gets to eat it with the one who baked it. No one is supposed to know whose pie they are bidding on, but everyone does. You would both enjoy it."

"Sounds like it. If nothing happens we'll be there," Cody assured her.

That brought a wide smile. She leaned close to Cody and whispered in his ear.

"Shhh, I'm bringing a cherry pie."

It was Cody's turn to smile and he did.

Ellen brought their steaks, along with fried potatoes, corn-on-the-cob and a basket of hot yeast rolls. They ate and talked. When closing time came, Cody and Lefty saw Miss Ellen safely home.

At the gate she stopped and turned to face them. A full moon lit her face almost like day. She reached out and touched both their cheeks with a hand.

"Everyone needs a friend. I'm lucky to have two of them."

A huge lump crawled up the back of Cody's throat. He swallowed. Then swallowed again, but the lump refused to budge. *Sure wish I was twenty-one already.*

Cody and Lefty stood and watched her as she hurried up the path to her house. At the front door she paused and looked back over her shoulder and lifted a wave. They stood motionless and watched until she closed the door behind her.

The three of them had shared a beautiful, almost sacred moment. There weren't many of those in a lifetime.

Neither fellow said a word as they walked side-by-side up to the main street. They turned and walked along the boardwalk. It was Saturday night. The saloon was going full blast. Piano music filtered through the open door and drifted on a soft evening breeze.

"Want a beer before we turn in?" Cody asked.

"Think that's a good idea?" Lefty returned the question. "That gunfighter more'n likely will be there."

"Maybe, but like I said, I ain't got no run in me. If we didn't stop by the saloon it would look like I was running from him."

"Whatever you say, partner."

Horses lined the hitching rails out front of the saloon. The music got louder. Cody pushed open the batwing doors and stepped inside. Lefty followed closely. Both stood just inside the doors and swept a slow gaze around the room.

The saloon smell greeted them. The stench of stale whiskey, long unwashed body odor and cigarette smoke filled the room. A blue layer of smoke hovered above the crowd of cowboys, businessmen, gamblers and saloon girls like a storm cloud. Flies circled a puddle of spilled beer that lay seeping through the cracks of the wooden floor.

Gamblers stood three deep around a poker table. All the tables were full and cowboys stood shoulder-to-shoulder at the long bar.

Someone at the bar recognized Cody and whispered to the cowboy standing next to him. He told his neighbor and so on until within seconds every head was turned, every eye gazed at the young shooter standing inside the door wearing the ragged serape.

Voices lowered to quiet whispers. The piano stopped playing. A deathly silence settled over the room. Men scooted sidelong along the crowded bar, making room for Cody and his friend. Cody nodded his thanks and walked over to fill the space. Lefty followed only a step behind.

"What's your pleasure, Kid? It's on the house." the bartender asked.

"Two beers and I'm obliged."

The barkeep brought their beers and Cody lifted the mug to his lips. When he did he saw the gunfighter, Vance Longley's, reflection in the long mirror behind the bar. The spectators around the poker table melted aside.

Cody watched as Longley removed a long, thin cigar from a vest pocket. He bit off the tip and spat it out and then ran the cigar in and out of his mouth, all the while keeping a level gaze fixed on Cody.

He clamped the cigar between his teeth and lit it, breathed in a long pull and let the smoke out in a thin line. He tipped back in his chair and fixed a stare at Cody.

The crowd waited in hushed anticipation.

"You're awful young to be a shooter," Longley said, his voice low, barely audible to those standing at the bar. His face wore an ugly smirk that was tainted by an arrogant smugness.

Cody sipped his beer and said nothing.

"What I can't figure out is how in the world you beat Billy Pike. That's what's got me buffaloed. Billy was fast. Not as fast as me, but then nobody is. They're saying you're chain lightening with that belly gun. That bothers me. Folks might get to thinking you're as fast as me and we can't have that."

Cody listened, but still didn't reply.

The batwing doors pushed open. Marshal Bell walked in followed closely by a deputy. Both carried double-barrel shotguns in the crook of their arms. The marshal looked straight at Cody.

"Make tracks, Kid."

Cody swallowed the last of his beer and sat the mug on the bar. He turned and fixed a flat stare at Longley. For a moment their gazes locked. Neither blinked.

"Move, Hondo!" the marshal ordered loudly.

Cody walked slowly toward the door. Lefty was only a step behind.

"We'll meet, Kid," Longley said loud enough that all could hear. "If not now, soon. Very soon."

Cody and Lefty left the saloon and headed for the hotel.

"Think you could take him?" Lefty asked.

"Hope I never have to find out," Cody replied.

Morning sun crested the eastern horizon as Cody and Lefty emerged from the hotel and headed toward the café for breakfast. Up the street, Vance Longley and his companion leaned against a post in front of the Waco Mercantile store directly across the street from the café.

"See 'em?" Lefty asked.

"I see 'em."

As they got closer to the café, the gunman stepped off the boardwalk and walked slowly to the middle of the street before stopping. He shrugged out of his suit coat and handed it to his companion without taking his gaze off Cody.

Cody and Lefty gave one another a look. "If it comes down to it," Cody told his friend, "just keep an eye on the other fellow for me."

"You got it, partner."

"Hey, Kid!" Longley shouted. "Just couldn't bring myself to leave town without finding out how fast you are. I'd always wonder."

"I don't want to fight you, Mr. Longley," Cody told him.

"Sorry Kid, but I ain't giving you a choice. You'll pull iron with me, sure enough, and I'll kill you."

"Not today," Marshal Bell said from behind the gunman. "I've got a double-barrel shotgun aimed at you and an itchy trigger finger. Unbuckle that gun belt and let it drop in the street."

Longley didn't as much as look in the marshal's direction.

He stood motionless in the center of the dusty street. His hand hovered within a hair's breath of the pearl-handled Colt on his hip.

Several early risers ventured onto the boardwalk to watch what was going on. Other faces crowded windows along the street.

"I don't give up my gun for anybody," Longley said.

In the stillness of the early morning, the sound of two hammers being thumbed back on the double barrel echoed along the street.

"I won't say it again, Vance."

Underneath his serape, Cody's hand made sweat on the handle of his Colt. He didn't dare flip his serape up and maybe do something that would cause Longley to draw. He stood motionless, waiting.

Finally, the gunman raised both hands shoulder-high.

"Okay, Marshal. You win this round. There'll be another day. I'm unbuckling my belt."

With his left hand Longley slowly reached down and untied the rawhide thong from around his leg. His hand moved slowly to unbuckle his gun belt. It fell into the dusty street.

"Now tell your partner to do the same," Marshal Bell ordered.

He didn't have to. The skinny fellow let his gun drop.

"Go pick up their guns, Sammy," the marshal told his deputy.

Cody hadn't even noticed the deputy who stood by the corner of the mercantile store with a shotgun in his hand. The second lawman walked to the middle of the street and retrieved the guns.

"Let's go," Marshal Bell said, stepping down off the boardwalk. "I got a nice jail cell waiting on the two of you."

"Just a matter of time, Kid," Longley said, looking at Cody. "All the marshal did was buy you a little more time. We'll meet again, mark my word."

"Shut up and start walking," Marshal Bell told him, urging him with the nose of the shotgun in his back.

Cody watched them go. When they disappeared through the door of the jail, Cody and Lefty turned and walked toward the café. Several customers had left their breakfast to crowd outside the door. Cody saw Miss Ellen standing in front.

As Cody drew near, the crowd stood aside to allow him and Lefty to enter. Ellen reached and took Cody's hand and squeezed it before leading him inside.

"Have a seat. I'll get you both some coffee."

The sign over the door indicated, *THE WACO COMMUNITY CHURCH.*

The church sat at the end of the main street at the far end of town. It was a small, white building that looked like it wouldn't hold more than two-dozen people. More than four times that many milled around two long tables covered with white tablecloths. It appeared at least fifty pies sat on the tables.

A wooden half-barrel stood on a small table nearby. A heavyset lady stood ladling red punch into cups. Cody and Lefty headed toward her.

They'd taken their first sip of the sweet-tasting punch when Miss Ellen hurried up.

"I'm so happy to see you two. I was beginning to think I was going to have to buy my own pie."

"Sorry if we're late," Cody said.

"No, you're right on time. It's just about to start."

As she spoke, a tall, scarecrow-thin fellow in a black suit and with thin hair on top of his head held his hands up asking for quiet. Miss Ellen leaned close and whispered. "That's Reverend Small, our pastor."

"Folks," the preacher said, "it shore is good to see all of you out tonight. I see lots of faces I haven't seen in a while. We'd like to see you next Sunday morning, too. Course, if all of you showed up we'd have to build a bigger building."

"Let me say just a few words before we get things started."

Someone hollered, "Don't make that speech too windy, Preacher, we're all hungry." A ripple of good-hearted laughter swept through the crowd.

"As you all know, every penny of the money that is raised tonight will go to help us put a steeple up yonder on top of our church. The nice ladies of our church baked up some delicious pies and I know you fellows are just itching to get to share them with these pretty ladies, so let's get started."

A heavyset fellow Miss Ellen said was one of the deacons served as auctioneer. He was pretty good at it, too. He held up a pie, told what kind it was, and started the bidding. Most pies sold for a dollar or two.

When the auctioneer picked up a pie and told the audience it was a cherry pie, Miss Ellen squeezed Cody's hand.

"What am I bid for this delicious-looking cherry pie?" the auctioneer asked. "Do I hear a dollar?"

A fellow standing down front raised his hand.

"A dollar!" the auctioneer shouted. "I've got a dollar. Do I hear two?"

Cody raised his hand.

"Two dollars!" the fellow shouted even louder. "I've got two dollars bid. Do I hear three?"

Again, the man in front raised his hand. The auctioneer began to get excited.

"I have three dollars bid, thank you, sir. Do I hear four dollars?"

"Five dollars!" Cody hollered, raising his hand with fingers spread.

"My goodness," the auctioneer shouted loudly. "Five dollars has been bid. Do I hear six?"

The crowd was silent. The auctioneer looked at the fellow who had been bidding against Cody. "I've got five dollars bid for this delicious-looking cherry pie. Do I hear six? I've got five dollars going once. I have five dollars going twice. Sold to the young man near the back."

A grin crooked its way across Cody's face. He slid a quick glance at Miss Ellen. She smiled broadly and squeezed his hand. He walked forward, proud as a bantam rooster and paid the lady collecting money. She handed him his cherry pie.

"Thank you," Ellen said.

Lefty laughed. "First pie I ever seen worth five dollars."

They found a spot under a big oak tree where the grass was green and soft. Ellen cut the pie and handed a large slice to both Cody and Lefty.

"Um," Lefty said, taking a large bite. "Best cherry pie I ever tasted, especially since it was the Kid's five dollars." They all laughed.

CHAPTER VIII

Justice—Texas Style

Cody and Lefty arrived back at the ranch just before midnight. All the other Lazy J hands already lay in their bunks, snoring loudly. Not wanting to disturb the sleeping cowboys, Cody and Lefty undressed in the dark and crawled into their bunks. A new workday would arrive all too quickly.

At breakfast the following morning, after the Brazos hands stuffed themselves with flapjacks covered with sorghum, Del Horton called them all together. "Everybody grab a cup of coffee and have a seat. I need to make some new work assignments."

The men sat around, sipped coffee, and waited to hear what the foreman had to say.

"As you boys know, this country is all open range. We keep our brood cows bunched in pretty close, but we let the rest roam the range pretty much anywhere they take a notion.

"There have been reports from other ranches that some of their cattle are disappearing. Maybe they're just bunched up somewhere in a thicket or something, but we can't afford to take any chances.

"Starting today, I want four of you riding the range. When you locate one of our herds put a bell cow with them. That will keep them bunched a little better and make it easier for us to locate them come roundup time.

"Keep your eyes peeled for anything unusual. Hondo, take Lefty with you and cover the north range. Grady, you and Slim cover the range to the south. Take enough trail supplies with you to last a week."

The morning sun was fresh born and an hour old when Cody and Lefty climbed into their saddles and headed north. Behind them a packhorse loaded with their trail supplies followed on a lead line, along with three of their older and wiser bell cows. Cody's dog trotted in front.

They rode all day in an ever-widening circle. It was nearing sundown before they found the first bunch of Brazos cattle. They were scattered in a draw, grazing peacefully among a heavy growth of mesquite and scrub cedar. Cody judged there to be near forty head.

"Let's turn one of the bell cows among 'em and keep 'em bunched in the draw till morning," Cody suggested. "We might as well make dry camp here for tonight."

Dark set in by the time they made camp and had a fire going. Lefty put coffee water on to boil from one of their canteens while Cody strung a picket line for their horses.

After a supper of cold biscuits and bacon, they leaned back against their upturned saddles and sipped their steaming coffee. The ink-black summer sky was sprinkled with a million twinkling stars. A three-quarter moon cast eerie shadows at the edge of the jagged circle of light from their campfire. The big dog walked over and lay down next to Cody. He reached a hand and rubbed the dog's ears.

"When I was just a kid we used to sit out on the front porch on a night like this and try to count the stars," Cody said. "I had a dog back then, too."

"What happened to it?"

"Indians killed him when they killed my folks."

"You miss your folks, don't you?"

"Yeah, I do. Your folks still living?"

Lefty took his time answering. "No, they both died when I was real little. I lived with my grandparents after Ma and Pa passed on. They're both dead now, too."

"You got any brothers or sisters?" Cod wanted to know.

"Nope, not even any kin that I know about. What about you?"

"I had an older brother, but I reckon he was killed in the war."

"Lonesome feeling, ain't it? Not having family, I mean."

Cody let that thought wrap itself around his mind for a spell. "Shore is," he finally said.

Silence settled. Both Cody and his friend lost themselves in their own thoughts of family. The night surrounded them with quietness. The soothing sounds of the crackling fire and an occasional lowing of the nearby cattle quickly brought sleep.

During the next two days they found three more bunches and several strays, which they drove back to join the nearest herd. On the fourth day they came upon something that caused both Cody and Lefty to step to the ground and examine closer.

Tracks of a larger herd, perhaps as many as a hundred head, were accompanied by the tracks of three shod horses. Clearly, three horsemen were driving the herd.

"What do you think, partner?" Cody asked.

"If them are Brazos River cattle they're driving, I think we better check it out."

"Reckon we best find out what brand they're wearin'," Cody said, stepping into a stirrup and swinging into the saddle.

They followed the trail the rest of the day. Just before sundown, a second herd of another twenty cattle, driven by two more riders, joined the first herd.

"There's five of them now," Lefty said. "What if those are Brazos cattle, we gonna tangle with all five of them rustlers?"

"Been thinking on it," Cody replied. "We've been gone four days already and it's another hard days' ride back to the ranch. I expect the boss will be wondering about us. Might be best if one of us rode back and told Mr. Horton what we found. I'll stay on their trail and see where they're headed."

"Watch yourself, Kid. I'll be back with some of the boys quick as I can."

Lefty wheeled his horse and kicked it into a ground-eating short lope.

Full dark shrouded the prairie, but even in the dimness of the night the trail was still visible. His gaze swept the horizon, searching for the glow of a campfire, but nothing he saw looked like it.

Just before midnight, the trail dipped into a deep arroyo that snaked its way through the east Texas prairie. Cody reached down and slipped his Henry rifle from its backward saddle boot and levered a shell. He didn't like the nervous knot in the pit of his stomach.

His eyes stared into the darkness of every twist and turn of the canyon-like arroyo. His ears strained for any sound that seemed out of place.

Then he heard it.

From around a bend up ahead, he heard the faint sound of cattle bawling. *Wonder if they'll have someone watching their back trail?*

His hand made sweat on the wooden stock of his rifle. *Sure would like to know if those are Brazos River cattle. This might turn out to be a wild goose chase.*

The more he thought about it, the more he convinced himself he ought to back off and wait until Lefty got back with some of the boys. *I'd hate to tangle with these fellows and then discover these ain't even our cattle.*

He turned Cincinnati and rode back to a small offshoot canyon he spotted about a mile back. He decided he'd make dry camp there and see how things looked come morning. He found the opening and rode a couple hundred yards around a sharp curve and reined up. After tying his pinto securely to a scrub cedar, he shook out his bedroll and fell asleep in minutes.

Cody lay awake well before first light. He decided to leave his pinto tied in the small off shoot canyon and take a look at things from on foot. He climbed the high canyon wall and peered over the rim carefully. Seeing nothing on the flat prairie, he trotted cautiously along the edge of the canyon.

Hearing cattle ahead, he slowed and proceeded with caution. When he figured he was above the herd, he bellied down and chanced a look over the edge.

Forty feet below, the long line of cattle plodded along at a slow pace. Off in the distance Cody could see a rider on a blood-red bay leading the herd. A single rider flanked the line on either side. Two more riders rode drag, urging the longhorns along with coiled ropes.

The men were a tough-looking bunch. They all rode single-rigged saddles. That told Cody these definitely weren't everyday, run-of-the-mill, cowboys. Any cowboy worth his salt wouldn't be caught riding a single-rigged saddle. Even from forty feet away, Cody could see the brands on the cattle clearly. They all wore the Brazos River brand on their hips.

Cody knew it would be at least another day before Lefty and the Brazos crew could catch up with the herd. All he could do was tag along and see where the rustlers were taking the cattle. He would have to be careful. He couldn't afford to let them know they were being followed.

By noon, the herd broke out of the canyon and moved steadily northeast. Cody had no idea where they were headed. But it was obvious they had someplace in mind and they felt safe making the trip.

Once they broke out onto open prairie, Cody was forced into dropping back and following from a distance to keep from being spotted. It was just after sundown when he glanced over his shoulder and spotted riders coming at a gallop. He recognized Del Horton and six of the Brazos River riders. He reined up and waited for them.

"How far ahead are they?" the foreman asked, as they reined up on sweaty horses.

"Couple of miles or so," Cody told him. "They seem to know where they're headed. What's up that way?"

"Town called Corsicana's the only town for miles. How sure are you these are our cattle?"

"I'm sure. I saw our brands plain as day. They ain't even tried to change them."

"Then let's ride. I want to catch them before they get where they're going."

Eight Brazos River riders gigged their horses to a gallop. They closed the distance in short order. As they rode within sight, Horton and his crew fisted their rifles and levered shells into the chambers.

The rustlers spotted them and spurred their horses into a run. The Brazos riders laid down a hail of bullets that knocked two of the fleeing outlaws from their saddles. The remaining three, seeing their companions hit the dirt, threw up their hands and surrendered. The Brazos River riders quickly surrounded them.

"Get them off their horses and tie them up," Del ordered.

The men were jerked from their horses, disarmed, and their hands quickly tied behind their backs.

"Which one is the leader of this pack of thieves?" the foremen asked.

Two of the rustlers cast quick, sideways glances at the tallest of the three. He was tall, scarecrow thin, and looked to be somewhere straddling thirty. He had small, hawkish eyes, a permanent squint look to them.

"What's your name?" Del demanded, fixing a level look at the man.

"Name's Talbot, Otis Talbot."

"You boys rustled the wrong cattle. Get 'em on their horses."

"What you gonna do, mister?" the tall man asked nervously.

"Do? We're gonna stretch your neck. That's what we're gonna do."

"But you can't do that! We didn't even get a trial or nothin'!"

"Take it up with the judge."

"What judge?"

"The one you're fixing to meet. Bring them on. I saw a tree a ways back that ought to serve the purpose. Grady, take some of the boys and head those cattle back toward home."

When they reached a large oak tree with a stout limb, Del called a halt.

"Drop a noose over their heads," he ordered.

"Please, mister," one of the rustlers begged. "Don't do this. I didn't mean no harm." The man broke into tears, his body jerking with sobs. "This ain't no way for a man to die!"

"Never seen a good way," the foreman told them. "You boys picked a poor way to make a living. If you got anything to say, you best get it said."

The skinny leader let loose with a string of curses, using words Cody had never heard before.

The third man, somewhat older, sat stone-faced and silent, seemingly accepting the consequences of his actions. At least he was taking his punishment like a man. He sat tall and erect, his gaze fixed straight ahead.

Cody knew the rustlers deserved what they were about to get. They had chosen the *easy* way, stealing what belonged to somebody else. But still in all, he couldn't help but feel sorry for them, especially the older fellow.

Del Horton guided his mount behind the three rustlers. He held a coiled lariat in his hand and paused for an instant, as if considering what he was about to do. Then he swatted the skinny leader's horse on the rump.

The horse leaped forward, dragging the outlaw from his saddle. The rustler dropped. When he hit the end of the rope, his neck snapped like a dried branch and crooked to one side. His feet jerked a few times, and went still.

Before the first rustler stopped kicking, Del swatted the second man's horse. The sobbing man's shrill scream was cut short when his weight broke his neck.

Del walked his horse behind the older man's mount. He paused.

"What's your name, mister?" the foreman asked.

"Sam Bodine."

"What are you doing ridin' with riff-raff like this? You don't look like the sort."

"Needed the money. Got a sickly wife."

"Where do you live?"

"Corsicana."

"Would you work if you had a job?"

"I've worked hard all my life, but since the war there just ain't no jobs."

"I'm Del Horton, foreman of the Brazos River Ranch. I was thinking, we've got a small cabin on the ranch, nothing fancy, but you and the wife could make a home there. We could use another man. We pay forty a month and found. The job's yours if you want it."

"Mister, that's an answer to prayer. I'll work hard, you'll see. I'll make you a good hand. I'm shore much obliged, Mr. Horton."

"You go on home and see to your wife. Soon as we get back to the ranch, I'll send a wagon and a couple of boys to help get you moved. Hondo, cut this man loose. He works for the Brazos Ranch now."

Cody smiled broadly. "Sure will, boss,"

CHAPTER XIX
Hide Peelers

A month passed. Then two. Summer turned to fall. The early spring calf crop was now young yearlings and required constant attention.

It was a busy time on the Brazos Ranch. Hay had to be put up for winter feeding, water holes needed to be cleaned out, and the chore of range duty to keep track of the herds kept the hands busy.

Most of the cowboys hated the monotonous duty of riding the range, but Cody looked forward to his turn. Lately, each cowboy on range duty rode alone. He enjoyed being alone, sipping coffee at night by a campfire, seeing the sun come up in the early mornings, soaking up the sights and sounds of nature. Dog always accompanied him.

He was halfway into one of his weeklong swings when he saw the tracks. The wide-rimmed wagon tracks bit deep into the prairie. His gaze followed the two lines until they disappeared in the distance. *Most likely a homesteader. They often pass through looking for a place to put down roots.*

Something else caught his eye. Far off in the distance, dark specks circled against a pale-blue sky. Turkey buzzards floated in a lazy spiral. Something was dead. Deciding he best check it out, he gigged his pinto into a trot.

What he discovered turned his stomach. The remains of at least twenty cattle lay scattered along a shallow swag in the ground. They had been skinned and the bloody carcasses left to rot. The scavengers from the air were feasting on what coyotes had left.

Hide peelers, he realized. The ranch hands had talked about them and described their handiwork. They roamed the range, searching for isolated herds of cattle, slaughtered them, skinned them and took only the hides, leaving the rest to rot. A load of hides brought tidy profits.

From a nearby grove of scrub cedar, a bawling calf caught Cody's hearing. He rode toward the sound. A young calf stood beside the carcass of its mother. Left on its own without the mother, the helpless young had no chance to survive. The sight sent waves of anger surging through him.

What kind of men would do this?. He decided he had to find out if these were Brazos cattle. He lengthened the lead line of his packhorse and reined Cincinnati around. He urged his mount into a short lope and followed the wagon tracks.

From the condition of the carcasses, he knew the slaughter must have happened the day before. Unless they found another bunch of cattle to skin, he had a lot of catching up to do. He hurried his horse.

By sundown he could tell by the freshness of the tracks he was getting close to the hide peelers. Up ahead he spotted a thin tendril of smoke. Not knowing what to expect, he broke open his double-barrel shotgun and thumbed in two shells.

Just after good dark he saw their campfire. Their campsite lay beside a small stream with a backdrop of large cedar trees. A heavy freight wagon sat up close. Two mules and three horses were tied to a line stretched between two trees a ways off from the campsite. Cody counted four men squatted near the fire inside the jagged circle of light. They were sipping coffee, obviously unaware of his presence.

He thumbed back both hammers on his shotgun and held it underneath his serape with his left hand.

"Hello the camp!" he hollered as he pulled rein forty yards away.

The men scrambled for their rifles that lay nearby.

"Who are ya and what you want?" one of the men growled out.

"Saw your fire. I'm alone. Shore could use a cup of coffee."

"Ride in."

Cody heeled his pinto ahead in a slow walk. He stopped just outside the circle of light and sat his saddle.

The men were a filthy-looking lot. Their clothes bore the signs of their trade. Their pants and shirts were dirty and covered with dried blood. All wore heavy beards and floppy hats. Cody could smell them from where he sat.

"I'd feel more welcome without them rifles pointed at me," Cody said.

"What'cha doin' way out here?" the leader asked, still holding his rifle pointed in Cody's direction.

"I ride for the Brazos River Ranch down south of here. Found some dead cattle back a ways without their hides. I need to take a look in your wagon and make sure they weren't Brazos stock. If they ain't I'll ride on."

"None of your business what's in our wagon," the man said, his voice rising. "You best turn that hoss around and ride out while you still can."

"'Fraid I can't do that, mister. My boss would have my hide if I didn't look in that wagon."

The speaker levered a shell and began raising his rifle. Cody lifted the edge of his serape and triggered one barrel of his shotgun.

The blast shattered the stillness of the night. The impact of the heavy double-aught pellets picked the man up off his feet and blew him backwards. He landed on his backside in the campfire. Sparks scattered in every direction.

One of the three remaining men raised his rifle for a shot. From out of the darkness Cody's dog suddenly appeared. It took two long bounds and locked its fangs deep into the man's arm, causing his shot to go astray. The other two men fled.

Cody jumped from his pinto and rushed forward. He swung his shotgun and struck the hide peeler on the side of his head with the heavy barrel. The man flew sideways into a heap on the ground.

From the darkness Cody heard pounding hooves. The two hide peelers had mounted and were galloping away.

"Let go!" Cody told his dog.

Only then did the dog loosen his deathly grip on the man's arm. Cody patted the dog. "Good boy."

Although it appeared the man he shot was dead, nonetheless, he decided he would rest easier after he double-checked. He grabbed a heel and pulled the leader from the campfire and dragged his body into the nearby bushes.

Walking over to the wagon he looked inside. Just like he figured, stacks of stinking hides wore the Brazos River brand.

He took his time tying the unconscious hide peeler to a wagon wheel. When he walked over to check the mules and horse the hide peelers left behind, he discovered in their haste to get away, they had left their saddles and fled bareback.

He knew it would be useless trying to track them down in the darkness. He decided to make use of their campsite that night and start after them come daylight.

He stripped saddles off his pinto and packhorse and tied his horses to a wagon wheel. That done, he stoked the fire and dropped a couple more sticks of wood on it.

Shaking the blackened coffee pot and finding it still had coffee in it, Cody picked up an abandoned cup, poured it full, and settled down for the night. Dog trotted over to lay down beside him.

Feeling confident his dog would alert him if the hide peelers should return, Cody stretched out against his upturned saddle and quickly fell asleep.

Sometime during the night, the fellow tied to the wagon wheel awoke and started moaning and cursing. Cody listened for a few minutes.

"Best shut your mouth or I'll conk you again."

His threat did the trick. The man quieted down for the rest of the night.

Cody was up before first light. He watered all the stock in the nearby stream and retied his packhorse to the wagon wheel. He threw his saddle on the pinto's back and threaded the cinch. The horse stamped its hoof and shifted itself when the girth drew tight. Cody untied its reins and stepped in a stirrup.

"Where you going?" the hide peeler demanded.

"Going after your friends."

"You ain't gonna leave me spread-eagled to this wagon wheel, are ya?"

"It's either that or kill you. Take your pick."

The man said nothing more. Cody reined his pinto around.

"Come on, Dog."

The fleeing hide peelers' trail was clear and easy to follow. By mid-morning Cody found where they stopped to rest their horses. Several cigarette butts told him they spent the best part of the night there before moving on.

Shortly after noon the trail led to the edge of a river. The riders had clearly crossed the river. Cody reined up. His slow gaze searched the far side of the river. A heavy growth of willow and underbrush hugged the far bank. It occurred to him this would be a perfect place for an ambush. If he got caught in the middle of the river, he would be a sitting duck for a man with a rifle hiding in the heavy underbrush of the far bank.

Making up his mind, he reined Cincinnati upstream. He rode for half a mile before guiding his mount into the water and crossed to the other side. Once on the far bank, he doubled back to pick up their trail where the others came out of the water.

He discovered his fears had been right. The hide peelers had been waiting in the underbrush to ambush him. He found where they left their horses tied and where they'd lain in wait.

When he crossed them up by riding upstream to double back, they hightailed it out of there. "Come on dog, we ain't far behind them now," Cody said to his furry companion.

The country he rode through appeared to be getting rougher. Rolling, rock-strewn hills hugged the trail Cody followed. He reined his pinto to a slow walk and levered a shell into his Henry rifle.

Dog trotted twenty yards in front with his nose low to the ground. Suddenly he swerved to the right, let out a deep, growling bark and broke into a run toward a jumble of large rocks. A shot rang out.

Dog stumbled and fell, tumbling along the ground.

Cody let out a loud scream. "No!"

He fired at the puff of smoke rising from among the rocks, levered another shell and fired again.

From somewhere to his left another rifle barked. A slug singed past his head. He swung a look and saw the outline of a man's bearded face and shoulders above a rock. Cody shouldered his rifle and fired a snap shot. He knew he had hit the man dead center of his forehead, a lucky shot. The man let out a strangled scream and disappeared from sight.

The sound of pounding hooves from behind the rocks to his right told Cody the first shooter was getting away. He paid the fleeing ambusher no mind. His first concern was for his dog.

He raced his pinto to the dog's side and swung to the ground to sit beside his friend. Dog lay still. One quick look told Cody that his faithful companion had no chance. The bullet had entered its body in the center of its chest.

Cody knew his friend had only short moments to live. The dog's big black eyes fixed squarely upon Cody. Reaching a hand he lifted Dog's head and laid it in his lap.

The animal blinked its eyes once, and then closed, never to open again. Cody bowed his head and cried.

The trail swung west toward the setting sun. The land in front of him yawned endlessly to the distant horizon. Cody's jaw set in a hard line as he leaned low over his galloping horse's neck. He reached a hand and patted his pinto, urging him to even greater speed. He was determined to overtake the fleeing hide peeler that killed his faithful, adoring companion.

In the purpling dusk he spotted movement up ahead. A lone horseman sky lined himself against a paling sky as he crested a distant hill.

That's him.

By the time he reached the hill, full dark shrouded the land. A thin sliver of moon made it near impossible for him to see the tracks. Then he slid off and led his pinto. He bent low as he walked, straining to see the barely visible tracks. He walked for hours.

A cold wind sent shivers over his body. He paused long enough to untie his sheepskin coat from behind his saddle and sleeve into it.

Sometime well after midnight, the smell of wood smoke reached him on a soft breeze. He paused and sniffed the air. No doubt about it, somebody had a fire going not far away. He tied his pinto to a sturdy bush, thumbed two shells into his shotgun, and moved ahead cautiously.

A faint glow rose from among some large boulders up ahead. Cody bent low, thumbed back the twin hammers of his shotgun, and crept forward. When he reached the rocks, he chanced a quick look.

The man he sought lay hunkered near a flickering campfire with no blanket, his legs drawn up, his body in a fetal position. He appeared sound asleep, his horse tied nearby.

Cody deer footed it to stand only a few feet from the sleeping outlaw. He kicked the man's feet. The bearded hide peeler jerked upright to a sitting position. He blinked himself awake. His eyes rounded when he stared up into the twin barrels of Cody's shotgun.

Cody saw the man cut a slanted glance toward his rifle lying within easy reach.

"Go ahead. Go for it. You might be quick enough, but I doubt it."

The man seemed to consider the move for only a second before slowly lifting his hands shoulder-high. Cody used the toe of his boot to rake the rifle out of reach.

"You killed my dog," Cody whispered through clenched teeth.

The man looked long into Cody's face. Whatever he saw caused him to begin scooting backwards, his head shaking from side to side.

"You ain't gonna kill me just for shooting your dog, are ya?"

Cody shook his head. "No, I ain't gonna kill you. That would be too easy. But you're gonna die, sure enough. Real slow."

Cody lowered the shotgun slightly and touched a trigger. The thundering blast shook the stillness of the night. A swarm of deadly double-aught pellets belched from the nose of the shotgun and tore through flesh and bone of the hide peeler's knees, shattering them into a thousand pieces. Blood and bone fragments splattered in every direction. A scream burst from the man's lips and pierced the night.

Cody picked up the rifle then removed the gun from the man's holster. He walked to the hide peeler's horse, gathered the reins and led it off into the darkness. *He ain't gonna need it anymore.*

Behind him, Cody heard the man screaming in agony, cursing, and begging through choking sobs for somebody to help him.

When Cody reached Cincinnati he swung into the saddle and led the hide peeler's horse behind him as he rode off into the night.

As the morning sun peeked over the eastern horizon, Cody buried his dog under a big oak tree near the river. He gathered the other dead hide peelers' weapons and tied the second horse on a lead line.

It was late afternoon by the time he arrived at the hide peelers' wagon. After searching the wagon for weapons and finding none, he hitched up the team of mules to it and tied the three extra horses to the back of the wagon. Afterward he untied the prisoner and pitched him a canteen of water.

"I expect you're a mite thirsty. Crawl up onto that wagon seat. You do anything but drive and I'll kill you, understood?"

The man nodded his head. Cody mounted his pinto and rode alongside the wagon as they headed toward home.

It took two days to reach the ranch. Someone spotted Cody coming and every hand on the ranch came out to meet him. Del Horton emerged from the ranch house and hurried up.

"What you got here, Hondo?"

He dismounted, the crew gathered around, and Cody told the whole story over a cup of coffee. The telling took a while.

They hung the last hide peeler just before sundown.

CHAPTER X
Long Trail To Missouri

Fall turned to winter and all too quickly, winter became spring. Cody made several trips into Waco during that time, all without encountering trouble.

Each time he went into town Cody stopped in to see Marshal Bell. He took a liking to the tough old lawman and felt as if the feeling was mutual. They often sat and talked for hours while sipping coffee at Miss Ellen's café.

While in town, Cody spent most of his time in the café. He knew that he and Miss Ellen could never be anything except best friends, because of his age, but he sure liked being around her.

"Mr. Horton said we was taking a herd up to Missouri come April," Cody told Miss Ellen and Marshal Bell one day while they were having dinner.

"Where in Missouri?" the marshal asked.

"A place called Sedalia."

"Yeah, I heard that was the nearest rail head to us. How many head you boys trailin'?"

"Thousand head, I think he said."

"It's a fer piece to Missouri."

"How long will you be gone?" Miss Ellen asked.

"Don't rightly know. I've never been to Missouri. Never been much of anywhere, matter of fact."

"Well, you ain't missed all that much," the marshal said. "I've been might near every place I ever heard of and seems I always come back to Texas."

"Just make sure you do the same," Miss Ellen said, looking squarely at Cody.

They pointed the Brazos River herd north at the crack of dawn on April 3, 1866, one thousand head of bawling, cantankerous longhorns that would rather be grazing peacefully on their home range than marching northward. The herd strung out in a dusty mile-long column. Leading the column was a brindle steer that moved to the front of the herd on its own and assumed leadership. The rest of the herd somehow accepted their role as followers and moved in behind the brindle.

For the eight cowboys in the Brazos Ranch trail crew, their day began well before first light and usually ended after the birds went to roost. After grabbing a quick breakfast while huddled around a campfire, they caught the first of a half-dozen horses they would wear out that day. Then they climbed into the saddle, their home for the next fourteen to sixteen hours.

Today Cody rode flank. His job was to keep the longhorns moving in the endless line. If an ornery old steer strayed from the bunch, he hazed it back with a slap from his coiled lariat. Generally it was a boring job, but one he came to love and be proud of, especially when Miss Ellen called him *cowboy.* He liked that. A slight grin played at the corner of his mouth at the thought of her.

If I was just a little older maybe she would think of me as more than just a friend. But a woman like Miss Ellen deserves more than a-dollar-a-day-and-beans-cowboy. She deserves a man who has made his mark. She deserves a man who is somebody. Right now I'm a nobody. But someday, someday, I'm gonna be somebody.

His thoughts scattered by the sound of Del Horton riding up alongside him on his big chestnut gelding.

"We're gonna push 'em hard today," the foreman said. "Maybe walk some of the juice out of 'em."

"You got it, boss."

The foreman reined his horse around to make the rounds of the other cowboys. Cody twisted in the saddle and glanced up at a clear sky. He squinted against the early morning glare. The sun was warm and golden in a cloudless sky. The day had scarcely started and already he craved a steamy hot cup of coffee.

The Brazos Ranch made him feel a part of something and yet, lately, he felt an itch for more. He had a yearning to see the land that stretched beyond the horizon.

The day wore on.

It was full dark before they watered the herd in Mustang Creek and bedded them down in a wide valley nearby. The cattle were trail-weary, having walked steadily for more than fourteen hours. It didn't take them long to belly down. At midnight they would climb to their feet, move about and bawl a while, before bedding down again until first light.

All hands, except the night herders, picked up a tin plate and stood in line for supper. Swede spooned their plate full of steaming hot beef stew and laid two Dutch oven biscuits on top. A tin cup of thick black coffee rounded out their meal.

Cody carried his plate near the campfire and sat down cross-legged next to Lefty. Del Horton walked up and sat down beside him.

"How'd it go today, boss?" Cody asked.

"I figure we made might near twenty miles."

"Good day."

"Yep. Few more days like today and we'll back off a bit."

They were sipping coffee around the fire when a deep voice called from the depth of darkness.

"Hello the camp!"

Del Horton set his coffee cup on the ground and stood to his feet. Cody thumbed the travel throng off the hammer of his Colt and stood beside his foreman.

"Who are you?" Horton called back.

"Charley Davis, Hill County sheriff."

"Ride on in."

The approach of horses and the squeak of saddle leather sounded at the edge of darkness. A big man, Texas tall, riding a big-boned buckskin walked his horse into the circle of light while his companions waited in the darkness. He stepped to the ground slowly, deliberately. Light from the campfire reflected off the gold star pinned to his leather vest. He stood a shade over six foot, whipcord lean, yet broad through the shoulders. His square jaw and weathered features gave him an all business look.

He hooked a thumb under his shell belt and knuckled back his gray, flat-brimmed Stetson. The sheriff's dark-eyed gaze did a slow sweep of the men sitting around the campfire. The effect of his gaze was close to scary, as if he looked at nothing and saw everything.

Del Horton stuck out a hand.

"I'm Del Horton, foreman of the Brazos River Ranch in the big bend of the Brazos in McLennan County."

The sheriff took the foreman's hand and shook it. "Where you boys headed?" the sheriff asked, still allowing his slow gaze to search the faces of the Brazos cowboys.

"We're taking a herd up the trail to Sedalia, Missouri. This is our first day out."

"Uh-huh. Seen any riders today by chance?"

"Don't think so," the foreman said, twisting a look at the cowboys sitting around the fire. "Any of you boys seen strangers today?"

All the Brazos crew shook their heads.

"Who you looking for?"

"Outlaw named Kinch West and his gang robbed the bank over in Hillsboro this morning. They shot up the town, killed the president of the bank, and got off with a passel of money. My posse's been trailing them. Lost their tracks after dark. Thought you boys might have seen them."

"Can't say we have. We've got hot coffee and plenty of it. You and your men are welcome to a cup."

"We're obliged, but we've got to get on. We need to catch these hombres before they get out of the county. If you happen to run across these boys, watch yourselves, they're a mean bunch."

"We'll keep an eye out. How many's in the gang?"

"There's four of them. One of them lost his horse and is riding double. They'll be looking for horses."

After the sheriff and his men rode off, the Brazos hands sat around the fire and jawed about the outlaws.

"Might be good if we doubled up on our nighthawks tonight," the foreman said. "If them fellows are looking for fresh horses, our remuda might look awfully tempting. Hondo, how about doubling up with Grady, come midnight?"

"Be glad to."

"Wish somebody had asked that sheriff if there was a reward on them jaspers," Lefty said.

"Why in the Sam Hill would you care?" Slim wanted to know.

"Just wondering, that's all. Never know, we might just happen to run across them fellows. I'd shore like to get my hands on some of that reward money."

"Most likely get yourself killed is what you'd get. You heard the sheriff. He said these boys were some kind of mean."

"I ain't scared of no two-bit outlaws."

"Might better be. You better forget about reward money and stick to nursin' cows."

Cody drained the last of his coffee in a swallow and stood.

"Where you going, Kid? It's still early."

"I'm on nighthawk duty at midnight. I reckon I better get to sleepin'."

Just before midnight, one of the nighthawks woke Cody from a sound sleep. He crawled out of his blankets, shook out his boots and stomped them on. He swung his gun belt around his waist and buckled it in place as he strode to his pinto.

He yawned and stretched before toeing a stirrup and swinging into the saddle, reining his mount away from camp to the remuda of horses. His and Grady's job was to keep the thirty head of horses bunched from midnight until first light.

Grady was already riding a slow circle around the horse herd when Cody rode up beside him.

"Everything quiet, Grady?"

"Yep. Shore hard to stay awake, though."

"I'll ease around to the other side of the remuda."

"Might be good."

Cody walked his pinto around to the other side. The horses were quiet and content with barely a snort. A ghostly stillness settled. Shadows danced in the thin, dim light of a quarter moon. His senses keened. It was way too quiet for Cody's liking.

The sheriff's words kept ringing in Cody's mind. *If you happen to run into these boys, watch yourselves, this is a mean bunch. They'll be looking for horses.*

He glanced across the horse herd into the darkness beyond. A murky outline of Grady's saddled horse was barely visible, but where was Grady? He wasn't in his saddle. *I better check just to make sure he's all right.*

He reined his pinto around and headed around the remuda at a trot. To be on the safe side, he threaded the rawhide loop on his shotgun around his left wrist and thumbed off the hammer thong on his Colt.

As he rounded the horse herd and drew closer, he looked again and Grady was back in his saddle, but was walking his horse away from the herd. *What's going on?* Cody wondered. He called out to his fellow nighthawk.

"Hey, Grady! You okay?"

The words barely left his mouth when something caught his eye. Someone lay sprawled on the ground near where Grady's horse had been. It was Grady! *Then who's riding Grady's horse?*

Whoever it was jammed heels into the horse's flanks. The horse broke into a gallop, making a beeline for a grove of trees a couple hundred yards in the distance. *It's got to be the bank robber the sheriff told us about.*

He hurried his horse and reined up near the body on the ground. He was out of his saddle in an eye blink and fell to his knees beside Grady. One look told him what he didn't want to know. Grady's throat had been cut from jawbone to jawbone. A growing puddle of blood formed where he lay.

Cody snatched the Colt from his holster and fired three rapid shots to alert the camp, as he grabbed hold of the saddle horn and swung into the saddle. He put heels to Cincinnati's flanks. The pinto went from a standing start to an all out run in three bounds.

The vague form of the fleeing bank robber was about to disappear into the safety of the trees. Cody leaned low in his saddle and urged his mount to greater speed, but it was too late. As he looked, the outlaw was swallowed up by the heavy growth of trees and underbrush. It would be nigh impossible to trail him until daylight.

Cody reined Cincinnati down and turned back toward the nervous horse herd. He swung to the ground beside Grady as the rest of the Brazos hands rode up.

"What happened?" Del Horton asked with concern in his voice, swinging out of his saddle.

"It's Grady. Somebody cut his throat and took his horse."

The foreman knelt beside his fallen cowhand. His features were set in a dour expression and there was a troubled cast to his eyes.

A silence stretched out.

"Think it was them bank robbers?"

"I figure. I didn't see but one man. I chased him, but lost him in the trees."

"We'll go after him at first light."

"Uh, boss, I ain't trying to second-guess you, but that fellow'll likely ride all night. It would take a couple of days to catch up to him. By that time the herd would be scattered from hell to breakfast."

"You ain't saying we ought to just let him go, are you?"

"No. Why not let me go after him?"

"You mean by yourself?"

"You could spare one man. You can't afford to lose the whole herd."

"But you'd likely find yourself facing all four of them fellows. You heard the sheriff. He said they were a bad bunch."

"They killed my friend. I can't let that go."

"Well, you're right about the herd. But I sure hate to see you go after them by yourself."

"I'll catch up to you in a few days."

"If you're dead-set on going after them, I reckon I can't stop you."

"I'll leave at first light."

* * *

A faint brush of dawn grayed the eastern sky. An early morning mist began to lift and the fog became a gentle rain. Cody pulled his rain slicker closer around his neck, stepped into a stirrup, and swung into the saddle. He did a half-hitch with the lead line to his pack horse.

Del Horton and the rest of the Brazos River cowboys stood near the chuck wagon with gazes fixed upon Cody.

He touched the brim of his hat with two fingers in goodbye. "I'll catch up to you in a few days," he repeated.

"See that you do," the foreman said, lifting a hand goodbye.

Cody reined his pinto around and kneed him forward. He didn't look back.

By the time good light settled, he found the tracks. No doubt about it, the killer was in a mighty big hurry. The length of the horse's strides told Cody the man had run the stolen horse flat out, even in the dark and through heavy timber. *Only a fool or a mighty desperate man would do that.*

As the day wore on, the weather worsened. A storm rolled in. Thunder rumbled like a continuous drum roll. Lightning cracked and flashed jagged streaks across the sky. A chilling wind blew in from the north and drove the rain in blinding sheets ahead of it. The wind tore at his body as well, chilling the blood in his veins and causing his muscles to ache. He pulled the collar of his slicker tighter, bowed his head low into the wind and breathed a silent prayer that the rain didn't wash out the killer's tracks.

He followed the trail all day. At times he had to dismount and bend low to the ground to find the faint tracks. The rain slacked off by mid-afternoon. Cobweb clouds hovered low and gray. A ground fog made dusk even more uncomfortable. When darkness hid the tracks, he made camp beside a creek running bank-full from all the rain.

Failing to find wood to build a fire that wasn't water-soaked, he tied his rain slicker between four saplings to ward off the rain and spread his groundsheet on the wet ground.

It's gonna be a long, cold, wet night, he thought, as he chewed on a piece of dried beef jerky.

Sometime during the night the rain stopped. Cody broke camp and swung into his saddle before first light.

Morning arrived bright and clear without a cloud in the sky. By the time the eastern sky began to gray, he found the trail. The trail twisted through rugged hills dotted with scrub cedar and stunted mesquites. He followed it all morning with his gaze alternating between the tracks and his surroundings. Didn't want to ride into a trap.

Just before the sun crested directly overhead, the trail led him to where the outlaws had camped the night before. The killer rejoined the rest of the band and now there were four of them again. The one-sided odds didn't particularly worry Cody; he'd just have to wait for the right opportunity to confront them or pick them off one by one.

By late afternoon the trail led into rocky, steepening hills. Deep canyon arroyos twisted and turned, crisscrossing the landscape. They threaded between steep, rocky hillsides where scrub cedar and mesquite clung precariously to narrow ledges on sheer bluffs. The canyon floors were littered with rocks and large boulders fallen from the walls forming them.

Cody reined Cincinnati to a stop and allowed his slow gaze to examine the landscape. It was worrisome country. If the outlaws posted a lookout, Cody would be an easy target.

He withdrew his Henry rifle and levered a shell, before kneeing his pinto slowly forward.

Cincinnati's iron horseshoes, and those of his packhorse, clicked against the rocks. The sound echoed along the canyon. Cody reined his mount to a stop and dismounted. He tied his horses to a small bush and moved forward on foot.

Snapping open his shotgun, he thumbed in two shells, closed it, and let it dangle on his left wrist by the leather thong. He eased forward, being careful where he placed his feet; he didn't want to dislodge a rock and reveal his presence. His slow, searching gaze swung back and forth, scanning every rock, every ledge and every bush for possible danger.

The sun slipped from sight and dusk descended. Still Cody eased forward, step by careful step.

A *feeling* swept over him. The hairs on the back of his neck tingled. He squinted. His quick gaze swept the area. He didn't see anything, didn't hear anything. But something was there. He sensed a presence. His senses keened and instincts took control. He ducked behind a large boulder just in time.

The crack of a rifle reached his hearing at the same instant a bullet gouged a large chip from the boulder only inches from his head, sending the fragments airborne. The sound reverberated along the canyon.

Cody hunkered down behind the boulder. *That was too close for comfort. Whoever this guy is, he's a good shot.*

On an impulse, he removed his hat and stuck it on the barrel of his shotgun. He wiped sweat from his hand holding his Henry rifle and climbed to his knees. *Let's see how quick on the trigger he is.*

Slowly he raised the hat just above the top of the boulder. Another shot rang out and the hat went flying through the air. Cody immediately rose up with his rifle to his shoulder.

A small puff of blue smoke hovered like a tiny cloud above an up-thrust rock no more than thirty yards away, a man's head and shoulders clearly visible. Cody feathered the trigger.

The soft smack of the bullet told him his shot found its mark. The head exploded in a shower of blood and bone fragments. *One down and three to go.*

He expected the man's companions to emerge from whatever

hole they were hiding in and come out shooting. It didn't happen. He braced himself and waited.

Silence lengthened. Night settled its shroud of darkness over the canyon. His eyes were of little use in the total blackness. He would have to rely on his hearing for any warning.

Simple logic told him the three remaining outlaws couldn't be far away.

Light from the newborn moon began to filter into the canyon, but it was mighty little. Cody could see no more than a few feet in front of him, but that meant the outlaws had the same problem. *Will they simply hole up wherever it is they are hiding and wait? Will they come storming out with guns blazing, or will they try to make a run for it under the cover of darkness? They'll likely think it's the sheriff's posse out here instead of just one man. My guess is they'll make a break for it.*

He waited.

A sound was faint, barely distinguishable. It was the soft click of metal against rock. It came from up the canyon. Cody cocked his head sideways and strained his hearing. Seconds stretched into minutes. There it was again. This time it came from farther up the canyon. They led their horses and escaped in the darkness. He had to follow them, but not on foot. Cody pushed to his feet and hurried back to where he left his two horses.

By the time he reached them the silver moon peeked over the horizon, bathing the canyon in pale light. He walked his horses slowly up the canyon. The stars told him it was nearing midnight when the canyon ended abruptly. It was a box canyon.

Then where did the outlaws go?

He stopped and searched the walls of the canyon carefully. Then he saw it. A steep, narrow, winding trail led up the sheer side of the canyon wall. He dropped to one knee. Hoof prints showed clearly in the soft, sandy soil.

If they can make it up that trail in the darkness, so can I.

He carefully tied the lead line to his packhorse to Cincinnati's tail, then gathered his pinto's reins and started up the steep trail. It was slow going. The trail was narrow and steep. One misstep would send his horses, and most likely him, over the edge to their death.

Step by slow step Cody inched up the trail, leading his horses behind him. He dared not look down, but kept his eyes focused on where his next foot must be placed. It took a while.

Suddenly he sensed something was wrong and stopped in his tracks. Nervous chill bumps tingled along his neck. He stood motionless, eyes squinting. His gaze crawled slowly along the trail ahead.

A movement in the dim darkness above the trail caught his eye. A narrow ledge led to a crack in the canyon wall. Something was there. *Is it one of the outlaws lying in wait?*

The vague outline on a large animal appeared over the edge of the ledge, was a mountain cougar.

If my horses catch the scent of that cougar it will frighten them and they'll likely go over the edge to their death.

He swiped the hat from his head and, turning, clamped it over his horse's nose. He couldn't reach the packhorse. He rubbed his hand gently along Cincinnati's nose, gentling him, while craning his head around to watch the cougar.

For what seemed an eternity the big cat stood motionless, staring directly at Cody and the horses. Then, as suddenly as it appeared, the cougar disappeared. Still Cody waited, giving the small breeze time to clear the air of the any lingering scent.

Finally, Cody inched his horses forward again, keeping a wary eye on the ledge where he first spotted the big cat. By the time he reached the top he was exhausted.

Cody patted both of his horses on the neck and breathed a long sigh of relief. He bent low to the ground and located the outlaw's tracks. They were headed north. He untied the lead line from Cincinnati's tail and looped the line around his saddle horn before threading a stirrup with his boot and swinging into the saddle.

The long strides of the three horses he followed told him the outlaws were galloping their mounts full out, putting as much distance as they could between them and their pursuers. Cody heeled his pinto into a ground-eating short lope. He rode steady the rest of the night.

Just as dawn was breaking over the horizon, the trail led into a shallow creek. Remembering the previous experience of his near ambush by the hide-peelers, Cody reined up and swept both sides of the creek banks with a long, searching look.

Seeing no sign of danger, he urged his pinto across the narrow stream. Then he searched the far bank, but could see no tracks coming out of the water. Reining up in the middle of the stream, he sat his saddle while his gaze searched the bank.

They must have waded their horses along the stream in an attempt to throw off, or at least slow down, anyone following. The question is, which way?

With no way of knowing, he reined Cincinnati upstream. He rode slow, searching both sides of the stream for tracks. He wouldn't put it past the outlaws for them to double back in a further attempt to throw off their pursuers.

He waded his horses in the middle of the creek half the morning. The sun was halfway to high noon and still he discovered no tracks where they came out of the water.

Reckon I guessed wrong. They must have gone downstream instead of upstream.

He almost missed it.

He was about to rein his horses out of the water and head downstream when he saw it. A deep scrape on a rocky ledge left by a horseshoe was the only evidence where they left the water. They had chosen their exit well. A rocky ledge extended to the waters edge where they came out.

Cody urged his horses out of the water and followed the tracks that continued a northerly direction. He rode the rest of the day, stopping only at brief intervals to rest his horses. The country through which he rode changed drastically. Gentle, rolling, tree covered hills stretched endlessly. Off in the distance, he could see a line of larger mountains. Fresh, swift-running streams wound their way to an unknown rendezvous. Birds fluttered about. A rabbit scampered for cover. A deer lifted its head from grazing and bounded to the safety of a grove of trees. It was a peaceful, beautiful country.

Topping a low-rising hill, he reined up abruptly. In the valley below, partially hidden by a grove of trees, Cody saw a small log cabin. Nearby, a dilapidated barn with an adjoining corral held three horses. One of the horses below was the sorrel with three white stockings Grady had been riding. No doubt about it, this was the outlaws' hideout.

A thin tendril of smoke trailed lazily from a rock chimney. The outlaws' trail led directly to the cabin. Obviously, this was their hideout.

Reining Cincinnati around, he retraced his steps to the bottom of the hill and into a thick grove of sycamore trees. Cody swung to the ground, loosened the cinch straps, and tied his horses where they could graze. Sitting on a fallen log he contemplated what his plan of action should be.

Eventually he decided he should wait until they went to sleep before approaching the hideout. Most likely the outlaws felt safe here, so they might not even post a guard. He stretched out on soft grass to relax.

The sun completed its daily arch across the sky and slipped out of sight. Dusk slowly gave way to a velvety curtain of darkness. Stars blinked above the silent hills. Cody dozed comfortably knowing his horses would alert him should anyone venture close.

When the stars told him it was near midnight, he rose, then double-checked his weapons to make sure they were all fully loaded. Slipping the leather thong attached to his shotgun over his left wrist, he levered a shell into his Henry rifle, and set out on foot.

The cabin's single window near the front door showed no sign of a light inside. Nonetheless, Cody approached cautiously. He bent low, slipping from one clump of bushes to the next, sticking to the cover of the trees until he drew less than twenty yards from the barn. He worried about the three horses; they raised their heads and watched his approach but didn't snort an alarm.

Relieved, he then worked his way to the end of the cabin, out of sight to anyone who might be watching from the window. Cody pressed his back against the logs of the cabin and listened intently.

No sound disturbed the silence.

He thumbed back the twin hammers of his shotgun. Slowly, cautiously, he crept around the front corner of the cabin, ducking low beneath the edge of the small window and paused just outside the heavy wooden door. Listening.

From inside he heard the sounds of loud snoring. A knot formed in his stomach. Muscles worked silently in his cheeks. He leaned his Henry rifle against the wall beside the front door. His hand made sweat on the wooden stock of his shotgun and he swallowed, then swallowed again.

Using as much stealth as he could muster, he reached his right hand to try the latch on the door. It lifted. Slowly the door eased inward. As he was about to step inside, a rusty door hinge let out a loud squeak.

The dim outline of a sleeper bolted to a sitting position and grabbed for a gun. Cody's finger tightened one of the a triggers and the shotgun roared.

The blast lit the inside of the small cabin like it was day. The heavy load of double-aught buckshot tore into the man, lifting him from his bedroll and tumbling him end-over-end.

A single, pitiful cry erupting from the man's lips sounded like a wounded animal.

The remaining two men scrambled from their bedrolls, snatching for their guns. Cody swung the nose of his shotgun in the nearest man's direction and fired. In the light from the blast he saw the man's head explode. Blood and bone fragments flew in every direction. The last man rolled to his knees with a gun in his hand. A finger of orange flame spat in Cody's direction. Something hot singed past his ear and buried into the log wall behind him.

His own Colt was in his right hand. He fired once, twice, three times, all in the space of an eye blink. The man's body whirled away, twisted by the force of the three heavy .44 slugs.

Moving cautiously, his gaze alert for any movement by the outlaws, Cody found a lantern on a table in the center of the room and lit it.

The small room was a shambles. Blood covered torn bodies lay sprawled where they fell.

The acrid stench of gunpowder and death filled the cabin. For a minute he stood motionless, gazing at the dead men. One outlaw's head was completely gone, only the bloody stub of neck where his head should have been, remained. Cody's stomach revolted at the sight.

Cody rode into Hillsboro, Texas, in Hill County, at mid-morning. Behind him, following on lead lines, trailed his packhorse and three saddled horses. Tied belly-flat in the saddles of the three horses were the bodies of three men.

All along the street, people emptied from stores to stare at the little procession. Whispered questions were exchanged and went unanswered. Men hurried along the boardwalk to stay abreast, lest they fail to find out who the dead men were and who the young fellow was who brought them in.

By the time Cody reined up in front of the sheriff's office, someone alerted the big lawman who stood waiting on the boardwalk.

"You're that young fellow from the Brazos River trail crew, ain't you?"

"Yes, sir."

"Thought so. I remember seeing you at the campfire. You were wearing that same serape. Who you got there, boy?"

"Got some fellows that need burying. They're getting a mite ripe."

"Yeah, I'd say so."

The sheriff walked over and grabbed a handful of hair and lifted, first one of the outlaw's head, then the other and gazed at them before he spoke.

"That's Kinch West and his boys, sure enough. Leastwise that's what's left of the three of 'em."

"The other one is in a canyon about twenty miles or so up yonder way," Cody said. "I didn't feel like going back to fetch him "Don't reckon you come across any money along the way?" the sheriff asked, fixing a look at Cody.

"Yes, sir. It's in one of them saddle bags."

"Well, glory-be. Didn't catch your name, boy?"

"They call me the Hondo Kid. That'll do, I reckon."

"Bill, you and some of the boys take these bodies to the undertaker's. Come on in the office, Kid, we've got some talking to do."

The following morning at daybreak, Cody rode out of town with twelve hundred dollars in his pocket and the gratitude of the citizens of Hillsboro. It turned out each of the outlaws had three hundred dollars reward on their heads, dead or alive.

It took Cody an entire week to catch up to the Brazos River

trail herd. He told them about his experience with the four outlaws and about taking their bodies to Hillsboro, but saw no reason to mention the reward.

The rest of the trip to Missouri was long, routine, and uneventful.

CHAPTER XI
Dying for a Reputation

The men circled the herd and bedded them down a mile or so outside Sedalia, Missouri. It was the middle of May, 1866. Brazos's crew finished their supper and sat around the campfire sipping coffee.

"I'm gonna ride on into town come morning," Del Horton told Cody. "I'd be obliged if you'd look after things here till I get back."

"Be glad to, boss. Hope you get a good price for the cattle."

"Yeah, me too. Last word I heard, beef was bringing a good price."

"Got something on my mind, Del. Need to have a word with you."

"What's on your mind, Kid?"

"Been thinking I need to move on."

"You mean leave the Brazos crew? Sure hate to hear that. I was hoping you would stay with us. Fact is I talked to the owner about making you my top hand. What would it take to change your mind?"

"It's not about money or anything like that, boss. You and the boys have made me feel like family. I just have an itch to see what's over the next hill before I put down roots somewhere."

"When you got in mind pulling out?"

"Soon as we get the herd sold and settled, I reckon."

"Well, if you're sure that's what you want to do. Just remember, if you ever change your mind, there'll always be a job for you on the Brazos River Ranch."

"I'm much obliged."

It was two days before the foreman returned. Half-a-dozen riders rode with him. Cody and some of the boys stood sipping coffee beside the chuck wagon as Del swung to the ground.

"Sold the herd. Cattle are bringing a good price. These boys with me work for the cattle buyer. They'll take charge of the herd and put 'em in a cattle pen. We'll make the final count tomorrow. You boys gather round and we'll settle up your wages. There'll be an extra fifty dollar bonus for each of you. Then, if you're of a mind, you can all ride into town and take a couple of days off."

That brought wide smiles from the Brazos crew. Cody lifted his cup in a salute to the foreman. As Del paid Cody what he had coming, he stuck out a hand.

"Been a pleasure working with you, Kid. Drop by to see us now and again if you're back down our way."

"Count on it," Cody said, shaking hands with the foreman.

Lefty walked up as Del and Cody were talking.

"Me and the boys are riding into town to wet our whistle," Lefty told Cody. "How about riding in with us?"

"Don't see why not."

The Brazos cowboys had a pocketful of money and two days off to celebrate. There was lots of laughter and cowboy yells as they mounted and headed to town.

* * *

A fiery sunset ignited the western horizon ablaze and boiled the blue from the sky as Cody and the Brazos River crew rode into Sedalia, Missouri. Even late in the day, the town was a beehive of activity. Buckboards, heavy freight wagons, men on horseback, and folks afoot scurried about, seemingly in a hurry to get wherever it was they were going.

The cowboys from the Brazos trail crew were no exception. They headed straight for the nearest saloon. The sign outside said it was the Golden Nugget.

The saloon was crowded, but the six cowboys found an empty space at the bar and filled it. They all ordered a beer and were taking their first sip when several newcomers arrived. They were a tough-looking bunch. The noisy saloon fell silent at their entrance.

Leader of the pack appeared a swaggering, twenty-something fellow who seemed to want everyone in the saloon to know he *was* the leader. He strode directly toward the bar. Those with him did what they seemed accustomed to doing—they followed.

He would be called *handsome* by most folk. A black Stetson with a silver concho hatband matched his black pants and bib shirt. A black gun belt and tied down, cut-away holster held a yellow-handled Colt. This was a gunfighter's rig. Cody counted six notches in the yellow handle.

The men at the bar, standing shoulder-to-shoulder, melted away to make room. The leader shouldered in beside Lefty, and in doing so, jostled Cody's friend and caused him to spill his mug of beer.

"Watch it!" Lefty told the man. "You made me spill my beer."

"What did you say?" the man demanded, darting a look at Lefty.

"I said for you watch what you're doing. You spilt my beer."

"Do you know who I am?"

"Nope, and I don't care who you are," Lefty told him. "You don't go around spilling beer on somebody."

"Sam!" the man called loudly to the barkeep, never taking his gaze from Lefty. "Gimme a beer here."

The bar man hurried up with a beer and set it in front of the loudmouth. He calmly picked up the mug of beer and slowly poured it down Lefty's shirtfront.

"Oops," he laughed, glancing at his companions for agreement. They joined him in raucous laughter.

Lefty's response was immediate and predictable. He swung around to face the bully, drawing back his fist for a swing. Quicker than an eye blink, the yellow-handled Colt appeared in the man's hand and pressed against Lefty's nose.

Lefty's fist froze in mid-air. His eyes rounded. A look of fear and desperation swept across his face. The gunman's cold gaze fixed on Lefty. The room fell deathly silent. Every man waited breathlessly, waiting for the blast they were sure would come.

"Back off, mister," Cody said evenly. "You've had your fun, now leave it lay."

The man slanted a quick glance at Cody, the Colt still pressed against Lefty's nose, the hammer at full-cock.

"Who are you?" the man demanded.

"I'm the fellow who's gonna blow your head off if you pull that trigger. Some call me the Hondo Kid."

Cody flipped the edge of his faded serape back over his shoulder, revealing the pearl-handled Colt in his belly holster. His right hand settled easy on his belt buckle mere inches from the butt of his gun.

The man's eyebrows dipped. His dark eyes squinted, seemingly searching his memory for the name.

"That supposed to mean something to me?"

"Not really, just wanted you to know who's fixin' to kill you."

"You sure don't look like much to be talking so all-fired big, friend."

"I was about to say the same about you. And I ain't your *friend*. Lefty's my friend. He don't carry a fast gun. I do. You wantta shoot somebody, try me."

For several heartbeats the gunman hesitated. Cody waited. Finally, the man thumbed off the hammer and twirled the yellow-handled Colt into his holster faster than the eye could follow.

"Maybe you don't know who you're dealing with. I'm Wade Boggs. I'm the fastest gun in Missouri."

"I'm from Texas," Cody said calmly, stepping away from the other Brazos cowboys and squaring off, facing the bully.

Just as El Diablo had coached him so many times, Cody fixed a hard stare directly on the gunman's eyes. A smirking smile puckered the corners of the bully's mouth. His look oozed confidence. He was about to add another notch in the yellow handles of his Colt, or so he thought.

When Cody saw the man's eyes squint, his hand reacted instantaneously.

The gunman's draw was a blur, too fast to see with the naked eye. One instant his hand was empty, the next heartbeat it held the yellow-handled Colt.

Two guns fired simultaneously, making a sound like a thunderclap. Cody heard the slug from the bully's gun thwack into the wooden floor only inches from his boot toes. His own bullet plowed into the gunman's chest, in the center of the bib shirt.

The man staggered, his Colt wavering. Not wanting the shooter to get off another shot and possibly hit a bystander, Cody shot him again, this time in the heart. The man spread-eagled over backwards, landing hard. He didn't move.

Cody swung the nose of his gun toward the gunman's companions, but quickly saw they wanted no part in the fight. Blue smoke curled upward from the nose of Cody's gun. He sleeved sweat from his forehead and holstered his Colt.

"Somebody better go fetch the sheriff," the bartender said loudly. A spectator darted out the door.

The barkeep lowered his voice and leaned close to Cody.

"None of my business, Kid; it was a fair fight, but you just killed Wade Boggs. His pappy is A. J. Boggs. He owns the biggest spread in these parts. He ain't gonna take kindly to you killing his boy. If I was you, I'd make tracks fast and far."

"Like you said, it was a fair fight."

The man who pushed through the batwing doors of the saloon was tall. His shoulders sloped downward. He wore a handlebar mustache that mantled his lip and a sheriff's star on his leather vest. His eyes took in the entire room in a single glance. He walked over to the dead gunman and stared down at him for a minute.

"Who shot him?" he asked, his head cocking slightly to sweep a gaze at every man in the room.

"I did," Cody answered.

The sheriff settled a long look on Cody.

Cody waited.

"I'm Henry West. 'm the sheriff hereabouts. What's your name, son?"

"Hondo. Folks call me the Hondo Kid."

"Where you from?"

"Texas. I'm from Hondo, Texas."

"But what's your real name?"

"My name is the Hondo Kid."

"What'cha doing in Sedalia, Missouri?"

"Come in with the Brazos River Ranch cattle drive."

The sheriff slanted a look at the bartender.

"Tell me about it, Sam."

"Well, not much to tell. Wade was his usual self. He came in bullying like always, like he was the cock of the walk. He shouldered into this fellow here, spilling his beer. When the fella objected, Wade ordered a beer and poured it down the man's shirt. Then he pulled that fancy gun of his and threatened to blow his head off.

"This young fella took up for his friend. One thing led to another and Wade pulled iron on the kid. Wade was fast, but not fast enough. The kid put two bullets in him quicker'n scat. Never seen anybody so fast. It was a fair fight. Wade drew first."

The sheriff turned to the B Bar B boys still leaning against the bar.

"Anybody see it different?

They all shook their heads without saying a word.

"I'll be needing that gun, Kid."

Cody raised his hands shoulder high. The sheriff lifted Cody's Colt from the holster and stuck it down behind his belt.

"Some of you boys get Wade over to the undertaker's office. I expect you boys better let his pa know what happened pretty quick. Kid, you come with me."

Cody followed the sheriff down the street to his office. The lawman took a seat behind a rickety-looking desk and fixed Cody with a long look.

"We got us a problem here, kid. That boy's daddy throws a wide loop in these parts. He's gonna be madder'n a wet hornet when he finds out about you killing his boy, no matter whose fault it was. A. J. Boggs is a man use to having his own way. When he says jump, all most folks ask is when and how high. He's got maybe fifty riders on his payroll. I know him. I've known him for years. He's gonna come looking for you. You can't run far enough and fast enough to get outta his reach.

"Now I'm gonna lock you up, not because you done anything wrong, but that's the only way I can keep you alive. If they come after you, I'll do everything in my power to keep them from hanging you."

* * *

Cody heard them coming. The sound of two hundred galloping hooves on the hard-packed street would be hard to miss. He swung his feet to the floor of his jail cell and looked through the bars of the small window toward the street.

Fifty riders charged up the street at full gallop. They reined to a stop in front of the sheriff's office. Each of them carried rifles in their hands. One carried a coiled lariat already fashioned into a hangman's noose.

A large man wearing typical rancher's clothing and a flat-brimmed black Stetson with a high crown, swung quickly to the ground and stomped toward the door to the office. *That would be the pappy of the fellow I shot. The one they call A. J. Boggs.* One didn't have to look too close to see the man had a full-size mad on. Cody could hear clearly when the big man slammed open the door to the sheriff's office. Another man followed Boggs close on his heels with his gun drawn.

"Where is he?" the big rancher demanded.

"Sit down, A. J., and let's talk about this."

"Don't want to talk. I want the man who killed my boy. You gonna march him out here or do I go in and get him?"

"Did your men tell you what happened?"

"Don't care what happened. All I need to know is that my boy's dead and the man who done it is gonna hang!"

"Nobody's hanging anybody! Wade came to town looking for a fight. He got it. It was a fair fight. Even your own men agreed Wade drew first. Now go bury your boy and let it drop."

"Ain't letting nothing drop. All I gotta do is say the word and my men will take this place apart piece by piece. If it's the last thing I do, that fellow's gonna hang for killing my boy."

"I can't let you do that, A. J. Don't make this any worse than it already is. Go on home before somebody gets hurt."

Cody heard a crunching sound, like metal on bone. The next sound he heard was a key turning in the heavy door separating the sheriff's office from the jail. The door swung open.

The big rancher strode toward Cody's cell. The other man followed closely, his gun still in his hand. Boggs stopped outside the cell. His face red with anger. His lips set in a cruel-looking scowl. His eyes blazed as he fixed a hard stare at Cody.

"So, you're him! You're the low-down snake that killed my boy!"

The rancher unlocked the cell door and pulled a Smith & Wesson from his holster.

"Get his hands tied," he ordered his man.

Cody's hands were quickly tied behind his back and they shoved him ahead of them as they marched from the jail into the office. The sheriff lay on the floor, out cold. A large blue lump on his forehead made clear what happened.

They shoved Cody through the door and onto the boardwalk.

"Get him on a horse," Boggs ordered.

Cody's heart pounded near out of his chest. One of the Boggs riders swung to the ground and lifted Cody into the saddle.

"Take him down to the livery," the rancher ordered. "We'll hang him from the overhang of the hayloft."

The horse Cody was on was led down the street. The other Boggs' riders followed. When they reached the livery, they tossed the noose over the overhanging arm and dropped over Cody's head.

Cody's breath nearly stopped cold. The horse he was on was turned facing the street. A crowd of spectators gathered and stood a ways off, watching the goings-on. All fifty Boggs riders sat their horses in front of him. Cody's gaze swept the faces of the riders with a look. What he saw wasn't hatred, or even anger. He saw only shame, at what was about to happen.

The big rancher reined his black stallion around in front of

Cody. For a long moment he sat silently, staring at Cody with hatred in his eyes.

"You got anything to say before we hang you?"

"Yes, sir. I'm sorry about your boy, but he pushed it. It was a fair fight. Your boy drew first. All I done was defend myself."

One of Boggs' men spoke up.

"He's telling it like it is, Mr. Boggs. Wade egged it on and drew first."

"You're fired!" the rancher screamed at his own man. "Get outta my sight!"

"Just hold it right there!" a voice from down the street hollered.

Cody twisted his head to look. Sheriff West staggered down the street with a long-barreled shotgun in his hands. He stumbled, and come near falling, then caught himself and hurried on. He stopped beside the horse Cody sat on.

"Get that rope off the boy!" he ordered, lifting the shotgun to his shoulder and pointed it directly at Boggs.

"NO!" the rancher screamed, and clawed his gun from its holster.

The explosion from the sheriff's shotgun shattered the stillness that had settled along the street. The force of the blast lifted the big rancher out of his saddle. He somersaulted over the back of his stallion, dead before his body hit the ground, his face and chest a mangled mass of blood and gore.

Cody's mount shied sideways, tightening the noose. The sheriff reached a hand and grabbed the reins of the horse, steadying it.

"Get that rope off him!" Henry West ordered again.

Two of the riders hurried to remove the noose and untied Cody's hands. Cody and the sheriff turned and elbowed their way through the crowd to his office. The lawman opened a desk drawer and handed Cody his gun and holster. He stuck out a big hand. Cody took it. They shook hands warmly.

"You're free to go, kid."

Cody strapped his gun belt in place and checked to make sure the weapon was loaded.

"I'm obliged for what you done," Cody said, turning to leave.

"All I did was what was right."

At the door, Cody paused and looked back over his shoulder.

"My *real* name is Cordell. Cody Cordell."

Part II

CHAPTER XII

The attack came just before dawn. Loud ringing of the alarm bell woke Buck Cordell from a sound sleep. He swung out of bed, jerked on his pants and shirt, and stomped on his boots.

"What is it, Buck?" Rebekah asked sleepily, sitting up in bed.

"Don't know. Could be nothing. Better get dressed just in case. Stay inside."

"No, I'll be in the cookhouse. Jewel will need help if someone is injured."

Buck slung his gun belt around his waist and buckled it in place as he hurried for the heavy front door. By the time he reached it he heard shooting, lots of shooting.

"Indians!" somebody from the wall shouted. "Indians!"

Longhorn men took up positions on the walkway along the wall, others poured out of the bunkhouse, rifles in hand, running for their assigned emergency stations. Buck raced toward the front gate. Chester was already climbing the ladder that ran the entire circuit of the wall. Buck took the ladder two rungs at a time. He grabbed a couple of the .52 caliber Spencer rifles they always kept fully loaded in racks placed along the walkway.

Bullets ricocheted off the thick adobe wall and whined off into the gathering dawn. All around him, Longhorn men fired time and again. Buck chanced a quick look over the top of the wall.

Black smoke billowed from the front gate. The attackers had dragged bundles of burning bushes against the gate in an effort to gain entry.

"Somebody dump a barrel of water on that fire against the gate!" Buck yelled.

Two Longhorn men rushed to comply.

In the half-light of early morning, Buck saw the fleeting outlines of a large force of Indians racing back and forth along the wall, firing in an endless barrage from repeater rifles. Indian war whoops from the hard charging warriors mixed with screams of pain and death as Longhorn men laid down a deadly barrage of fire from their Spencer rifles.

"Hanging their chief musta made 'em mad," Chester shouted, ducking his head below the top of the wall as a bullet whistled past.

"Wonder where they got hold of those repeater rifles?" Buck yelled, over the sound of gunfire.

Chester's answer was drowned out by the deafening sound of gunfire. One of the Longhorn men near Buck let out a scream and grabbed his neck. A bullet hole in his throat pumped blood like a geyser with each beat of his heart. Buck snatched a bandana from his pocket and stuffed it in the hole.

"Over here!" Buck yelled. "Help me get this man to the cookhouse!"

Two men grabbed the wounded man and lowered him to the ground. Others picked him up by the feet and arms and hurried him to the makeshift hospital set up in the cook shack.

"Look out! They're coming over the wall!" someone shouted.

Buck swung a look. Sure enough, brown, painted bodies scrambled over the top of the wall. He jerked his Spencer to his shoulder and found a target. His shot blew a warrior backwards over the wall. He levered another round and sent another screaming Indian to the happy hunting ground.

Buck jerked a quick glance over the wall. He discovered a new appreciation for the Comanche's skill at horsemanship. Warrior after warrior raced his mount along the high wall of the compound with a rifle on a slung on his backs. At precisely the right moment, they stood to their feet on the back of their racing ponies and leaped to grab hold of the top of the wall and pulled themselves over. It was an amazing feat of bravery and agility, and was usually met with sudden death from Longhorn rifles.

The battle raged for what seemed an eternity, but in reality lasted less than an hour. When it was over, the report of the dead and injured saddened all those in the compound. Four Longhorn men lay dead, six others were wounded but would recover.

Later Buck and Chester walked slowly along the battlefield outside the compound wall. This was a gruesome sight, a sickening sight. Scores of dead and dying warriors lay scattered along the wall.

"Reminds me of the war," Chester said.

Buck only nodded in reply.

The soft rains of early March did their job. Fresh blades of green grass sprang from the earth in a magnificent rebirth that happens each spring; a rebirth conceived in the mind of the Creator to multiply itself in an endless chain of life.

"The spring calf crop was a good one," Rowdy Sloan said. "The calves sired by *El Toro* are something to behold."

"If you think this year's crop is somethin', just give me a couple of years and you won't believe what that monster bull will produce," Pappy promised.

Buck glanced around the long table. All of the top hands of the Longhorn were sipping coffee and discussing the operations of the ranch and the upcoming drives.

"Yeah, since those newspaper articles came out about your bull, we've had all kinds of inquiries from some large ranches wanting to talk about renting him," Buck told them.

"You ain't thinking serious about it, are you?" Pappy asked. "We can keep that big fellow busy breedin', right here on the Longhorn."

"Not at this point," Buck said. "Maybe later on we might think about something like that. Rowdy, the first herd from Mexico will be arriving in less than two weeks. Where you got in mind to put 'em?"

"I checked the north pasture along the Sycamore River just yesterday, boss. The grass is up and ready for 'em. It'll handle five thousand head for two weeks without a problem."

"Ray, you'll be leaving with the first herd of twenty-five hundred on April first. Is your crew ready?"

"We're ready. My crew is chomping at the bit to get on the trail. Wash will be our trail cook again, just like last time. One of the newer men, Sam Becker, will be my top hand."

"What about you, Smokey? Your crew ready to pull out right behind Ray?"

"We're ready, boss."

"Good. Buster Keene will be following you two weeks later with another twenty-five hundred head in herd number three. Slim's herd will be the fourth herd in line, a day behind Buster. Artie Blaine and Link Stone will head up the next two drives. Pedro Sedillo, Carlos Rodriguez, Cleveland Sims, Dirk Phelps, Dave Hannibal, and Burt Langer will follow them. All together, we'll have twelve trail drive crews, each with a cook and a twenty-man crew.

"It's important each of you make the turnaround in three

months 'cause you'll be taking another herd up the trail as soon as you get back. Each crew will make two drives this year. We're gonna take sixty thousand head up trail this year, come hell or high water.

"Chester will be the overall trail boss. He'll be drifting from herd to herd, making sure things run smooth. If you run into a problem you can't handle, get word to Chester; he'll do what needs done. Got anything you want to say, Chet?"

Chester climbed to his feet. He took a minute to let his slow gaze sweep the faces of their top hands gathered around the table.

"You fellows were picked as our top hands to lead these drives because we believe you're the best in the business. We've got a long, tough year ahead of us. Each one of you will be making two trips to Missouri and back this year. Far as we can tell, nothing like this has ever been done before. You boys are gonna be making history. Let's do it right. Like Buck said, you run into a problem, word to me."

Chester lifted his coffee cup in a cowboy salute to the leaders of the Longhorn trail crews before sitting down.

"Anybody got questions?" Buck asked, pausing to wait. "That's it then, daylight's wastin'. We've all got a lot to do and not much time left to do it. Let's get at it."

Rebekah lay quietly, staring with sleepless eyes through the dimness of the night at the ceiling. Only a single, flickering candle disturbed the darkness. After a time she twisted her head to nestle it closer against Buck's wide shoulder. His even breathing told her he was asleep.

His fresh-bathed scent filled her nostrils. She breathed deep and raised her eyes to gaze at his face. A smile lifted the corner of her lips as she watched him; she often lay awake, delighting in watching her husband sleep.

The three months since their marriage had been the happiest time of her life. And now…this.

As she stared through the darkness at his face, an overwhelming surge of love enveloped her. Soft tears leaked from her eyes and trailed down her cheeks. An irresistible urge to kiss him overtook her. She raised her head and touched soft lips to his in a long, tender kiss.

Suddenly his eyes opened, instantly awake. His strong arm drew her closer into his embrace, into his kiss. It was a long kiss, long, and searching, and wonderful. With blood burning in her cheeks, she opened her lips to his, reaching a hand to gather a handful of his long, corn silk hair and pulling him to her.

When the kiss ended, his lips trailed over her chin, her neck, until…But then his lips contacted tears. He jerked his head up and stared at her with a concerned look.

"You've been crying. Is something wrong?"

A huge lump suddenly developed in her throat. She swallowed, and then swallowed again, taking a deep breath and letting it out before words would come.

"No, my darling cowboy. Something is wonderfully *right*. We're…we're going to have a baby."

When construction on the Longhorn compound was completed, Juan Santos and his crew were given a new assignment to build a bank in Del Rio. They would also construct a house in town for Sam and Kathleen Colson. Sam agreed to accept the job as president of the Del Rio, Texas bank that Buck and Chester wanted to open, and once he made the decision to accept the job, both he and Kathleen became excited about their new life.

Until their new home was completed, they moved into temporary quarters in a rented house. Kathleen's days were spent making the small, three-room house livable. Sam spent his days supervising the construction of the new bank and visiting with various businessmen in town.

Del Rio, Texas was growing.

John Walker found himself forced to double the size of his store and feed operation with the dramatic increased needs of the Longhorn. Neither Buck nor Rebekah were surprised when they learned John hired Elvira, his widowed friend, to help in the business.

Several new businesses were opening in town, and with the thousand dollars donated by the Longhorn, the businessmen met and formed a town council. Their first order of business was to begin a search for a town marshal.

With all the new construction going on, Selena and her mother's business was also booming.

They had to hire two new helpers just to take care of the increased custom in their café.

News that Buck and Rebekah were going to have a baby spread throughout the Longhorn Ranch like wildfire. As they went about the daily routine of ranch life, they received congratulations and pats on the back from all they encountered.

At the request of both Buck and Chester, Rebekah took charge of the books at the Longhorn. She immediately organized the accounts to reflect the many expenses, as well as the income. She spent long hours sorting out receipts, itemizing expenses and sorting through folders and boxes of paperwork Buck hadn't had time to handle properly.

With Jewel's help, Rebekah also reorganized the work assignments of the increasing number of help needed to run the support operations of the ranch. They now had well over two hundred people living and working on the ranch, which took a lot of food preparation, ordering of supplies, and kitchen help.

Days were long on the Longhorn. Both Buck and Rebekah rose well before daylight and finally went to bed, totally exhausted, sometime before midnight. Ranch life was hard. It demanded the best each of them had in them. But the Longhorn was flourishing, and so were both Buck and Rebekah.

The two made it a point to save time for one another. They spent time together in the large bathroom pool Juan Santos constructed for Rebekah. That was their private time, their personal time together.

One night, near midnight, Buck got home to find Rebekah still in the office, poring over stacks of papers. Fatigue and frustration showed clearly on her face.

"I love you dearly, Buck Cordell," she told him as he approached cautiously. "You are the perfect husband and you will be the best father known to mankind, but keeping your finances straight is definitely not one of your strong points."

"Hmm," Buck said, leaning over the chair and pushing aside her long, red hair that hung loose around her shoulders. He lowered his head and trailed soft kisses along her neck.

"Your *perfect* husband is going into the kitchen, warm some water, and make a nice hot bath. When it's ready, and if you can tear yourself away from these books, you could—"

The vaqueros of the Silver Spur Ranchero in Mexico arrived with the herd of longhorns on the *exact* day they were scheduled. *Señor Antonio Lopez* himself led the herd of five thousand head of cattle. The date was March 15, 1867. Carlos, Buck, and Chester rode out to greet him.

After introductions, all four went into the compound and made themselves comfortable in the large den in Buck and Rebekah's home. A Mexican house girl brought coffee for everyone.

"We are pleased to have you in our home," Buck told his guest. "We hope you will honor us by having dinner with us and spend the night."

"I would be honored to be your guest, *señor.* You have a remarkable place here."

"My men will assist your vaqueros in moving the herd to our holding ground and conducting the count. Allow me to congratulate you on arriving with your herd on the precise date we specified.

"Shall we get our business out of the way? Then we will be happy to show you around the Longhorn. I believe the agreed price was four dollars a head plus one dollar bonus for timely delivery. How many head did you bring us?"

"We started out with five thousand-one hundred head. Unfortunately, we lost sixty head on the trip. I am delivering five thousand-forty head of the finest Longhorns in all *Mexico*."

Buck went to his desk and withdrew a leather satchel. From a drawer he added a packet of bills. He set the satchel on the table in front of the owner of the Silver Spur Ranchero.

"There's twenty-five thousand-two hundred dollars there. Feel free to count it if you wish."

The ranch owner glanced briefly inside, and then closed the satchel.

"That will not be necessary. It's a pleasure to do business with honorable men."

Dinner that night was an elaborate affair and was the very first time they had entertained guests in their home. Rebekah went all out.

Chester, Selena, Carlos, Buck, Rebekah, and their guest, Antonio Lopez, sat around the large dining room table.

Jewel personally oversaw the servants who served their dinner. Large steaks cooked over a mesquite fire, baked sweet potatoes, stewed cabbage, and homemade yeast rolls with honey were served in Rebekah's new dinnerware, each piece emblazoned with the Longhorn brand.

Rebekah was the perfect hostess.

Buck couldn't have been more pleased. He was amazed at her ability to make their guest feel welcome and special.

After dinner they visited over coffee in the spacious and elaborately furnished den.

"May I compliment you, *Señora* Cordell, on your lovely home. I have not seen its equal in all of *Mexico*."

"Thank you, S*eñor Lopez*. We are delighted to have you as our guest. I hope I will have the honor of meeting S*eñora Lopez* sometime, perhaps on your next trip."

"I assure you, she would be delighted to meet you."

"Speaking of the next trip," Buck said, "would you be able to supply another herd next year if it's needed?"

"I'm sure that could be arranged."

"Good. Then Carlos will be in touch with you and make the arrangements."

"It will be a pleasure."

After a while the ladies excused themselves, but the men talked cattle talk far into the night.

The next two weeks passed all too quickly. On April 1, 1867, Chester and Ray Ledbetter led the first herd of twenty-five hundred head across the Sycamore River and north toward Missouri.

The following day, Smokey and his crew splashed another twenty-five hundred head across the river.

Two weeks later, two more herds of twenty-five hundred

each pulled out one day apart. That same day, April 15, ten thousand head arrived from the *San Carlos Ranch* in the *San Fernando River* Ranch.

Señor Manuel San Carlos accompanied the large herd. As before, he accepted their invitation to spend the night, and again, Rebekah, Jewel, and her crew served a wonderful dinner.

"You're getting right good at entertaining our guests," Buck told Rebekah, as they lay in the warmed pool of water in their bathroom that night.

"You think so, huh?" Rebekah said, shoving Buck's head under the water playfully.

He came up sputtering and returned the favor. They both laughed and shared a hug.

"You sure you ain't trying to do too much? Don't forget you're carrying my son in there."

"Oh? How do you know it's going to be a son?"

"Of course it's gonna be a boy. No question about it. I want two sons and a beautiful daughter, in that order, please."

"Yes, sir, Mr. Cordell. Coming right up," she said, saluting smartly.

They kissed.

Chester and Smokey sat their saddles on a small rise overlooking the Red River crossing.

It was mid-April. Ray Ledbetter's herd number one made the crossing the day before, but heavy rains upstream had the river running bank-full. They were forced to delay attempting a crossing with the second herd.

"Way I see it, we've got no choice," Chester told Smokey. "We're liable to lose some drovers and no telling how many cattle if we try a crossing with the Red running this deep. Let's circle 'em in that grassy valley we passed a couple miles back. We'll give it a day or so and see if the water goes down a tad."

"Think you're right. It's too dangerous to try a crossing with the water that high."

"I'd rather lose a day or two than lose one of our wranglers. Let's ride back and tell Joshua to set up camp."

It took two days before the river receded enough to make the crossing. On the second day Zack Gibbs appeared.

"We got a little worried when your herd didn't show up behind us," the scout said. "Ray thought I better ride back and check on you."

"We got delayed by the river being up," Chester told Zack. "But the herd's well rested," Chester said to Smokey. "Let's drive 'em hard for the next few days to catch up with Ray's herd."

"I figure if we cover twenty miles a day driving hard, it'll take us a week to make up for the time we lost," Smokey replied.

"Sounds about right. Let's do it. Me and Zack are gonna wait at the river for Buster and Link and their herds to get across. We'll catch up to you in a couple of weeks or so."

Smokey said, "Ride careful. We'll see you up the trail."

It was the better part of two weeks before Buster's herd number three showed up.

"You're right on schedule," Chester told him. "Smokey's herd got delayed a couple of days because of high water. Decided me and Zack would wait here and make sure you and Slim's herd got across safe.

Buck says the Red is the worst river crossing between here and Missouri. I'm gonna leave Zack here until all the herds are across. Some of the newer boys might need some help. Don't let them take any unnecessary chances. We don't want to lose anybody."

"Might be right nice to lay around for a couple of months." Zack grinned at his own joke.

"More like five months. Don't forget, we'll be crossing a herd every two weeks from now until the end of September."

"You got it, boss. We'll get 'em across safe."

After Buster and Slim's herds were safely across the river, Chester left Zack at the river and headed up trail. It took a week for him to catch up with the lead herd.

"Any problems back there?" Ray asked.

"The river was running too high and we had to hold Smokey's herd a couple of days until the water went down. I left Zack at the crossing to help with all the herds. He knows that river like the back of his hand."

"Good idea."

Chester sent a serious look. "Seen any Indian signs?"

"No, but that don't mean much. Like Buck says, you don't see an Indian unless he wants you to see him. By then, it's usually too late."

"Well, tell the nighthawks to keep their eyes peeled. Our remuda might look too tempting."

The raid came shortly after midnight. A dozen dark figures swooped out of the nearby woods, stampeded the horses, and disappeared into the night before the two sleepy nighthawks knew what hit them. They managed to kill two of their attackers before the horse thieves were swallowed up by the darkness.

"We can't track them until first light," Chester told Ray. "Come morning, I'll take a few of the boys and track them down. May take a while. We've got to have those horses. All we've got are the saddled mounts we keep at the camp."

"We'll have to drive slow days until you get back. With just one horse, the boys will wear them out pretty quick. Who you got in mind to take with you?"

"I'd like to take Monty Montana, Artie Sells, Rich Maxwell, and that Mexican we just hired not long ago. What's his name?"

"Jose Vazquez."

"Yeah, that's the one. Seems to me he's a fellow with plenty of sand."

"You got him pegged, boss. Word is he's a crack shot with a rifle, too."

"Have Wash load a couple of packhorses with enough supplies for two weeks. We'll try to be back before then."

"You boys ride careful."

They rode out at the first crack of dawn. Each man carried a rifle in his saddle boot and plenty of ammunition. They rode at a steady, ground-eating short lope. Chester allowed his gaze time to take each man's measure.

Monty Montana was a young, clean-cut, cocky sort of fellow, the kind of cowboy everybody liked immediately. His wide shoulders and thin waist made him seem taller than he really was.

He had a clean-shaven face with a square jaw and dark, flashing eyes. His denim shirt couldn't hide the bulging muscles in his arms. He was the sort of fellow you wanted on your side when push came to shove, either with fists or guns.

Artie Sells was a scarecrow of a man. He was tall, skinny as a fence rail, with the kind of face that made womenfolk turn and look away. His leathery skin stretched tight over a protruding chin and cheekbones. Artie was a quiet man who pretty much kept to himself. He was a hard worker that did his job and did it well. The well-oiled, worn holster and bone-handled Colt told Chester that Artie Sells knew his way around a gun.

Rich Maxwell was an ex-lawman and former Texas Ranger. He was an experienced tracker and man hunter. Rich Maxwell was a good man to have riding by your side in a situation like this one.

Jose Vazquez was everyone's idea of what a vaquero ought to look like. Chester slanted a look at the Mexican. Handsome. That's the singular description most folks would use to describe Jose. Chester made a mental note not to introduce Jose to Selena. The man sat tall and erect in the saddle. His dark, flashing eyes swept from side to side, looking at nothing, seeing everything.

They picked up the trail just as dawn lightened the eastern sky. It would have been hard to miss. A hundred frightened horses running as a herd made the trail easy to follow.

Chester knew that, to an Indian, horses were everything. Horses were the measure of their wealth; their very standing in the tribal structure. They were willing to risk their lives to possess them.

Chester and his men followed the trail for three days. Near sundown of the third day, the tracks told them two things. First, the Indian horse thieves knew where they were headed and they weren't in a particular hurry to get there. They were driving the horses at a walk.

This worried Chester. These horse thieves were too confident, too relaxed. They didn't seem worried in the least they might be followed.

Then something suddenly dawned on Chester. *They're getting close to home! They're not worried because they are so close. They feel safe.* Finally he gave voice to his thoughts. "I got a feeling we best ride slow and keep our eyes peeled. I figure these fellows are close to home."

"Think you're right," Maxwell agreed, keeping his voice low. "Look over yonder."

They all looked in the direction Maxwell pointed. Several faint tendrils of light gray smoke trailed upward.

"Looks like their camp," the ex-ranger said. "That's most likely supper fires."

Chester nodded in thought. "Maybe we best not get any closer until dark. Let's water the horses in that little creek over there and try to figure out how we're gonna get our horses back without getting scalped in the process."

Chester and his four men squatted beside the small creek with reins in their hands while their horses drank their fill.

"What's your feeling on the matter, Rich?" Chester asked, slanting a sideways gaze at the ex-lawman.

"I figure they'll be celebrating tonight. Stealing a horse is one thing, stealing a hundred horses is a big deal. Them horse thieves are big men in camp tonight. The whole camp will likely celebrate most of the night. Yes, sir. They'll break out the mescal jugs tonight for shore."

"What do the rest of you think?"

"Makes sense," Monty agreed. "Maybe if we wait a while they'll all be too drunk to put up much of a fight."

"What about you, Artie?"

"Reckon that's as good a plan as any, better'n most."

"What do you think, Jose?"

"You are the boss. I will do as you say."

"Okay then," said Chester. "We'll wait until midnight or so. Give them time to get liquored up. No killing unless we have to. I don't want any women or children getting hurt, understood?"

They all nodded.

They left their horses on the shoulder of a hill overlooking the Indian village. It was a small collection of wickiups, no more than forty or so, bunched tightly together along a small stream winding through the small valley. For more than two hours Chester and his men lay belly-flat, watching the drunken celebration. The bonfires gradually burned themselves out, leaving nothing more than smoldering piles of hot coals.

The large horse herd grazed peacefully among the tall sycamore trees that lined the stream. Three of the younger Indian boys were left to guard the herd.

Chester decided it was time.

He lifted an arm and moved it forward. His four men stepped into stirrups and swung into their saddles, sliding their booted rifles free, and levering. They walked their horses over the crest of the hill and down the hillside.

As they drew near the horse herd they fanned out, getting within a hundred yards before the alarm sounded. One of the young Indians spotted them and let out a long, piercing yelp.

Chester and his men put heels to their mounts and quickly closed the distance between them and the horses. His men were well experienced at herding horses and quickly had the entire herd galloping up the hillside away from the village.

It had happened so quickly the young Indians didn't have time to put up any resistance. Chester crooked a look back over his shoulder and saw the drunken Indians rushing from their wickiups, but with most of their horses gone, had no way to pursue. He felt good. It was a successful raid. Not a shot had been fired.

The days grew long on the Longhorn Ranch. A constant stream of longhorn cattle arrived weekly from the Mexican ranchers. Supply wagons arrived daily, bringing much needed supplies for the departing trail crews, two each week.

Buck and Rebekah rose well before first light every day. Though he encouraged her to let someone else take part of her workload, she would have none of it. She helped Jewel oversee the cooks. They fed two hundred hungry cowboys a hearty breakfast daily. After breakfast she spent long hours in the office keeping the books updated.

A growing part of her duties was playing hostess, entertaining Mexican ranch owners delivering their herds who often spent the night. Texas cattlemen visited in increasing numbers and were frequent overnight houseguests. Rebekah assumed the additional responsibility of planning elaborate dinners for these important men. Mostly, the ranchers came to see El Toro, the *super bull,* as the newspapers called him. They wanted to see for themselves if the stories they were hearing were fact or fiction.

Buck stayed on the run from early morning until near midnight every day. A pre-dawn breakfast, followed by a daily meeting with his top hands, was over well before daylight. Trail herds had to be organized, new cowhands interviewed and hired, emergencies dealt with, and visiting ranchers given his personal attention.

Richard King, along with two of his foremen and a six-man security escort, arrived unannounced at the Longhorn Ranch in late April 1867. Rebekah immediately dispatched one of the ranch hands to fetch Buck.

Buck was on the north range organizing the next herd that would be moving out the following day. When the ranch hand galloped up with the news that King had arrived, Buck turned the task over to the trail boss in charge of the herd and rode back to ranch headquarters to meet his famous guest.

Buck had already heard of the famous *Running W Ranch* and its owner, but had never met him. King, his two foremen, and Pappy were leaning on the corral fence staring at the now famous bull. Buck rode up, stepped to the ground and approached them. A black covered buggy and sleek, matching black horses stood nearby.

"I'm Buck Cordell," he said, extending his hand. "You must be Richard King?"

The man who reached to shake his hand was a large, rather heavy-set fellow. He wore a dark business suit, a white shirt, with a string tie. His black mustache matched his collar-length hair underneath the black, high-crowned Stetson. Buck's greeting was met with an almost stern, businesslike expression.

"It's a pleasure to finally meet you, Mr. Cordell. This is Carl Summers and Harvey Mills, two of my foremen."

Buck shook hands with the men.

"Say howdy to Pappy. He's my bush popper here on the Longhorn and the man who captured and trained El Toro."

"You and your ranch are causing quite a stir in cattle country, Mr. Cordell."

"Call me Buck. We don't hold much on formalities here on the Longhorn."

"Forgive me for arriving unannounced. I was in San Antonio on business and took the opportunity to visit. That bull of yours is the talk of Texas. After seeing him with my own eyes, I can understand why."

"He shore is something to behold, ain't he?"

"That he is. That he is. Your entire ranch is impressive. It's everything I've heard and more. I've never seen so much activity. It's hard to believe you've been able to organize all this in less than two years."

"Well, I've had a lot of help. We've all worked hard."

"I've heard you're trailing ten thousand head a month to Missouri. That's hard to imagine. No one has ever attempted such a massive movement."

"Well, like I say, I've got a lot of good help."

"Have you been able to breed this bull yet?"

"Yes, sir, his calf crop is right over yonder. Would you like to see them?"

"I certainly would," Richard King replied.

Together they walked past a long line of corrals and stopped at a large enclosure. Inside the corral was a herd of mother cows. The calves by their side were unusually large, almost as large as the mother cow.

"How old are these calves, Pappy?" Buck asked.

"Most are less than a month old, some a tad more."

Richard King's eyes went wide.

"They're near three times the size of a normal calf that age," the famous rancher exclaimed.

"Yes, sir," Buck agreed. "We're expecting these calves to grow up to be like their papa."

"I've never seen anything like it," King said, shaking his head in wonder and staring at the calves. "I'd like to discuss a business proposition with you."

"Can you and your men spend the night?" Buck asked. "Maybe we could talk business after dinner."

"We'd love to, if it's not an imposition."

"None at all. Pappy, have someone inform Rebekah that we will have three guests for dinner. I'll show Mr. King and his foremen around the ranch."

"I'll handle it," Pappy said.

After touring the ranch, and an elaborate dinner, Buck and his guests settled into the large, comfortable leather sofas in the den.

"Thank you, Mrs. Cordell, for that excellent dinner," Richard King said.

"I'm happy you enjoyed it. It's good to have you in our home. If you gentlemen would excuse me?"

They all stood as Rebekah left the men to their cigars and coffee.

"I must say, Buck, your wife is stunning, as well as a perfect hostess."

"I'll pass on your compliments."

"As I said earlier, I'm very impressed with your ranch, especially with that exceptional bull and the calves he sires. As you may know, I'm very interested in crossbreeding and upgrading my own herds. It is obvious to me that you have similar ambitions. Perhaps together, we could revolutionize the cattle industry in Texas.

"I'd like to acquire a few of those bull calves you showed me earlier today. Would you consider selling some of them?"

Buck took a space of time before he replied. In his mind he weighed the pros and cons of the proposal. *Should I keep El Toro's offspring here on the Longhorn and use them to build our own herds or should I consider the larger picture of improving the entire cattle industry in Texas?*

He took a swig of coffee and settled a long look on his famous guest. *No doubt about it, King has huge ambitions, just like my own. Word is he's dead set on building the largest cattle and horse ranch in Texas. He's an impressive fellow. He just might do what he's set on doing. Maybe working with him, rather than in competition, we could both accomplish more.*

"Might consider it," Buck said. "The price would be high."

"Name it."

"I'll sell you a dozen young bulls, once they're six months old, for a thousand dollars each."

"Sold. Write out the bill of sale and we'll settle up. I'll send for them in five months time."

"They'll be ready and waiting," Buck said, extending his hand to seal the bargain.

CHAPTER XIII

Chester and Ray Ledbetter rode into Sedalia, Missouri on June 4, 1867. They noticed the cattle pens were mostly empty and a line of railroad cattle cars stretched as far as the eyes could see.

"Looks like they're expecting us," Ray said.

Chester grinned. "Seems so."

They rode down the street and reined up at the hitching rail in front of the hotel.

"Ray, How about getting us a couple of rooms? I'll mosey down to the cattle buyer's office and let him know we're here."

"Sure will."

Buck had explained that Harvey Owens' office was just a short distance from the hotel. Chester walked down the boardwalk, found the office, and knocked on the door.

"Come in," a voice from inside called.

He opened the door. "I'm Chester Colson, Buck Cordell's partner."

Harvey Owens stood quickly and hurried around the desk with his hand extended.

"It's good to meet you, Chester. Buck told me all about you. I've been expecting you."

"We've got some cattle for you."

Harvey continued pumping Chester's hand. Finally he seemed to realize it and motioned Chester to a chair in front of the desk.

"That's the best news I've had in a long while. How many you got and where are they?"

"If all went as planned, by now we ought to have thirty-thousand head strung out all the way from here to Texas. We've got twenty-five hundred head, give or take a few, about five miles south of town. There's another herd a day behind us. They'll be coming in every two weeks, five thousand head at a time."

"Never heard of such a thing. You boys beat all. I'll get hold of my men and have them ride out and start bringing them in. Who will you have working with my man on the count?"

"Ray Ledbetter. He's getting us settled in the hotel."

"Of course. I already know Ray. Good man. Could you have dinner with me at the hotel dining room tonight? We'll work out the details."

"Sounds good."

"Fine. See you about seven then."

After a lengthy discussion about the future of the cattle market over dinner, Chester agreed to a fixed price of forty-two dollars a head for all of the Longhorn herds that year.

"My bosses at *Armour & Company* are pleased with the quality you boys are delivering," Harvey said. "They are gearing up for quite a year, thanks to you and Buck delivering a steady supply of beef. Since the war ended, folks in the east are clamoring for beef. We're having trouble supplying enough."

"That's what we like to hear," Chester said, sipping on his coffee.

"You boys run into any trouble down the trail?.

"None to speak of. Why do you ask?"

"Oh, it's most likely nothing, but for some time, a gang of rustlers has been stealing herds coming up the trail. Talk is a fellow who calls himself a cattle broker named Nate Bonner is behind it all. The gang rustles the herd, and then Bonner winds up with them.

"When Buck was here the first time, he and his men helped a rancher from east Texas recover his herd. He confronted Bonner, but of course, he denied knowing anything about it. Buck told Bonner to get out of town or he would kill him the next time he saw him. Thought you might have run into them."

"Buck told me about it. This Bonner fellow, is he still in town?"

"Oh, yeah. He keeps coming up with herds real regular."

"Can't the law do something about it?"

"Not so far. Bonner always has a bill of sale to show he bought the cattle. Bonner is a ruthless no-count. He's got a gunslick named Frank Vines that hangs around real close. I figure Vines is the head honcho of the rustlers. Just thought you'd want to keep your eyes peeled just in case."

"We'll do it. Obliged for the warning."

"How long you staying in town?"

"Just long enough for the count on the first couple of herds. I need to get back down the trail and check on the other herds. I'll be back and forth most of the year, I expect."

"I sent word about moving to Abilene, Kansas the first of next year. I hope we can continue our arrangement there."

"Don't see why not."

"How you want to handle payment for the rest of the herds you're bringing in this year?"

"Me and Buck talked about that. We decided on certified checks, made out to the Longhorn Ranch, in care of the San Antonio Bank. We'll be wanting to change that as soon as we get the bank in Del Rio open."

"Good. I'll talk to Andrew Simmons over at the bank. Your money will be ready for you as soon as the count is done."

"Buck told me you were a man to do business with. He told it right."

They moved the first herd into the cattle pens the following day. Ray Ledbetter and Cheyenne Morgan, Harvey's top hand, worked together on the count.

Chester and Harvey Owens sat their saddles and watched the endless line of longhorns being driven into the pens. As they entered the gate they were counted and loaded directly into the waiting cattle cars.

"It's quite a sight, ain't it?" Harvey said.

"Like nothing I ever thought I'd see," Chester agreed.

By nightfall, three trainloads pulled out and were already on their way to the Armour packinghouses in Chicago.

The following day Chester and Harvey Owens sat in the office of A. C. Simmons, president of the bank. I believe you gentlemen have agreed on a count of four thousand, six hundred and forty-five head for the first two herds. At forty-two dollars a head, that comes to A hundred ninety five thousand, ninety dollars. Here are the certified checks for that amount, made out as you instructed."

Chester glanced down at the checks in his hand. He blinked, and then blinked again. His mind whirled. It was more money than he had ever seen in his life. He swallowed the lump in his throat.

"If it goes as you gentlemen have outlined to me, there will be more of those checks twice a month for most of the year," Simmons said. "Will you be picking up the checks?"

"Most of them, I reckon," Chester told him. "I may ask my man in charge of the herd to pick them up from time to time."

"Very well. It's a pleasure doing business with you," the bank president said, standing to his feet and extending his hand.

Chester tucked the check into his pocket and shook the banker's hand. After leaving Harvey Owens, he walked across the street to the marshal's office, opened the door and stepped inside.

Henry West looked up from some papers on his desk and climbed to his feet.

"I 'spect you'd be Chester Colson, Buck's partner. Heard you were in town. Pleasure to meet you," the lawman said, extending a big, gnarled hand.

Chester took the hand and shook it. "And you'd be Henry West. Buck told me all about you."

"Well, hope he didn't tell you everything. That partner of yours is a big fellow in more ways than one."

"You got him pegged right. Known him a long time. Just wanted to stop in and say howdy. I've got my business done, leastwise for now. Fixing to ride back down the trail and check on the other herds. I'll be back from time to time."

"Has your partner heard anything more about his brother?"

"No, he's got the Pinkerton people looking for the boy. Maybe they'll come up with something before long."

"Shore hope so. Took a liking to that young fellow."

"Harvey Owens tells me Buck had trouble with a fellow named Bonner. Know anything about him?"

"I know he's a shady character. It's rumored he's involved in rustling trail herds, but so far, he ain't broke no laws, leastwise, any that I can pin on him."

"Where could I find him?"

"He's got an office over the Golden Nugget Saloon. Hope you ain't planning on starting trouble."

"No, just thought we ought to come to an understanding about our cattle."

"Watch yourself."

"I'll do that, Marshal. I'm obliged."

Chester returned to the hotel and found Ray. His top hand had his bedroll packed and ready to ride. Chester handed him the check the banker had given him.

"You and your crew about ready to head back toward home?"

"We're ready. Where you headed?"

"I've got one more stop to make before I head back down the trail. You and the boys ride on ahead, I'll be along."

Chester left the hotel and walked up the street to the Golden Nugget saloon. He pushed through the batwing doors and swept a look around the large room.

A half-dozen cow nurses lounged against the long bar. A poker game was in progress with five local businessmen. But Chester's gaze fixed on two men sitting at a table near the back wall.

One was a heavy-set fellow who wore a black three-piece business suit. He had black, slicked-down hair and a matching mustache. He fit the description Harvey Owens had given him of Nate Bonner.

The other man at the table was Frank Vines, no doubt about it. He had gunfighter written all over him.

Chester walked to the bar, ordered a beer, and then strode directly to the table where Bonner and Vines were sitting. Without a word he pulled out a chair and sat down. The gunfighter flicked a questioning look at Bonner, who creased his forehead with a frown.

"Your name Bonner?" Chester asked, his hard stare boring a hole in the big fellow's face.

"Yeah, I'm Nate Bonner. Who are you?"

"My name don't matter. What I've got to say does. Me and my partner own the Longhorn Ranch down Texas way. We'll be trailing a bunch of longhorns up the trail over the next few months. My job is to make sure every single one of them critters gets here safe and sound."

"What's that got to do with me?" Bonner asked, cutting another glance at the gunman sitting to his left.

Chester slanted a look at the gunman across the table.

"Talk around town is that herds have a way of disappearing along the trail lately. I aim to see that don't happen to one of our herds."

For the first time, the gunman spoke. His voice was raspy and came out in a loud whisper.

"That sounds like a threat."

Underneath the table, Chester slipped his Colt from its holster and pointed it at the gunfighter's stomach.

"Take it any way that suits you. But if either one of you mess with my cattle, I'll kill both of you. Are we clear on that?"

Chester saw anger flare in the gunfighter's eyes. The man's face flushed crimson. In one quick motion the gunman jumped to his feet and kicked his chair backwards. His right hand dipped to the Colt in the cut-away holster at his side.

Chester waited.

When the man's gun cleared leather, Chester thumbed back the hammer of his own Colt and feathered the trigger. The bullet entered the man's stomach just above his belt buckle even as the gunfighter's slug punched a hole in the floor at his feet.

Frank Vines staggered backwards like a drunk. A groan whispered from his mouth. He tried to raise his gun, but he was dying on his feet. The weapon curled from his hand. He grabbed his stomach with both hands and looked down. Blood oozed between his fingers and colored the front of his shirt. He raised his eyes and stared with a disbelieving look on his face. His eyes fixed with a blank, lifeless stare. His knees buckled and gave way. He fell to the floor.

Chester swung a look at Bonner. The big man sat with a stunned look on his face. Beads of sweat popped out on his forehead. The cigar hung slack in his open mouth. He had a frantic look in his eyes.

Chester stood to his feet. His hand still held the smoking Colt. He swept the room with a quick glance. No one seemed inclined to side the fallen gunfighter.

With his free hand, Chester gathered a handful of shirt and pulled Bonner to his feet, the man's face an inch from his own.

"You got a choice," Chester spat the words at the fat man. "Get out of town before I finish my beer or I'll kill you, no two ways about it."

Holstering his Colt, Chester opened Bonner's coat and removed a gun from a shoulder holster. He stuck the weapon underneath his own belt and pinned the fat man with a look.

"You ain't got much time, I drink fast."

He shoved the man backwards. Bonner headed for the front door in a staggering run. Chester calmly sat down at the table and sipped his beer.

"I've got a meeting in Del Rio this morning," Buck told Rebekah over morning coffee at the small breakfast table in their kitchen. "Want to ride into town with me?"

"I wish I could, Buck, but I've got so many things around here I need to get done."

"Come with me," he said, reaching across the table to squeeze her hand.

"Well, since you put it that way," she said, smiling. "I guess those things can wait. It's been a while since I've seen Dad. I need to check on him and Elvira, that widow *friend* of his."

"Good. I'll saddle our horses and wait for you by the corral."

They rode out of the compound just as the sun was peeking over the eastern horizon. The red sun ball announced its arrival by painting the blue sky with crimson-gold. It splashed streaks of golden rays onto the puffy-white clouds and set them ablaze with breathtaking color.

"Oh, Buck, look at that!" Rebekah exclaimed.

They reined their horses to a stop and spent a few moments soaking up the beauty of nature.

"I love the early mornings like this," she said, reaching across the space between their horses to take his hand.

"Makes a man feel awfully small, don't it?"

They arrived in Del Rio at mid-morning and reined up in front of Walker's Store. John Walker, with Elvira close by his side, walked out to greet them.

"It's about time you two took time off to ride into town," John said, taking Rebekah's reins and looping them around the hitching rail. "I was beginning to think you had disowned your father."

"I know, Papa, but we've been so busy. Seems like there's never enough time."

Buck dismounted and reached to help Rebekah to the ground.

"How are you, Elvira?" she greeted the woman.

"I'm fine. It's good to see you, Rebekah. You look wonderful."

"Thank you," She smoothed the loose blouse she wore over her riding pants. "I feel wonderful. I'm beginning to show."

"I was starting to worry," John told Buck. "I was afraid you weren't gonna make it to our meeting."

"Am I late?"

"No, you're right on time. We can walk down to the church together. That's where the town council meets."

Rebekah smiled. "I'll visit with Elvira, and then I want to walk over to see if Kathleen and Sam are getting settled in. Will the meeting be over by noon? Maybe we could meet at Selena's café for lunch? I need to visit with her too."

"Yeah, I'll meet you there."

Buck and John walked on to the white church at the end of the street. A dozen businessmen stood outside talking. Sam Colson was among them. Buck shook hands all around.

"Looks like everybody is here," John Walker said. "Let's go on inside and get started."

When everyone was inside and seated, John raised his hand for quiet.

"Well, since you men elected me head of the town council, I reckon it's up to me to get things started. Unless a man is blind in one eye and can't see out of the other, it's easy to see that our town is growing, and growing fast.

"Last time I looked we had four new businesses being built. New folks are moving in most every day. Our brand new bank will be open before you can say scat. Sam Colson's on our council and I expect he's already been around to see all of you.

"It ain't no secret my son-in-law here and his partner are responsible for most of the growth of our town. The Longhorn Ranch has might near as many folks working on it as we have in Del Rio. Besides that, I think most of you already know they gave a thousand dollars to help get this council going. We all owe a big *thank you* to Buck Cordell and Chester Colson."

The businessmen broke into a loud round of applause.

"I'd like to see if Buck's got a few words to say."

Buck's face flushed red. He sat with his head lowered for a minute before climbing to his feet.

"Don't hardly know what to say." He swept the businessmen with a look. "We just want to be good neighbors. Whatever we can do to help, we'll do."

He sat back down.

"Thanks, Buck. I reckon the first thing we need to talk about is how we're coming along on finding a town marshal. Ben Harding is heading up that committee. What you got to report, Ben?"

The lumberyard operator stood to his feet. He was a big, rugged fellow with arms as big as most men's legs. His head seemed to sit directly on his wide shoulders with no neck that one could see. He wore a friendly look about him. Buck liked the man immediately.

"I'm afraid we ain't got much to report. We've put out the word that we're looking. We've contacted the Texas Rangers and most of the sheriffs around Texas that we could get hold of. Oh, we've had a few ask about the job, but nobody we'd be interested in. If any of you men know somebody you could recommend, we'd like to hear about them."

He sat back down. Buck glanced around the room at the faces before raising his hand.

"Something else you'd like to say, Buck?" John Walker asked.

"Well, don't know if he'd be interested or not, but we've got a man working cattle for us that used to be a lawman. I think he was a ranger for a spell, too. His name's Bud Cauthorn. Might be someone you'd want to talk to."

"Sounds like it," the lumberman said. "Where can we find him?"

"He's somewhere between here and Missouri on a cattle drive right now," Buck said. "He ought to be back in a few weeks. If you think you'd want to talk with him I'll send him in."

"Sounds like he might be what we're looking for. If it's all right with you, ask him if he would come and talk with us."

"Sure will."

"I think all of us would like to hear from the president of our new bank, Sam Colson," Walker said. "Stand up, Sam. Tell us when you'll be open for business."

"Most of you have stopped by and eyeballed the construction of our new bank, so you know it's coming along right on schedule. Our state-of-the-art vault is completely installed. It's the latest and most secure bank vault in existence. For added protection, we'll have four armed guards on duty twenty-four hours a day, seven days a week. We want you to know your money will be safe in the Del Rio Bank.

"Our plans are to open our doors for business on October first. Stop in and let's do business."

After they discussed the merits of several new town ordinances, John Walker adjourned the meeting. Buck headed for the Del Rio café.

Rebekah was already there. The café was so crowded she was helping Selena and Nita, Selena's young cousin, serve tables. Buck poured himself a cup of coffee and lounged near the front door until a table finally opened up.

"Busy place," he told Rebekah, as she hurried around the room refilling everyone's cup.

"It sure is. Selena says it's been this way for the last few months. She says they are talking about either expanding or building a completely new and larger café. "

"They need to talk to Juan Santos if they are thinking about building." Buck told them. "I've never seen anyone better."

Selena hurried by, balancing four plates of food expertly on her hands and arms. Buck watched her as she rushed about, waiting on her customers in the packed café. Although she worked the room extremely fast, she never seemed to rush her interaction with the diners. She appeared to make each person feel they were the most special person in the room.

It took a while, but finally the last customer left. Selena and Rebekah joined Buck at the table.

"Rebekah tells me you're thinking about expanding your café."

"Yes, we just don't have enough room. Our customers have to wait too long to be seated and even longer to be fed. Mother and I feel badly about keeping them waiting so long."

"From what I see, you not only need more room, you also need more help. I don't see how you and your mother feed this many people in such a small place."

"It's very hard."

"Think about talking with our builder, Juan Santos. He could build you a café as large as you wanted. He'll be finished with the bank building and the house for Sam and Kathleen Colson before long."

"I'll talk to Mother about it and let you know. Have you heard any word from Chester?"

"No, not yet. Ray Ledbetter and the first trail crew should be getting back in a couple of weeks. We'll know something then."

"I really miss him."

Rebekah reached a hand to squeeze Selena's arm.

"I know how you feel. Those three months Buck was on the trail were the longest three months of my life."

Ray Ledbetter and Smokey Cunningham and their crews rode into the Longhorn Ranch compound the first week of July. Buck hurried out to meet them, shook hands all around, and invited his two top hands into the main house for a cup of coffee and a report on the drive.

After they were settled and sipping their steaming coffee, Buck looked at Ray anxiously.

"Hope that grin on your face means good news."

"Don't rightly see how it could be much better," Ray told his boss. "So far, at least, we haven't lost a single hand. Our loss in terms of cattle has been less than five percent; far below the average ten percent most drives lose.

"Chester contracted all of our herds coming up the trail this year for a fixed price of forty-two dollars a head. He said he was betting that with the increased supply the market price would slide. By having a guaranteed price of forty-two we didn't run the risk of a steep downturn in the market."

Ray withdrew a leather moneybag and handed Buck the checks for the first two herds. Buck stared at the checks for a minute, shaking his head from side to side.

"Sounds like good thinking. Sure is a lot of money."

"Chester said the trail bosses of the other herds would be carrying the check for their herd."

"Run into any major problems on the trail?"

"Nothing other than the usual. High water on the Red delayed Smokey's herd, but they caught up. Indians stole our whole remuda, but Chester and a few of the boys stole 'em right back without firing a shot. All-in-all, I reckon the drives are going pretty good."

"When's Chester coming back?"

"Don't know. He said he most likely wouldn't be back until the season was over. He's riding up and down the trail tending to business. I tell you, boss, that young fellow's a wonder."

"Why you say that?"

"He braced that fellow named Bonner and the gunslick that sides him. Chester killed the gunman quicker'n scat and run Bonner out of town. Told Bonner if he was still in town by the time Chester got through drinking his beer he'd kill him. Bonner took off like a jack rabbit with a coyote on his tail."

"Chester's a good man."

"You shore got that right. Two more of our trail bosses and their crews ought to be getting back in the next couple of weeks.

"Oh, yeah, ain't that new man, Bud Cauthorn, in your crew?"

"Yeah, something wrong?"

"No, not at all, I'd just like to have a word with him."

"I'll send him right in."

"You boys get some rest. Tell your crews to take a week off before you start back up the trail with another herd."

After his men left, Buck sat alone in his den, staring at the checks. *I've got to make another trip to San Antonio and cash these. We'll need money to pay off the other Mexican cattle ranchers and the hands. We'll need cash for operating funds to open the new bank, too. I'll see if Rebekah would like to go with me.*

Buck's thoughts were interrupted by a knock on the door of the den.

"Come in."

The door opened and Bud Cauthorn stepped into the den.

"Ray said you wanted to see me."

"Have a seat. How'd the drive go for you?"

"Went good. Long way to Missouri, but it was a good trail drive. You've got a salty bunch of men working for the Longhorn."

"I understand you used to be a lawman?"

A questioning look wrinkled Cauthorn's forehead.

"Yes, sir, I was town marshal in a couple of places before I joined up with the Texas Rangers."

"How'd you like being a lawman?"

"Liked it fine. It just didn't pay enough for the job you gotta do."

"What if it did? Would you be interested?"

"Maybe."

"The town council over in Del Rio asked me to talk with you. Del Rio is growing like a newborn calf. Folks are moving in every day. New businesses are springing up most every week. We're building a new bank. We need a good man as town marshal."

"What does the job pay?"

"Not enough, I reckon. Don't know what they have in mind, but whatever it is, I'll match it."

Maxwell was quiet for a minute, clearly mulling over what Buck had said.

"You say you'll match what they offer. What kind of strings would be attached to the Longhorn money?"

"No strings. The new bank I mentioned is a Longhorn bank. I just want a good man in the marshal's job as added protection for our bank, that's all. Other than that, you wouldn't owe the Longhorn anything."

"Just wouldn't want to be a bought-and-paid-for lawman no matter who was doing the buying."

"I understand. I appreciate that."

"In that case, I'd be glad to talk with them."

"Good. Ride in and talk with a fellow named Ben Harding. He runs the lumberyard. If he ain't around stop in the general store and see John Walker. Tell them I sent you."

"Thanks, Mr. Cordell. I like it here on the Longhorn. I'd hate to leave."

"You've got a job on the Longhorn as long as you want it."

"I'm obliged."

It was hot. The boiling late July sun cooked the bone-dry countryside like an egg frying on a hot griddle. A scalding westerly wind made matters worse. Sweat dripped from the matched team of horses pulling the covered buggy.

The twenty security outriders that flanked the buggy slumped in their saddles, but their gazes continually searched the trail ahead for any sign of hidden danger. The thin trail they followed for the better part of two days opened into a well-traveled road.

"We're only a few miles from San Antonio now," Buck said, slanting a glance at his companion in the buggy.

His wife smiled up at him. "Thanks for asking me to come with you."

"You've been working too hard. Thought a little break would do us both good."

"There's so much going on. Seems like there's never enough time to do what needs to be done."

"You ever been to San Antonio?"

"No, and I'm so excited. I've wanted to go for a long time, but just never had the opportunity."

"You'll like it."

Their arrival caused quite a stir. Folks along the boardwalk stopped to watch the black buggy and the heavily armed escort as they made their way up the street and stopped in front of the Menger Hotel. It was the newest and most exquisite hotel in San Antonio.

Buck and Rebekah climbed down and their luggage was quickly unloaded by one of the Longhorn security riders. Buck took Rebekah's arm, escorted her into the hotel and arranged for rooms for himself and his wife and his entire crew.

"I'm Buck Cordell," he told the manager at the front desk. This is my wife. We'd like your best suite. We'll be staying several days."

"Welcome Mr. Cordell. It's a pleasure to have you with us," the manager said, smiling widely. "You and Mrs. Cordell will be in our finest suite. You'll find it at the top of the stairs on the third floor. It's our Presidential suite. Suite Number 1."

"This is Wade Thomas, the head of our security detail. We'll also be needing several rooms for his men."

"Splendid. If there's anything we can do to make your stay more enjoyable, just let us know."

They found their room and opened the door with the key the manager had given him. The suite consisted of a sitting area and a separate bedroom. Both rooms were well furnished with expensive furnishings. Thick, soft-colored Persian rugs covered both floors. A large, white-canopied bed dominated the bedroom and a porcelain bathtub sat against the wall. It had a circular rod with pull drapes for privacy.

"Oh, Buck, it's beautiful," Rebekah said smiling, wrapping her arms around Buck's neck and hugging him close.

"You talking about me or the room?"

"Both. Thanks again for bringing me with you, cowboy."

"My pleasure. I'm gonna walk over to the bank. I'll arrange for them to bring up a bath for you. There'll be two security men right outside the door while we're here. Just wanted you to know. After you've had a chance to rest and freshen up, meet me down in the hotel restaurant."

Buck touched a hand to the money belt beneath his shirt as he descended the stairs. Two of the security detail waited in the lobby and followed close on his heels as he crossed the street and headed for the bank.

C. V. Seymour jumped to his feet and hurried around his desk when Buck entered the bank.

"Well, well. It's good to see you again, Mr. Cordell. I heard you were here. News of your arrival is the talk of the town."

They shook hands and Buck followed the banker into his private office.

"What brings you back to our fair city?"

"Business and pleasure," Buck said, taking a seat in the chair in front of the banker's large desk.

"Here's the business," he said, scooting the four cashiers' checks his trail bosses had brought back across the desk.

The banker picked up the checks and looked at them. His eyes grew larger. He finally looked up at Buck.

"Oh, my!" he said, scribbling the totals onto a piece of paper and adding up the column. "That comes to four hundred twenty-thousand dollars."

"I'd like it in cash. How long will it take to get it here?"

"Uh, well, I'm not sure. I can send a telegram to the bank in Austin. It will take at least two days, even if they have that much cash on hand."

"Good. I'd be obliged if you'd keep this as quiet as possible. I reckon you understand. My wife and I are staying over at the hotel. Let me know," he said, standing to his feet.

"Of course, I'll send word as soon as I get a reply."

Buck left the bank and headed for the Pinkerton office next door to the telegraph station.

He knocked on the door and waited for an invitation to enter. Mel Sloan, the Pinkerton agent greeted him with a friendly handshake.

"It's good to see you again, Mr. Cordell. It's been a while."

"Yeah, it has." Buck folded into the chair in front of the desk. "I was in town on business and wondered if you had heard anything about my brother?"

"Yes and no. We traced him to a cattle ranch outside Waco. It seems he worked there a while for the Brazos River Ranch. While he was there he built himself quite a reputation as a fast gun.

"We talked to the marshal in Waco. All of his gunfights were on the up and up. He's not wanted by the law as far as we can tell. We talked to the foreman of the ranch where he worked. They all liked the boy and spoke highly of him.

"He went on two cattle drives with them, one to New Orleans and one to Sedalia, Missouri. He had a run-in with a local fellow in Sedalia and killed the man. Turned out his daddy was a local big fish and there was a lot of trouble.

"The father of the man Hondo killed and his men tried to lynch the boy. The marshal in Sedalia intervened and killed the old man. After that incident Hondo left town and hasn't been actually seen since then.

"Our man in Fort Stockton barely missed him a while back. We haven't seen or heard of him since then."

"Fort Stockton, huh? That must have been after he visited our folks' graves. Well, stay on it. I sure would like to locate him."

"We'll find him, we always do. It's just a matter of time."

"Do I owe you any money?"

"No, the retainer you gave me earlier was enough."

From the Pinkerton office Buck stopped in to see the Mexican attorney, Manuel Rodriguez. The man greeted Buck warmly. "How's the cattle business?"

"Doin' good. Got a question for you."

"What is it?"

"Don't reckon you'd know of any land for sale in our general area, would you?"

The attorney scratched his chin in thought.

"How much land would you be interested in?"

"The more the better. As long as it's got grass and water."

"Not at the moment. But I'm working on securing the broker rights on a rather large tract of land that you might be interested in."

"Where is this land?"

"It's about two hundred miles northwest of your ranch, near the Big Bend country along the Rio Grande."

"How much land we talking about?"

"A half million acres."

"Let me know if you get that contract. We might consider riding up and taking a looksee."

Buck stopped by the barbershop and got a haircut and a bath before returning to the hotel. Rebekah was waiting for him in the dining room.

"I stopped in at a ladies clothing shop this afternoon," she told him as he folded into a chair. "I found a couple of dresses I'd like you to look at when you have time."

"We'll be here two or three days. If you feel up to it, I'd like for us to drive over to Hondo. I want to take some flowers and put them on Ma and Pa's graves."

"Of course. I'm seven months pregnant, but I'm not helpless. I'd love to see where you grew up and visit your folks' graves. When are you thinking about going?"

"At first light in the morning."

"I'll be ready."

"Think we could find some flowers somewhere?"

"I saw a flower shop next door to the dress shop. It might still be open."

"Let's walk over and see. If the dress shop is still open we can look at those dresses."

They left the dining room and walked slowly along the boardwalk. It was late afternoon, but the streets were still bustling with folks making their way somewhere.

"Busy place," Buck commented. "They say the population of San Antonio is over ten thousand. The army is building a new fort here called Fort Sam Houston. There's a new railroad coming in a year or so. That will bring even more folks. Once it's here we may want to look at shipping our cattle to market from here, instead of driving them all the way to Missouri or Kansas."

"I've never seen anything like it. What do all these people do for a living?"

"The area around San Antonio has lots of cattle ranches. It's the main mercantile marketing and distribution center for all of south Texas. Most of the goods your father orders come through San Antonio."

Luckily both the flower shop and dress shop were still open. After explaining to the floral shop owner their need, both Rebekah and the florist agreed that a live rose bush would be the best choice.

"We can plant it near the graves and it will bloom each year," Rebekah suggested. "If we took fresh flowers they would be wilted by the time we got there."

"I like that idea," Buck agreed.

After leaving the flower shop with a rose bush wrapped in a wet tow sack, they went next door to the ladies dress shop.

Rebekah showed Buck the dresses she looked at earlier that day. She held them up in front of him and did a little twirling pose.

"What do you think?" she asked.

"I think they were made for you," he told her. "Take them both."

Buck and Rebekah, escorted by their security riders, arrived at Buck's old home place in late afternoon. As they drove slowly up the long lane toward the place, he related memories from his childhood.

"We grew cotton in that field over yonder," he said, pointing toward a grown-up field near the lane. "I've spent many an hour chopping and picking cotton out there."

Rebekah listened intently.

"Wish I had known you then."

He slanted a look at her and offered a nod. The Longhorn riders moved on toward where the home place once stood to set up camp for the night.

Buck pulled the buggy to a stop near the graves under the big oak tree. Weeds had overgrown the small mounds of dirt. He sat motionless for a long moment. A lump filled his throat. He blinked to clear his moistening eyes.

Rebekah must have sensed his emotions because she reached to take his hand and squeezed it. Buck climbed from the buggy and helped his wife to the ground. Hand in hand they walked the few steps to the graves.

Buck dropped to one knee beside his mother's grave. With bowed head he spent the next few minutes in quiet reflection. His mind flashed a picture from his memory of the last time he had seen his folks.

I remember looking back as I rode down the lane. They were standing together on our little front porch. Pa's strong arm was wrapped around Ma's shoulder. I remember seeing Ma crying with body-shaking sobs as she lifted a hand in goodbye.

Buck felt a hand on his shoulder.

"They must have been wonderful people," Rebekah said quietly.

Buck nodded. "Yeah, they were. They deserved more than what they had."

The two spent an hour pulling the weeds and planting the rose bush near the head of the two graves. When the work was finished Buck leaned against the shovel and swiped beads of sweat from his forehead. The sun slipped almost reverently behind the western horizon. In the same direction it appeared the sky was ablaze with a crimson inferno. As if in tribute to those resting beneath the little mounds of dirt, blazing streaks of gold shot across the sky in a dazzling display of nature.

The money coach arrived from Austin two days later. As before, its arrival brought everything in San Antonio to a standstill. Folks poured out of stores and houses to witness the arrival of the specially built stagecoach.

"What's all the commotion about?" Rebekah asked, seeing folks rushing out of the dining room where she and Buck sat eating lunch.

Overhearing her question, the restaurant manager answered as he rushed past.

"It's the money coach."

"Come on," Buck said. "This is something you've got to see."

They hurried outside and joined the gathering crowd in front of the hotel.

The unusual-looking stagecoach moved rapidly down the street. A double-team hitch of high-spirited black horses pulled the heavy coach along with little effort.

The entire box of the coach was built of heavy iron with only small gun ports in the sides to allow the guards inside to fire through. Ten heavily-armed outriders escorted the coach. They rode with their rifles propped butt down against their legs.

It was an impressive sight.

Buck leaned close and spoke quietly.

"Our money has arrived."

Rebekah swung a quick, questioning look at him.

"You mean?"

Buck only nodded and offered a small smile.

Buck learned that a touring company from back east was performing that very night. He arranged for box seats in the newly constructed San Antonio Arts Theatre. Rebekah was ecstatic when he told her about it. Her first comment was *I don't have a thing to wear.*

She finally decided that one of the new dresses she just bought might do for the special occasion.

Escorted by four Longhorn security men, Buck and Rebekah arrived right on time and were seated only minutes before the play began. Rebekah looked beautiful in her new dress and Buck told her so. Her face glowed with excitement as she looked at all the people looking back at her.

In the adjoining box, an army officer along with a dark haired gentleman, sat with their wives. The officer wore the bars of a full general. He saw Buck looking at him and stood.

"I don't believe I've had the pleasure of meeting you," the officer said. "I'm General Phillip Sheridan."

Buck was taken aback. *Here stands the general I fought against in the war. The man I would have shot on sight if I had laid eyes on him.*

Buck stood to his feet. His height towered over the smaller man.

"It's a pleasure to meet you," Buck said, offering his hand. "I'm Buck Cordell."

The general took his hand and shook it warmly. "This is our newly elected governor of Texas, James Throckmorton. He will be sworn-in next month in Austin."

The governor stood and shook Buck's hand.

Buck introduced Rebekah to the men and their wives.

"May I ask what business you are in, Mr. Cordell?" the governor asked.

"I'm in the cattle business. Me and my partner own the Longhorn Ranch down on the Rio Grande, not far from Del Rio."

"Oh, yes," the governor said. "Your name was mentioned just yesterday by my friend, Richard King. "He says you and your ranch are causing quite a stir in the cattle business in Texas."

"Didn't know he was in town."

"I believe he left this afternoon."

The lights dimmed in the theatre signaling that it was time for the play to begin. Buck and his neighbors took their seats.

The orchestra struck up a song and the curtains opened. Neither Buck nor Rebekah had ever seen anything like the play they enjoyed. Rebekah sat in total silence, her unwavering gaze glued to the events on the stage. Buck couldn't get interested in the production for watching Rebekah's glowing face.

Finally the play ended to loud applause and the appropriate number of encores. The audience stood to their feet in a standing tribute to the cast. Governor Throckmorton turned to Buck.

"We're having a small get-together in the dining room of the hotel. Could you and Mrs. Cordell join us?"

Buck glanced at Rebekah for approval. She nodded and smiled.

"We'd be glad to. We're obliged for the invitation."

The "small get-together" turned out to be half a hundred. The room was packed with officers and their wives, the general's aides, and local would-be political types. The large dining room had been cleared of tables. Those in attendance stood in small groups sipping cocktails and listening to whoever had the group's attention at the moment.

Governor Throckmorton saw Buck and Rebekah enter and motioned them over to join their group. General Sheridan and his wife were part of the group.

Buck saw Colonel Callahan from Fort Clark standing in another group of junior officers nearby and nodded to him. The colonel left his group and walked over.

"Mr. Cordell. It's good to see you again. How is your partner, Mr. Colson?"

"He's doing good. In fact, he's somewhere between here and Missouri, driving our herds to market."

"You're Colonel Callahan from Fort Clark, I believe," General Sheridan said, extending his hand to shake the junior officer's hand.

"Yes, sir."

"I don't believe we've ever met before." The general said.

"No, sir."

"I see you already know Mr. Cordell?"

Buck didn't like the way the conversation was going. He was in danger of having the lie he told the colonel about being friends with general Sheridan exposed.

"Yes, sir. Mr. Cordell has...visited the fort several times."

"Splendid."

"Have you moved your headquarters to San Antonio?" the colonel asked.

"No, I'm here to look over the progress of the construction of Fort Sam Houston. I'll be returning to the gulf coast in a few days."

"Well, it was a pleasure to meet you, general," the colonel said. "I better get back to my wife before she feels abandoned." He excused himself and Buck breathed a big sign of relief.

After a few long moments of boring chitchat and smiles, the governor turned to Buck. "I'm glad you decided to come. There's a matter I'd like to discuss with you in private if you have the time."

"I'd be glad to, but we'll be leaving at first light in the morning."

"Perhaps we could get together for a few minutes tonight then?"

"I suppose."

"Why don't you and Mrs. Cordell come up for a cocktail? We're in room number eight."

"We'll pass on the cocktail. We're coffee drinkers, but we'd be glad to talk."

Buck and Rebekah accompanied the governor and his wife up to their room. After they were seated an aide brought cocktails and coffee.

"I'll get right to the point," the governor said, scooting forward to the edge of his chair. "As you know, Texas is going through reconstruction. We've got our problems and lots of them. One of those problems is finding the caliber of people willing and capable of helping rebuild Texas.

"Richard King spoke highly of you. He says you are a leader with vision and the determination to get things done, the kind of man we need in the Congress of Texas.

"You mentioned your ranch was near Del Rio. We desperately need someone from that part of Texas to run for Congress. We need a man who's not afraid to speak his mind and stand up for the people in his district. In short, we need you, Mr. Cordell. Texas needs you."

Buck was dumbfounded. The thought of being in politics had never crossed his mind. Besides, he had too much going at the ranch to go to Austin and listen to a bunch of long-winded politicians make speeches.

"Well, needless to say, I'm flattered, but I just can't see myself as a politician. Afraid I would ruffle too many feathers."

"That's precisely why we need you. We need men who're not afraid to *ruffle feathers,* as you put it. Just promise me you'll think about it."

"We'll see," Buck said, standing to his feet. "I'm afraid you'll have to excuse us. We're leaving mighty early and my wife needs to rest. I'll think on your suggestion."

"Splendid. We'll talk again."

After shaking hands and saying their goodnights, Buck and Rebekah returned to their own room.

"What a wonderful evening," Rebekah said as they were preparing for bed. "Just think, we actually met the governor of Texas and the most famous general of the war, both in the same night."

"They put their britches on one leg at a time like everybody else," Buck said.

It was still dark when Buck and two of his Longhorn men walked quickly from the bank carrying bulging satchels of banknotes. It took two trips to transfer the twelve money bags to the buggy and cover them with a blanket. Eighteen more Longhorn security men stood facing away from Buck with rifles in hand, their gazes searching every shadowy corner along the street where the threat of danger might lurk.

By the time the first hint of dawn colored the eastern horizon, the Longhorn procession was several miles out of San Antonio, headed home.

"That looked like an awful lot of money," Rebekah mentioned as they continued along the road.

"It *is* an awful lot of money, almost a half-million dollars, to be exact."

"Oh, my! I can't even imagine that much."

"Takes money to make money. We've still got a lot of cattle coming from the Mexican ranchers that we have to pay off when they deliver. We've got over two hundred on the payroll we have to pay and feed, and we've got to have seed money to open the bank."

"I know. You've accomplished so much in such a short time it's almost beyond comprehension. I'm so proud of you." She leaned her head on his broad shoulder. "Have you thought any more about what the governor suggested?"

"You mean about getting into politics?"

"Yes, he seemed pretty determined."

"I've got too much to do."

Buck was nervous. Having nearly a half-million dollars in cash in the back of the buggy wasn't something one does every day. His gaze swept both sides of the road and lingered long on any arroyo, any canyon, or thick groove of mesquite or cedar, anywhere anyone could lay in wait to ambush them. His hands sweated inside his gloves.

The twenty Longhorn riders rode with their rifles in hand, constantly alert for any sign of hidden danger. Two rode far ahead, but within sight.

It was a long and nerve-racking trip.

When they sighted the Longhorn compound ahead, Buck breathed a long sigh of relief. They made it.

"It's good to be home," said Rebekah.

"You can shore say that again."

When the twelve moneybags were locked in the large safe in the den, Buck finally relaxed.

"Hope we never have to do that again," he told her.

CHAPTER XIV

The third week of August was hot in Sedalia, Missouri.

Chester sat with Carlos Rodriguez and Cleveland Sims in the saloon sipping lukewarm beer. His two trail bosses arrived two days before with their herds. The cattle were now counted and loaded onto the cattle cars. Carlos kept the two checks tucked safely away in his money belt.

"You boys ready to head back to Texas in the morning?"

"Sure am, boss." Sims said, taking a long swallow from the mug of beer in his hand.

"The last trail herd is supposed to leave the Longhorn September first. That's only a week from now. Figuring two months for it to get here and another three weeks to get home, I ought to be back to the ranch by Christmas."

"You've been gone a long time. Bet you'll be glad to get back home," Carlos said.

"Yeah, I'm missing that pretty sister of yours. Sure would like to see her."

Chester heard someone enter the saloon. He crooked a look.

Sheriff Henry West walked casually over and stopped near their table.

"Afternoon, boys."

"Sheriff," Chester said lifting his half-empty mug. "Can I buy you a beer?"

"I'm obliged, but no. You Longhorn boys have shore been keeping the trail hot between here and Texas. How many more herds you bringing in?"

"Last herd ought to be leaving the ranch in a week or so," Chester replied. "There ought to be eight already on the way."

"Never heard of such a thing. Has Buck heard any more about his little brother?"

"Not that I've heard."

"Well, better mosey on up the street, I reckon. Tell Buck I said *howdy* when you see him."

"We'll do that."

Harvey Owens entered the saloon as Sheriff West was leaving.

"Pull up a chair and have a beer with us."

"Don't mind if I do," the cattle buyer said, scraping out a chair and settling into it.

The bartender brought them all another round.

"We bringing you enough cattle?" Chester asked, already knowing the answer.

"Sure are. My bosses in Chicago are very pleased."

"I heard the operation in Abilene, Kansas is up and running. Tell me what you know about Abilene."

"Well, as you already know, the Kansas shorthorn growers convinced the legislators to pass a law banning all Texas cattle from crossing the line into Kansas. A fellow named Joseph McCoy somehow got the governor to lift the ban along a mile-wide corridor from the state line to Abilene.

"He also convinced the railroad to run their line to his town. He built a two-story hotel and cattle pens and announced he was open for business. The only problem is that he hasn't been able to talk the Texas cattle growers, like you, into driving their herds to Abilene.

"My feeling is that, to get the herds to come to Abilene, McCoy and other buyers like me are gonna pay top dollar. The ranchers who get there first with their cattle are gonna cash-in big. I'll be moving my operation there soon as your last herd comes in."

"Sounds like something we need to think about."

"Like I told you before, I'd like to work a deal to buy all the cattle you bring up the trail, but I realize that you'll want to explore the market. All I ask is a chance to quote you a price before you decide."

"Seems fair."

Two months passed quickly. It was the deepest part of the night. Rebekah woke with a gnawing backache. She turned over onto her side trying to relieve it, but it wouldn't go away. She slipped out of bed quietly, trying not to disturb her husband's sleep.

After a trip to the bathroom the ache seemed to go away and she went back to bed. Soon, however, it returned; this time even stronger. *Maybe this is it,* she thought. *Maybe the baby is coming. Should I wake Buck or should I wait until I'm sure?*

She decided to go into the kitchen and make a pot of coffee. She just got the fire built and the water on when the next pain hit her, this time even sharper than the others. She held on to a chair until it subsided.

Then she added the ground coffee beans to the boiling water and went to the bedroom. She lit the lamp. Buck was sleeping soundly. She hated to wake him. He looked so peaceful and she loved to watch him sleep.

Rebekah touched his bare shoulder. His eyes blinked open. A concerned frown furrowed his brow.

"What's wrong? Are you okay?"

"I'm having pains. I think our baby's coming."

Buck leaped out of bed instantly. He grabbed his pants and shoved one foot into the leg while standing, but crow-hopped a couple of steps before he could get the other foot in, all the time searching the room for his boots.

"Calm down, Cowboy, it isn't that close."

"I've got to ride into town and get the doctor," he said, sleeving into his shirt.

"No, get Jewel. She has probably delivered more babies than Doctor Williams."

"Oh, okay. I'll be right back," Nervously, Buck hurried from the room.

Jewel arrived within minutes and calmly took charge.

"Has your water broke yet, child?"

"No."

"Then just lay there and try to relax, might be a while yet. I'll put this folded blanket under you just in case."

Buck hovered by the bedside, holding Rebekah's hand.

Time inched by. The pains grew more frequent and severe as daylight arrived. Shortly after sunup Rebekah's water broke without warning.

"Won't be long now, I reckon," Jewel said. I'm heatin' hot water. Mr. Buck, you might just as well get yourself a cup of coffee or go check on your cows or somethin', you gettin' my meanin'?"

"You're wanting me to leave?"

"Might be best."

Buck leaned over and kissed his wife. She offered a weak smile.

"I won't be far. Just holler if you need me."

"Oh, I'm sure I will be hollering, but don't worry, Jewel and I can handle this."

Buck reluctantly went to the kitchen and poured himself a cup of coffee. He paced the floor, sipping the steaming liquid. Every few minutes he stopped to listen. When he heard Rebekah's stifled scream he wanted to rush to her side. He put his coffee down and hurried toward the bedroom, but stopped outside the closed door.

The screaming stopped. Complete quiet settled.

Another high-pitched scream pierced the silence. This time it wasn't Rebekah. It was a baby's scream. His heart leaped. A huge lump crawled up his throat and lodged there. The bedroom door opened. Jewel stood there with a baby in her arms. It was wrapped in a blanket. She was grinning from ear to ear. She handed the baby to Buck.

"Is Rebekah all right?" he asked anxiously.

"Miss Rebekah is just fine. She done good. You got yourself a fine-lookin' boy, Mr. Buck, a mighty fine lookin' boy."

Buck looked down at the tiny baby through watery eyes. His heart was so full it was about to burst. Emotion welled up inside him. He stared down at the tiny miracle of life. Reaching a finger he touched the cottony-soft cheek of his son, *his son!*

He carried his baby into the bedroom, stopped beside the bed and stared down into the face of his wife. She looked tired, but her face shone with a radiant glow.

"Hey, Mrs. Cordell."

"Hey, Mr. Cordell."

She smiled. Buck didn't speak. He couldn't. He was so full no words would come out. He swallowed again and again.

"Have you decided what to name our son?"

"Been thinking on that. I'd like you to meet Cody Walker Cordell, if that's all right with you? I'd like to name him after my little brother and your father. "

"Oh, Buck, that's a wonderful name."

"That's it then," he said, looking down into the face of their son. "Welcome to the world, Cody Walker Cordell."

It was September 2, 1867. The last herd had pulled out for Missouri just one day earlier, but that was nothing compared to the birth of his first child.

The Longhorn Bank of Del Rio, Texas opened its doors for business October 1, 1867. Sam Colson stood beside Buck and watched the line of customers waiting to make their first deposit.

"Looks like business is good," Buck said.

"Yeah, folks are tired keeping their money under the mattress. It's been like this all day. Folks were waiting in line outside before I opened this morning."

"How's Kathleen?"

"Doing fine. She's staying busy furnishing our new house. Buck, I shore appreciate all you and Chester have done for us."

"It's worked out good for everybody."

"When are you looking for Chester to get back?"

"He sent word to look for him by Christmas. He wanted to stay until all the herds got there safe. Soon as he gets back with the last of our checks we'll need to arrange for a delivery of money from Austin."

While they were talking, Bud Cauthorn walked up to join them.

"Howdy, Buck. Mr. Colson."

"Howdy, Bud," Buck said. "How's the new job as marshal working out?"

"So far, so good. The council is building us a new jail and marshal's office. It ought to be finished in a couple of weeks."

"Town's sure growing," said Sam. "I reckon it's near doubled just since I got here."

"Had any trouble yet?" Buck asked the marshal.

"None to speak of. I've had to lump a couple of heads, but nothing serious."

"Got time for a cup of coffee?"

"Always."

"Can you join us, Sam?"

"No, thanks, I need to hang close and visit with my depositors."

Buck and the new marshal walked up the street to the Del Rio café. Selena spotted them as they pushed through the door and took a seat at a table. She brought cups and poured coffee.

"How's Rebekah?" she asked.

"She's doing good. Trying to do too much too soon, but you know Rebekah. She's got a mind of her own."

Selena laughed. "All women do, Mr. Buck, you ought to know that. How old is the baby now?"

"Almost five weeks and growing like a weed. If he keeps that up he's gonna be bigger than me."

"I doubt that. I've got to find time to get out there and see him again. I've only seen him that one time right after he was born. Heard anything more from Chester?"

"Just that he's expecting to be back in time for Christmas."

"Sure hope so. I miss him."

As they were talking, the door opened and four men tromped in. Both Buck and Bud swung a look.

Clayton Dawson, followed closely by three rough-looking companions, walked in and sauntered to a table near the back wall. Selena flicked a sideways glance at Buck as she approached the toughs with a coffee pot and cups.

Buck's hard gaze fixed upon the leader of the bunch and stayed there.

"Trouble?" Bud Cauthorn asked quietly.

"The worst kind. That's Clayton Dawson and his bunch. Chester had a run-in with them a while back."

Cauthorn didn't say a word. He scraped back his chair and rose, then strode deliberately to the trouble-makers' table.

"You boys finish your coffee and ride on," the lawman told them. "We don't want your kind in Del Rio."

"Who're you?" Dawson asked sarcastically.

"I'm Bud Cauthorn. I'm the law in Del Rio. That's more'n you need to know. Don't be in town by the time your coffee gets cold."

"We breaking any law, *marshal*?"

"Yep. We got a law against polluting the air. You boys' stench is breaking it. You've been told. I won't tell you again."

Cauthorn returned to Buck's table and sat down. Dawson and his gang cast long glances of smoldering black hatred, sipped their coffee, and carried on whispered conversations. After a few minutes they rose and stomped from the café. Through the window Buck could see them ride out of town.

"You handled that real good," Buck told the marshal, "but I expect you haven't seen the last of that bunch."

"I expect you're right."

Bud Cauthorn walked slowly down the darkened street. It was late, most likely only a couple of hours before midnight. He pulled out his pocket watch and confirmed his estimate.

The streets of Del Rio were rolled up for the night. Even Sam had already closed the saloon unusually early for a weeknight.

Marshal Bud Cauthorn. He liked the sound of it. He hadn't realized how much he missed being a lawman, but a man's gotta do what a man's gotta do.

He strolled slowly along the darkened street, making one last round before calling it a day. He was tired and anxious to get to his small cot in the partially constructed marshal's office. All was quiet. He stepped up onto the boardwalk in front of John Walker's store and checked the door. It was locked.

As he stepped off the boardwalk into the dusty street a stray cat scurried from under the boardwalk near his feet. The suddenness of the cat's appearance caused him a start. He spun around, his hand instinctively palming the Colt .44 from its holster. His sudden movement is probably all that saved him.

A slug burned the air an inch from his head. The post beside him splintered into a dozen pieces. The loud crack of a rifle echoed along the canyon-like deserted street.

Bud saw the lingering light from the rifle blast. It came from the small alleyway between the new ladies dress shop and the barbershop next door.

All this he saw even as he wheeled and made a beeline around the corner of Walker's store. He rounded the corner just in time. Another shot ploughed into the wall he had just ducked around.

Bud raced down the narrow space beside Walker's store and across the back loading dock. He skidded to a stop at the far corner of the store and chanced a look. Across the street, the sound of a galloping horse from behind the barbershop echoed in the night. Whoever the shooter was, he had lit a shuck.

The shots brought lamplight to life in several windows along the street where the owners kept living quarters in the back of their businesses. Old Pete hurried up the street lugging a long-barreled shotgun. Others rushed to see what all the commotion was about.

"What's all the shootin'?" the liveryman asked, as he hurried up.

"Reckon somebody don't like their new marshal," Bud said. "Fellow tried to drygulch me. Would have, too, if it hadn't been for a stray black cat. I'm gonna find that critter and give him a home for life."

"Who would want to shoot you?" Sam Taylor the barber asked while glancing anxiously up and down the street.

"Don't know, but I intend to find out. It's all over folks," he told the knot of townspeople gathered nearby. "Go on back to bed."

They slowly complied, still speculating, aloud about who might have done something like that. Bud speculated too. Far after he pried off his boots and bedded down on his small cot, he lay awake staring at the darkened ceiling, searching his memory.

To be sure, there were men from his past years in law enforcement who had good reason to kill him. Men he sent to prison, relatives of men who chose to fight rather than surrender to arrest. It was a lengthy list. But standing at the head of the line were the hard cases he had braced in the Del Rio café earlier that day. *What did Buck say the fellow's name was? Dawson. That was it. Clayton Dawson.* Bud nodded his head and pursed his lips. *He's my man. I'll bet my boots on it. It was either Dawson or one of his men. Most likely he left one of his men behind to do his dirty work, while he sips tequila in a cantina somewhere across the river.*

"We'll meet again, Mr. Dawson," the lawman spoke aloud into the darkness. "I expect we'll meet again."

Buck sat his saddle on the shoulder of a flat butte. The Sycamore River snaked through the center of the long valley below and offered nourishment to the thick bunch grass on which his cattle thrived.

It was not yet sunup. He gazed through the haze of early morning and counted four herds grazing peacefully. Half-dozen Longhorn wranglers lounged lazily in their saddles, keeping watch over the herds.

A cold breeze from the north chilled the air. He pulled the collar of his sheepskin coat closer around his neck. It was late December, only a few days until Christmas. *Chester should be getting back any day now. Last word was that he would be back before Christmas.*

A growing worry gnawed at him with each passing day.

All in all, things were coming together. For over a year they had been selecting the *best of the best* from the thousands of young heifers that passed through the ranch. These were set aside as part of their brood herds and bred to the high-powered Mexican bulls they bought from their friend, *Antonio Rivas*. The calves they produced were prime stock, but were nothing compared to those from *El Toro*.

The *Super Bull*, as the newspapers were calling him, was like nothing else in existence. Pappy had convinced Buck that *El Toro's* offspring were destined to change the entire cattle industry in Texas.

Little Cody was growing like a weed. Buck delighted in the fact that when he entered the room and spoke, his son always cracked a big smile and turned his head toward Buck's voice.

Rebekah assumed more and more responsibility for the day to day operation of everything inside the sprawling compound. She oversaw the dozens of workers, did all the books and payroll, and ordered the supplies necessary to keep the Longhorn Ranch running smoothly. Buck was amazed how much she had matured in the short year of their marriage. Everyone acknowledged her as the matron of the Cordell family and the Longhorn Ranch.

When Buck was on the ranch, he made it a top priority to spend some time with his wife and son nightly. He delighted in watching Rebekah feed little Cody.

"The way this boy eats he's going to be even bigger than you," Rebekah often told Buck.

"He needs to be big. Someday he'll take over the Longhorn."

"He'll have mighty big boots to fill," she said then, smiling at Buck with her eyes.

The Longhorn Bank in Del Rio did even better than Buck

expected. Sam Colson submitted a monthly report that deposits far exceeded the many loans the bank made for new businesses and expanding old ones. Del Rio was booming.

John Walker doubled the size of his mercantile and feed store. He now had a line of large warehouses through which he supplied not only the Longhorn Ranch, but numerous smaller ranches nearby. He now employed a dozen or more full-time workers, including Elvira, who acted more like the boss than an employee.

Shore will be glad when Chester gets back, Buck thought, as he unwound his leg from around the saddle horn and gigged his dappled grey toward the compound for breakfast and his regular morning meeting with his top hands.

The fresh born sun peeked its golden head over the eastern horizon and announced a new day. Chester saw the distant smoke from the Longhorn compound. It sent a surge of excitement through him. *The cooks are cooking breakfast for the hands.* He could almost smell fresh bacon frying, eggs sizzling in the pan, and oven-baked biscuits smothered with thick-n-gravy. *It shore is good to be back home.*

Chester left his mount and packhorse with the Mexican stableman and hurried to the mess hall. At least a hundred times on the long trip home he pictured how it would be—and that's how it was. The aroma sped his steps.

Buck and the top hands of the ranch sat around a long table. Each held a cup of coffee in his hand or in front of him. Buck swung a look when Chester walked in and leaped to his feet. They met halfway, pumped one another's hand in a warm handshake.

"It's good to have you home," Buck told his partner. "I was beginning to get a mite worried."

"I rode on ahead. The others ought to be here late today or tomorrow."

The handshakes and howdies took a while.

When Chester finally poured himself coffee and sat down, one of the workers brought him a heaping plateful of breakfast. He leaned over it and took a deep inhale before he picked up a fork and dug in.

"Smells good and tastes even better," he told Jewel, as she refilled everyone's coffee cup.

Chester was finishing his second plateful when Rebekah walked in carrying little Cody. He jumped up and hurried to meet her, using a finger to push aside the blanket Rebekah wrapped her baby in to protect him from the chilly morning air.

Chester's mouth dropped open. A grin split his face from ear to ear. He gazed at the rosy face before swinging a look at Buck.

"Gonna be the spittin' image of his daddy. He's got your red hair though," he told a smiling Rebekah. "How old is he?"

"Born September 2," Rebekah said proudly. "He's almost four months old."

"Say *hello* to Uncle Chester," Rebekah told Cody, using a finger to tickle his full chin.

"What did you name him?"

Buck spoke up. "Cody Walker Cordell."

Chester jerked a look at Buck and smiled.

"That's a good name. That's a very good name."

Buck and Chester spent half a day talking. It took a while for both of them to fill each other in on all that was going on.

"You did a great job, Chester," Buck told his partner. "Forty-two dollars a head is a good price."

"Got no idea what it all comes to. I just know it's a heap of money."

"You can say that again. Rebekah said we took a total of fifty thousand, two hundred forty head up the trail. According to the final tally, we actually got there with forty eight thousand, seven hundred twenty head. At forty-two dollar a head, that comes to a tad over two million dollars."

Chester's mouth dropped open. *"Two million dollars?"*

"Yep. Can you believe it?"

"Not in two million years," Chester said, still shaking his head. "Does that mean I've got enough money to get married?"

It was Buck's turn to split a wide smile and he did. He grabbed Chester in a big bear hug.

"You and Selena? It's about time! No way could I be happier."

"We've kinda skirted around talking about it, but I ain't actually asked her yet. I've been gone the best part of a year. She mighta got tired of waiting and found somebody else."

"What are you talking about? That lady's been burning her eyes out for two weeks looking up the road watching for you."

"Think I'll ride on into town."

"Can't say I blame you."

Selena and her three helpers were feeding a full-house supper crowd. Several people stood at the door waiting for an empty table when Chester excused himself and pushed past them.

Selena glanced up, spotted Chester, and promptly dropped a tray full of coffee cups that went crashing to the floor. Everyone in the room looked in time to see Selena race across the room and leap into Chester's open arms.

Happy tears streamed from her eyes. For a small slice of eternity they held one another. Selena didn't say a word. She couldn't. Words just wouldn't come. They just held each other and cried, oblivious to the applause that broke out from her customers.

Later, after the crowd finished eating and left, Selena and

Chester went for a walk. Chester slipped his arm around her and pulled her close as they strolled along the darkened street.

"I missed you," she told him.

"I missed you too. I thought about you every single day I was gone."

Suddenly realizing they were in front of the little church at the end of the street, he stopped and cleared his throat. He swallowed hard, searching for words. "There's something...there's something I need to ask you, Selena. Reckon this is as good a place as any."

Reaching into his pocket he pulled out a small, velvet-covered box and opened it. Light from a full moon reflected off the golden band. "Could you, I mean, *would* you...be my wife?"

Selena closed her eyes and pointed her face to the sky. Then, reaching a hand, she took the ring. Her gaze found his. He retrieved the ring and slipped it gently on her finger.

"What took you so long, Chester Colson? Of course I will be your wife."

Their lips found each others, sealing their long-awaited hopes.

CHAPTER XV

Christmas, 1867 at the Longhorn Ranch turned into a grand affair. Rebekah told Wash and Jewel and their staff to go all out. They did.

The big event happened on Christmas Eve, the large chow hall decorated. A Christmas tree proudly presided from the corner of the room with a present for every child under it. The cooks served a dinner fit for a king. Every employee received a special Christmas bonus of fifty dollars. Christmas carols sung by all resonated far into the night.

Sam and Kathleen Colson invited Chester, Selena and her mother, John Walker and Elvira, Buck and Rebekah, and of course little Cody to have dinner with them in their new home on Christmas Day.

Kathleen was so proud of her new home. She was all smiles as she gave the ladies a tour of the house, while the men folk sat and drank coffee and talked cattle talk.

Kathleen hired extra help to prepare and serve the dinner. Golden-brown turkey and dressing, potato casserole, corn on the cob, and oven-fresh rolls were enjoyed by all. Both apple and pecan pies finished out the meal.

Chester was too nervous to enjoy the elaborate dinner, because what no one knew except Chester and Selena, was arrangements were made for Reverend Baxter to show up at two o'clock that afternoon to perform a wedding—Chester and Selena's wedding.

What a surprise it was when Sam Colson answered the knock on the front door and found the preacher standing there.

After inviting him in and asking him to join them for dessert and coffee, Reverend Baxter declined and explained that he had decided to start a new tradition on Christmas day, that of performing a marriage.

"I was wondering if perhaps there might be someone here who would like to help me begin this new tradition."

Everyone in the room glanced at one another, puzzled by the minister's strange request. Everyone except Selena and Chester. They slowly lifted their hands. Suddenly it dawned on the others what was going on. Shrieks of joy, laughter, back patting, and many happy tears finally subsided and the wedding got underway.

"Chester Colson. Selena Rodriguez. You have come to me expressing your desire to be united in marriage. If you now wish to be joined as husband and wife, please signify that desire by joining your right hands."

Chester looked into Selena's eyes. She smiled. He reached out and took her hand.

"Marriage is an honorable estate and has existed since the beginning of time. God created Eve and presented her to Adam to be his companion. Jesus of Nazareth honored the marriage covenant with his presence at the marriage ceremony in Cana of Galilee and future blessed it by choosing its beautiful relationship as the figure of that union between himself and his church.

"Those who take these vows are brought into the closest

and most sacred of all human relationships. Their lives are blended as the waters of merging streams are mingled and thereafter must share the joys and sorrows of life together. Thus the two, forsaking all others, become one.

"Chester Colson, wilt thou have this woman to be thy wedded wife; to live together after God's ordinances in the holy estate of matrimony? Wilt thou love her, comfort her, honor and keep her, in sickness and in health, in poverty as in wealth, and forsaking all others keep thee only unto her as long as ye both shall live?"

Chester gazed into Selena's dark eyes. Tears breached his eyelids and escaped from the corners of his eyes. He swallowed back a lump before he could speak. "I do," he finally said.

"Selena Rodriguez, wilt thou have this man to be thy wedded husband; to live together after God's ordinances in the holy estate of matrimony? Wilt thou love him, comfort him, honor and obey him, in sickness and in health, in poverty and in wealth, and forsaking all others keep thee only unto him for as long as ye both shall live?"

Large tears streamed across Selena's golden-brown cheeks. Her lips trembled through a smile.

"Yes, I do," she whispered.

"Then by the authority as a minister of God, I pronounce you are now husband and wife. You may kiss your bride."

And he did.

The bunkhouses on the Longhorn Ranch were jam-packed with over two hundred-forty wranglers since the cattle drives wouldn't resume until April, but that didn't mean they had leisure time. There was more than enough work to keep every hand working from first light until dark.

Pappy's bush poppin' operation moved several miles

downstream. The crew was expanded in order to capture more of the wild longhorns from the thickets along the river.

Longhorn purchased more dragging wagons to make up for the added distance and built more corrals to take care of the wild longhorns until they became tame enough to mix in with the regular herd.

It was a busy time.

Carlos and his team were sent back into Mexico to contract with the Mexican growers to purchase more cattle.

"So we'll be trailing to Abilene, Kansas this year instead of Missouri, huh?" Buck asked Chester over early morning coffee. "Hope this new operation Harvey told you about can handle the kind of numbers we'll be bringing."

"Harvey says this Joseph McCoy fellow knows what he's doing, says the Abilene setup is first-class. He shore wants to talk with us before we make a deal with any of the other cattle buyers. No doubt about it, he wants our cattle bad. I got a feeling we might get more than forty-two dollars a head this coming year."

"Far as I can tell, he's been straight with us right down the line."

"Believe so."

"How's your new house coming along? You and Selena about ready to move in?"

"Well, yes and no. She's running her legs off between here and Del Rio. Between the new café they're building in town and our new house here, she's got a plateful."

"How's she gonna handle running the café and being a wife, too?"

"She's hired some help for the café. They have a cousin who ran a café down in Monterrey. She moved up here and is gonna manage the new café for Selena and her mother. They also hired a couple more cooks and waitresses. Selena says as soon as they get the new café open she will have more time to concentrate on furnishing our house. It's still pretty bare right now."

"It'll all work out," Buck told his friend.

* * *

The money wagon from Austin delivered their money to the Del Rio Longhorn Bank the middle of January. Both Buck and Chester were on hand for the delivery. Del Rio came to a standstill as the armored wagon rolled down the street pulled by two teams of high-spirited horses. Twenty-four heavily armed outriders rode alongside the coach on either side. More armed guards rode inside. The townspeople had never seen anything like it. The boardwalks were crowded with people standing shoulder to shoulder. Chester and Selena stood beside Buck in front of the café.

"How much of our money is in that coach?" Chester asked, leaning close and speaking softly.

"Over a million," Buck replied.

Chester just shook his head.

"It still blows my boots off. When we were eating grub worms in Virginia, would you ever have dreamed of anything like this?"

Selena jerked a look at her husband and frowned. "You ate grub worms?"

"Shore did, and glad to get 'em, too. You remember that jar of canned green beans you found in that abandoned cellar? Man-oh-man, I can still taste those. Best green beans I ever ate."

"Those are some of those *good old days* I'm not hankering to go back to."

The money coach reined up in front of the bank. Its guards dismounted and formed a corridor from the coach to the front door of the bank. Two bank guards and tellers lugged the heavy strongboxes inside. When the transfer was completed, the guards remounted and the coach rolled out of town as quickly as it came in. The entire transfer took less than thirty minutes.

Buck, Chester, and Selena went inside the café and sat down over coffee. It was the middle of the afternoon and the café was empty.

"Think all that money is safe in the bank?" Chester asked. "Shore would look mighty tempting to some jaspers hankering to get rich without working for it."

"It's about as safe as we can make it. That vault your pa has in the bank is the best there is. The company that built it says its dynamite proof. We've got two armed guards posted inside the bank and two outside in front of the bank. Besides that, Bud Cauthorn and his new deputy keep an eye on the bank, too. The fellows who take the notion to rob our bank have to be either really dumb or awfully smart."

"I ain't never heard of a smart bank robber," Chester said.

"I've got it all planned out," Clayton Dawson told the dozen men gathered around him in the deserted shack. "We'll drift into town one at a time over the next few days. Anyone asks, we're looking for work. Stay out of trouble and don't draw attention to yourself.

"We'll hit the bank just before closing time on Thursday. There won't be as many people in town during the week. By the time they get after us, it'll be dark. There ain't no moon this week and they can't follow us in pitch dark. By morning we'll all be long gone.

"Cliff Bell cased the place. He says they brought in a whole coach load of money about a week ago. Word is there's over a million bucks in this small town, hick bank. We're gonna relieve 'em of it. That means almost a hundred grand apiece. We can all live on easy street after this caper."

"Why don't we just hit 'em at night, blow the safe, and hightail it outta town?" Herb Hicks asked. "I don't hanker getting shot by some town do-gooder."

"Like I told you, Cliff looked this place over to see what's what. Far as I'm concerned Cliff knows more about blowing safes than anybody in the business. He says this vault can't be blown. Why don't you tell 'em yourself, Cliff?"

A tall, gangly man unlimbered from the upturned nail keg and stood. He spent a minute letting his slow gaze slide over each man in the room.

"Dawson is telling you like it is. I've been around safes and bank vaults all my life. Blown more'n my share of 'em. You can forget blowing this one. This whole bunch couldn't pack enough dynamite to even put a dent in it. If we're gonna rob this bank it'll have to be when that big vault door is already open."

"They've got two guards posted outside on each side of the front door. There's two more inside the bank. We've got to take care of them first rattle outta the box. After that it's a cakewalk. Anybody else got a question?" Dawson asked, sweeping a look around the room.

"Yeah, I've got a question," Rafe Hicks spoke up. "You said earlier that when we leave town we scatter, every man riding a separate trail by himself. I never heard of such a thing. Where we gonna meet back up and when? Who's gonna pack the money?"

"That's exactly why we're gonna be doing it like I said. You can bet your boots there'll be a posse after us, but which trail are they gonna follow? We're gonna scatter like a bunch of quail. Some will head across the river into Mexico, some going north, some east, and some west. They shore can't follow all of us and they ain't gonna know which one of us has the money. We'll meet back up in Piedras Negras one month from now."

"You still ain't said who *is* gonna carry the money," Hicks persisted.

"*I'm* gonna carry the money!" Dawson shot back angrily. "*I'm* the one that planned this little shindig, remember? I'm the boss of this outfit. Best you all remember that. If it don't suit you, you can hit the trail right now."

"Don't get all riled. I just asked a question, that's all," Hicks replied.

"The meeting's over," Dawson said, still hot from being questioned. "First couple of men starts drifting into town tomorrow."

Dawson turned on his heels, slammed out the door, mounted his horse and rode away.

"Lucky you didn't get your head blowed off," one of the outlaws told Rafe. "Not many question Clayton Dawson and live to tell about it."

Bud Cauthorn headed over to the café with his new deputy J. D. Summers to have a cup when he saw the stranger. This was the second one he had seen today. Bud stopped and took the man's measure.

The stranger was a tall man, tall and skinny as a rail. He had a beak nose; one a fellow wasn't likely to forget after you saw it. He rode a slat-ribbed sorrel that looked like it hadn't been fed in a week.

"Something wrong?" the new deputy asked when he noticed the marshal eyeing the stranger.

"That fellow on the sorrel. I've seen him before. He was in town a few days ago, hanging around. He's the second stranger I've seen in town today."

"Lots of newcomers in town. Del Rio's growing. Why else would they need a couple of badge-toters like us?"

"Yeah, maybe. I don't like the looks of the ones I've seen today. Something about them just don't seem right. Let's keep our eyes peeled. You see any more hard-looking strangers, let me know."

They headed on to the café, got seated and blew steam from their coffee as old Pete from the livery hurried in, out of breath.

"Marshal, I'm shore glad I found you. Been looking all over for you."

"What is it, Pete? What's wrong?"

"You asked me to let you know if I saw any strangers. Well, sir, we've had two just today. Hard looking fellows. Wore tied-down guns. Not the kind that would be looking for a job nursin'cows. They both stalled their horses. Both of 'em paid for two days. Thought you'd want to know."

"Yeah, we saw one fellow ride in as we were walking over here. I'm obliged. Let me know if you see any more."

"Shore will, Marshal."

The day wore on. Two more strangers arrived before dark; both riding alone, but both somehow connected, at least in Bud Cauthorn's thinking.

Worry gnawed at him that night. He had trouble going to sleep. *Something's going on. It just ain't natural for that many strangers to show up in just a couple of days. Just ain't figured out what the connection is.*

When the marshal spotted three more tough-looking characters ride in the following day, he knew his suspicions were right. *These boys are all part of the same bunch. Something's going down. It's got to be the bank. That's it! They're gonna hit the bank!*

"Want you to do something for me," Marshal Cauthorn asked J.D when he arrived on Wednesday afternoon for his night shift. "Want you to ride out to the Longhorn Ranch and talk to either Buck or Chester. Tell them I need to borrow his security men for a couple of days. Might be nothing that will amount to a hill of beans, but I've got this gut-shot feeling all these strangers that's showing up are part of the same bunch. I got a hunch they're gonna take a run at the bank."

"The bank?" the wide-eyed deputy said, surprise written all over his face. "You really think so? I never lawed in a town that had a real bank robbery."

"Keep this quiet. Don't tell anybody except Buck or Chester. Tell them to have their men ride in the back way and hide their horses. Then have them wait in Mr. Walker's feed warehouse until whatever happens, happens. They'll know what to do. Tell'em to come running."

Deputy Summers hurried from the office to carry out his mission.

Bud Cauthorn spotted three more ride in late in the day on Wednesday. With each new stranger that arrived, Bud grew more certain his assumption was correct. He talked privately with John Walker and asked for the use of his warehouse. John gladly agreed. The marshal then went to see Sam Colson just before closing time.

"Don't mean to worry you, Sam, but we may have a problem. I'd like to have a talk with your four security people, if you've got no objections."

"Of course. I'll get them in here. What's wrong?"

"Go ahead and ask them to step in. I'll fill you all in at one saying."

The banker locked the doors and called his four armed security men into his office. "The marshal's got something to say. Hear him out."

Bud Cauthorn let his gaze crawl slowly over the four bank guards. They were good men. All four were Texas tough. Two were ex-lawmen. All four were crack shots with both the rifles they carried in their hands and with the side arms on their hips.

"Might be nothing," Bud told them, watching their reaction closely. "But we've had a lot of strangers ride into town in the last couple of days. These boys ain't just down-on-their-luck cowboys looking for work. These are hard men. I've seen their kind before. I got a feeling they're gonna make a try for the bank.

"If I'm right, they'll most likely make their move either when you first open or just before you close. One thing for sure, it'll be when the doors to that big vault are open.

"Keep your eyes peeled and stay on your toes. If and when it happens, it will be sudden and without warning. Which two work the outside by the front doors?"

Two of the guards lifted a finger.

"I'm Slim Ballinger," the tall one said.

"My name's Henry White," the other guard said.

"Good. I know you fellows give everybody the once-over as they approach the bank. My advice is to extend your field of vision farther out. We're not looking for the little old lady coming to withdraw money for groceries. We're looking for hard-looking men who look out of place, like they don't belong. You know the type.

"If you see something that don't look right to you, don't take the chance. Turn and get inside. Lock down the bank as quick as you can. Drop that bar on those heavy front doors and stay inside until we can get help to you.

"I'm surc Mr. Colson would rather apologize to a customer who got the door slammed in his face, than get robbed. Anybody got a question?"

"Got any idea who these men are?" the guard called Ballinger asked.

"Nope, but if they are up to no good, I reckon we'll find out who they are."

Deputy J. D. Summers rode in front of a long line of twenty-four Longhorn security men. All were heavily armed with Spencer saddle guns and extra ammunition. Some carried short-barreled shotguns. All carried two side arms on their hips.

It was dark as they drew near Del Rio. They veered off to the right into a thick growth of cedar and mesquite trees. They reined up in a brush-choked draw about a hundred yards behind Walker's large feed warehouse.

They loosened cinches and tied their horses securely before moving quietly to the sprawling warehouse. Once inside, they lit a lantern and spread their ground sheets and bedrolls.

"The marshal said to stay inside and out of sight. He said if you hear shooting to block off both ends of the street as quick as you can. He'll stop by in the morning."

"Buck told us to stay as long as we're needed," Wade Thomas told the deputy. "We'll be here and ready if something happens."

Marshal Cauthorn and his deputy made their rounds Wednesday night just like always. Everything appeared quiet with nothing out of the ordinary going on. Bud finally returned to his office and went to bed around midnight. He tossed and turned, worried if he had done everything he could do to prevent the robbery, if indeed there was going to be one.

Thursday morning broke clear and hot. Marshal Cauthorn rubbed sleep from his eyes and stomped into his boots. After a trip out back to the outhouse, he washed, shaved, and sleeved into a clean shirt. He buckled on his Colt and headed for the café to eat breakfast.

Merchants along Main Street swept the boardwalk in front of their businesses. Heavy freight wagons pulled by dual-team hitches rolled along the street heading somewhere. Stray dogs nipped at the horses' hooves and barked, their shrill sounds echoing along the street, a typical morning.

Clayton Dawson rode into Del Rio just before sundown. His head swiveled from side to side as he walked his Bay horse down the street. His searching gaze swept both sides of the street. Close inspection revealed no reason for alarm. Everything looked normal.

He saw, but didn't acknowledge, his men scattered along

the street. Some lounged on a bench in front of the saloon, others stood at hitching rails along the street, fumbling with their cinch straps. All were trying to be inconspicuous.

Down the street he saw two of his men casually approaching the bank from different directions. It was their job to take out the two bank guards standing beside the front door of the bank. If all went well, in a few short moments they would have the bank's money packed in the saddlebags tied behind his saddle and be long gone.

Over his shoulder he saw his other men mounting and following him toward the bank. He turned in his saddle and swept a look along the street, seeing no reason for alarm. People appeared to be going about their business, paying no attention to the strangers riding along the street.

He slanted a look at his two men approaching the bank. All still seemed to be going as planned. Then suddenly he saw the two guards turn and rush into the bank. The big heavy doors slammed shut.

Clayton looked about frantically. Something had gone wrong. He jerked another look toward the bank. He saw Dingus and Gus drag iron and wheel around. They took off running toward their mounts as fast as they could. A shot rang out from the nose of a rifle barrel poking through the glass window.

He saw Gus turn and fire a running shot at the window even as a slug tore into his back. His body arched forward. He stopped dead in his tracks, clutching at the hole in his back. Clayton watched as his man toppled forward, falling face forward into the dusty street.

This wasn't the way it was supposed to be. Everything had gone wrong. *We've got to get outta here!*

He jerked the reins to his bay, spinning it around. Out of the corner of his eye he saw the marshal and a deputy rush from the jail across the street. A hail of bullets came from the windows of the bank. Suddenly his horse shuddered and went down. Dawson kicked free and hit the dirt with a jolting thud. Rolling to his feet, he swung his head, frantically searching for a place to take cover. There wasn't any.

Guns popped all around him as his men returned fire even as they spurred their mounts back up the street. His man, Cliff Bell, appeared beside him and reached a hand. He took it and swung up behind the saddle of Bell's slat-ribbed sorrel.

Bell slammed spurs into his mount. The horse tried gamely, but the weight of two riders on his back slowed his movement to a fast trot. Clayton knew they would never make it riding double.

Without hesitation, he jerked his Remington from its holster, jammed it into Bell's back, and pulled the trigger. With his free arm he swept the outlaw from the saddle and scooted forward into Bell's empty saddle.

He jerked his head about, taking in the confused scene in a glance. A shotgun roared. Another of his men tumbled from his saddle. The deputy swung the shotgun, searching for another target.

A slug singed dangerously close to Clayton's ear. He swung his Remington and snapped off a shot at the marshal who was standing in front of the jail, feet spread apart, handgun held at arm's length and pointed directly at him.

He jammed spurs into the slow-running sorrel, hoping to get more speed out of it, but the horse was no runner. Clayton knew if he was gonna make it out of this, he needed another horse.

A long-legged black tugged frantically at the reins holding him to a hitching rail in front of the saloon. It was his only chance. He reined toward it, leaped from his saddle and jerked its reins free, yelled into the horse's ear and slapped it on the rump with his open hand.

The frightened horse wheeled and took off in a leaping run. At the same time, holding onto the saddle horn, Clayton took a couple of running steps and swung into the saddle. He hovered low over the galloping horse's neck and crooked a look back. His men were falling like flies under the withering fire from the marshal and his deputy.

When he looked forward again his heart leaped into his throat. A dozen men with rifles to their shoulders formed a line across the street, blocking any hope of escape in that direction. Already his men ahead of him were blown from their saddles.

Dawson hauled back on the reins and jerked the black horse around, meaning to head back down the street. He bent low, viciously slapping the black horse with the long reins, torturing it into more speed. When he glanced down the street he couldn't believe what he saw.

Just like the scene behind him, another dozen men stood shoulder to shoulder with rifles in action, emptying the saddles of Clayton's men. *Who are these guys?* He wondered. *Where'd they come from so suddenly? It's like they appeared out of nowhere!*

He saw some of his gang throw down their guns and raise their hands, choosing years in prison rather than death in the dusty street.

That wasn't for him. He would never give up.

Clayton spotted a narrow alleyway between two buildings, and reined that direction. He entered the alley at a hard gallop as slugs tore holes in the walls of the buildings on both sides.

Behind the buildings a thick grove of trees loomed ahead. *If I can just make it to those trees I've still got a chance.* He jammed his spurs deep into the horse's sides and glanced backwards.

A man with a rifle appeared in the alley. He saw a blossom of red bloom from the nose of the rifle. A sharp pain stabbed his left shoulder slamming him backward. He reeled in the saddle and grabbed for the saddle horn, holding on for dear life as the stolen horse plunged into the safety of the trees.

CHAPTER XVI

A six member army detail approached the gate of the Longhorn compound at mid-morning. The guards on the gate challenged them and inquired as to the nature of their business.

"We're here to deliver a personal message from General Phillip Sheridan to Mr. Buck Cordell," the spit and polish sergeant replied.

"Just hold on," the guard told him, ringing a nearby bell.

Several men appeared, seemingly out of nowhere, with rifles in their hands. The guard hollered down to them.

"These army boys got a message from General Sheridan for Mr. Cordell."

"I'll go let him know," one of the men said, turning and trotting toward the sprawling main house.

In a few moments the guard reappeared and waved the army detail forward. They dismounted and the sergeant was escorted into the den. Buck and Rebekah sat at a large desk with a stack of papers in front of them. Buck rose as the sergeant entered.

"I'm Buck Cordell. I understand you have a message for me?"

"Yes, sir," the man said, withdrawing an official-looking leather folder from his tunic. "I'm supposed to wait for your reply."

Buck opened the folder and read the letter inside. When he finished he sat down, quickly scribbled his reply on a piece of paper and placed it inside the folder.

Without a word the sergeant did an about-face and left the room.

"What was that all about?" asked Rebekah.

"General Sheridan's coming for a visit. His note said he needed to talk with me on a matter of importance. He'll be here within the week."

"Hmm, wonder what it could be about?"

"Got no idea, but when the General in charge of reconstruction for all of Texas wants to talk, I reckon I ought to listen to what he's got to say."

General Sheridan arrived at the ranch five days later accompanied by a full platoon of bluecoats. Buck was made aware of their approach and waited at the gate when they rode up.

The general rode a high-stepping white stallion. He stepped to the ground as Buck walked up to greet him.

"Welcome to the Longhorn," Buck greeted, extending his hand to his former enemy.

"Thank you, Mr. Cordell, for allowing me to invite myself to your home. What a surprise to find such a large complex out here in the middle of nowhere. I could hardly believe my eyes."

"Well, it's built more for protection than comfort, I'm afraid. Seems the Indians don't cotton to us setting up housekeeping in their hunting ground."

"Ah, yes, the Indians. We'll be forced to deal with them shortly, I'm afraid. Nonetheless, I've never seen a more impressive layout."

"Come on inside."

"Would it be convenient for my men to set up camp somewhere nearby?"

"Of course. One of my men will show your lieutenant a good campsite down by the river."

Buck escorted the general to the sprawling hacienda. Rebekah met them at the door.

"Welcome to our home, General Sheridan."

"Mrs. Cordell," the officer said, bowing and kissing the back of her hand. "Your wife is even more breathtaking than the first time I saw her."

"You're very kind," Rebekah said, blushing broadly. "How long will you be able to stay with us?"

"Only until tomorrow, I'm afraid. Would it be possible to show me around your ranch?"

"Be glad to."

They took a walking tour of the compound. Buck showed him the row of bunkhouses, the chow hall and stables.

"My, my," the general said. "How many men work on your ranch?"

"Two hundred sixty-eight, at last count. We have several crews that don't actually live on the ranch; they're off in the thickets catching longhorns. Our trail crews are usually on the trail between here and Missouri or Kansas, but they're between drives and are here right now."

"We trailed forty thousand head to market last year. Most likely do the same this year. Right now they're all busy branding and getting ready for this year's drives."

After the tour of the compound they mounted and took a riding tour. Buck showed the general herd after herd of cattle, all under the watchful eyes of several cowboys. They watched several branding crews as they burned the Longhorn brand into the hides of young stock calves.

As they sat their horses watching, Chester rode up.

"This is my partner, Chester Colson. Chester, this is General Phillip Sheridan."

Chester reached a gloved hand across the space between their horses and shook the general's hand. "It's a pleasure to meet you, General. Buck told me about meeting you in San Antonio. Good to have you on the Longhorn."

"It's good to be here. You and Mr. Cordell have quite an impressive ranch."

"It's growing, sure enough. Will you be staying with us a few days?"

"Only until tomorrow, I'm afraid."

"Have you showed the general *El Toro* yet?" Chester asked Buck.

"Not yet. I was saving the best for last."

"Ah, yes, *the monster bull*," General Sheridan said. "I believe everyone in Texas has heard of your famous bull. My friend, Richard King, was quite impressed by it."

"We'll stop by the corral and take a look on the way back to the compound," Buck said. "Will you and Selena be able to join us for dinner tonight?" he turned and asked Chester.

"Looking forward to it. I'm gonna have the boys move the young brood herd over to the north pasture. The grass is better."

"Sounds good. We'll see you at dinner tonight."

After Chester left, Buck and the general rode back toward the ranch and stopped by the large corral and adjoining barn that housed their famous bull. Sheridan's eyes rounded as he saw the huge animal.

El Toro stood in the middle of the corral. He swung his head toward them as they dismounted and leaned on the fence. He snorted and shook his massive head in defiance. White foam bubbled from his flaring nostrils. His black eyes seemed to blaze as he stared at Buck and the general. Great hooves pawed the ground, throwing dirt in a cloud over his shoulders and back.

"Oh, my!" the general exclaimed, as he stared wide-eyed. "No wonder the newspapers are calling him the monster bull. I've never seen anything like it."

"He's a big one, sure enough," Buck agreed. "Looks like the calves he sires are gonna be might near as big as their papa, too."

"How did you ever manage to capture the beast?"

Buck told him the story. The general listened intently. After the telling, General Sheridan shook his head in amazement.

"That story needs to be recorded in a book. Everyone needs to hear it. Are you a reader, Mr. Cordell?"

"No, I'm afraid not. I've been too busy just surviving to spend much time reading."

"Did you serve in the war?"

Well, here it comes. I knew we would get around to that question sooner or later. Do I tell him the truth? How much should I tell him? Wonder if he heard about the ambush and the missing payroll? Could he tie me to that somehow?

"Yes, sir. But I was on the losing side, I'm afraid."

"Ah, yes, Captain Benjamin *Buck* Cordell. You rode for Colonel John Singleton Mosby, I believe. The ones we called *Mosby's Raiders*. You were a constant thorn in the Union Army's side, Mr. Cordell, especially in the Virginia campaign. You did your job well."

"I see you've done your homework. Well, the war is over, I'm glad to say."

"I think we can all agree to that. And yes, I've looked into your background. The matter I've come to discuss with you required it."

"Just what is it you want to discuss, General?"

"It's rather complicated, I'm afraid. It involves the reconstruction of Texas. As you are aware, no doubt, we're in the difficult process of forming a new government in Texas. You met James Throckmorton, our newly installed Governor, although I'm already beginning to regret that appointment. The man is simply not up to the task.

"But be that as it may, I'm in the process of choosing representatives for the various districts of Texas. They will be the men who write legislation, make laws, and represent the citizens of their districts. They will be the real power of the government. The governor is largely a figurehead, anyway. The real power of our new government will rest in the legislature.

"That's where you come into the picture. I'd like you to accept an appointment to represent the citizens of southwest Texas. Your district would extend all the way from the Gulf of Mexico to the New Mexico line.

"Your district would encompass thousands of square miles of mostly uninhabited land, land on which we need settlers, lots of settlers. Part of your responsibility would be to write legislation providing a means to recruit those settlers and provide them with land where they can raise their families.

"If Texas is to be the great state we believe it can become, we need men with vision in positions of authority. In short, Mr. Cordell, we need you. I'd like you to consider accepting the appointment. Think it over. I'd like to have your answer before I depart tomorrow."

Buck was stunned speechless. Governor Throckmorton had alluded to something like this, but Buck hadn't given any serious thought to it.

"I'm afraid I wouldn't make a good politician, General. I've got a way of speaking when I ought to be listening. I'm not much at playing around with words. I say what's on my mind no matter whose feathers it ruffles."

"Several have told me as much. That's precisely why you are the right man for this job. We don't need a man who just goes along to get along. We need a man with vision, a man who's not afraid to stand up and say what's on his mind. I'm convinced you are that man, Mr. Cordell."

"Besides, as you can see, we've pretty well got a plateful right here on the ranch. Just don't see it would be fair for me to run off to Austin and dump a bigger workload on Chester and my wife. But I'm obliged for the confidence. I'll think on it. I'll give you my answer before you leave."

Nothing more was mentioned about either the war or the political appointment at dinner that night. The conversation revolved mostly around the ranch, *El Toro,* the cattle drives, and of course, little Cody, who was the center of attention.

After an elaborate dinner they all moved to the den where Rebekah's house girls served everyone coffee.

"Thank you for the wonderful dinner. I need you to teach our Army cooks how to prepare food, Mrs. Cordell."

"I'm afraid I can't claim credit for the meal, general. In fact our chef was a former cook for the army."

"I should fire the officer that let him get away."

After an appropriate time, Rebekah and Selena excused themselves and left the men to their cigars and coffee. It was late when the conversation ended and they all retired for the night.

Rebekah was still awake when Buck undressed in the dark and slipped quietly into bed. She snuggled into the hollow of his shoulder and kissed his chest. "Did he tell you why he came?"

"Yep."

She waited. Finally, deciding he either couldn't or didn't want to talk about it, she snuggled deeper against him. She was almost asleep when he spoke.

"He wants to appoint me to be the representative for this part of Texas. I'd have to go to Austin some."

Rebekah raised her head to stare through the darkness at Buck's face for a long moment. "What did you tell him?"

"Told him I'd give him my answer in the morning before he leaves."

"Are you going to do it?"

"Don't know. What do you think about it?"

"What would you be doing?"

"Writing legislation, making laws, stuff like that, I reckon."

"You'd be good at it."

"You think so?"

"No, I know so."

PART III

CHAPTER XVII

Cody Cordell, sat beside a small campfire in a remote area of extreme northwest Texas. For the past year he had kept on the move, avoiding larger towns. When he was forced to replenish his trail supplies he tried to find a small community or trading post, someplace where it was unlikely folks had heard of the Hondo Kid.

But even in these small isolated places, it seemed somebody usually recognized him. When this happened, there was always some local yokel who fancied himself a gunfighter and wanted to make a name for himself by gunning down the Hondo Kid.

Mostly he kept to himself, living off the land, rising every morning anxious to see what lay beyond the next hill. His wanderings took him across most of Texas, Missouri, Arkansas, Louisiana and the Indian Territory. He knew he was searching for something, but he couldn't figure out what that something was.

Each night he spent at least two hours practicing with his Colt; sometimes more. The weapon felt as natural in his hand as his fingers. He could tell his speed was much faster than even a few months earlier. He knew his life depended upon how fast he could draw and fire his weapon.

A far off coyote disturbed the quiet with a high-pitched series of yelps. Others answered, filling the night with their musical ritual. Cody picked up his small blackened coffeepot and refilled his tin cup.

He was about to bring his cup to his lips when his pinto snorted. Cody immediately recognized the warning. He had company.

Snatching up his nearby Henry rifle, he rolled away from the jagged circle of the campfire just as the swish of an arrow pierced the saddle he'd been leaning against. He took cover behind a large boulder and jacked a shell into his rifle. Swinging his head back and forth, he searched for the location of his attackers but saw nothing.

Quiet settled in.

He didn't know where they were or how many they were. *Figure it's a small group or they would have attacked me in force right off, maybe a small hunting party, no more than two or three.*

He blinked his eyes several times to adjust them from the light of the campfire to the darkness.

As Cody lay there waiting for his enemies to make the next move, the old bitterness returned. A picture of his parents flashed before him. He felt sick to his stomach as he remembered finding his mother lying nude on the ground, her body brutalized beyond belief. He remembered how they had tied his father to the corral fence, scalped him and used his body for target practice. He felt a flush of anger race up his neck and burn his face.

His senses keened, honed sharp from several similar encounters during his travels. His searching gaze swept back and forth, his eyes squinting to pierce the darkness as he listened for the slightest sound.

Still he waited.

It wasn't what he heard; it was what he *felt*. Cody reacted instantly, rolled to his back just in time to see the silhouette of an Indian flying through the air in a headlong dive. One upraised hand held a war ax.

He jerked the nose of his rifle up and fired pointblank. The shrill scream of the warrior cut short in mid-flight. The attacker landed facedown in the dirt and didn't move. Cody jerked his head around at a sound from his right. Another attacker raced toward him, long lance held at the ready. Working the lever of his Henry, he aimed from waist-high and touched the trigger. A blossom of fire bloomed from the nose of his rifle. The Indian staggered, stumbled, and fell at Cody's feet.

He squatted against the boulder. His head swiveled back and forth. His hands made sweat on the wooden stock of his rifle. His body felt tense; tight. He waited expectantly for another attack.

Long moments passed slowly. Still he waited.

Finally deciding there must have been only two of them, he pushed to his feet and examined the two dead Indians. Apache. The red headbands clearly identified them. Cody knew he couldn't rest easy until he was certain there had, indeed, been only two Indians. He went looking for their horses.

He found them tied in a small cluster of mesquite bushes. One was a half-starved looking roan, hardly worth keeping. The other was a beautiful paint. He decided to keep the paint and turn the roan loose.

Leading his new horse by its single Indian style bridle, he returned to his camp, tied the paint alongside Cincinnati and his packhorse, and dropped a handful of small sticks on the fire. Picking up the coffee cup he had dropped, he filled it from the coffee pot and squatted on his heels beside his fire.

Killing had become a way of life. What troubled him most was that it didn't bother him, especially killing the Indians. His deep-seated hatred for all Indians was born the day he found his parents and the feeling had grown in the two years since then.

As far as the others went, it was a matter of survival. He never picked a fight in his life, but he saw a growing number go down in front of his Colt. *How many is it now?* He wondered. *Twenty. Maybe twenty-one. I've lost count. I'm sixteen years old and I've killed twenty men, not counting Indians.*

Two weeks after the encounter with the Apache, Cody rode into the small community of *Las Cruces,* New Mexico to restock his trail supplies. The town wasn't much different from dozens of others he visited in the past year.

He saw a collection of adobe houses laid out along crooked, dusty streets. One of the buildings on the edge of town was a sprawling livery with an attached pole corral containing three scrawny-looking horses. Cody reined over.

A big, unhappy-looking fellow emerged from one of the stalls with a pitchfork in his hand. He eyed Cody up and down before his gaze swung to the paint Indian pony on a lead line.

"Howdy," Cody offered. His greeting brought no response, not even a sideways glance.

"I'd like to sell the paint. You interested?"

The liveryman thought on the question for a time. Finally he spat a large stream of tobacco juice and ran his hands up and down the paint's forelegs, pried open the horse's lips and examined the teeth before replying.

"Maybe. You got a bill of sale?"

"Nope. It belonged to an Indian who tried to ambush me."

The liveryman scratched his whiskers in thought. "Give you twenty dollars."

"That's a fine horse, mister. It's worth twice that."

"Not to me, it ain't," the man said, turning his back and heading back toward the stall.

"Okay, twenty dollars," Cody said, untying the lead rope from his saddle horn.

The liveryman took the lead rope and counted out twenty dollars into Cody's hand. He stuck it into his drawstring moneybag and put it back in his saddlebag.

A sun-bleached sign hanging on the front of a small building across the street identified it as the General Store. He reined his horses toward the hitching rail and stepped down. Swiping his floppy hat from his head, he beat the dust from his clothes with it before replacing it on his long, wheaten hair.

A baldheaded fellow with a dirty apron watched him from the wooden boardwalk in front of the store.

"Hot day," the storekeeper greeted.

"'Fraid so," Cody replied. "Need some supplies."

"I got 'em, if'n you got the money. I don't do credit with strangers."

Cody came down off his horse and looped Cincinnati's reins around the hitching rail and followed the man through the open door into the store. He glanced around. The shelves were mostly bare. Several skinny chickens inside the store scattered out of the way as the storekeeper hurried behind the counter.

"Need a bag of coffee if you got it," Cody said.

"I got it."

The man scooped a cloth bag full of coffee from a small barrel and set it on the counter. "What else?"

"Bag of salt. Small bag of sugar."

"Looks like you're stocking trail supplies."

"Yep."

"Which way you be headed?"

"Don't know yet. Thought I might head up Colorado way."

"Then do yourself a favor, boy. Take one of those canvas tarps with you. This time of year those Colorado rains get mighty nasty."

"I'm obliged. I'll take one. You got a slab of salt pork?"

"Shore do," Taking up a dirty butcher knife and turning to a wooden box. He reached inside and withdrew a large slab of meat. He shooed away the flies from it and laid the knife against one edge. "'Bout there suit ye?"

"That'll do," Cody said, picking up a book from a nearby table. The title caught his eye; *Gulliver's Travels, by Lemuel Gulliver*.

"How much for the book?"

"Aw, a dime I reckon. Ain't much call for books in this neck of the woods."

Cody added it to his growing pile of purchases.

"Where ye hail from, young fellow?"

"Oh, here and there. Why do you ask?"

"Just wondering, that's all. There was one of those Pinkerton fellows through here a while back. He was looking for a young fellow that sounded a lot like you. Said the man he was looking for called himself the Hondo Kid. But it's a big country. Lots of folks come and go, I reckon. Might be a good idea if you done the same. That fellow might take a notion to come back"

"I reckon." Cody said. "Figure up what I owe you."

"That comes to four dollars."

"Don't reckon there's a place a fellow could get a bath around here?"

"Shore 'nuff. Right down the street at the barbershop. Ole Grumpy will fix you right up."

Cody touched his hat with a crooked finger and left the store. He stowed his supplies in his pack and led his two horses down the dusty street. *Why would a Pinkerton man be looking for me? I haven't robbed anybody. Far as I know there ain't no wanted posters out for me. Strange.*

Two tough-looking men with low-tied guns lounged on a bench in front of the saloon. They eyed Cody as he walked his horses down the street and tied them in front of the barbershop.

The heavy-set barber was asleep in the barber chair. Cody shook him awake.

"Fellow up at the store said I might get a bath and haircut here. Are you Grumpy?"

"That's my name, not my disposition." he said, rising from the chair like it was the hardest piece of work he had done in a while. "Which you want first?"

"Don't matter to me. The haircut, I reckon."

"Then have a seat right here, young fellow. I'm gonna fix you right up."

Cody folded into the recently vacated chair.

"How much you want cut off?"

"About to my shoulders, I reckon."

"You ain't from around these parts are you?" The barber went to work on Cody's long hair.

"Nope."

The man let a long silence fill time before he said anything more. "Didn't think I seen you before, but something about you seems familiar."

"I ain't been through here before," Cody assured him.

The barber finished cutting Cody's hair. "Say you want a bath, too?"

"Yep, if you got one. My horse is starting to shy away from me lately."

The man cackled like a bantam rooster. "Got a bath waiting right out back under the lean-to. Ain't been but one other fellow in it all day."

Now that's a comforting thought. Cody paid the man and walked through the open back door. A large metal tub sat on the ground underneath a shed. He looked at the gray scum coating the top of the tepid bathwater. *Maybe there's only been one to take a bath in that water today, but no telling how many there's been in the last week.* He decided to wait a while longer on that bath.

As Cody rounded the corner of the barbershop, the two men he had seen earlier were rummaging through his saddlebags and the packs on his packhorse.

"Can I help you fellows find something?"

The two men jerked around, surprised at getting caught rifling his supplies.

The older of the two was maybe just shy of forty. He had a week's growth of whiskers and hair that needed cutting. He was a barrel-chested man with a black Stetson and a tied down Remington on his hip.

The other man looked young, slim, and had an evil look about him. He too, wore his gun low and tied to his right leg.

"We, uh…we were looking for something," the older one said, flicking a sheepish look at his partner.

"And just what would that be?" Cody asked, eyeing his drawstring moneybag in the fellow's hand.

"This here bag. It was stole from me just last night."

Cody felt another presence off to his left. The barber must have overheard the loud voices and stepped through the open front door of the barbershop.

"Mister, that bag in your hand is mine, not yours. Just put it back in the saddlebag where you found it and we'll forget all about this."

"We ain't forgetting nothing, kid. This is my moneybag and I'm taking it. If you think you're big enough to stop me, you got another think coming."

Cody flipped the *serape* back over his shoulder revealing the bone-handled Colt in his belly holster. He took a step backward and squared around facing both the men. When he spoke, his voice was as flat and cold as a slab of slate, barely above a whisper. "Put the bag back. I won't say it again."

The man holding Cody's moneybag stared at the gun in Cody's holster. His eyes rounded. He flicked a glance at his partner then back at Cody. A sneer crooked the man's lips.

"You ain't nothing but a snot-nosed kid with a gun. Beat it kid, or we'll kill you where you stand."

"That might be easier said than done."

As if by some prearranged signal they both went for their guns. In the blink of an eye Cody's Colt was in his hand. It roared once, twice, three times. Neither of the *would-be* robbers got off a shot. Their guns barely cleared leather before falling from their hands to the ground. The men doubled over and staggered backwards, falling into the dusty street.

Behind him the barber let out an excited shout.

"Whoohee! I seen it, but I didn't see it! I mean that was so fast a fellow couldn't see it. Them two jaspers been bullying this town for over a month. Nobody had the sand to stand up to them until you come along. Young fellow, you done this town a big favor by killing that scum. What's your name anyway?"

"You ever heard of the Hondo Kid?" Cody asked as he leathered his Colt.

"The *Hondo Kid?* Are you really him? Might near everybody's heard of you. You're right famous. Fact of the matter, there was a Pinkerton detective come through looking for you not long ago."

"Yeah, that's what I heard. Is there a lawman in this town?"

"Only law in *Las Cruces* is the one you're wearing in your holster."

"Well, somebody needs to stick these fellows in the ground."

"Ole Jed down at the store takes care of the burying."

Cody gathered the lead lines to his packhorse and toed a stirrup. He swung into the saddle and reined Cincinnati down the street without another word.

"You come back this way again sometime, Kid," he heard the barber call as he rode away.

Riding east out of *Las Cruces* in the failing light, Cody figured he had an hour, two at the most, before he needed to find a place to make camp.

The country was barren. Sandy soil packed hard by a relentless sun. Scattered patches of scrub cedar and mesquite sapped the last dregs of moisture from the ground leaving nothing for other vegetation. Large fingers of rock protruded from the ground and pointed skyward. It was an unforgiving land, a land where man was not welcome and where few could survive.

As the night gathered around him Cody took note of the flight of the desert birds. He had learned they knew the location of water and would visit before good dark. He followed their path.

He found the desert spring in a draw surrounded by a grove of scrub cedar. It bubbled out from under a rock shelf and formed a small pool of clear, fresh water. Cody reined up nearby and tied his horses to a sturdy bush.

Swinging his searching gaze in a circle and settling his mind that he was the only visitor, he bellied down and scooped a handful of water to his mouth. It was fresh and sweet. He buried his face and drank long.

After letting his horses drink their fill, he made camp in a small clearing among nearby rocks. He gathered sticks and built a small campfire and put coffee water on to boil.

He was about to add a handful of coffee to the water when

Cincinnati let out a deep, rumbling snort. Cody immediately dropped the coffee and crouched, palming his Colt.

His gaze peered through the gathering darkness and glimpsed something move. Someone was there.

From among the rocks two figures emerged. Both had a blanket wrapped about their shoulders. It was two elderly Indians, an old man and an old woman. Both moved forward slowly, feebly; taking weak, shuffling baby steps.

They moved past Cody without so much as a glance, making their way to the water. Both folded to their knees weakly, and, with cupped hands, scooped water to their thirsty mouths.

Cody look nervously about, searching for others who might be with the two older people, but could find no sign of anyone else. He watched the elderly man and woman. When they finished drinking, they shuffled a few feet from the water and sat down cross-legged, huddling together under their blankets.

Cody was dumbfounded. He stared at them for a long while, not knowing what to think. Finally, assuring himself they meant him no harm, he made coffee and sliced some salt pork into a frying pan for supper.

He ate while keeping an eye on the two old people. Guilt overcame him and he pushed to his feet, dropped several slices of meat onto a tin plate and walked over to where the old people sat.

He stopped before them and held out the plate of food. The old man looked up at him. His skin was deeply wrinkled with age. His tired-looking dark eyes met Cody's and held for a long moment. Cody saw large tears escape and run down the old man's face as a bony hand emerged from the blanket and accepted the plate of meat.

Cody watched as the old man shared the food with his wife. They both ate like they were half starved. Without a word Cody returned to his campfire.

For a long time Cody lay awake thinking about the old couple. *Who are they? Where did they come from? What are they doing out in the desert alone?*

Then he remembered.

He had heard stories of certain tribes that turned out their elderly when they could no longer care for themselves. They were banished to die alone in the desert without weapons, water, or food.

Could this be the case with his visitors? How could a family send their parents into the desert to die?

As strong as his deep-seated hatred for all Indians was, still his heart hurt for these two helpless old people. *Come morning, I'll see what I can do to help them,* he determined in his mind just before he drifted off to sleep.

Cody woke at the first crack of dawn. His first thought was of the two old people. He swung a look at where he had last seen them. They were gone. For a minute he sat staring at the spot, wondering about them. He felt an overwhelming compassion for them.

Trying, but failing, to put the two old Indians out of his mind, he broke camp and saddled up. He couldn't help searching both sides of the trail for them as he left the area of the spring.

Then he pointed Cincinnati's nose northeast. Maybe there was a place in Colorado that had never heard of the Hondo Kid.

CHAPTER XVIII

It was unusually cold for February. A strong chilly wind from the north tugged at Buck's flat-brimmed Stetson. He snugged it tighter onto his head and held it in place with a gloved hand as he guided his covered buggy through the gates of the newly constructed Fort Sam Houston.

The sentry saluted smartly and waved him on through. Buck pulled his matching black horses to a stop in front of the headquarters building. A young private walked briskly forward.

"Good afternoon, sir. Will your business take a while? I'll see to your horses."

Buck nodded his head once. "I shouldn't be that long. I'm here to see General Sheridan."

"Yes, sir. Right inside."

Buck climbed the three steps onto the wide wooden porch that fronted the building and opened the heavy front door.

A sergeant sat at a desk beside another closed inner door. "Can I help you?"

"I'm here to see General Sheridan. I'm Buck Cordell."

The sergeant rose and tapped on the closed door to the general's office.

"Enter," a deep voice from inside the office invited.

The sergeant opened the door as Buck waited. General Sheridan saw him through the open door and rose quickly from behind a large desk. "Buck Cordell, my friend. It's good to see you. Come in. Come in," he said, as he came around the desk with an outstretched hand. "How's your beautiful wife and that new son of yours?"

"They're both good."

"Have a seat. So you're on your way to Austin?"

"Yep. I understand the first meeting of the legislature is scheduled for a week from now. Thought I'd get there a day or two early and sorta get the lay of the land, so to speak."

"Good idea. Good idea. See Governor Throckmortan when you get there. He'll help you get settled in."

"So he's still our governor?"

"For now. My subordinate, General Charles Griffin, believes Throckmorton to be disloyal. Throckmorton is a former Confederate, but not all former Confederates are disloyal, are they my friend?"

"Of course not."

"I'd be obliged if you would keep our conversation just between you and me."

After they were both seated, the general reached into his desk drawer and withdrew an official-looking paper. "Here's my proclamation appointing you as the State Representive for all of southern Texas. Your district will be by far the largest, perhaps not in numbers of citizens just yet, but in area. As we discussed earlier, I'd like you to put your mind to the task of convincing more folks to homestead in southern Texas. I realize the hostile Indians are a problem in that regard, but we're laying plans to deal with that.

"I'll work on it," Buck promised.

"Splendid. When are you going on to Austin?"

"At first light."

"Would you do me the honor of joining me for dinner tonight?"

"Be glad to."

"Are you staying at the hotel?"

"Yep."

"Then why don't we meet in the dining room, say about seven?"

"I'll be there," Buck said, pushing out of his chair.

They shook hands again and Buck left the office. He drove into town and left his buggy in front of the hotel, then glanced up and down the street before walking inside.

"Mr. Cordell," the hotel manager behind the desk greeted with a wide smile. "It's good to have you again. Will you be staying a while with us this trip?"

"Just tonight. I'll need a room and a bath."

"Yes, sir. You'll be in your usual suite. I'll arrange for the bath right away."

Buck took the key from the manager and climbed the stairs to his room. He went inside and pitched his travel bag on the floor, removed his hat and coat and flopped onto the bed with his head resting on his arm. He stared up at the ceiling for a long time.

A soft tap on the door interrupted his thoughts. He rose and opened the door. It was a couple of young Mexican ladies, both with two large buckets of hot water. They smiled and entered as Buck stood aside.

Three more trips filled the large bathtub. The girls left a bar of soap, a brush, and two towels before they curtsied and left. Buck locked the door and undressed. The steaming-hot water felt good as he settled down into it. He leaned his head back on the edge of the tub and closed his eyes. His first thought was of Rebekah and those wonderful times they enjoyed together in her large bathing pool at home.

A thin smile tugged at the corners of his mouth. *How could I be so lucky to have her for my wife and the mother of my son? She's the best thing that ever happened to this cowboy.*

Chester sat his saddle with one leg crooked around the saddle horn. He leaned forward, propped his arms on his leg and swept the valley below with a gaze. A vast herd of longhorns stretched from one side of the valley to the other. As far as the eye could see, the Longhorn cattle grazed contentedly on the lush green grass of the Sycamore River valley.

In another month the herds from Mexico will begin arriving, he thought. *We're as ready as we can be, I reckon. We've put together a good crew. They all know their job and don't have to be told what needs doing.*

He glanced westward at the fading sun slipping behind the horizon as Link Stone rode up and reined his chestnut gelding to a stop beside Chester.

For several minutes neither said a word. They sat staring down at the herd.

"Quite a sight ain't it?" the top hand finally said, still staring across the herd.

Chester just shook his head and blew out a draft of air. "It's something, sure enough. Never in all my born days thought we'd own something like all this."

"I got a hunch we ain't seen nothing yet."

"Reckon I better be heading back to the ranch."

"Can't say I blame you none," Link said grinning. "If I had somebody like your wife waiting supper on me, I'd be making tracks that way, too."

Chester just grinned and unwrapped his leg from around the saddle horn, then reined his black gelding toward home.

He short-loped his mount all the way to the ranch compound, turned his mount over to the Mexican stableman and walked briskly toward his and Selena's house. She must have been watching for him, because she met him at the front door. He stopped in his tracks and just stood staring at her for a long moment.

She wore a long, floor-length black skirt, and a white blouse gathered just below her shoulders. Her black, silky hair appeared recently brushed so that not a hair was out of place. She stood there, smiling and waiting.

"What a picture," he said, shaking his head from side to side.

She closed the distance between them and melted into his open arms. He hugged her close. The warmth of love that encompassed them was overwhelming, breathtaking. It was like they were no longer two, but one. With gentle fingers he lifted her face and saw tears working trails down her cheeks. He wrinkled a worried look. "Is something wrong?"

She shook her head.

"Nothing's wrong, my love. These are just tears of the heart."

Rebekah drifted aimlessly from chore to chore, going through the motions, her mind clearly someplace else.

"What's wrong with you child?" Jewel asked, as Rebekah stood several minutes with a large pan in her hand, staring off into space.

Rebekah jerked her mind back to reality at the words. "Oh, it's nothing. Buck's barely been gone three days and I miss him already."

"I know how you feel. I 'bout went crazy when my man use to be gone for months at a time. I reckon that's how it is with us womenfolk, seems like we always waitin' and wantin' our man right close by."

"I suppose."

"Say, how's *Rosetta* working out taking care of little Cody?"

"She's a marvel. I couldn't ask for anyone better."

"That little boy is growin' like a young calf, won't be long until he be running all over the place."

"Well, he eats like a young calf, too. It keeps me busy running back and forth to let him nurse."

"Yessiree, that boy is gonna be a big fellow just like his papa," Rebekah's black friend chuckled.

That night, long after little Cody was sleeping peacefully and Rebekah had taken her bath, she lay alone in their large bed. She stared up at the ceiling through the dim light of the small lamp.

Oh, Buck, I miss you so much. I know what you are doing is important, and I know I'm being selfish, but I sure do miss you.

Unconsciously her hand drifted across the bed to rest where her husband slept. Somehow the touching made him feel closer.

Buck arrived in the hotel dining room just before seven. The waiter showed him to a special table reserved for the general and his important guests.

"Would you like some coffee while you are waiting, congressman?"

The comment startled Buck for a moment. *Congressman. I suppose I best get use to the term.* "Uh, yes, coffee would be good."

He seated himself and swept the room with a look. It was crowded. Every table was full. He couldn't help noticing folks staring in his direction, whispering to one another in hushed voices.

Obviously word of his appointment already made the rounds of the *upper crust* of San Antonio.

General Phillip Sheridan swept into the room like a king.

In a way, I reckon there's not much difference, when I stop to think about it. Buck watched the officer approach. He stood and they exchanged handshakes.

"Thank you for joining me for dinner, my friend," the general said, scooting out a chair and sitting down. "I hate eating alone."

"Are you a married man, general?"

"Yes. Yes, I am. Unfortunately, we get to spend very little time together. Part of the price for serving your country, I suppose."

"I reckon. Any children?"

"No, I'm afraid not. Like I said, we aren't able to spend much time together. But what about you, I understand you were married only recently?"

"Yes, a little over a year. We were married on Christmas day."

"Well, you have a wonderful family. In fact, I'm a bit jealous at the level of success you've achieved in such a short time. I must tell you, you and your ranch are the talk of Texas."

"I've done nothing compared to you, general. You, of all people, know that success is the result of a lot of hard work and lady luck smiling down on you."

"Each must struggle in his own arena of life, I suppose. I've been summoned to Washington. I leave tomorrow. I've got a meeting with President Johnson, General Grant, who is now the Secretary of War, and Orville Browning, the Secretary of Interior. I suppose they have some outlandish scheme cooked up they want me to carry out.

"I've a feeling they want me to assume total command of the Fifth Military district with headquarters in New Orleans. The Congressional Republicans have recently passed a series of sweeping legislation regarding reconstruction. I suspect they want me to see the new laws are implemented."

"Sounds like a mighty big job."

"Politicians are fickle bedfellows, my friend. You'd be wise to remember that."

Congressman Benjamin *Buck* Cordell arrived in Austin on February 21, 1867. He checked into the newly constructed Williamson House, the largest and most modern hotel in town.

The next day after arriving in town he walked into the waiting room of Governor Throckmorton. A stiff-necked older lady looked up from her desk and peered at him over the top of horn-rimmed glasses.

"May I help you, sir?"

"Yes, ma'am. I'd like to see the governor. I'm Buck Cordell."

"I don't recall anyone by that name having an appointment. The governor doesn't see anyone without an appointment," she informed him coolly.

"He's expecting me. Just tell him I'm here, if you don't mind."

"Humph," she muttered, as she rose abruptly and tapped on the door to the governor's office and entered without an invitation from inside.

She emerged momentarily with a decidedly improved attitude.

"The governor will see you now," she said, standing aside and allowing Buck to enter.

"Mr. Cordell. It's good to see you again," the governor said, standing and reaching a hand across the desk. Buck took the offered hand and they shook warmly.

"I received a letter telling me of your appointment. I couldn't be more pleased."

"I'm obliged. General Sheridan asked me to stop in. He said you might be able to show me the ropes around here."

"Indeed. I'll have my aide take you over to Congress and introduce you around. He'll help you locate your office."

Buck sensed a tense feeling in the man. The governor wasn't the enthusiastic statesman Buck remembered from their meeting in San Antonio. Maybe he'd somehow got wind that he was on the way out. "That will be good. I'm obliged for your help," Buck rose from the chair. "I know you are a busy man. I'll run along."

"Hold on. Let me send for my assistant. Miss Pendergrass!" he called loudly.

The stiff-necked secretary appeared.

"Would you ask Mr. Sheffield to show Mr. Cordell to the Congress, please?"

After a fifteen minute tour of the Congress under the guidance of the governor's assistant, Buck figured he knew as much about the workings of Congress as the assistant, which was nothing.

He did find his office. It was almost as big as Rebekah's bathroom. The furnishings consisted of a worn out desk with three legs and a chair that looked so flimsy he wouldn't dare trust his weight in it. He stood in front of the desk with his legs touching it, and his backside touching the door.

Welcome to Congress, Congressman Cordell.

As he was seriously questioning his decision to accept the appointment, he became aware of someone behind him.

"Are you Congressman Cordell?"

Buck turned to find a short fellow with a bulging stomach hanging over a belt that must be there somewhere but couldn't be seen. His full hair was snow white and his face was puffy-looking like he'd had way too many after dinner drinks.

"I'm Buck Cordell. I'm not used to the *congressman* part yet."

"I'm Congressman J. W. Wentworth. I'm the speaker of the House and leader of Congress. Just stopped by to welcome you."

"I'm obliged. I was just looking over my *office*."

The man swept a look around the tiny room.

"Aw, yes, it is a bit small, but I'm afraid this is all we have available. We have very strict budget restraints, you know."

"Apparently. I understood there was to be an assistant and a secretary?"

"I'm afraid not. That budget thing you know. It is so annoying. We have to keep a close eye on every penny. There's just no available funds for additional personnel at this time."

"I see. Well, I sure wouldn't want to burden your *budget*."

"Yes, well, if there is anything at all I can do, just let me know. My office is always open to our *freshman* congressmen. You'll find my office on the second floor, suite 100."

"But isn't this the first session of the Texas Congress? Aren't we *all freshmen* congressmen?"

"Well, technically, yes. But some of us have been around politics a long time. We're experienced in this sort of thing."

"I see. Well, I'll be sure to stop by."

Over the next few days, Buck did visit the offices of all twelve congressmen, starting with the *leader* of congress.

Congressman J. W. Wentworth's *suite* of offices consisted of four rooms. The first was a large waiting room at least four times as large as Buck's entire office space. Then his private four *assistants* had an office they shared. Next was Wentworth's *private* secretary's office. She was a shapely blonde who gave the impression her talents lay in some area other than secretarial work.

The distinguished *leader* of congress's office was something to behold. Spacious, elaborately furnished with original paintings on the walls, floors sanded to a high sheen with oriental rugs, huge oak desk, and his own private, well-stocked built-in bar.

No wonder the budget is used up. Nonetheless, he decided to bite his tongue until he got the lay of the land.

The first session of Texas Congress opened a few days after

Buck arrived in Austin. It consisted of twelve congressmen who represented all the districts of Texas. The *distinguished leader* gaveled the meeting to order at ten o'clock sharp.

It was a joke.

For an hour they listened to Wentworth go on and on about absolutely nothing. He recessed the meeting at eleven for lunch. "We'll meet back here at two o'clock sharp for an important afternoon session. I urge all congressmen not to be late."

Buck was stunned beyond belief. He sat in his assigned seat, which was in the very back row, and looked around at his other eleven fellow congressmen. They were laughing loudly, backslapping one another, and having a big ole happy time.

Is this what I came to Congress for? I don't think so.

Over the space of the next several days Buck stopped by the General Mercantile store and ordered himself a desk, chair, and filing cabinet and paid for it with his own money. He also special-ordered a newfangled invention just come out called the typewriter. It was a weird-looking contraption used to print words on paper so you didn't have to write them out.

Next, he went to an agency in Austin that specialized in locating workers. He arranged for several interviews with potential secretaries. After eight interviews, he hired Ms. Sarah Johnson, a thirty-something widow who had three children. She was very efficient and personable and previously worked in lower level politics.

"You'll need to be both my secretary and my assistant, if that's all right with you," Buck told her.

Buck offered her a very generous salary. She happily accepted the job.

"I'll need you to start on Monday."

There wasn't room in the office for two desks so they both shared the same one. In a week she had the office all set up and ready. Mrs. Johnson spent lots of time talking with the other secretaries and assistants, learning how to prepare bills and generally how things worked.

Now if I can just figure out what I'm supposed to be doing other than sitting and listening to a bunch of windbags that like to hear themselves talk.

His first chance to speak came on the eighth day of the current session. The leader asked if anyone had anything to say. He would live to regret the question. Buck rose from his seat.

"Mr. Speaker, I'm Congressman Buck Cordell from the southern district. I'm new at this, but since this is the first session, I suppose we are all new. I'm not a politician, I'm a cattle rancher and I'm not much on playing around with words so I hope you will understand if I'm a bit blunt.

"I accepted the appointment and came here to do something worthwhile for the citizens of my district and for Texas. So far, in the eight days we have been here, I haven't heard one single thing that would help anybody except those sitting in this room.

"I didn't come here to play around with a bunch of words or back-slap one another. I came here to make a difference in the lives of my citizens. If this is the way we represent the folks, it's no wonder they think we're nothing but a bunch of crooks.

"I've been working on a bill that I will be presenting in tomorrow's session. It calls for an open election of this body to elect the speaker instead of some *back room* appointment by a small group that got together and decided on their own.

"One other thing. I also talked to the editor of the Austin Sentinel newspaper. They will have a reporter sitting in the visitors' galley during every session from now on. He agrees with me that the folks we're working for have a right to know what's going on.

"I'm obliged for the time, *Mr. Speaker.*"

All over the room his fellow congressmen nodded their heads in agreement. Buzzing of loud whispers between them sounded like a beehive and drowned out the noise of the wooden gavel red-faced J. W. Wentworth pounded on the desk. Clearly many, if not most, of his fellow congressmen agreed with Buck.

"This session is adjourned!" the angry *leader* shouted before turning and storming out of the room.

More than half of the congressmen made a point to come by to shake Buck's hand and express agreement with his comments.

"It's about time somebody had the guts to say what lots of us have been thinking for the last several weeks," one of his colleagues told him. "When your bill is introduced, you have my full support."

Others expressed the same sentiment. Buck went back to his office feeling good.

"I don't know what you said in there this morning," Mrs. Johnson said as he entered the office, "but whatever it was, it must have been good. Everybody in the building is talking about it."

"That bill we've been working on…is it ready to go?"

"Yes, sir. I've double-checked it to make sure every *T* is crossed and *I* is dotted. They'll have a hard time rejecting it on a technicality."

"Good. Some reporter from the Austin Sentinel is supposed to contact me about being in tomorrow's session."

"He already has. His name is Bill Bradley. He stopped in to tell you his boss has given him this assignment and that he would be there tomorrow."

"I'm obliged, Mrs. Johnson. You are very good at what you do."

"Thank you, Congressman Cordell. I can say the same about you."

One of J. W. Wentworth's assistants appeared at the door. "Congressman Wentworth would like to see you in his office."

"Tell the congressman I'm pretty busy right now and that I'll stop by as soon as I find the time."

The man looked flabbergasted. He stuttered and stammered

and had a helpless look about him. "With all due respect, congressman, I believe he's expecting you now."

"Then he'll be mighty disappointed."

The assistant turned abruptly and left.

Mrs. Johnson held a grin on her face stretching from ear to ear. She ducked her head to keep from laughing out loud.

When Buck walked into Wentworth's offices a good hour later, he had a good mad worked up. He strode through the waiting room and into the secretary's office. Without a word, the blonde jumped up and entered the congressman's office without knocking. She came back in seconds and held the door open for Buck. He noticed she closed the door behind him.

Congressman Wentworth sat in his chair looking out the window at the busy streets of Austin. His back to Buck, he didn't turn around or acknowledge Buck's presence for several minutes.

Finally, he swiveled his chair around. His puffy face looked beet-red, his mouth hard-set and his eyes cold and hard. "Why did you deliberately challenge me in there this morning?"

"I was challenging the system. It needs changed. I'm gonna do all I can to change it. Unless I'm wrong, General Phillip Sheridan appointed you to congress just like the rest of us. Unless that appointment was as the *leader* of congress, I'd like to know how you got the job?"

"Well, some of us got together and decided I should serve in that position."

"And as the *leader* you control the budget no doubt?"

"Of course. That's one of the many responsibilities of the position."

"Who's the *some of us* you referred to?"

"I, I don't have to give you names."

"No, sir, I reckon you don't. But what you have to do is accept the bill I'm going to introduce tomorrow and bring it to a vote. If you don't, your refusal will be the next day's headlines in the Austin Sentinel."

"You'll get your vote!" the enraged man shouted. "It's plain you are nothing but a pig-headed cattle nurse. Now get out of my sight!"

Buck took a step forward and reached across the wide desk and grabbed a handful of the starched white shirt. He jerked the congressman forward, pulling him halfway across the desk.

"Now you listen. The only reason I don't throw you out that window is you might hit somebody when you land. Don't you *ever* talk to me like that again. I'll be having a heart-to-heart talk with General Sheridan as soon as he gets back from Washington."

Buck released the blubbering politician and left the room.

True to his word, the reporter was in the galley taking notes when Buck introduced his bill the next day. Wentworth begrudgingly accepted the bill and the court clerk read it before the house.

When it was put to a vote it passed by a count of ten to two.

After Wentworth announced the outcome of the vote, Buck rose to his feet.

"Mr. Speaker, in accordance with the bill we just passed, I make a motion that we elect a new leader of this congress."

One of his fellow congressmen jumped up and shouted, "I second the motion!"

Another congressmen stood up. "I nominate Congressman Cordell as leader of the congress and that he be elected by acclimation."

Yet another seconded that motion. In less than five minutes, his fellow congressmen elected Buck Cordell as their new leader.

CHAPTER XIX

Most years springtime arrived shyly with little warm winds that encouraged new sprigs of grass, pretty little buds on trees, and flights of geese in their long V formations heading south. This spring was different. It rained for six straight days.

Cody hunkered under the canvas canopy he stretched between some trees and thought a thank you to the old timer back in *Las Cruces* who talked him into buying the canvas tarp.

He figured he was getting close to Colorado, most likely somewhere in northern New Mexico. He hadn't seen a soul in almost a week and it was all right with him. Actually, he would rather be alone. It seemed every time he went into a town there was trouble. He was tired of all the killing. Learning to use a gun most likely saved his life on several occasions, but at what cost?

Cody lay under his makeshift tent with his head propped on his saddle. He liked the sound of the rain on the stretched canvas canopy. Other than the rain, it was so still he could almost hear his heart beating.

Sometime after dark the wind picked up. It rushed down

from the north with a fury, bringing with it an icy chill. Cody snuggled deeper into his bedroll and pulled his blankets tighter around his neck. Last night's fire burned down to no more than smoldering coals, but it was too cold to get up and add wood to it.

He decided to stay put as long as the rain continued. He had no place in particular to go and he was in no hurry to get there.

The next day he shot a large buck deer that came to the nearby mountain stream for water. He hung it from a limb, skinned it out and dressed it. *At least I can eat good while I'm waiting for the rain to stop.*

The rain continued for two more days before it stopped. By the time it quit raining, Cody had read *Gulliver's Travels* from cover to cover four times.

Cody woke to a clear sky. The stars twinkled like fireflies on a summer evening. Before the day was fully born he finished breakfast, broke camp and sat his saddle. Both he and his horses were fully rested and ready to hit the trail. He gave Cincinnati his head and let him set his own pace. Cody just settled in the saddle and went along for the ride.

The country dwarfed him to ant size. Off in the distant north he could see the purplish outline of tall mountains, their lofty peaks seemingly poking holes in the sky. Most of them wore white caps on top. This was new country to Cody. He couldn't have imagined there was country like this.

He followed close to a river he figured likely was the Canadian River. The terrain became more and more difficult to ride, forcing him to divert often because of high steep mountains and deep treacherous canyons.

It took him two days riding to locate a high mountain pass to negotiate the line of unbelievably tall mountains, bigger than a boy from west Texas flat country could ever imagine.

As he came down the mountains through which the pass was located, he was shocked to see a small town below in a deep valley. A month on the trail had dwindled his trail supplies. He needed to re-supply and decided to stop in the town.

A small sign beside the trail identified the town simply as *Trinidad.* Cody walked Cincinnati and his packhorse slowly along the hard-packed street. He reined up at a small livery stable and blacksmith shop on the edge of town.

A huge man with Texas-size shoulders wearing a leather Smitty's apron sauntered out to Cody.

"Afternoon," the blacksmith greeted cheerfully.

"Afternoon. Need to stable my horses for a day or two. Full grain."

"That'll be two-bits a day for stalling and grain, too. In advance."

Cody stepped down from the saddle and raised a stirrup to off-saddle his mounts.

"I'll take care of that," the liveryman said.

Cody fingered the change left in his pocket. He was running out of money. He figured he had less than four dollars left to his name. He needed to find some kind of work. Fishing four bits from his front pocket, he paid the man. "Is there a hotel in town?"

"Nope. There's a boarding house called Molly's. It's the white house at the other end of the street. Might get a room there. Just passing through? We don't get many strangers way up here."

"Yep. Just kinda chasing the wind. Am I still in New Mexico?"

"Nope. You crossed into Colorado when you come through the pass."

"Any work in this part of the country?"

"Not unless you're willing to dig a hole through solid rock in the side of the mountain looking for gold."

"Anybody finding any?"

"Not that I know anything about, but that don't stop 'em from diggin'."

"What's work like that pay?"

"Not near enough. Four to six-bits a day is about average."

Cody untied his saddlebags and slung them over his shoulder. He slid his Henry rifle from the saddle boot. "Obliged for the information," Cody said, touching a finger to his hat brim and heading up the street on foot.

Trinidad, Colorado was a busy town. Folks went every which way. Gold miners with picks or shovels over their shoulders, women in long dresses that touched their shoe-tops with two or more small kids holding onto their dress tails, heavy freight wagons pulled by a two-hitch team, and old men lounging in front of three saloons.

The sun was still only an hour or so high and already the saloons sounded noisy. Cody figured Trinidad must be a pretty rowdy place.

He passed a general mercantile store that looked well-stocked, a small café, a barbershop, a government claims office, and opened the gate in the white picket fence in front of *Molly's Boarding House*.

The house stood two stories with a wide front porch out front. A wooden porch swing hung from small chains. It appeared an inviting-looking place. He knocked on the front door.

The woman who opened the door was as shapeless as a barrel and just as round. Her snow-white hair wound on top into a bun. Her face was full and puffy with a wide, full-lipped mouth. Cody figured her to be somewhere on the sundown side of fifty. She grew a wide smile when she saw Cody.

"Ma'am, the fellow down at the livery told me I might get a room here."

Her smile widened. She stepped back and opened the front door wider. "Got one waiting. Come on in this house. What's your name? My name's Molly, course you already knew that, I reckon. Where you from, young fellow? If I was a betting woman, which I ain't, I'd lay odds you was from Texas. Am I right?"

Cody had never heard so many words strung together without even taking a breath. He swept his hat from his head as he stepped inside the door.

"Afternoon, Miss Molly. I'm called the Hondo Kid."

"Hmm, funny name for a handsome young fellow like you. Why they call you that? Don't you have a *real* name? Oh, well, none of my business anyway, I reckon. Come on in, your room is right in here, first door on the right."

"Mostly they call me that because I'm from Hondo, Texas."

The room was nice. It had a big wide bed, a dresser with a blue-speckled pitcher and washbasin, a straw-bottom rocking chair, a braided rug on the floor, and pretty lacy curtains over the window. He liked it. He liked it a lot.

"How much for the room?"

"Two-bits a day unless you want to eat, four-bits if you do. I serve two meals a day, morning and night. I got three other boarders. One fellow snores loud, but I put him upstairs by himself."

"I'll take it, food too."

"How long you gonna be staying?"

"Not sure yet. We'll see. Is there a place to take a bath?"

"Shore is. Try the shed out back. Water pump is right beside it. Help yourself.

"Supper is at eight o'clock. We eat late because most of my boarders don't quit work until dark."

"That's fine. I'll be there."

Cody stashed his saddlebags and rifle in his room and sat down on the soft featherbed. He sank about a foot into the mattress and broke a smile. Never had he slept on a featherbed. He was anxious to take a good bath and try out that swing on the front porch. Rummaging through his saddlebags, he found a clean pair of pants and shirt and tucked them under his arm to head out back.

He pumped water and filled the longish bathtub in the little wooden shed and settled himself into it. The water was cold, but felt good. He soaked until good dark before climbing out of the tub, dressing and heading toward the aroma of food he'd smelled for the last half-hour.

Two men sat on either side of the long dining table with a red and white-checkered tablecloth as Cody entered. All four looked to be straddling forty. One by one they stuck out work-calloused hands and shook his hand. He didn't bother giving them his name since they didn't give theirs. There was an empty chair at both ends of the table. He scraped one out and folded his tall frame into it.

The table was filled with food. Fried chicken, green beans, mashed potatoes, and hot rolls, with a quart jar of fresh honey sitting in the middle. Miss Molly brought a blackened coffee pot and filled each man's cup.

If this is the way we eat every night, I'll be bustin' buttons off my shirt in a week.

Miss Molly finally got everything on the table and took her seat at the other end of from Cody. Conversation from the four boarders was sparse, but Molly made up for it. *She can talk more and say less than any woman I've ever seen.* He just kinda let it go in one ear and out the other. Mostly he concentrated on his third plateful of food. He did manage to hear her when she announced apple pie for dessert.

He crowded in two pieces of pie before setting back with another cup of coffee. The four boarders retreated to their rooms. Miss Molly still talked like a runaway wagon. When she stopped to draw a breath Cody chanced an edgewise word. "You shore set a fine table, Miss Molly."

"Why, thank you, Kid. I feel funny calling you *Kid.* You shore you don't have a real name? Most folks who come through here don't use their real name, though. Don't know why. A person's name is real important. Separates him from everybody else. My whole name's Molly Murphy. My folks come from Ireland. You ever been to Ireland? I ain't either, but from what I hear it's a pretty place. Heaven on earth, one fellow told me. Course I got no idea how he knew, he was from Germany, I think it was."

Cody was amazed. All them words without taking a breath. He'd never heard anything like it.

"Think I'll step outside and enjoy that porch swing I saw when I was coming in," he said, rising. He could hear her still talking when he reached the porch.

The night was clear and cold. He shivered as he sat down in the swing. *Never sat in a porch swing before. Someday when I get my own place I'm gonna have me a swing like this.* For some reason the thought reminded him of Ellen Richardson from back in Waco, Texas. *Wonder how she's doing? Strange I would think about her. She's most likely married by now. Let's see, I'm seventeen. That would make her twenty-two or so. Don't matter none, I'll most likely never see her again. She shore was a nice lady, though.*

His thoughts shattered by gunshots from down the street. He automatically leaped to his feet without thinking. Just then Miss Molly pushed out the door casually, as if she hadn't even heard the shots.

"Reckon what the shooting's all about?" Cody asked.

She briefly flicked a glance down the street before sitting down beside Cody in the swing.

"Oh, that? Don't pay it no mind. That goes on most every night. Probably some miner got himself shot in a poker game. I swear, our graveyard is gonna have more folks in it than our town before long. The businessmen have been trying to hire a lawman, but Trinidad's got such a bad reputation nobody will take the job. We've had two so far, neither one of 'em lasted more'n a week. One got shot. The other hightailed it over the mountain. I swear to my time, don't know what the world's coming to."

Clearly Cody wasn't gonna get to enjoy the peace and quiet of the front porch and the swing for Miss Molly's non-stop ramblin'.

"Think I'll stroll down the street a while," he said, pushing to his feet.

"You watch yourself, young fellow. Some of those jaspers don't have to have an excuse to pick a fight. Not long ago the one they call Snake Tucker shot a fellow just because he didn't like the hat the man was wearing. He's a mean one, poison mean, that Tucker fellow. Everybody's afraid of him. He walks around like it's his private town, never pays for nothing. Folks are afraid to say anything. You watch out for that fellow."

Cody strode outside the gate and headed down the street before she took the next breath.

The first saloon he came to was called *The Golden Nugget*. From his earlier observations it was by far the nicest of the three he counted. He was about to push through the swinging batwing doors when a fellow come flying out through them, head over heels.

The man landed flat of his face in the dusty street. The giant that obviously did the throwing followed him outside carrying the man's hat, which he threw down beside the prone man.

"Don't come back," the giant growled before turning and going back inside.

Cody picked up the man's floppy hat and took the fellow by the arm and lifted him to his feet. He staggered a couple of times and shook his head before he got his bearings. "You hurt?"

"Naw, been throwed outta better places than that."

"Why'd they throw you out?"

"Caught the house dealer dealing from the bottom of the deck. I called him on it. Ole Bruno throwed me out. I shoulda known better than to say anything. Some get shot for less. They're crooked. They're all crooked. Everybody knows it, but ain't nothing anybody can do about it. I was lucky. Fellow got shot a little bit ago for doing less than I did."

"Pretty rough place, huh?"

"Mister, I been all over and I ain't seen worse. Much obliged for helping me get on my feet."

"Don't mention it," Cody said, turning and entering the saloon.

It was a fancy place to be way up here in the middle of nowhere. Two roulette wheels, two crap tables, and three green-covered poker tables, all of them crowded.

Two bartenders worked the long mahogany bar where men were standing shoulder-to-shoulder. Half a dozen saloon girls worked the room hustling drinks and men. A tinny-sounding piano sat on a small stage at one end of the room. The fellow doing the playing never looked at the keys, his eyes were fixed upon a young blond-haired girl sitting on a miner's knee nearby. It was obvious even to a newcomer like Cody she was the piano player's girl, or at least he thought so. He missed several notes when they rose and headed up the stairs together.

There were no empty chairs so Cody shouldered into an empty space at the bar.

"How much is a beer?" he asked the big barman when he wiped the bar in front of him.

"Ten cents," the man replied gruffly.

Cody laid a dime on the bar when the man set a heavy mug of beer in front of him. He turned his back to the bar and sipped while he looked over the room.

Most of the men were rough-looking miners. The clothes they wore marked them as such. A few seemed to be cowboy types, clearly down on their luck. The local businessmen in the room were dressed differently from the first two groups.

Cody spotted the man Miss Molly told him about right away. He was nattily dressed in black from head to toe, easy to see why they called him Snake. His hatband was made from a rattlesnake skin. He wore two pearl-handled Colts tied low on his legs. He had an evil-looking hatchet face in which his pale green eyes sat close together. Just like Miss Molly said, he never paid for anything. *Must be nice.*

The man sat at a poker table with shapely lady with dishwater blond hair, on his knee. She had one arm around his neck and the other hand held a glass from which she sipped continually. Now and then she moved her glass to his lips and let him take a long swallow.

Cody decided to walk over and watch the game. He carried his beer with him. They were playing five-card stud. Five players sat in the game. Snake Tucker had a nine showing in front of him on the table. The player to his left was the first man to bet and had a deuce showing. He folded. The second man to bet had a king on the table and bet two dollars. The third man folded the six of hearts. The next man folded. Snake called the two-dollar bet.

Another round of cards was dealt. When the man with the first king thumbed his card to look, Cody saw another king, giving the man a pair of kings, a strong hand in five-card stud. The man bet five dollars. Tucker didn't even bother to look at his card.

"I'll call your five dollars and raise you ten," he said, shoving fifteen dollars into the pot.

Cody heard several gasps of surprise at Tucker's call and raise without looking at his card.

The third round of cards was dealt. The pair of kings drew a ten. He bet another five dollars. Again, Snake showboated it by not looking at the card dealt him.

"Call and raise you another ten," Tucker said loudly, smiling and looking around the room, obviously showing off for the onlookers.

The last card hit the table. The kings thumbed up his card slowly, cautiously. Cody stood right behind him and saw a second ten. That gave him two high pairs, almost an unbeatable hand with Snake's nine showing on the table. The man bet ten dollars.

There was already forty-two dollars in the pot, a huge amount for the miner with the two pair. He was smiling. Without so much as a glance at his card, Tucker said louder than before, "I call your ten dollars and raise you twenty."

The miner looked bewildered. His opponent not only called every bet, but raised the bet each time, all without even looking at his cards. He hesitated before pushing the last of his money into the pot.

"Call," the man said nervously as he turned over his two pair.

"Two pair. Good hand, but not good enough. I've got three nines," Snake announced loudly as he reached both hands and raked in the huge pot.

The man looked confused. He glanced frantically around the table. "You've got to show them," he said meekly as he reached for Snake's cards.

Tucker jumped to his feet, grabbing the man's hand before he could turn over the cards. In the process, he dumped the blonde saloon girl to the floor, causing her to spill her drink down his fancy yoke-buttoned shirt.

"I said I had three nines!" Snake shouted, one of the pearl-handled Colts suddenly appearing in his hand like lightning. "You calling me a liar?"

The unarmed man turned white as a sheet. His eyes rounded like saucers. His tongue made a circuit of his obviously dry lips. He dropped his head and shook it from side to side before turning and walking away

Snake watched the man until he disappeared through the front door. Then reaching a hand, he grabbed a handful of the blond hair and jerked the girl to her feet, his face red with anger.

"You spilled a drink on me!" he yelled, swinging the gun in his hand sideways. It struck the girl across her cheek. Pieces of her teeth and blood spewed from her mouth. A gargled scream burst from her throat before she crumpled to the floor unconscious.

Rage boiled up from deep inside Cody. Before he realized what he was doing his own Colt whipped out. He swung it backhand. The blow struck Snake Tucker square on his right ear. The force of it knocked him backwards over the poker table, spilling everyone's money. Tucker lay unconscious on the floor. It all happened in the space of a few heartbeats.

Folks scattered in every direction. The giant bouncer who had thrown the man out the door earlier came lumbering toward the melee. Cody saw him coming out of the corner of his eye and swung his Colt up just as the giant arrived. He stuck the Colt against the giant's large flat nose. Without a word, the bouncer raised his hands and took two steps backwards. Cody's lightening glance swept the room and saw no threatening movement.

"Cheating at a poker game is one thing," Cody said loudly. "Pistol whipping a lady for spilling a drink is something else again."

A large man in a black business suit approached cautiously.

"I'm Blackie Bishop. I'm the owner here. I'm beholden to you for what you done for my girl, so I'm gonna give you a little free advice. Don't be inside a hundred miles of here when Snake wakes up. Your life won't be worth a plug nickel. He's the best with those guns of his I ever seen."

"I'm obliged to you for the advice, Mr. Bishop, but I ain't run from nobody in my life and I don't mean to start now."

The saloon owner shrugged his shoulders. "It's your funeral."

Cody stepped over to the unconscious man and poured the rest of his beer into Tucker's face. He sputtered, groaned, and shook his head. A purple knot the size of a man's fist grew still larger on the side of his head.

"This town got a jail?" Cody asked.

A fellow dressed like a local stepped forward. "We got a jail. We just don't have a town marshal."

"Where would the key to the jail be?"

"I believe it's hanging on a peg by the door to the cells. Why you asking?"

"If you don't have any objections, I'm gonna lock this fellow up until he settles down some. You can let him out in the morning."

"He'll come looking for you sure as shootin'."

"I won't be hard to find."

Cody reached down and picked up the gun Tucker had dropped and stuck it under his belt before grabbing Snake under one arm.

"Help me get him to the jail," Cody told the local fellow.

The businessman helped lift Tucker to his feet. Together they half-dragged the man from the saloon and down the street to a small square rock building. The businessman pushed open the door. Once inside they found the keys to the cell located in an adjoining room. They placed Tucker in a cell and locked the door.

"Hope you know what you're doing, young fellow."

"Me, too," Cody replied, pitching the keys to the businessman.

"Didn't catch your name." the businessman said.

"Hondo Kid."

The man wrinkled an eyebrow. For a long moment the man stared at Cody. "I've heard of you. No wonder you weren't worried about Snake Tucker. He's fast sure enough, but I've heard you are the best there is. I'm Ed Hamilton. I own the General Mercantile store. I'm also the head of the town council.

"I saw how you handled that bad situation in there tonight. We're looking for a town marshal. Don't reckon you'd be interested?"

"What's it pay?"

"Hundred a month, if you last till the end of the month we'll raise it to a hundred and a quarter."

"You got a judge in this town?"

"Shore do. Judge O. J. Goodson. He's also the undertaker and the local doctor."

"Convenient. Who makes the laws?"

"The town council. I'm the president."

"Would the council back me up?"

"Son, if you can last the first month it'll be a site longer than the last two marshals we had. Long as you're enforcing the law we'll back you. You start making up your own laws then we got a problem. By the way, you ain't wanted by the law anywhere are you?"

"Not that I know of. I reckon you got yourself a town marshal."

"Just hold on right there. I'll go get the judge and get you sworn in all proper-like before you back out."

Fifteen minutes later, Cody was sworn in and had a town marshal's badge pinned on his *serape*.

CHAPTER XX

Buck Cordell had made an enemy. He knew Congressman Wentworth wouldn't forget Buck had cost him his cushy job as leader of the congress, even though Buck went out of his way to assure the *dethroned* congressman's assistant there would be no changes in office assignments under Buck's leadership.

Buck didn't know the first thing about what he was supposed to do as leader here, but he hadn't known anything about the cattle business, either.

Congressman Sullivan, from east Texas, was the parliamentarian of congress. It was his job to make sure the business of congress was conducted according to the law. Buck invited him to his office for a meeting.

"I'm gonna lay my cards on the table face up, congressman," Buck told him. "I haven't got a clue how or what I'm supposed to do as the leader. I want to do things by the book. I need help. Can you help me?"

"It's about time we had a leader who wants to do something besides talk. I'll help you any way I can. What can I do?"

Over the next two hours, Buck laid out the details of the bill he wanted to bring before the congress. As Buck explained the details, Congressman Sullivan became visibly excited. He smiled and nodded his head in agreement. When Buck finished, his colleague slapped his knee with a hand. "That's the most ambitious and far-reaching plan I've ever heard. If we can get this passed into law, it will revolutionize the state of Texas."

"So how do we get it passed?"

The first herd of the 1868 season arrived from Mexico on March 15th. Only two weeks remained until the first Longhorn drive of the season was scheduled to leave for Abilene, Kansas.

The ranch was a beehive of activity. Supplies for the long two-month drive had to be packed into the chuck wagon and supply wagon. Extra harness, ropes, chains, and wheels were taken along as backup.

Each trail crew consisted of twenty men plus two cooks and two helpers. Each cowboy was responsible for selecting and breaking five green range mustangs that would make up their personal string of mounts during the trip. These would become part of the two, fifty-horse remudas. A horse wrangler was responsible for each remuda.

Each drive consisted of five thousand head split into two separate herds of twenty-five hundred head each and separated by one day with a trail boss was in charge of each drive.

The Longhorn now employed twelve trail crews totaling almost three hundred men.

Chester allowed his slow gaze to fall upon each of his twelve trail bosses sitting around the large table in the chow hall. Cooks busied themselves preparing for the hungry cowboys soon to be pouring in for breakfast.

"Men, we've got just two weeks before the first drive pulls out. Each of you should double-check everything and then go back and check it again. If you forget something, it's too late once the drive pulls out.

"Like last year, Ray Ledbetter will lead the first herd. Smokey will be in charge of Ray's split-off herd that will pull out the next day. I've posted a lineup on the wall over yonder showing each trail boss and the day their herd will pull out.

"I can't tell you how important it is to keep your herds on schedule. Last year we got held up at the Red River because of high water. Something like that can't be helped. Work through it. If you run into trouble you can't handle, send for help. That's why we keep the herds only a day apart.

"Remember, we don't cut our herds for anybody. Giving the Indians a few cattle from the back of the herd is one thing, allowing some *regulator* or state *inspector* to cut your herd is something else again.

"Like last year, I'll be roaming back and forth along the trail. You need me, send a rider to find me. Anybody got a question?"

Chester waited a couple of minutes. "Then let's stretch our bellies and get to work. It will be light soon."

By daylight, over three hundred cowboys had been fed and headed out for a long day that wouldn't end until after sundown.

Rebekah and Selena arrived in the chow hall as the last bunch of cowboys was leaving. Each cowboy touched a finger to his hat brim in respect to the ladies. Chester sat at the long table sipping coffee.

The ladies filled their plates, poured a cup of coffee and sat down at the table with Chester.

"Thought I was gonna have to roust you ladies out of bed this morning."

"We overslept," Selena told her husband, leaning to kiss him good morning before she sat down to breakfast.

"I reckon the bosses' wives ought to have a few extra privileges," Chester kidded them. "Heard anything from Buck?"

"Got a letter yesterday. The postman sent it out from town by one of the supply wagons. He said he expected to be home before the first drive left."

"Did he say how things were going up there in Austin?"

"Yes, he said they got off to a rocky start, but things had settled down now and they were starting to get some things done. Guess what? Buck's the new leader of the congress. He said he'd explain when he got home."

It was well past midnight when Cody returned to Miss Molly's boarding house. A single lamp still burned dimly from a table in the hallway. He picked up the lamp and carried it to his room. After removing his holster and Colt, he laid them on a bedside table within easy reach.

Lying on the soft feather bed in the dark, his mind wandered.

A lawman? Leaping lizards. What have I got myself into? Trinidad seems like a nice enough town. Reminds me a little bit of Waco. Waco. Now there's a place I could settle into. Reckon how Miss Ellen is doing? Prettiest lady I ever seen. Maybe I'll go back there someday. Maybe someday.

The aroma of fresh coffee woke Cody from a sound sleep. He sat up in bed, stretched, and suddenly remembered he'd become the new town marshal. He swung out of bed, hurriedly dressed, washed up, and stomped on his boots.

The other boarders obviously already ate breakfast. They left as Cody walked into the dining room and poured a cup of coffee from the big pot.

"Morning, young fellow," Miss Molly greeted loudly as she came in from the kitchen carrying a plateful of scrambled eggs, sausage, flour gravy and hot biscuits. "I figured you'd be late so I left the lamp on for you last night."

"Yes, ma'am. I'm obliged."

The boarding house matron set the plate of food in front of Cody. As she did, she saw the marshal's badge pinned to the front of his *serape*. Her eyebrows arched. "What's that?" she asked, clearly taken aback.

"I took the job as town marshal last night."

"Why would you go and do something like that?" Concern shone her face. "I told you what happened to the last two. That job is the next thing to suicide. There's some around here who use that badge for target practice."

"Yeah, I met one of them last night," Cody said around a mouthful of biscuit. "Fellow called Snake Tucker."

"You didn't! The way I hear it he's the worst of the lot. Don't tell me you had a run-in with that sidewinder? He's the one who killed our last marshal. Shot him dead right in the middle of the street."

"Yes, ma'am. Fact of the matter, he's locked up down in the jail. I had to conk him on the head last night. More'n likely he ain't in too good a mood this morning. Reckon I best fetch him some breakfast."

"You watch yourself, young fellow. They say that Tucker fellow is meaner than the snake he's named after. Lordy me! Never figured you for no lawman."

"Me neither," Cody said, sopping the last of the gravy from his plate with a biscuit. "Sure was good, Miss Molly. What time is supper?"

"Same time every night, just after good dark, but I'll save you some in case you're late."

"I'll be here."

Cody stopped by the livery and picked up his sawed-off double barrel shotgun and a box of double-aught buckshot to have at the jail, just in case the marshal's job turned out to be as tough as they said it was.

His next stop was the small café across the street from the marshal's office. He ordered a plate of breakfast and a pot of coffee to take to his prisoner.

Opening the door to the marshal's office, he put his shotgun and shells in the drawer of a rickety desk.

"Hey!" Tucker called from the jail cell in the next room. "Whoever it is out there, let me out of here!"

Cody opened the heavy wooden door that separated the jail from the office. The prisoner wore a knot beside his ear the size of a man's fist and a king-size mad on.

"Brought you some breakfast," Cody said, holding the plate of food in one hand and the pot of coffee and a tin cup in the other.

"It's you! You're the one who blindsided me last night. What're you doing wearin' that badge? You ain't the law."

"I am now."

"What you got me locked up for anyway? I didn't do nothin'!"

"You pistol whipped a saloon girl last night. That's why I hit you over the head."

"You mean Sadie? She ain't nothin' but a common saloon whore."

"What she is or ain't's got nothing to do with it. You can't go around pistol whipping folks just because you feel like it. Better eat the breakfast I brought you. It may be a while before the judge gets around to a trial."

"Don't want no breakfast. I want out of here!"

"Suit yourself," Cody said, setting the plate of food on the floor just out of the prisoner's reach.

"Didn't you hear me, boy? Let me out of this stinking place!"

"Does smell kinda rank, don't it? Maybe I can find a bucket of water and mop so you can clean the place up some."

"Ain't cleaning nothin'."

"We'll see," Cody said, picking up the pot of coffee and stepping through the door to his office and locking the door.

Cody poured himself a cup and sat down in the chair behind the rickety desk just when Ed Hamilton, the storekeeper and councilman strode in. "I see you're still on the job," he commented, settling into the only other chair in the office.

"You think I wouldn't be?"

"Well, I suppose you've already heard the life expectancy of a town marshal in Trinidad is usually a week or so."

"Yes, sir, I heard something like that."

"And you ain't scared?"

"Scared will get a man killed quicker'n scat."

"Where you from, kid? Didn't get a chance to ask you last night."

"From a little place called Hondo, Texas. It's less'n a day's ride west of San Antonio."

"Where you staying?"

"Over at Miss Molly's boarding house. She shore sets a good table."

"Molly's a fine woman."

"How's our prisoner this morning?"

"Bellyaching about getting out."

"You gonna let him out or haul him up in front of the judge?"

"I figure it's about time Mr. Tucker learned how to behave around womenfolk. What do you reckon the judge would give him for pistol whipping a woman?"

"Don't know. Most likely a fine and a few days in jail."

"Yeah, sounds about right. I'll stop in and talk to the judge after while."

"Well, reckon I better get over to the store. Somebody might actually want to buy something today."

Before Cody finished his coffee, the door opened again and the judge walked in.

"Stopped by to see if we still had a town marshal this morning."

The undertaker and part-time judge was a tall skinny fellow with a long handlebar mustache curled up on both ends. He wore a three-piece black suit and faded white shirt.

Cody motioned to the pot of coffee sitting on the pot-bellied stove.

"You're welcome to a cup," Cody said. "Just brought it from the café for our prisoner, but he don't feel much like eating, I don't reckon."

"Aw, yes, Mr. Snake Tucker, the town's bully. You gonna charge him with something or let him out?"

"Ain't it against the law to pistol whip a lady?"

"Last I heard it was."

"Then I'm gonna charge him with pistol whipping a lady."

"That's called *assault* and *battery.*"

"What'll he get for that?"

"Oh, I'd say a ten dollar fine and ten days in jail ought to be about right."

"When can we have the trial?"

"How about tomorrow? I'll get Ed Hamilton to be here and we can do it right here. Shouldn't take more'n a few minutes."

Cody nodded his approval.

"I've gotta be going. Got a lot of sick folks."

"Don't tell me you're the doctor, too?"

"Yep. Only one within two hundred miles."

"You're a busy man."

The next day, the judge, Ed Hamilton, and Cody stood outside Tucker's cell for the trial. Tucker couldn't have heard a word the judge said because he was shouting obscenities the whole time. The judge held a handkerchief to his nose during the entire proceedings, which took no more than three minutes.

"Mr. Snake Tucker," the grim judge said. "You're charged with one count of assault and battery for hitting Miss Sadie in the face with a handgun. I find you guilty as charged and order you to pay a fine of ten dollars and spend ten days in jail."

With that said, the judge turned on his heel and walked out, followed closely by Ed Hamilton and Cody.

"It smells like a hog pen in there," the judge complained.

"I'll see about getting it cleaned up in the next day or two," Cody told them. "How do I know what's against the law and what ain't?"

"Just do what you figure's right," the judge told him. "We'll let you know when you're wrong."

Cody wrinkled an eyebrow. He'd have to think on that a while.

By the third day, Snake Tucker couldn't stand the smell any longer and decided to use the mop and bucket of soapy water Cody set just outside the bars of his cell.

"When you get it clean, I'll bring you something to eat," he told his prisoner.

"I'm gonna kill you, kid!" Snake shouted.

"Yeah, you've told me that a hundred times already."

"I mean it. You're a dead man!"

Cody discovered being the town marshal of Trinidad was mostly a nighttime job. During the daytime he lounged around the office trying to find something to keep him occupied. Nighttime in Trinidad was something else.

When the miners got off work or when the cowboys from one of the ranches the other side of the mountains came to town, they wanted to let off steam in one of the town's three saloons. That meant drinking, gambling, and fighting. Most of the time the fights were with fists and whatever happened to be within reach, sometimes it meant gunplay.

This was his third night on the job. He made it a practice to patrol the streets after dark and check the saloons regularly until they closed, which was usually around midnight. He always carried his sawed-off double barrel with him after dark.

Halfway to midnight, Cody strolled along the dark street. Up ahead the light from a small saloon called the Trail's End painted a square pattern in the dusty street. It had been a quiet night with only a couple of fights.

Suddenly a shot rang out up ahead from inside the saloon. Another followed only a few seconds later. Cody broke into a trot.

He paused at the open front door and looked inside.

A young cowboy stood in the middle of the room. He held a gun in his hand, waving it back and forth around the room at a bunch of angry miners. Blue smoke curled upward from the barrel. In his other hand he held a whiskey bottle by the neck from which he took frequent long swallows.

On the dirt floor lay a man in miner's clothes in a gathering pool of blood. He wasn't moving. Cody took a deep breath, thumbed back the twin hammers of his shotgun and stepped through the door. "Drop the gun! I won't say it again."

The drunken cowboy swung a look in Cody's direction. He blinked his eyes and squinted. For a moment he stared hard at Cody. Their gazes caught one another's and held. Several men moved silently out of the line of fire.

Cody waited. A hushed silence hovered over the room. He saw the cowboy's lips tighten and knew the meaning. The man whirled in Cody's direction, raising the gun in his hand.

The explosion of the shotgun going off in the saloon was deafening and rocked the small room. The heavy load of buckshot lifted the cowboy off his feet and propelled him backwards. He landed flat of his back unmoving.

Cody stepped over, removed the gun from the cowboy's lifeless hand and stuck it behind his belt. He bent and felt for a pulse on the miner the cowboy shot. There was none. The man was dead. Two bullet holes in his chest leaked blood onto the floor.

Cody turned to the bartender. "Tell me what happened here."

"The boy's name is Trace Higgins. His pa owns a big spread across the mountain. He comes in every now and then. He's sweet on Etta Mae. Her and Mike, the fellow on the floor, had been in the back room. They were just coming out when young Higgins got here. He saw them. They argued. Trace shot him. That's about all there was to it. You know the rest."

Cody bent and searched the dead man for a weapon. There wasn't any.

"Did the dead man go for a gun or anything?"

"Nope. He didn't wear a gun."

"Anybody else here from the Higgins ranch?"

Two cowboys stepped forward. One was a young fellow about the same age as the Higgins boy. The other was an older man, maybe straddling forty or so. The older fellow spoke up.

"Trace was drunk. He didn't know what he was doing."

"Drunk's no excuse. He shot a man who didn't have a gun. That makes it murder."

"His pa ain't gonna like this one bit."

"Mister, tell your boss what happened here. Tell it like it happened. Whether he likes it or not is no concern of mine."

The two Higgins riders hurried from the saloon, mounted and hightailed it out of town.

"He was right," the bartender told Cody. "Old man Higgins thought that son of his hung the moon. He's gonna be looking for blood when he finds out you shot his boy."

"Somebody get the undertaker," Cody said, ignoring the bartender's comments.

As it turned out his request wasn't needed. *Undertaker/Judge/Doctor,* O. J. Goodson walked into the saloon followed closely by Ed Hamilton. The councilman watched anxiously as *Doctor* Goodson knelt to check both of the dead men. After examining each man he looked up and shook his head.

"What happened?" the councilman asked.

"Young Higgins was sweet on one of the saloon girls. He walked in as she and the miner there was coming out of the back room. They argued. The Higgins boy pulled out his gun and shot the miner. The miner wasn't wearing a gun.

"I heard the shots. When I came in he was still holding his smoking gun. I ordered him to drop it. He didn't. He turned the gun on me and I shot him."

Hamilton thought a minute. "This is bad. This is *real* bad. Arlis Higgins is a hard man. He's got a big spread. He swings a wide loop in this part of Colorado. I've known him and been selling him supplies for years. He's gonna be hoppin' mad when he hears about his boy. Somebody's got to ride over there and break the news to him. I sure don't wanna be around when he finds out."

"Two of his riders were here with the Higgins boy. They lit out after it happened."

"This is bad," the man repeated. "No telling what Higgins will do. If he takes a notion, he might burn this whole town to the ground. Did you *have* to shoot the boy?"

Cody gave the councilman a sideways frown. When he

answered his voice was hard. “It was either shoot or get shot. What would *you* have done?”

“I’m not faulting you. I suppose you did what you had to do. I’m just saying there’s gonna be trouble over this.”

“We’ll just have to cross that creek when we come to it,” Cody said.

They charged into Trinidad at a gallop near high noon the following day. Arlis Higgins rode out front on a high-stepping golden palomino. Twenty men followed closely, each with a rifle propped upright on their leg. A wagon pulled by matching black horses brought up the rear.

Higgins reined up in front of Hamilton’s store. His men spread out along both sides of the street and sat their horses. The wagon pulled up in front of the undertaker’s office. Cody watched the arrival from in front of the jail.

Ed Hamilton stepped out onto the porch to meet him. Even from the distance, Cody could tell the councilman was cowed in the presence of the big rancher. Cody couldn’t hear what was being said, but it was plain the rancher did most of the talking.

After a few minutes, both men stepped off the porch and headed in Cody’s direction.

Higgins was a big man, big and tall and rangy with wide shoulders. His face looked weathered down to its elements. He walked with the self-assurance of one used to being in charge.

He wore Levis and a khaki shirt with a leather vest over it. His boots were polished to a high sheen and the wide-brimmed Stetson over his salt and pepper hair most likely cost more than Cody’s entire month’s wages. He also wore a holster around his waist that carried a bone-handled Colt. Hamilton struggled to keep pace with Higgins’ long-gaited steps as the two men approached. Cody leaned his back against the wall of the jail and waited.

"You the one who shot my boy?" the rancher demanded, his deep voice loud and angry.

"Yes, sir. He murdered an unarmed man. He was waving his gun around at other folks when I walked in. I told him to drop the gun; instead, he turned it on me. I had no choice. I had to kill him or he would have killed me, and maybe other innocent people."

"He was drunk! He didn't know what he was doing!"

Anger ripped up Cody's spine. He skewered Higgins with a look and bit down hard on what he wanted to say, instead he said evenly. "Explain that to the man he murdered. Your boy killed a man in cold blood, Mr. Higgins. He would have killed me too, if I hadn't stopped him. I'm sorry your boy is dead, but wrong's wrong and shooting down an unarmed man is as wrong as you can get."

"You'll pay for this!" Higgins snarled through closed teeth, his angry eyes flashing pure venom. "Mark my word. You'll pay for this. I'll see to it!"

The rancher spun on his heels and strode across the street toward the undertaker's office.

Ed Hamilton hadn't moved nor said a word during the conversation. He stared at the toes of his boots.

"You can have my badge, if it'll help," Cody told him.

The councilman shook his head slowly.

"No, you done what you had to do. We can't ask more than that. It may cost us, but we'll stand behind you."

Cody just nodded. Hamilton turned and walked slowly back toward his store. Across the street, Higgins stood by with his head down as four men loaded a wooden coffin into the wagon for the long trip back to the ranch.

CHAPTER XXI

It was only two days before the first Longhorn herd was supposed to pull out for the long drive to Abilene, Kansas. Rebekah was expecting Buck's return from Austin for the past week. She grew more and more anxious with each passing day.

Little Cody was asleep under the watchful eye of Rosetta, his caretaker. Rebekah grew restless. She walked outside. The night air fet crisp and cool. The velvety night wrapped itself around her. She peered up through the pale wash of moonlight at the stars. One particular star was brighter than the others, *their* star. Her gaze fixed on it. A raw ache rose from her heart and lodged in her throat. She felt tears escape her eyes and trail across her cheek.

His last letter said he would be home before the first drive left. Maybe something happened to him on the long trip home.

"Mrs. Cordell, are you okay?" one of the guards asked as he made his rounds.

Rebekah's thoughts scuttled away like mice before lantern light at the sound of the guard's voice. She scrubbed away the tears with the back of her hand and drew a shaky breath. "Yes, thank you. I'm just enjoying the beautiful night."

"Goodnight, ma'am," the man said as he moved on about his rounds.

Buck reined his buggy through the gates of the Longhorn compound just shy of sundown. The guards on the wall shouted their *welcome home* and waved him through with a sweep of their rifles.

It's shore good to be home. He pulled the team of horses to a stop beside the barn. The old Mexican stableman hurried out to take charge of the horses. Young Christopher Lopez, the boy Buck and Carlos rescued from the banditos down in Mexico, trotted up and took Buck's luggage from the buckboard.

"Gracias, Amigo," Buck said, as he ruffled the boy's hair.

Young Christopher flashed an ear-to-ear grin that showed a mouthful of pearly-white teeth.

"Where's Mrs. Rebekah?" Buck asked the boy as they headed for Buck's *hacienda.*

The boy pointed to Chester and Selena's home.

"I see you're doing better on understanding English. That's good."

"Si, I learn *rapido."*

Buck smiled and pointed to his luggage and then to his house. The boy nodded and hurried on toward Buck's home. Buck angled toward Chester's house.

They were having dinner when Buck walked in.

Rebekah turned her head, saw him, and leaped from her chair. She rushed into his open arms, wrapping her own arms around his neck and planted a long kiss on his mouth.

"Maybe I need to go away more often," he joked, after the kiss ended.

"It's so good to have you home," she said, circling his waist with an arm as they walked to the table.

"Welcome back," Chester greeted, standing and sticking out his hand. Buck took his partner's hand and shook it warmly.

"It's good to be home."

"Have you eaten?" Selena asked, as she stood and placed a plate in front of an empty chair.

"I'm starved."

While Selena poured Buck some coffee, Rebekah disappeared and returned momentarily with little Cody. Buck stood and took his son in his arms.

"He's grown so much since I've been gone."

"Yes. He's already sitting up and crawling."

Buck hugged his son and held him close for a time.

"So," Chester said, "how was Austin? Did you get those politicians straightened out?"

"No, I can't say that, but I can say we passed some important legislation that's gonna change Texas for the better."

"How's that?"

"Well, for one thing, we passed a law expanding an existing homestead act and provided for the recruitment of immigrants. Southern and southwestern Texas, from here and including the big bend country, has been slow in developing. Those who have homesteaded are isolated and vulnerable to renegade Indian attacks. We've asked the army to establish several new forts to protect them.

"Once the forts are in place, we will actively recruit new settlers and grant homestead rights for as much as one hundred-sixty acres to each head of household."

"Any danger of the homesteaders settling on our land?" Chester asked.

"No, we're talking about public land. Most of it is north of Del Rio. But enough about politics. How are the drives shaping up?"

"We're ready. Ray leaves with the first herd tomorrow. Smokey and his bunch leave the next day. I'll be leaving with the third herd in a week.

"Carlos and his boys did a good job down in Mexico. The Mexican ranchers have delivered right on schedule. Things are looking good."

Rebekah said, "When will you have to go back to Austin?"

"Not until September. I've decided to go along on this year's drives to help Chester and the boys, though."

Buck saw the look on Rebekah's face. He knew she would require more of an explanation than this.

The four friends enjoyed their meal, brought Buck up-to-date on all that went on during his absence, and visited far into the night. It was the other side of midnight when Buck and Rebekah made their way home.

"The house girl prepared a warm—" Rebekah left the thought unfinished, giving Buck a long, slanting look.

"Bet I can get in it before you can," he laughed, prying off his boots as he crow-hopped across the floor.

In record time they were soaking together in the warm water, wrapped in one another's arms.

"I missed you so much," Rebekah whispered, her voice breathy and low.

He looked down at her for a very long time, his eyes unfathomable, his gaze holding hers. "I missed you too, pretty lady," he said, finding her inviting lips with his own.

Later, they stared at the ceiling in the afterglow of love. Buck spoke softly through the darkness.

"I want to explain why I think I ought to go on the drives. I know I've been away several weeks and I hate leaving again so soon, but I don't feel it's fair that Chester shoulder all the responsibility of this year's drives. He went alone last year. I can't ask him to do it alone again this year."

Rebekah was quiet for a long minute before reaching to take his hand.

"I know. I'm being selfish. I know you should go. It's just that I miss you so much when you're gone."

They hugged. Moments later they fell asleep in each another's arms.

A blind cow could have followed the trail. Old Baldy, their bell cow, with two round trips the previous year, lit out at a brisk walk. She followed the wallowed-out trail scarring the countryside left by forty thousand longhorns that made the journcy the year before.

Chester left with the third herd led by Buster Keene. Buck waited another week and accompanied Link Stone's herd. It was the third week of the driving season and they now had six herds on the trail to Abilene with twenty-five hundred head in each.

As usual, the first few days on the trail were the worst. The half-wild longhorns had seemingly only one thing they wanted to do; return to the thickets which had been the only home they knew since birth.

Bunch-quitters were a constant problem. Cowboys with coiled lariats swatted them back in line. Drag riders spent their days eating the dust of twenty-five hundred cows and keeping the stragglers moving.

The first few days they were in the saddle from dark to dark, usually changing horses every two hours. It was always full dark before they got the herd circled and settled down for the night. By then, after sixteen hours on the trail, they were ready for a nights' rest and gave the night herders little trouble.

The trail-weary cowboys straggled into camp, almost fell from their saddles, wolfed down supper, and after a long cup of coffee around the campfire, crawled into their bedrolls. They knew Cookie would have them up, fed, and back in the saddle before first light.

Buck ranged up and down the trail, visiting each herd along the way. He made it a point to spend a night or two with each crew.

It took thirty-three days to reach the Red River crossing. Zack Gibbs, their scout, and Chester waited there for Buck.

"I scouted all the way to the Kansas line," Zack told them. "It's gonna be a rough drive from here to there. We got five more rivers to cross after the Red. On top o' that, the Indians are thicker than fleas on a mangy dog. Offhand I'd say the worst part of the drive is still in front o' us. But the graze is good and there's plenty of water."

"Sounds like a piece of cake," Buck joked. "Are the lead herds already headed that way?"

"Ray's lead herd is still a week or so from the Washita River crossing," Chester said. "I told him we'd catch up to him before that."

"Sounds good. Any signs the Indians might give us trouble?" Buck asked their scout.

"Saw plenty of 'em, but they were mostly tolerable."

Buck and Chester stayed at the Red River crossing until the next two herds crossed safely before riding north. As they rode they kept a sharp eye out for Indians. A week later they caught up with Ray's lead herd.

"We figured to cross the Washita first thing tomorrow," Ray told his bosses.

"I scouted the river for several miles in both directions," their scout told them. "The banks are steep and the bottom is boggy, but this is the best crossing I could find,"

"Whatta you think, Ray?" Buck asked.

"We'll make do."

* * *

The water wasn't deep, but like Zack had said, the bottom was soft. Several longhorns got bogged down. When they did, two cowboys threw ropes over the critters' head, did a half-hitch around their saddle horns and pulled them out.

By the time they got the first herd safely across the river, Smokey's second herd was approached. Fortunately, only three head were lost during the two days it took to get both herds across the Washita. Up ahead, just two days' drive away, they faced the wide and sandy-bottomed South Canadian River.

Indians appeared in an eye blink. The fresh-born sun hadn't crested the hilltop off to their right when one of the cowboys spotted them and alerted the crew.

"Indians!" He pointed with an upraised arm.

Buck and Chester rode beside Ray Ledbetter and Zack Gibbs in front of the first herd. They were a day shy of the North Canadian crossing. The cattle were snatching mouthfuls of April fresh green grass from the long narrow valley they traversed.

The three men joined the rest of the trail crew as they crooked their necks to look. Sure enough, at least half-a-hundred bare-chested Indians sat atop their ponies on the crest of the hill.

For several minutes the Indians sat motionless, staring down at the vast herd of cattle stretched in a thin line from one end of the long valley to the other. Buck and his men stared back at the onlookers.

Ray said, "What you reckon they got in mind?"

"If'n I knew what an Indian was thinkin,' I'd be drawin' more'n fifty a month and found," Zack said. "Most likely they're waiting to get a look at our herd of horses."

Bucked shifted in his saddle. "We'll wait 'em out."

They didn't have to wait long. Three of the Indians separated from the others and heeled their ponies down the hillside toward Buck and his men.

"Tell your men to keep the herd moving until we see what they want," Buck instructed. "But tell them to keep their Spencers handy just in case things turn sour."

Ray wheeled his horse back to issue Buck's orders. Buck, Chester, and Zack urged their mounts forward to meet the Indians.

"The tall one in the middle would be the leader," Zack said without diverting his gaze from the oncoming Indians.

Buck and his men reined to a stop and waited. As the three Indians approached, Buck took the leader's measure.

He was tall for an Indian; tall, thick-chested, and slender of waist. His long black hair hung in two braids across broad shoulders. A single eagle feather protruded from his hair.

His face was dark brown and weathered, high cheek bones. His coal-black eyes were expressionless and stared straight ahead. He carried an army-issued 1861 model Springfield rifle musket propped against his left leg. The Indians reined to a stop about ten yards from Buck and his two companions. Buck noticed the horses the three leaders were riding. They were old and slat-ribbed.

For a long moment the Indian leader sat motionless, staring with a fixed gaze directly at Buck. He moved a fisted hand to touch his chest.

"Me called Kotkoshyok. Chief of Akaka Choctaw."

Buck mimicked the chief by touching his own chest with his fisted hand. "My name is Buck Cordell. These are our cattle."

"You cross Choctaw land. You pay or no cross."

"How much pay?"

"Ten horses," the chief said emphatically, eyeing the high-bred black gelding Buck was riding.

Buck shook his head and fixed a stern look on the chief. He turned a slanted look at Zack Gibbs.

"Tell the chief we'll give them a reasonable number of cattle from each herd that comes through, but we won't give him horses."

Zack used a combination of English, Choctaw, and sign language to relay Buck's message to the chief. As the scout spoke, Buck watched the chief's face closely for any change of expression. The stone-faced leader's gaze swung between Zack and Buck.

After several minutes of negotiation they all agreed ten cows must be cut from each herd for the privilege of crossing Choctaw land, but none of their cattle or horses would be bothered.

The chief agreed and Buck shook the chief's hand to seal the bargain. After the handshake Buck swung his leg over the saddle and loosened the cinch strap. He slid his saddle off the black and handed the bridle to the chief.

The stone-faced chief's face softened. His eyes went wide with surprise.

"Tell the chief I give him two gifts, the black horse and my friendship. Tell him that I wish him long life and many sons."

The scout relayed Buck's message. The Choctaw chief stared at Buck for a long moment. He nodded his head just once, turned his worn out pony around, and led his new high-spirited black horse away at a gallop.

"That was a mighty nice thing you did, Pard," Chester said. "But it's sure a long walk to Kansas."

"I was hoping to ride double with you."

Chester grinned and reached a hand to help Buck swing up behind his saddle.

They reached the South Canadian River a day later and were delighted to find it at low level. The first two herds were able to wade across with little trouble. *So far so good,* Buck thought.

"That's the last troublesome river we've got between here and Kansas," Zack told his bosses. "All that's left are the North Canadian, the Cimarron, and the Salt Fork of the Arkansas. They won't give you no problem."

"Then I reckon I best ride back down our back trail and check on the other herds," Chester told Buck. "I'll let our trail bosses know about the deal we reached with the Choctaw. I'll catch up with you in Abilene."

Three weeks later the first herd crossed the Kansas state line. They wouldn't have known except for the scrawled *unwelcome* signs posted every quarter-mile as far as the eye could see.

THIS IS KANSAS
Texas cattle ain't welcome!

Buck, Ray, and Zack reined up and read the sign.

"Now that ain't very neighborly," Ray said.

"It's the shorthorn cattle growers in this area. They're up in arms about Texans bringing our cattle into Kansas. They say our longhorns carry some kind of *fever* or something with the ticks our cattle carry," Buck explained. "Seems the ticks drop off and then infect their shorthorn cattle. Their breed of cattle can't tolerate the ticks like longhorns can. So they passed a law banning our longhorns from entering the state.

"A fellow named Joseph McCoy built a town where there wasn't anything but a few mud huts, talked the railroad into running a spur line to it, and somehow convinced the governor to allow Texas cattle into the state inside a mile-wide corridor that starts at the state line and ends in Abilene."

"Maybe we didn't hit the line at the right place."

"Why don't we hold up the herd until I can scout around," Zack offered. "Maybe I can find that strip, if there is one."

"Might be good," Buck agreed. "We don't want any trouble unless it's brought to us."

They allowed the herd to graze in a grassy meadow for the rest of the day. Zack rode off to look for the so called *Texas corridor.*

Supper was over and the Longhorn cowboys sat and sipped around the campfire just when Zack rode into camp. He dismounted and turned his horse over to one of the wranglers as Ray handed him a cup of coffee.

"Any luck?" Buck asked.

"Yep. It's there all right. We missed it by about four miles. The signs were torn down but the corridor is there and clearly marked. I ran into an old timer who lives in a small shack by a creek.

"He said a bunch that called themselves *jayhawkers* watches corridor like a hawk. Said they were a bad bunch and we better watch ourselves if we was bringing a herd through."

Peering over the lip of his coffee cup, Buck said, "*Jayhawkers,* huh?"

Then Ray spoke up. "I've heard about them, but I thought they were just a bunch of makeshift vigilantes using the Civil War as an excuse to rob, rape, burn towns, and murder innocent folks."

"That's all they were," Buck explained. "You've heard about Quantrill's Raiders? "They're all cut from the same cloth. Sounds like they're up to their old tricks. Only now they're using this tick scare from Texas longhorns as their excuse. We better sleep with one eye open between here and Abilene. Because of our delay, our second herd is only an hour or so behind."

They posted extra guards, especially around the remuda and the camp.

The following day they threaded the herd into the corridor leading to Abilene. The lead riders of the herd were no more than a mile or so into Kansas when they spotted riders approaching from the north. Buck and Ray saw them, too, and signaled the rest of the Longhorn hands. Another man galloped back to the second herd with word to bring their men forward.

Buck judged there to be near twenty in the approaching band. The leader rode a dappled gray marked much like Buck's. As they drew near they spread out, forming a wide line. Each of them carried a rifle in his hands. They reined up thirty yards away. The leader separated from his men and walked his mount forward.

Buck, Ray, and Zack sat their horses and waited.

The leader was an average size fellow. He carried a new model Henry rifle lying across his saddle. "Howdy. Where you fellows headed with those cows?"

"Who's asking?" Buck said.

"Name's Colonel Henry Bledsoe of the Kansas Cattlemen's Association. It's my job to intercept Texas cattle and turn them around. The law says Texas cattle ain't allowed in Kansas."

"Is that right? It's my understanding this corridor is exempt from that law."

"You understood wrong, mister. You got a choice. Either turn the herd around and head 'em back where they came from, or I'm authorized to impound your herd and place them in quarantine."

"That's how it is, is it?"

"That's how it is. Course we're reasonable folks here in Kansas. If you don't want to drive your cattle all the way back to Texas I'm authorized to give you a fair price for 'em."

Buck stalled for time. He could see by the expression on the Jayhawker's face that the Longhorn riders were arriving and taking up positions. The man's eyes kept shifting from Buck to the Longhorn men. "And just supposing I was willing to sell my herd to you. What are you offering?"

"Oh, I think a dollar a head ought to be fair."

"Then you'd take them into Abilene and get forty dollars a head for them. Ain't that right?"

"No, they'd be held in quarantine until they can be inspected."

"Well, *Mr. Bledsoe*. Let me tell *you* how it is. I ain't about to sell my cattle to a bunch of cattle rustlers posing as some sort of official.

"Now you got a choice. You and your men can ride out of here *in* your saddles or *over* them. If you ain't outta rifle range in two minutes we're gonna start emptying saddles, starting with you."

A look washed over the man's face. His eyes widened as he flicked a look at forty men facing him with Spencer saddle rifles to their shoulders. He jerked his dappled gray around and motioned his men to turn around and ride away.

Buck rode into Abilene, Kansas at mid-afternoon on June 5, 1868. He saw what seemed to be an endless complex of stockyards stretching endlessly along a single railroad track.

As he rode along Texas Street he counted over a dozen saloons, half that number of mercantile stores, and a three-story, box-looking hotel called the Drover's Cottage. Next door to the hotel sat the largest livery stable he had ever seen.

He reined up and stepped to the ground as a black man waited to take his horse. He untied his saddlebags and slid his rifle from the saddle boot.

The hotel was a wooden structure with a lengthy shaded veranda. It was painted beige with green-louvered shutters framing each window. Buck stepped up onto the porch and through the double wide front doors that included stained glass in their top halves.

The inside of the lobby appeared elegant beyond anything he had seen before. It featured a large chandelier, elegant oriental rugs, a restaurant, a billiard room, a bar, and fifty spacious, lavishly furnished rooms, according to what he'd been told.

"May I help you, sir?" the desk clerk asked stiffly, casting a disparaging look at Buck's dirty trail clothes.

"I'd like a room, the best you got."

"I'm sorry sir, but I'm afraid we're completely full. There are no rooms available. You might try the small boarding house down the street."

Out of the corner of his eye he was aware of two men walking out of the restaurant, but he didn't bother looking their way until one called his name.

"Buck Cordell, is that you?"

He swung a look and recognized Harvey Owens, the cattle buyer who had contracted to buy all their cattle.

"Hello, Harvey," Buck said, accepting the offered hand.

"It's good to see you. I'd like you to meet Joseph McCoy. He's the one who built Abilene from the ground up." Buck turned his gaze to the man beside Harvey.

Joseph McCoy was a tall, thin fellow with a longish face, high cheekbones, a moustache and beard that hung to his collar. He had a high forehead, bushy eyebrows, and dark, piercing eyes. He wore a dark business suit and a white starched collar shirt with a string tie.

McCoy stuck out his hand. Buck took it and shared a warm, friendly handshake.

"It's good to meet you, Mr. Cordell. Harvey was just telling me about you. He said you were bringing lots of longhorns up the trail to our little town."

"More'n a few."

"Are you just checking in?" Harvey Owens asked.

"Well, I was, but I understand there are no rooms."

"Nonsense," McCoy said, turning to the red-faced desk clerk who'd been listening and shifting nervously. "Give Mr. Cordell the governor's suite," he ordered.

"Yes, sir," the desk clerk said, hurriedly handing Buck a key.

"I hope you enjoy your stay," McCoy told him.

"I'm much obliged."

"Could you join Harvey and me for dinner tonight?" McCoy then asked.

"Don't know why not."

"What say we meet in the restaurant around seven?"

"Good. That will give me time to wash off some trail dust." He shook hands with the two men again.

After arranging for a bath to be brought up shortly, Buck walked up the street to a large mercantile store and purchased a new suit of clothes, new boots, and a gray Stetson. Returning to his room, he found a steamy-hot bath ready and waiting.

It took a while, but the soap, hot water, and long relaxing bath soon soothed his saddle-sore body. Afterward he dressed and went downstairs.

Joseph McCoy and Harvey Owens were waiting for him at a special table near the back. They stood as Buck walked up, exchanged handshakes and sat down. A waiter in black pants and white shirt hurried up with a silver coffeepot and poured Buck a cup.

"How far out is your first herd, Buck?" Owens asked.

"Couple of days. The second herd is another day behind the first."

"Harvey tells me he contracted with you for all your herds this year. He says you have one of the largest ranches in Texas."

"Not really. We've only got ten thousand acres."

"Really? Judging by the number of cattle Harvey tells me you are bringing up the trail this year, I would have guessed your ranch to be much larger."

"No, we just catch a lot of longhorns out of the thickets."

"I would say you do. How many cattle do you expect to deliver to us this year?"

"In the neighborhood of forty thousand head, more or less."

"My, my, that's a large neighborhood. Well, we certainly appreciate you bringing your herds to Abilene. As I'm sure Harvey has told you, I own the bank as well as most of the businesses in Abilene. It will be a pleasure doing business with you."

"Looking forward to it."

They enjoyed a wonderful dinner and talked cattle talk for another hour after the meal.

Buck pushed back from the table and stood.

"I hope you gentlemen will excuse me. It's been a long trip and I'm looking forward to that feather bed upstairs."

He spent three weeks in Abilene. During that time six herds arrived, were counted, and loaded on to waiting cattle cars. He rode out of Abilene with checks for fifteen thousand head, totaling $630,000.00.

CHAPTER XXII

Cody opened the heavy door leading to the jail area and stood in front of Snake Tucker's cell.

"The judge gave you a ten dollar fine and ten days in jail. Your ten days are up. If you can pay the ten dollar fine I'll let you out."

"I've got ten dollars," the man said with a snarl. He fished the money from his pocket and threw it through the bars at Cody's feet. "Like I said before, I'm gonna take pleasure in killing you as soon as I get out."

"Do yourself a favor and ride out of town," Cody told him, as he inserted the key and swung open the door to Snake's cell.

Cody stepped back away from the door and handed Tucker his holster and gun.

"In case you're wondering, I took all the shells out of your gun and belt."

"I'll be seeing you again real soon," Tucker stomped out of the office shouting back over his shoulder. "You're a dead man. You hear me? A dead man!"

Cody watched him through the office window. He headed for Hamilton's mercantile, most likely to buy some shells.

His suspicions were right. A few minutes later Tucker emerged from the store. He stopped on the boardwalk and loaded his gun before stepping into the street and heading back toward the marshal's office. Ed Hamilton came out of his store and followed along the boardwalk.

Cody figured it would come to this. He knew a man like Tucker couldn't—or wouldn't—let bygones be bygones. A man whose very existence depended upon his ability to bully and intimidate others couldn't live with everyone knowing he had been bested at anything.

Withdrawing his Colt, he checked the load; it was full. He replaced it in his belly holster and covered it with his serape…and waited.

He didn't have to wait long.

"Hey, kid!" Tucker shouted from the street. "Come on out and face me like a man!"

Taking a deep breath, Cody let it out in a long, slow slide. Delaying what was about to happen wouldn't change anything. He opened the door and stepped outside.

Tucker stood in the middle of the street facing the office, thumbs hooked under the front of his gun belt in a braggart's stance.

"I told you I was gonna kill you!" Tucker screamed even louder now that he had an audience. "You can't hide behind that tin star! Nobody pistol whips Snake Tucker and lives to tell about it! Nobody!"

Cody glanced up and down the street. Town folk gathered on the boardwalk and in doorways all along the street. Others peered cautiously through windows. Ed Hamilton stood in front of the undertaker's office beside Judge Goodson.

"Walk away, Tucker," Cody said. "You don't have to prove anything. Walk away."

"Not on your life. Get it?" Tucker laughed. "*Not on your life!*"

"Okay," Cody said, frustration sounding in his voice. "Have it your way."

He used his left hand to flip the edge of his serape back over his right shoulder and stepped off the boardwalk into the street.

Is this it? Cody asked himself. *Will this be the time? Will my life end here in a dusty street in Colorado? Is this what life is about; proving you are faster than another man just to stay alive? There's got to be more to life than this.*

He wiped the thoughts from his mind and fixed his attention on the latest face to stand before him, the face of Snake Tucker. Cody's unblinking stare locked upon his opponent's eyes.

Time stood still. Seconds seemed like a lifetime. For a short slice of eternity the two men stood facing one another. The balance of a life would be determined in the next moment. One would live. One would die.

He saw it in Tucker's eyes an instant before he clawed for his gun. The braggart's eyes squinted. His lips compressed. His hand flew like a lightening bolt to the gun on his hip.

Instinct, born of natural ability and untold hours of practice, took control of Cody's body. He was only vaguely aware that his own Colt was magically in his hand, that it sent shock waves racing up his arm once, and then again. It was like a dream in slow motion when he saw Snake Tucker stagger backwards on wobbly legs, his unfired gun curling from his fingers and falling toward the ground.

Cody watched in trancelike awareness as the gunman before him toppled over backwards. It seemed to take a very long time for the body to land on its back in the dusty street. Tiny puffs of dust rose around Tucker and hovered over the fallen man like a small cloud of demons waiting to claim his soul.

Blue-gray smoke curled upward from the nose of Cody's weapon. Only then did he realize he held a great breath of air locked inside him. He let it out in a long sigh and replaced his Colt in its holster as wide-eyed people rushed forward.

"Never seen anything like it." the storekeeper exclaimed. "I didn't even see you draw, it was so fast."

Cody said nothing. He just lowered his serape, turned, and walked back into his office.

As was the custom, Trace Higgins lay in his coffin in the living room for two days. All work ceased on the Higgins Ranch during the time of mourning.

Mrs. Higgins was a sickly woman, bedridden and unable even to be carried downstairs to view her son's body. The news about his death drove her even deeper into the silent world in which she existed for the past two years.

Juliana, Trace's younger sister by two years, was shattered by her brother's death. She moved about the house in a trancelike state, refusing even to look at the body.

In happier times she was a bubbly, happy-go-lucky person, always able to find something good in most anything. But now she moped around and took long walks alone around the sprawling ranch.

She had returned from an exclusive school for young ladies in Denver only two weeks earlier. She knew Trace was a showoff and braggart. He always had been. Still, that was no reason for him to be gunned down in a filthy bar in an argument over some common saloon whore.

Juliana pulled the crocheted white shawl closer around her shoulders against the chilly mountain breeze. Touching the shawl reminded her of happier days.

This is the shawl mother made for me before I went away to school.

Thoughts of her mother hurt her heart. She liked to remember her mother the way she was before she got sick. Folks from far and near talked about how beautiful Leona Higgins was with her long, coal-black hair that hung almost to her waist, her dark, flashing, laughing eyes. Her full lips always seemed to be smiling. Juliana always thought of her mother as the most beautiful woman she had ever seen. It made her feel embarrassed when people said she was her mother made over.

She had always been closer to her mother than to her father. Trace was her father's favorite of the two children. Whatever Trace did, her father made excuses for. He always had.

Like the time he slipped around and crippled a neighbor boy's horse by cutting its leg tendons because it could outrun Trace's horse.Or the time he caught a poisonous mountain rattler and tied it under the covers of one of the hand's bunk because he dared argue with Trace.

The story her father told about the shooting over in Trinidad didn't make sense.

Why would some lawman shoot Trace down in cold blood over an argument about some saloon girl? When Trace is buried and things settle down a bit, I'm going to find out exactly what happened. I've got to know.

Without even realizing it, she had walked the two miles from their house to her favorite place in the whole world. It was a small, bubbly mountain stream meandering down from the high mountains. It slid lazily over rounded rocks and through a small clearing bordered by tall pine trees that reached toward the heavens.

As a young girl, Juliana used to lie on the moss covered bank for hours staring up at the puffy-white clouds, her childish mind forming them into all kinds of images.

Once she even saw her knight in shining armor, riding a charging white steed, coming to sweep her up and take her away to some far off castle to live happily ever after.

Now, she sat down on the soft bank of the stream and cried.

* * *

The funeral was over. Arlis Higgins had buried his son, his only son. His racking grief gave way to raging anger.

They'll pay! He swore over the grave of his son. *They'll all pay! That lawman who murdered my boy will die slow. Very slow. I want him to have time to think about what he did. I want him to suffer the way my son suffered, the way I'm suffering.*

I want that town to pay for what they done, for hiring that murderer and calling him a lawman. I've got to make them pay! I'll burn the town! I'll burn it to the ground. I won't leave enough for folks to know there was ever a town there.

The day after the funeral, Arlis called his foreman into the den. "I've got a job for you," Higgins told him. "I want you to ride into Denver. I want you to hire twenty of the toughest gunmen you can find. Promise them top wages. I want men that ain't afraid to use a gun and know how to follow orders."

"They'll be wantin' to know what they'll be expected to do for their money. What do I tell 'em?"

They'll find that out when they get here. If that don't suit them, they're not the men we're looking for."

"Mr. Higgins, I've worked for you for fifteen years. Not once in all that time have I questioned an order you gave me, but this time I've got to ask. Are you sure you want to do this?"

Arlis Higgins's face flushed blood-red.

"If you can't do the job I'll fire you and send someone else!"

The foreman cowed in the face of anger like he had never seen from his boss.

"Whatever you say, boss."

"Don't come back without twenty men who will do whatever we tell them to do, understand? And keep this quiet. I'll tell the others I sent you to Denver to buy a breeding bull. Don't bring them here to the ranch. We'll put them up at the old abandoned silver mine north of here."

Higgins handed his foreman a leather billfold with a thick wad of money in it.

"Don't let me down on this, Roy."

"I won't, Mr. Higgins. I'll be back as soon as I can."

"I'm going to ride into town tomorrow," Juliana told her father at dinner.

He jerked his head up and stared hard at his daughter before replying.

"I don't want you in that town," he said emphatically. "I don't want you having anything to do with those people."

Juliana was dumbfounded. She wrinkled her forehead in surprise.

"Why not? I want to see my friend, Mary Ann. It's been two years since I've seen her and I also want to pick up a few things from the store."

"Because they murdered my son—*your brother*—that's why."

"But it's been two weeks since we buried Trace. Blaming them won't bring him back. You've never objected to me going into town before. What's different now?"

"I told you. That bunch *murdered* my son. I forbid you to set foot in that town ever again."

"That's ridiculous. Besides, it's the only town within two hundred miles. I'm riding into town tomorrow, with or without your permission."

Juliana jumped up from her chair and stormed from the room. She climbed the stairs and stopped just outside her mother's room. For a moment she paused, listening for any sound from inside.

The door opened and Louisa, her mother's personal caregiver, stepped from the room.

"Is Mother awake?"

"*Si.*"

Juliana stepped into the room. Her mother lay in the big mahogany poster bed near the window. She was covered to just above her chest with a white sheet. She wore a creamy-white nightgown. Juliana could smell the lingering aroma of a fresh bath. Her mother's long black plaited hair lay over her chest.

Juliana hated seeing her mother like this. She didn't even know if her mother was aware of her presence. She visited several times every day since returning from school in Denver.

She sat by her mother's bedside, holding her hand or caressing her face, sometimes for hours at a time. She was always met with the same blank, expressionless stare. It was like her mother was in another world; a world without feeling or pain or hurt. It seemed to be a peaceful world.

It was late when Juliana left her mother's room and went down the hall to her own bedroom. A hot bath waited, prepared by the two Mexican house girls. She quickly undressed and stepped into the tub.

After a long leisurely bath she slipped her nightgown over her head and sat down in front of the large mirror on the dresser. She spent a half-hour brushing her long black hair and gazing at her reflection in the mirror and thinking.

Why was father so adamant against me going into town? We've done business in Trinidad for as long as I can remember. We've got lifelong friends there. It's the only town for hundreds of miles. It makes no sense.

The reflection staring back at her in the mirror was that of an eighteen-year-old girl who had matured into a woman in the past year. She saw a picture of what her mother must have looked like when she was Juliana's age.

Juliana saw her own creamy, golden-brown flawless skin with high cheekbones that reflected her Indian heritage, dark, flashing eyes, a slim-waist, but possessing womanly features that turned the head of nearly every man she encountered.

She tossed her shining hair over her shoulders, blew out the lamp, and climbed into bed. Sleep evaded her. For a long time she lay awake reflecting on the events since her return from Denver.

It's not the same as I remembered. Everything has changed.

The next morning at breakfast her father seemed in a better mood. Juliana came down dressed in her riding clothes and sat at the table without a word.

She wore black riding pants, black high topped boots, and a blood-red, buttoned blouse open at the neck. A matching red ribbon held her long hair together as it hung down her back to just above her waist.

"I see you're still dead-set on riding into Trinidad?" her father said, not looking up from his coffee cup.

"Yes, I am."

"I don't want you to go, but if you insist, at least take a couple of the ranch hands with you. The way things are around here these days there's no telling what kind of riffraff you might run into."

"I will. It's too far to make it back today. I'll be back sometime late tomorrow. I'll either spend the night at Mary Ann's or in Miss Molly's Boarding House."

"Be careful, and don't listen to some of those wild stories you're liable to hear about your brother's murder. No telling what kind of lies they're spreading."

Juliana rode out right after breakfast on her favorite horse, a high-stepping, solid white mare named Snowflake.

Two of the older hands from the ranch accompanied her. It was a four hour ride into town. They rode most of the way in silence. The ranch hands had been instructed by her father not to speak to his daughter unless they were spoken to.

They rode into Trinidad just shy of noon. She told the hands to meet her in front of Hamilton's Mercantile at noon the following day. They touched finger and thumb to their hat brims and rode off to find the nearest saloon.

Juliana walked her white mare through town toward her friend's house. She had been told that Mary Ann and her husband lived about a quarter-mile west of town.

Cody stepped out of his office just as Juliana rode past. He took one look and stopped dead in his tracks. *Who is that? I've sure never seen her before.* His gaze followed her as she rode slowly down the street. He couldn't take his eyes off her. *That's the most beautiful woman I've ever seen.*

As she rode past she happened to glance in his direction. For one brief instant their gazes met. A soft smile lifted the corners of her lips. He smiled back. Then she was gone. He watched her until she rode out of sight. For several minutes more he stood motionless, staring down the road after her.

As he went about his duties that afternoon he couldn't get the picture of the pretty lady out of his mind. The memory of her kept flashing before his mind's eye, he remembered every detail of her brief smile, those flashing, dancing eyes, and her long, silky-black hair.

Unable to shake her memory, he walked over to Hamilton's store. "Afternoon, Ed."

"Afternoon, kid. Seems pretty quiet in town today."

"Yeah, well, just wait until tonight. The rowdies don't come out of their holes until after good dark."

"Suppose you're right. But it's been pretty peaceful even at night lately. We haven't had a shooting in almost a week. That's a new record. It's got to where a fellow can get a little sleep without getting woke up by gunshots."

"Say, Ed, I saw a lady ride through town earlier on a solid white mare, real high-stepper. The mare I mean, but the lady was real pretty too. Any idea who she might be?"

"Would you be asking *officially* or *personally*? Though I can't blame you, she's a mighty pretty lady. That would be Juliana Higgins, Arlis Higgins' daughter. She's been away at school in Denver for a couple of years. I heard tell she was back."

"She just rode through town like she was headed somewhere."

"She was most likely headed out to the Jessup place about a quarter mile west of town. Her and Mary Ann Jessup's been friends since they was knee-high to a jack-rabbit. Mary Ann's married to a no-good named Harvey Jessup. He's lowdown. Won't work. He ain't worth shooting. Steals anything that ain't nailed down. It's a wonder you ain't had a run-in with him before now."

"Miss Higgins is sure a pretty thing," Cody commented, hardly hearing a word the storekeeper was saying.

"She is that, sure enough, but the fellow who throws a loop over her head will have his hands full. Besides, look who they'd have to put up with for a father-in-law."

"Yeah, I see what you mean. Well, just curious, that's all."

Juliana reined up in front of the rundown shotgun shack and couldn't believe her eyes. *Mary Ann lives here?* She couldn't believe it. The tiny two-room shack looked as if it would simply collapse in the first strong wind.

Knee-high weeds choked the front yard. Trash lay strewn about the yard. The only window in the front of the house had rags stuffed in the holes where glass should have been. Half a dozen mangy-looking hounds announced her arrival as they emerged from under the front porch.

Her friend had married Harvey Jessup only a few weeks after Juliana left for school on her sixteenth birthday. Rumors were she was with child and had to get married. The rumors turned out to be true. Less than ten months later she had their second baby.

Juliana was shocked and repulsed to see her friend was living this way.

Her first thought was to turn her mount and ride away, not because of where her friend lived, but because Mary Ann would be embarrassed to have Juliana see how she lived. But just as Juliana was about to leave the door opened.

A scroungy-looking, shirtless, barefooted man with two weeks' growth of whiskers, and hair that hadn't seen a comb in months, stood there gawking at her. "Who are ya and what do you want?"

"Is this where Mary Ann Ledford lives?"

"Name's not *Ledford*. Name's Jessup."

"Yes, I'm sorry. I forgot. Is Mary Ann here?"

"She's here. What you want?"

"I'm Juliana Higgins. Mary Ann and I are best friends."

"Higgins, huh? You kin to that Higgins fellow who got himself shot a few weeks back?"

"That was my brother. Is Mary Ann here? Can I see her?"

"Yeah, she's here, but she's busy right now cooking vittles."

"Who is it, Harvey?" Mary Ann's voice called from inside the house.

"Some high-fallutin' woman who says she's a friend of yourn. Name of Higgins."

"Juliana!" Mary Ann shrieked and rushed to the door. The person who squeezed past the man didn't remotely resemble the Mary Ann Juliana remembered.

She was barefooted. Her dress hung on her thin body. Her hair looked a mess and she had a naked child propped on one hip. She quickly passed the child to her husband and leaped from the doorway to the ground. There was no step.

Juliana stepped from her white mare to the ground just as Mary Ann flung herself into Juliana's arms. They hugged for a long minute. When they loosed one another Juliana noticed her friend's black eye, bruised cheek, and split lip.

"I didn't know you were back." Mary Ann said through tear-wet eyes. "When did you get home?"

"A few weeks ago. I would have come sooner, but mother is very ill and with my brother getting killed and all…"

"I heard about that. I'm sorry."

"Yes, it was tragic. My entire family is upset."

Mary Ann seemed to suddenly become aware of her appearance. She smoothed her flimsy dress and ran her fingers through her stringy hair and looked embarrassed.

"I…I'd invite you in, but, well, the house is a mess. Could we just maybe walk together?"

"Of course."

They strolled side-by-side along the road. No words were spoken for several minutes. "Mary Ann, I don't mean to pry, but are you okay?"

Her friend looked at the ground and slowly shook her head. Tears welled from her eyes. She lifted a hand to gingerly touch her bruised cheek.

"Did your husband do that?" Juliana's anger was evident in her voice.

A sob squirmed its way up Mary Ann's throat. "It's not his fault," her voice frayed as she spoke. "It's only when he gets drunk. He hurt his back and isn't able to work. Sometimes it gets to him and makes him angry. Maybe if I was just a better wife—"

"Stop it." Juliana interrupted. "Stop making excuses for him.

This is *not* your fault. Why do you put up with a husband who beats you?"

Again her friend ducked her head and slowly shook it from side-to-side. She raised her frantic gaze to Juliana. "What else can I do? All my folks are dead. I have two kids. I've got nowhere else to go. Besides, Harvey loves me."

Juliana drew a shaky breath. She felt her face flush hot. Anger boiled over and gushed out through her voice. "I can see how much he *loves* you. Mary Ann, you don't have to live like this. Come home with me. I'll have father give you a job there on the ranch. We'll take care of you and your children. You mustn't live like this."

"But I couldn't leave Harvey. He needs me. He's the father of my children," she protested.

Juliana drew a long, shaky breath and let it out on a sigh. It was clear she was wasting her words. Her friend had resigned herself to the conditions in which she lived and wasn't ready to change. Juliana sadly nodded her head.

"Okay, but just remember. If you ever decide differently, the offer still stands. I'll be there for you and your children."

They stopped and hugged for a long time before turning around and walking back to the house. Juliana took up the reins to her mare and climbed into the saddle. She looked back just once. Her friend stood in front of the house with the baby on her hip. Mary Ann lifted a hand and waved goodbye. Juliana returned the wave.

It was a long and sad quarter of a mile back to town. She tried to comfort herself that she had done all she could do for her friend. Until Mary Ann decided to make a change, there was nothing anyone could do.

She decided to go to Miss Molly's boarding house and arrange for a room for the night, but first she needed to care for her mare. She reined up and stepped down in front of the livery stable.

"Howdy to you, Miss Juliana," the liveryman greeted, taking the reins to her mare as she untied her saddlebags. "Ain't seen you in a 'coon's age."

"Good afternoon, Mr. Cox. I've been away at school in Denver."

"Real sorry about your brother."

"Thank you. I'm going to stay at Miss Molly's tonight. Will you see to my mare?"

"Shore will. Good to see you again."

Juliana raised her hand to acknowledge his words as she walked away. She made her way along the boardwalk and nodded a hello to several folks who recognized her and spoke.

The sun was sliding its way toward the distant mountains. *Sundown comes earlier here in the high country than it does in Denver.* The air was crisp and chilly.

Miss Molly's boarding house still looked the same as it did when she was a little girl. It would be good to see her old friend again. She stepped onto the porch and knocked on the door.

Molly screamed when she opened the door and saw Juliana. She wrapped her inside those big arms and hugged her to her ample bosom.

"Land sakes alive, child," she said pushing Juliana to arms length, but still holding onto her hands. "Look at you. You're all growed up into a beautiful woman. I'm not surprised though. I always said you was the best looking girl in Colorado. Come on in this house. Where you been so long? I heard you went off to school in Denver. Real sorry about what happened to your brother."

"Thank you, Miss Molly. I need a place to stay tonight. Do you have a spare room?"

"Well, you better know it. Come on in. I got a room all ready and waiting on you. I'd put you in the front bedroom, but I've got a nice young man staying with me. Say, come to think of it, you need to meet him. He's right nice. He's from Texas. You ever been to Texas? I hear tell it's hot as all get out down there. I don't like hot weather myself. Right in here. Make yourself at home. I'm in the middle of cooking supper. I tell you, these men can put away more vittles than you can shake a stick at. When you get all settled, come on in the kitchen and let's talk while I'm cooking. We've got some catching up to do."

The last few sentences Molly spoke as she walked away headed for the kitchen. Juliana didn't even bother to answer her. Molly hadn't changed a bit in all the years she had known the woman.

Juliana closed the door to her room and hung her saddlebag on the post of the rocking chair. She was tired. The long ride into town and the upsetting visit with Mary Ann had sapped the strength from her.

I'll just lie down for a few minutes before supper.

The aroma of food woke her. It was dark. She had fallen asleep. She swung her booted feet to the floor and splashed sleep from her eyes with water from the speckled wash pan, patted her face dry, brushed her hair with a brush from her saddlebags, and headed for the dining room.

Juliana was late. Everyone was already seated and spooning platefuls of delicious-looking food from bowls piled high. All the men stood up when she entered the room, including Cody.

Somewhere in Cody's mind he heard Miss Molly talking, but he was so taken aback by the pretty lady he didn't hear what she was saying. He couldn't take his eyes off the beautiful creature that just walked into his life.

The others had already sat down and Cody was still standing, his head spun like a child's toy top. The pretty lady pulled out her chair, glanced quickly at him and offered a small smile before sitting down. He felt himself blushing from ear to ear.

Suddenly realizing he was the only one still on his feet, Cody ducked his head in embarrassment and sat down. He tried hard to look down at his plate and not stare toward her, but as hard as he tried, his eyes wouldn't obey his mind. They kept sneaking looks toward the end of the table. Before she entered, he had been starving. Now he couldn't force himself to eat a bite.

Miss Molly kept up a steady stream of talk, mostly about next to nothing. Cody didn't hear a word she said anyway, his mind could think of nothing except the pretty lady at the end of the table. He did manage to pick up her name from Miss Molly's rambling. Juliana. What a pretty name. He said it over and over in his mind, though he knew there was no way he would ever forget it. Juliana. Even if she *was* the daughter of Arlis Higgins, she was still the most beautiful woman he had ever seen.

Supper was finally over and the other men straggled out one by one, leaving Cody alone with Molly and the pretty lady.

I suppose I ought to leave too.

Miss Molly stood and started gathering dishes from the table.

"I'll help you," the woman called Juliana said, beginning to rise.

"I won't have it," Molly said. "You're a guest in this house. I won't have you doing dishes. You just sit right there and enjoy your coffee."

Juliana settled back into her chair and picked up her coffee cup.

"What did Miss Molly call you?" she asked, giving him a look over the rim of her cup.

Cody had to swallow the lump in his throat before he could answer. "The Hondo Kid," he finally managed.

"What a strange name. I believe she said you are from Texas?"

"Yes, ma'am. I'm from a place called Hondo, Texas. That's why folks call me by that name."

"And you're a lawman, I understand?"

"Yes, ma'am, well, sorta anyway. Never done anything like that before, but I needed a job and that's all I could find to do. I'm not a *real* lawman, though."

"How long have you been here in Trinidad?"

"Not long, just a few weeks."

"Are you planning to stay?"

"Well, don't rightly know, ma'am. It's a nice place. I like it here. Might decide to stay, but haven't made up my mind yet."

"Would you do me a favor?"

The question surprised him. He stammered before he could answer. "Well, yeah, sure. What can I do?"

"You can stop calling me *ma'am*. My name is Juliana. Please call me Juliana."

"Yes, ma—I mean, yes. Of course. Do you live around here close? In town I mean?"

"No, I live a few miles over the mountain. My father has a ranch there. We raise cattle and horses."

"I see. I worked on a cattle ranch one time. I liked it real good."

"Oh? Where was that?"

"Down in Texas. The ranch was called the Brazos River Ranch. Real nice place. I liked it a lot."

"Why did you leave?"

"Oh…don't rightly know. Been trying to figure that out myself. Just got a hankering to see some of the country, I reckon."

"I've been away to school in Denver for two years. I just returned a few weeks ago."

"Never been to Denver yet. Might go someday. I hear tell it's a big city. Not much on big cities myself. Reckon I'm more of a small town fellow. How'd you like it?"

"Oh, it was okay, I guess. Like you, I prefer a smaller town. Would you like to take our coffee and sit on the front porch in the swing?"

Cody was shocked speechless. *Did I hear what I thought I heard? Did she actually ask me to sit in the porch swing with her?*

"Uh, yeah, I mean, yes, m—I mean, yes, I'd like that a lot." He stood on shaky legs and moved to help her with her chair, but she beat him to it and was already up by the time he got there. She smiled at him and picked up her coffee cup and headed toward the front porch. He followed along. His legs still wouldn't work right.

They sat down, side by side. His leg accidentally brushed against hers when they sat down. He quickly moved it like he had touched a red-hot stove. They sipped their coffee.

It was a star-studded night. The velvety night sky was littered with twinkling stars. They seemed so close it was as if one could reach out and gather a handful. Cody felt nervous as a cat in a roomful of rocking chairs. He had run out of words and couldn't think of anything to say that wouldn't sound really dumb, so he just waited…and enjoyed the moment.

"I love this time of the day," Juliana said. "It's my favorite time. When I was a little girl I use to sit on the front porch almost every night and look up at the stars. See that one right there, the brightest one?" She leaned close and lifted a hand to point. "That's my star. I claimed it when I was just a little girl. I used to look at it and make a wish and believe it would come true. Did you ever do that?"

"No, don't reckon I did. Did your wish ever come true?"

"Not yet, but it will. I still believe it will."

"I heard somebody say one time that if you believed something enough it would happen," Cody said. "How long are you gonna stay in town?"

"Just tonight. I'm going back home tomorrow about noon. Why do you ask?"

"Oh, no reason, I just thought maybe…"

"Maybe what?"

"I was just kinda hoping you might stay longer, that's all."

"I can't. At least not this time, but I'll be coming back to town before long. Will you be here?"

"Yeah, sure. I mean, I'm not planning on going nowhere."

"Good. Then I'll look forward to seeing you the next time I come." she stood then. "I better get to bed. It's been a long day."

"Yeah, and I need to get to work," he said, pushing to his feet with hat in hand.

"To work? You work at night?"

"Yes, ma'am—uh Juliana. That's when most of the rowdies come out. I'm a lawman, remember?"

"Yes, yes, I almost forgot. Will you be late?"

"Most of the night I reckon, at least till the saloons close down."

"Is it dangerous—being a lawman I mean?"

"Aw, I don't know. I reckon it could be sometimes. I don't worry much about it, though."

"Then I'll worry about it for you. Be careful tonight, okay?"

"Yeah. Yeah, I will, thank you."

She turned and started inside. Cody watched her go. At the door she stopped and glanced over her shoulder at him and smiled.

CHAPTER XXIII

Buck met Chester and one of the herds at the Cimarron River crossing. They sat their horses and watched the longhorns plow across the river.

"How'd it go in Abilene?" Chester asked.

"Went fine. Saw Harvey. Got a check in my pocket for the first six herds; six hundred thirty thousand dollars with more where that came from."

"All this is still hard for me to believe."

"Yeah, but this horse won't keep running forever. One of these days the railroads will reach down into our country. When that happens, the trail driving days will be over."

"Yeah, I reckon you're right," Chester agreed. "Just hope we get our share before those days come."

"Oh, there'll still be a market for beef, but I figure the days of the big profits won't last much longer. When the railroads get into our neck of the woods, the Mexican cattle ranchers will figure out they don't need us to market their cattle."

"Sorta hate to see it come to an end. I kinda got used to living high on the hog."

"By then, we ought to have our Longhorn Ranch cattle upbred and large enough where we can still make a healthy profit."

"You heading back home, Buck?"

"Thought I'd take it slow and spend some time with the other herds along the trail. How 'bout you, Chester? You going on into Abilene?"

"Thought I would. Kinda like to see the place."

"It's something else. Met the fellow who built it. His name's Joseph McCoy. Right nice fellow. Look him up when you get to town."

"I'll do that."

"He owns the bank and most everything else in town. I figured you'd be riding in. I told him to hold the other checks until you got there."

"You spending the night or riding on?"

"Riding on, I think. Seems like the drives are going well."

"Yeah, we had a small stampede a couple days back. Delayed us a day gathering the strays, but all in all it's going good."

"When you planning on heading back toward home?"

"Think I better wait till the last herd gets there. Tell Selena I miss her and I'll be home as soon as I can."

"I'll do it. So long, partner." They shook hands and Buck heeled his dappled gray south.

Buck made camp that night near a small creek. After a supper of bacon and beans, he sipped coffee beside his small campfire and thought about Rebekah and little Cody.

Sometime during the night, Buck's horses snorted. He came instantly awake, rolled out of his bedroll and had his rifle in his hands in two heartbeats. He hunkered down behind his saddle and listened.

It was a moonless night. Almost total darkness surrounded the dim light from his dying campfire. He heard nothing, and that was the problem. No night birds, no tree locusts. Nothing. That told him something, or someone, had disturbed them. Something was out there in the darkness.

"Cordell," a voice from the heart of blackness whispered. "Me, Kotkoshyok."

Buck couldn't believe his ears. It was that Choctaw chief he had given the horse to. *What's he doing out here in the middle of the night?*

"Come on in," Buck said softly, not sure why they were being so quiet.

From the depth of darkness the Indian chief stepped into the dim circle of light. He raised his right hand in a universal gesture of peace. Buck returned the greeting.

"Bad Indians come," the chief said. "They follow you. Steal horses. Kill you. I follow. I come help you. You my friend. They come now," the chief said, repeatedly glancing over his shoulder and speaking softly.

The only cover nearby was a large fallen sycamore only a few yards from Buck's camp. It would have to do. They quickly bunched a horse blanket under Buck's bedroll and hunkered down behind the log.

They didn't have to wait long. When the attack came, it came suddenly, without warning. One second the night was still, quiet. The next second, three dark silhouettes materialized out of the darkness. As silently as death they crept toward the bunched bedroll.

Buck and his Indian friend fired almost at the same instant. Two of the attackers went down instantly; the third one wheeled and made a dash for the edge of darkness and safety. He didn't make it. A slug from Buck's Spencer overtook him. He arched backward before toppling over onto his back. Buck's friend shook a nod and offered a thin smile. "You saved my life, my friend," Buck said, reaching to grasp the Choctaw chief's hand.

The Indian looked deep into Buck's eyes and smiled. Then he was gone without another word.

* * *

It took Buck three weeks to make it back home. He arrived in time to see the last herd leave the Longhorn headed for Kansas. It was August 16, 1868. With this herd, they had sent fifty thousand longhorns up the trail that year.

He rode into the Longhorn compound just shy of dark. The alarm bell in the guard tower sounded, announcing his arrival.

Rebekah sat at the desk working on books when she heard the bell. She could tell by the ring that it was announcing someone's arrival rather than an emergency. She cocked her head and listened. Again it sounded.

A surge of excitement raced through her as she jumped up and hurried to the front door, hoping against hope that it might be Buck. Through the dimness of fading light she saw the dappled gray. *It is Buck*. Her husband was home.

She raced to meet him. He saw her coming and broke into a run. She leaped into his open arms, buried her face in the hollow of his wide shoulder and laughed and wept happy tears.

"It's so good to have you home, my husband," she whispered.

"I missed you," he said on a heavy sigh.

Arm in arm they walked slowly home.

Later, after spending an hour with his small son, Buck and Rebekah bathed together. Lying in their bed in the dim light of a single candle, his knuckles traced a line along her cheek to settle under her chin. Gently he lifted her face to his and gazed into her tear-moistened eyes. Rebekah caught her breath in a long gasp.

Barely breathing, she shifted nearer and raised her lips to his; taking his wide, warm mouth with the fullness of her own. Buck drew her to him with the strong, sure sweep of his arm.

She closed her eyes and gave herself over to the sensation of his nearness, nestled closer and breathed him in.

* * *

Chester arrived in Abilene as the sun was settling behind the flat prairie. He checked into the Drovers Hotel and arranged for a bath to be brought to his room. After a leisurely wash, he dressed in the cleanest clothes he had in his saddlebags, which weren't all that clean, and went downstairs to the restaurant he spotted while checking in.

His steak order came with all the trimmings and was about to take his first bite when someone stopped at his table. He looked up and recognized Harvey Owens.

"Welcome to Abilene, Chester," Harvey said, sticking out a hand.

Chester stood to his feet and shook hands with the cattle broker. "Let me tell you, Harvey, it's a far piece from south Texas to Abilene."

"Yes, I suppose it is. Did you just get in?"

"Yep. A little while ago. Can you join me?"

"Don't mind if I do, at least for a cup of coffee."

"There's another herd just outside town. They'll be bringing them in tomorrow."

"You and Buck have done something no one else has ever done, a remarkable job. My bosses in Chicago are very pleased."

"Good. We want to keep them happy. Have the herds been arriving on schedule?"

"They have. Mr. McCoy has several checks he's holding for you. Buck told us you would pick them up when you got here."

"The last herd should be leaving our ranch right about now. It should be here in about two months."

"Well, it's been a great year. No doubt about it, you boys have stood the cattle industry on its ear."

Chester and Harvey talked cattle talk for an hour before the cattle broker excused himself to go to another meeting. Chester sipped another cup of coffee and then went to his room and turned in for the night.

Noise from the street woke him. He jerked upright, shocked to see it was well past daylight. He had overslept, something he almost never did.

He jumped out of bed, freshened up, and dressed, then hurried from the hotel and went directly to the livery stable. Then he saddled and gigged his horse out of town to meet the herd.

Chester met up with Link Stone and his herd just outside town. "Morning, Link." "See you got things under control, as usual."

"I've got a good crew. Something needs done, they do it. They don't have to be told. They're an easy bunch to work with."

"Yeah, the whole Longhorn crew is the best in the business. Cheyenne and his boys will be waiting for you by the stockyards. I'll wait there for you. Tell the boys we'll pay 'em off after the counting's done."

"It's been a long drive. They're ready to let off a little steam."

The counting ended just before sundown. Chester and Link were ready and waiting to pay off the hands. Each cowboy walked away from the pay table smiling with a hundred dollars cash money in their hands for two months' work.

Most made a bee-line for the nearest saloon. After finishing off the biggest steak the Drover's Cottage Restaurant had to offer, Chester and Link found their men in the Bull's Head Saloon.

Cigar and cigarette smoke hung like a thick fog. The stench of stale whiskey, unwashed bodies, and the brown splotches on the sawdust floor of expelled tobacco juice, was a recipe to turn most men's stomachs, but the half-drunk cowboys who crowded the room didn't seem to notice.

Like the other saloons in Abilene, this was a rough, tough, rip snorting place. If a fight didn't break out at least twice an hour it was considered a quiet evening. Most were simply disagreements that ended in fist-a-cuffs, but sometimes things got more serious and settled with gunplay.

Twenty Longhorn riders crowded around two tables pushed together filled with a mess of whiskey bottles, empty or nearly so. The noise in the saloon was deafening. Loud laughter from half a hundred cowboys and the shrill, playful screams from a score of saloon girls mostly drowned out the piano player's efforts at entertainment.

Chester strode to the bar and returned with six bottles.

"This round's on me," he announced as he set the bottles in the middle of the tables. "You boys enjoy yourselves tonight, but make sure you're ready to ride at the gray of first light."

They all let out a chorus of Texas whoops and grabbed for the nearest bottle. Chester watched his men enjoying themselves after two long, hard months on the trail and smiled.

One of the Longhorn men, a smallish fellow named Dink Wilson, announced loudly he had to make a necessary trip out back. His buddies all laughed as he rose, staggered a step or two, and headed quickly toward the back door on wobbly legs.

In his haste, he accidentally bumped into a fellow returning from the bar with a drink in his hand. The glass of whiskey jolted from the man's hand and thudded to the sawdust floor.

The man had all the markings of a gunfighter. He wore a bone-handled Colt in a tied-down, greased holster.

"Hey, drunk!" the fellow shouted. "You spilled my drink!"

"Oops, sorry." said the Longhorn cowboy as he staggered on his way toward the back door.

"Sorry don't get it!" the fellow shouted. "Turn around!"

The Longhorn cowboy stopped, staggered around to face the angry man, and had trouble focusing.

"I said, I'm sorry," Dink slurred his apology.

"That ain't good enough. I'm gonna teach you a lesson. You're wearing a gun. You got half a minute to go for it or I'm gonna kill you where you stand."

Chester had heard enough. He pushed up from his chair and thumbed the traveling loop off his Colt. He stepped between the two men who faced one another.

"Mister, you're talking to one of my men. He apologized for spilling your drink. I'll buy you a whole bottle if it will settle this without gunplay."

The gunfighter looked Chester up and down. His searching gaze settled on Chester's Colt tied to his right leg and his thumbs hooked under his gun belt on either side of his buckle.

"Then maybe I'll kill you first and then him."

The music and laughter suddenly stopped. A deathly silence settled over the room. Men hurriedly scattered out of the line of fire.

"You can try."

Chester's calm words caused the gunman to pause. For several heartbeats he stared hard at Chester.

"Who are you?" he asked.

"I'm the man who's gonna kill you if you push this."

"That's mighty big talk."

"Talking's over. Walk away or die. Your choice."

"You're bluffing."

"I don't bluff."

Chester saw the man's eyes go hard. They squeezed together at the corners. His hand streaked to grasp the handle of his Colt. It was halfway out of his holster when Chester's Colt bucked in his hand. Once, twice, three times.

Three .38 caliber slugs bored holes in the gunfighter's chest. A man's single hand span could have covered all three. The gunman's eyes rounded the size of a half dollar. His feet did a backward dance of death before his knees collapsed and he crumpled backwards into the sawdust.

"Is there a law in this town?" Chester yelled as he reloaded his Colt.

"Nothin' 'cept the law of the quick and the dead," one of the bartenders said. "You're either *quick* or you're *dead*. He weren't quick enough."

It was a slow night in Trinidad. Cody only arrested three for drunk and disorderly conduct and conked one miner on the head with his sidearm. Things settled down when the saloons all closed at two o'clock in the morning. It was another hour before the last straggler disappeared for the night. He made the rounds checking locked doors before heading to Miss Molly's.

As he walked toward the boarding house he thought of Juliana once again as he had many times during the night. A picture of her flashed across his mind. He remembered the way she looked at him; the way her gaze seemed to linger an instant longer than normal, like she was looking past his eyes directly into his heart. He replayed every word of their conversation again and again.

The lamp was still lit in the hallway. He paused, lifted the globe, and blew it out. Then he slipped into his room and quietly closed the door. Undressing, he flopped down on the soft bed. For several minutes he lay awake staring up at the ceiling, picturing Juliana in the next room sleeping peacefully. With those thoughts clutched close, Cody drifted into a dreamless sleep.

"I'm real sorry about your brother," Molly said, as Juliana helped her prepare breakfast.

"Who killed him, Miss Molly?"

"Why, I thought you knew. It was our new town marshal. You met him last night. The way I hear it, your brother gave him no choice. Trace shot a miner that was messing with one of the saloon girls he was sweet on. The man he shot didn't even have a gun. Your brother gunned him down in cold blood.

"When the marshal got to the saloon your brother was waving his gun around looking for somebody else to shoot. Hondo told him to drop the gun. Instead, Trace turned it on the marshal. That's when Hondo shot him. Lots of folks seen it and said the same thing."

Juliana felt stunned. Somehow she knew it hadn't happened the way her father said it did. But still, Trace was her brother.

The man I sat on the porch with last night is the one who killed Trace. Instantly she was struck by a sense of betrayal, anger, and disappointment. On one hand she knew she should be angry at Hondo for killing her brother, but on the other hand, if it happened the way Miss Molly said, how could she blame him for doing what he did?

Questions she'd smothered with her grief and drowned with her tears over her brother's death slithered to the surface.

What Molly told her about her brother's death was completely different from the way father said it happened. What really happened? Did the marshal have to kill her brother? There's got to be more to it than what Molly says. I've got to know the truth.

Tears welled up and escaped her eyes. Molly saw the tears and wrapped Juliana in a hug.

"I'm sorry, child," Molly said, "I thought you knew how it happened."

All Juliana could do was shake her head and run from Molly. She fled to her room and threw herself across the bed, burying her tear-wet face in the pillow.

Questions without answers swirled through her mind and gave birth to anger. It festered, boiling like a volcano in the pit of her stomach.

When Miss Molly told Cody that Juliana knew he was the one who killed her brother, his heart exploded. Molly explained that Trace Higgins had been in and out of trouble most of his life, but his father always used his power, influence, and money to get him out of it.

Cody was devastated. He felt he had to explain to Juliana what had happened, so he went to her bedroom door and tapped softly.

"Who is it?" Juliana's voice from inside the room called out.

"It's me, Hondo. Can I talk with you a minute?"

"Go away!" Juliana half-shouted, bitterness evident in her voice. "You killed my brother!"

"If you'd just let me explain."

"I'm not interested in your explanations. My brother's dead! *You* killed him! That's all I need to know."

Cody sadly turned and walked away.

Inside the bedroom Juliana smothered her anger and retreated back into her confused thoughts.

How could he? He seemed so nice. I was actually attracted to him. Now I find out he's the one who killed my brother. I can't believe it happened the way Molly said. Surely Trace wouldn't shoot down an unarmed man. There must be a mistake. I've got to find out the truth. I've got to know.

Rising from the bed, she splashed water on her face from a pan on the dresser, rose, and walked with determined steps down the street to Hamilton's Mercantile. Ed Hamilton had been a friend of her family since she was a little girl. *He'll tell me the truth about what happened to Trace.*

"Good Morning, Juliana," the storekeeper greeted as she stepped into the mercantile store. "I heard you were in town. Glad you stopped by."

"Good morning, Mr. Hamilton. I need to talk with you if you have time."

"Why, of course. What can I do for you?"

"It's about my brother and the way he was killed. Father told me one story and Miss Molly tells me something completely different. I've got to know how he died. Will you tell me?"

"I wasn't actually there when it happened, mind you, but I talked to more'n a dozen men who were, and they all say the same thing. Your brother thought he had staked a claim on one of the saloon girls, a girl named Etta Mae. He walked into the saloon as her and one of the local miners was coming out from the back room. They argued. Your brother went crazy. He pulled out a gun and shot the miner dead. The man didn't even have a gun.

"Our new marshal heard the shot and came running with that short-barreled shotgun he carries. Trace was still waving his gun around and turned it on the marshal. The marshal did what anybody would have done. He shot your brother.

"I don't know what your father told you, but that's the straight of it."

Juliana lowered her head and slowly nodded.

"Was Trace drunk like father said?"

"Not according to those who saw it, but even if he was, drunk ain't an excuse to kill an unarmed man. Our marshal had no choice. He did what he had to do."

Juliana closed her eyes and nodded. "Thanks, Mr. Hamilton."

From the mercantile store she headed for the saloon. She had never been inside a saloon in her life. The overwhelming stench greeted her as she pushed through the front doors. It was mid-morning so only a couple of men sat at a table nursing a drink. Juliana headed directly for the bar.

"I want to see a girl named Etta Mae," she told the bartender.

"Doubt she's up yet," the man said, eyeing Juliana suspiciously.

"I need to talk with her. I'm Juliana Higgins. It was my brother who was killed in here a couple of weeks ago."

"Oh, yeah, the Higgins boy, I remember. Saw the whole thing."

"Is it true he shot an unarmed man?"

"Shore is. It's a living wonder he didn't shoot somebody else, too. Most likely would have if the marshal hadn't stopped him."

"Where can I find this Etta Mae?"

"She sleeps in the back, second door on the right. She ain't gonna be too happy getting woke up this time of the day."

"She'll just have to get over it," Juliana said over her shoulder, as she headed toward a door in the back wall.

She paused before the second door on the right and pounded loudly with her fist. She waited a couple of minutes then repeated her pounding even louder.

"Go away!" a sleepy voice from inside the room shouted harshly.

Juliana turned the knob and pushed open the door without answering. A girl with rumpled brown hair raised her head and peered at Juliana through sleepy eyes.

"Who are you?" Etta Mae demanded to know.

"I'm Juliana Higgins, Trace's sister."

"Who?"

"Trace Higgins, the young man who was shot and killed in here about two weeks ago."

"Oh, him."

"I understood you and my brother were close."

"*Close?*" the girl asked, letting out a dry chuckle. "We were only together twice I think it was and he beat me up both times. No, I wouldn't say we were *close*."

"He must have thought so."

"Sissy, in my business lots of guys *think* so."

"The man my brother shot. Did he have a gun?"

"Mike?" again the woman let out a dry chuckle. "I doubt

Mike would know one end of a gun from another. No, sissy. Your brother shot Mike like he would shoot a stray dog. I think he would have killed me, too, if the marshal hadn't killed him first."

Juliana had heard enough. She turned on her heels, walked from the room, and went directly to the livery. She quickly saddled Snowflake and rode out of town at a gallop.

CHAPTER XXIV

By the time Juliana arrived back at the ranch, she was madder than a wet hen. She reined up, turned Snowflake over to the horse wrangler, and went looking for her father. She found him at his desk in the den.

"Why did you lie to me?" she blurted, storming into his office. She leaned over his desk, her reddened face only inches from his.

"Lie to you about what?"

"You know *about what!* About how my brother was killed. That's *what!*"

"Don't talk to me in that tone of voice. I'm still your father. I told you not to go into town. I forbade you to go! You're headstrong just like your mother and you went anyway, against my wishes. I knew this would happen. They filled your head with a bunch of lies and you come back here accusing *me* of lying to you."

"You did. I talked to Miss Molly, Ed Hamilton, the bartender, and even to the saloon whore Trace claimed to be sweet on. She said they were together only twice and that he beat her up both times. They all told me the same story. Trace got jealous over a common whore and shot down the man who was with her in cold blood. The man was *unarmed!* He had no gun!

"What's even worse, if such a thing were possible, Trace was about to shoot the girl and anyone else who got in his way.

"In all my eighteen years you've never lied to me until now. Why now? Why did you think you had to lie about this?"

Arlis Higgins appeared shamefaced. He knew his daughter posed questions he couldn't—or wouldn't—answer. He couldn't tell her that an irresistible craving for revenge had taken control of his life since his son's death. He couldn't or wouldn't tell her that he would stop at absolutely nothing to punish the entire town and everybody in it for his son's death. He couldn't or wouldn't tell her that, even now, his foreman was in Denver hiring men to wipe Trinidad, Colorado off the face of the map along with everybody in it. *I'll teach them a lesson they'll never forget. They can't murder my son and get away with it.*

"Aren't you going to answer me, Father?"

Arlis Higgins just shook his head and turned his back on his daughter.

Juliana stormed out of the room. She climbed the stairs and tapped softly on the door to her mother's room before opening it and stepping quietly inside.

Louisa rose from the bedside chair where she had been applying a damp cloth to Leona Higgins's fevered brow. A look of concern wrinkled the woman's face.

"What's wrong?" Worry pulled Juliana's eyebrows together. "Is mother all right?"

The woman lowered her head and shook it slowly. "She took worse yesterday. Fever very high."

"Didn't you tell my father?" she asked, her voice rising.

"I tell him. He say she will be all right. She is not all right."

Juliana hurried to her mother's bedside and placed a hand on her forehead, immediately jerked it back as if she had touched a red-hot stove. "She's burning up" Juliana said, her voice cracking with panic. She whirled and ran from the room and down the stairs. Her father still sat in his chair, staring off into space with a faraway look in his eyes when she rushed in.

"Mother's burning up with fever. Did you send for the doctor?"

He continued to stare at nothing as if he didn't hear her.

"Father!" she screamed at the top of her voice. "Did you send for the doctor?"

He jerked back to reality and stared at her with a blank expression. "What? What is it?"

"Louisa said she told you yesterday that mother had taken a turn for the worse and had a high fever. *Did you send someone for the doctor?"*

"She's done this before. She's just grieving over our dead son the way you ought to be. She'll be all right in a day or two."

"I can't believe this. Your wife is lying up there burning up with a fever and you haven't even sent for the doctor? What's come over you?" Juliana shrieked. "If you won't send for the doctor I'll go myself!"

"I'll send Roy."

"I thought you sent Roy to Denver to buy a breeding bull?"

"Oh, yeah, I forgot. Well, send one of the other hands then."

Two ranch hands happened to be near the barn. Juliana raced to where they were working on a corral fence. "Saddle up and ride to Trinidad as quickly as you can. Take an extra horse. Bring Doctor Goodson. Mother's taken a turn for the worse. She's burning up with fever. Please hurry."

"Yes, ma'am," the men said, hurrying into the barn to saddle their horses.

Juliana raced back to the house. As she passed the open door to the den she saw him still sitting in his chair with that same faraway look. She shook her head and raced up the stairs, taking them two at a time.

For the rest of the day and half the night she sat by her mother's bedside, bathing her face, arms, and chest with a damp cloth.

Leona Higgins died just before midnight, an hour before the doctor arrived.

"You did all you could do, Miss Juliana," the doctor told her. "That first stroke she had weakened her. She's been going downhill ever since. With the fever and all she just didn't have the strength to withstand this last one."

Juliana nodded sadly and shook Doctor Goodson's hand. "Thank you for coming, Doctor. You're welcome to spend the night."

"No, I need to get back to town. Mrs. Tuttle is expecting her baby any time now."

"I understand. Our men will escort you back."

Juliana closed the door to her mother's room quietly. She went downstairs. The door to her father's den was closed. She tapped on the door and opened it. Arlis Higgins still sat where Juliana had last seen him earlier that day. It seemed he hadn't moved. His chair was turned around with his back to her.

"Father? Are you all right?"

He twisted his neck to look at her with a blank look in his eyes. Juliana had never seen her father like this.

"Are you all right?" she asked again.

"Huh? Yes, of course I'm all right. Why wouldn't I be?"

"Didn't you hear the doctor come and go? I thought you would have come upstairs to check on Mother."

"The doctor? Why was he here?"

"I sent for him, remember? He came to see about Mother."

"Oh, yes, how is she?"

Juliana was stunned. Stunned and confused. *What's happening? First my brother is killed. Now mother is dead. And father sits here in the den and doesn't even bother to come upstairs and check on her? This is crazy!*

"How is she?" Juliana screamed. "How is she? Mother died an hour ago! You didn't even bother to come upstairs and check on her. How *could you do that?* How could you sit down here grieving over your no-good son and let your wife die right upstairs and not even tell her goodbye? What's happened to you? You're not the man I've known for eighteen years. Something's happened to you."

They buried Leona Higgins two days later. Six ranch hands carried the coffin to the small graveyard with a white picket fence around it. Juliana and her father followed the procession on foot. They laid her to rest beside her son.

Arlis Higgins moved through the motions, but seemed not to even be aware of the events going on around him. Juliana couldn't bring herself to even speak to her father. She wasn't sure she could ever forgive him for treating her mother so poorly.

She kept to herself for the next three days, spending lots of time in her room, taking long walks and rides in the beautiful mountains surrounding their large ranch. The first snowfall of the year left the mountain peaks white. She loved the Colorado winters.

She was returning from one of her rides when she spotted Roy Self, their foreman, coming back from his trip to Denver. He saw her coming and reined to a stop. She rode up.

"Hello, Roy. See you made it back from the big city. Did you find us a breeding bull?" Juliana noticed an odd look sweep over the foreman's face. It caused her to wonder.

"Uh, no, ma'am. Couldn't find what we needed."

"That's too bad. I'm sure father will be disappointed. Mother passed away while you were gone. Father's not feeling well. I've never seen him like this. I'm worried, Roy."

"Yes, ma'am. I am, too. I've worked for Arlis Higgins for fifteen years. He's not himself since your brother got killed."

"I know. I just don't know what to do. He just mopes around, hardly ever leaves his den, and just sits there staring off into space."

"Yes, ma'am. Well, I better be getting on. I need to report to Mr. Higgins."

"I'll ride to the ranch with you," Juliana said, gigging Snowflake in the flanks.

After eating supper alone, Juliana decided she needed to be alone and do some thinking. It was such a beautiful crisp night she decided to take a ride to her favorite spot. She didn't want to disturb the horse wrangler so she saddled Snowflake, threaded a boot through the stirrup and swung into the saddle.

She rode slowly, enjoying the star-studded night. A slight breeze crept down the mountainside and brought with it the sweet smell of fresh pine. She loved the freshness of the mountains, the quietness, the vast feeling of space.

Quite a contrast to the non-stop noise and stench of the big city, she thought. *I don't understand how people live that way.*

She found her spot beside the little bubbling mountain stream and tied Snowflake in a small clearing nearby so the mare could graze. Juliana sat down on the soft mossy-bank and leaned her head back to gaze her up at the three-quarter moon.

Her gaze came to rest on star. Immediately her mind flashed back to the night she and the young marshal sat on Molly's front porch and looked up at that star. Her thoughts lingered on him for a time.

I wasn't fair with him. He tried to explain and I wouldn't listen. I should have gone back and apologized to him after I found out the truth about how my brother died.

Miss Molly was right. It wasn't his fault. I need to ride back to Trinidad and explain that I found out the truth. I will. I'll ride into town tomorrow.

A sound broke the silence of the night. The sound of horses reached Juliana's hearing. Fear gripped her and raced up her spine. *Is it Indians?* She rolled to her feet and slipped quietly to where her horse was tied. She slid her rifle from its saddle boot and tiptoed into a small stand of Aspen saplings nearby. She levered a shell and listened.

The voices of two men reached her hearing. As they drew nearer, she realized both were familiar voices. *It's Father and Roy.* She started to call out, but something stopped her. *What are they doing out here in the middle of the night?*

Through the dim light of the moon she saw them as they passed within twenty yards of where she stood. They were leading a packhorse. Her curiosity kept her silent. *What could they be doing? Where are they going? Why were they leading a packhorse?*

After the voices faded she hurried to her horse, mounted, and followed them, keeping far enough behind not to be heard, but close enough not to lose them. She felt guilty following her own father, but somehow her suspicions told her something was going on she needed to know about.

They climbed steadily, winding around great up-thrust rocks, through thick groves of aspen and pine, and through wide mountain valleys. Far ahead, on the shoulder of a sloping mountainside, she caught sight of a flickering light. It seemed to be a campfire.

She found a thick stand of pine and tied Snowflake inside the grove of trees. Taking her rifle she moved ahead on foot. As she drew closer she could make out the dark silhouettes of many men sitting around the fire. They laughed loud and talked as they passed bottles from one to another.

Curiosity got the best of her and she crept closer. Their voices became clearer. Her father spoke then.

"I'm Arlis Higgins. I own a large spread not far from here. I sent Roy to hire you men because I've got a job I want done. He tells me you are the best at what you do. He says you know how to follow orders and ain't the kind of men that worry about what you have to do to earn your money.

"There's a town not far over the mountains west of here called Trinidad, Colorado. I want it burned to the ground. I want it wiped off the face of the earth. I don't want anything left standing."

"What about the people who live there?" one of the men spoke up. "What if they don't cotton to their town being burned?"

"I don't want anybody walking away to tell what happened. Is that understood?" Juliana's father shouted. "If any of you got a problem with that, you best saddle your horse and head back where you come from right now."

Juliana couldn't believe her ears. *My father just told those men to burn Trinidad and kill everyone there! This is insane! What has gotten into him? I can't believe he would do such a thing!*

"When're we doing this?" another fellow asked.

"Tomorrow," Higgins said flatly. "I want it done tomorrow night. I'll meet you here at sundown. I'm riding with you. After it's done, we'll meet back here and I'll pay you off. After that, you can scatter and go wherever you want."

Juliana heard enough. She deer-footed back to where she tied her horse and walked it quietly out of hearing.

I can't let this happen. Mounting, she kicked Snowflake into a hard gallop. *Somehow I've got to stop this.*

She pointed Snowflake's nose toward the west, toward Trinidad.

CHAPTER XXV

It was now late November. All the trail crews were back safely. Buck, Chester, Rebekah, and Selena sipped coffee in front of a roaring fire in Buck's den.

"We've had a good year," Buck told them. "Rebekah tells me that even after expenses we banked over a million dollars this year for the second year in a row. Sam's doing a good job with our bank in Del Rio and our breeding stock is flourishing. The army's presence has cut down on our Indian problems and I don't have to be back in Austin until early March. Life is good."

"Do you think the cattle market's gonna hold up for another year?" Chester asked.

"Well, seems like Harvey Owens and Joseph McCoy think so. I think we ought to tell Carlos to go ahead and contract with our Mexican ranchers for another year. What's your thinking on the matter?"

"Don't see why not. Like I've heard you say more'n a few times, '*let's ride this horse 'till it quits running.*'"

"How's your new café working out, Selena?" Buck asked her.

"It is doing well. We built it larger than we thought we would need, but the business just keeps growing. Mother is happy and my cousin is doing a good job managing it for her."

As she spoke, she slanted a look at Chester and gave him a questioning look. Buck saw his partner smile and nod.

"Chester and I have some more good news we wish to share. We're going to have a baby."

Rebekah whooped and leaped from the sofa. She wrapped her arms around her friend and they both mixed laughter with tears of happiness.

"That's wonderful," Buck said, leaning over and shaking Chester's hand. "Congratulations. When is the happy occasion?"

"Sometime in June," Selena said happily.

"That means no trail drives for you next year then, partner," Buck told his friend.

"What're you talking about? Of course I'll be on the drives," Chester said.

"Not on your life," Buck told him. "You need to be here with Selena when your son is born. She'll need you."

"Son?" Selena questioned. "Why are you so sure it's going to be a boy?"

"Of course it'll be a boy," Chester said. Buck had a boy. I'm gonna have one too."

"I had a little something to do with our son," Rebekah corrected him. They all shared a good laugh.

Chester grinned. "Yeah, I reckon you did at that,"

"Come on Selena," Rebekah told her friend. "Let's go check on little Cody and I've got lots of clothes he's outgrown I want you to have for your *son*."

After the girls left, Buck and Chester sipped their coffee in silence for a time.

"Heard anything more about finding your brother?"

Buck took a long sip of his coffee before responding. "No,

afraid not. The last report I got from the Pinkerton folks was that the trail had gone cold someplace in New Mexico. They're still looking, but I'm getting worried. They're telling me that Cody's reputation as a gunfighter is growing by the day. The word is he's the fastest there is."

"That kind of word spreads fast and far, Buck. It brings all the wanna-be's out of their holes looking to build a quick reputation by beating the best. Like the sheriff up in Sedalia told you, *there's always somebody faster.* Maybe the Pinkertons will find him soon," Chester tried to reassure his friend.

"Yeah, maybe."

The emergency bell from the guard tower brought both Buck and Chester from their seats. They ran for the door and across the compound yard toward an approaching rider. It was J. D. Summers, the deputy from Del Rio.

"The bank's been hit!" the deputy shouted as he slid his mount to a stop. "The marshal sent me to get you. He wants you to come right away."

"Get our security team together!" Buck shouted to the guard on the wall.

Chester was already racing for the stable to saddle their horses. Within minutes Buck and Chester led a group of two-dozen Longhorn riders as they rode hard for town.

It was near midnight when they galloped into Del Rio and headed for a large gathering of men and lanterns around the bank building. Bud Cauthorn and Sam Colson hurried to meet them as they dismounted.

In the light of the lanterns Buck could see the bank building was a shambles. A huge hole was blown in the side that you could drive a team and wagon through.

"It was Clayton Dawson again. He had twenty or so men with him this time. Some of his men caught us in the marshal's office and pinned us down while the rest of them pulled a field cannon into town big as life. They acted like they had all night. They set up and blowed that hole in the bank vault and then loaded all the money in a wagon and hightailed it out of town. They took everything, cleaned out the vault to the bare walls. They had us cold, Mr. Cordell. There wasn't anything we could do. We managed to get four of them as they rode out of town. One of them is still alive."

"Which way did they go?" Chester asked.

"They headed west toward Mexico. We followed as far as the river, where we found the cannon on this side. We searched the riverbank on the other side, but never could find where they came out. The other wagon and riders just disappeared."

"More'n likely they went either upstream or down to a place they'd already picked to come out of the water," Chester suggested. "This Dawson fellow ain't no dummy. I figure he planned all this out right down to the nubbin. Come first light I'll take some of the boys and go after them."

"I'm coming with you," Bud Cauthorn said. "Dawson robbed a bank in my town. I take that right *personal.*"

"First, I want to talk to the one who's still alive," Chester said. "Where is he?"

"He's over at the jail. I had the doctor take a look at him. Doc says he'll live. He got hit in the shoulder."

"Let's go have a chat with this fellow."

Bud Cauthorn and Chester walked across the street to the marshal's office and jail. The marshal retrieved the keys from the desk drawer and opened the door that separated the office portion from the jail. He started to step into the hallway that fronted the cells when Chester reached a hand for the keys.

"Mind if I talk to the prisoner alone?"

"Oh, well, no, I reckon it will be all right."

"I'll call if I need you." Bud walked back into the office and closed the door behind him.

* * *

A half hour later Chester walked back into the marshal's office.

"Did he tell you anything?"

"Yeah, he spilled his guts. They're headed for a little Mexican village called El Sueco. It's about three days' ride northwest into Mexico. We'll need packhorses, supplies, and lots of water. I'll have a couple of the boys get things together for us."

"How'd you get him to tell you where they're headed?"

"You don't want to know, but you might want to ask the doctor to look in on him again."

As the first hint of gray tinted the eastern sky Chester and Bud Cauthorn splashed across the Rio Grande River followed by twenty heavily-armed Longhorn security riders. They urged their horses out of the river and quickly picked up the tracks left by the wagon. The outlaws came out of the river a half mile upstream. The tracks headed northwest.

Chester and his men followed the tracks at a steady, ground-eating short lope. There was little conversation. Each man knew he had a job to do and would do whatever necessary to get it done.

They rode the day away, made dry camp and rode again. Even in early November the sun was unmerciful. Dust-caked sweat dripped from both horse and rider. The rider's faces were drenched with beads of sweat. White foamy lather dripped from the horse's nostrils and formed around their rigging.

They stopped often to allow the mounts a few minutes' rest, but no shade was available to escape the boiling sun. The area through which they traveled was barren. Nothing but sand and patches of white caliche with occasional scrawny mesquite trees and tumbleweed as far as the eye could see. Little plumes of dust lifted from their horses' hooves, immediately swept away by a hot westerly wind gusting around them. This was a land not fit for man or beast.

The only sound to disturb the desert quietness was the squeak of saddle leather and the constant screeching of the *chichada* locust. They clung to the brush choked draws and wind tossed mesquite limbs that sapped the last dregs of moisture from the ground. A desert hawk soared above them along a fast moving current of air and screeched a cry.

Just before noon they came upon one of the outlaws' horses. It had been wounded by a stray bullet during the robbery and couldn't go any further. At least the robbers had enough compassion to put the horse out of its misery.

Chester's gaze followed the faint wagon tracks cutting parallel lines in the shifting desert sand. Their horses' hoof prints were already mostly erased. The hot wind and shifting sand was wiping all traces of the outlaws passing.

"Good thing I was able to find out where they're headed, Chester thought. *Without knowing that, there's no way we'd ever catch them.*

They plodded on toward an uncertain encounter.

Clayton Dawson and his eighteen men who survived the robbery in Del Rio straggled into the tiny village of El Sueco at sundown. Their exhausted horses moved ahead with their heads low, barely able to put one hoof in front of the other.

At first glance the village appeared deserted. A hot wind swirled along the single dusty street. Here and there scrawny-looking chickens scratched the sand, searching for some morsel of food.

Clayton swept the scattering of small adobe houses along the single street with a look, searching every doorway, every window for anyone who might offer a threat. He had little worry. One of his men, a Mexican bandito named Emilio, called this flyspeck village home and assured Clayton it would make a safe place to hole up for a while.

They guided their tired horses to the large building the Mexican said was the cantina.

"Take the horses to that livery down the street and see they're taken care of," Clayton told the youngest member of his band. "Unhitch the wagon and leave it here. I don't want to be far from all that money. You can take the team with you."

"Is there a hotel in this one-horse town?" he asked Emilio.

"No, señor."

"Then we'll have to make do. We'll bed down in the cantina. At least we'll be close to the liquor. Some of you boys unload those sacks of money and tote 'em inside. I'm anxious to see how much we took 'em for. Shore seems like a big haul. Cat, you come with me."

Clayton swung off his horse to the dusty street and handed the reins to the young outlaw. He slipped his rifle from the saddle boot and swung his saddlebags over a shoulder. "The rest of you round up everybody that lives in this sorry excuse for a town and bring 'em all to the cantina. I want to look them over."

His men scattered to do his bidding. Clayton and his right hand man walked to the open door of the cantina and stepped inside. It was nothing more than a shell of a building. The hard-packed dirt floor gave witness to many spilled drinks, tobacco juice, and bare feet.

A board stretched between two upturned barrels served as a bar. Two rickety tables with straw bottomed chairs wore an inch of dust on them. One short, whiskered old Mexican smiled a toothless welcome. *"Buenas tardes, señor."*

"Tequila and lots of it," Clayton ordered, swiping his hat from his head and sleeving sweat from his forehead. He drew back a chair and slouched into it tiredly.

The old man shook his head. *"No tequila. Mescal."*

"Wouldn't you know it; no bed, no whiskey, no tequila, nothing 'cept *mescal."* the outlaw chief complained.

"I hate that stuff." the one called Cat grumbled. "I tried it once down in Monterrey. It ain't nothing but cactus juice strained through a rag, ain't fit for a man to drink."

"You might as well get used to it, we'll be here a while."

"Might drink it," Clayton's number one man said. "Nothing says I have to like it."

"As soon as the heat from this job blows over you can afford to drink anything you want."

"Think they'll follow us way down here?"

"They'll try. Ain't no way they could follow us though. Tracks disappear in a day or two in the desert. All we have to do is lay low for a while. Then we can all live like kings for the rest of our lives."

"Sure ain't gonna be no fun lyin' around this rat trap very long without something to drink."

Several of the gang members herded the residents of the village into the cantina. Mostly they were old and stooped in homespun goat herders' clothing. Only a few children were among the two dozen villagers.

One girl drew particular attention. Clayton judged her to be somewhere in her late teens, maybe as much as twenty years of age. She had flawless, olive-colored skin, long black hair, and wore a drab, ankle-length skirt and a shoulderless blouse gathered at the top. Like most of the others, she was barefooted.

Cat fixed his gaze on her and smiled an evil smile.

"Well, now. Maybe this won't be so bad a place to hole up after all." He said, leering at the pretty Mexican girl.

"Settle down, Cat," Dawson told him. "There'll be plenty of time for that. Right now we need to get some grub in our bellies and whiskey in our gut.

"Emilio, tell these women we want some food and lots of it and we want it pronto. Tell them nobody will get hurt if they do exactly what they are told. Anybody gives us trouble and we'll kill everybody in the whole village. Make sure they understand."

The Mexican bandito explained what Dawson said. The cowed villagers huddled together with their faces pointed to the floor. Afterward they were shooed from the room and allowed to return to their homes.

The rest of the gang straggled in and found room to sit or lie around the cantina. They grabbed bottles of the golden-colored mescal and promptly proceeded to get drunk.

Clayton Dawson and Cat began opening the tow sacks full of money and stacking the wrapped bundles into twenty equal-size piles.

"Why are you counting out twenty piles," Cat wanted to know. "There ain't but eighteen of us left."

"Because I get three shares," Dawson told him.

"Three shares! How come *you* get three shares and everybody else just gets one?"

"Because I set the job up, that's why. I planned the whole thing. Without me the rest of you would still be robbing some poor drummer for whiskey money."

"Okay, okay, I just asked. Don't go getting' all riled up."

"I don't like being questioned when I say something. If you don't like the way I run things, just say so and we'll find out if you're as good with a gun as they say you are."

"I could take you anytime I felt like it."

"One way to find out," Dawson said, locking a hard look on the gunman. "Anytime, anyplace."

Dawson continued stacking the money into piles while his

men downed the strong mescal. Finally the gang leader pushed back with a smile on his face. "The way it works out, each man gets a hundred and twenty-five thousand apiece."

The small cantina rocked with whoops and yells. "We're all rich!" they yelled, lifting their bottles in celebration.

Chester and his men spotted the thin tendril of smoke trailing upward up ahead just before sundown.

"That's got to be El Sueco," Chester told Bud Cauthorn. "How d'you think we ought to play it?"

"Well, unless I miss my guess they'll be a mighty tired and thirsty bunch, just like we all are. Don't know how long they been there, but I'd say they'll be celebrating and counting their money right about now. In a couple hours they'll be so drunk they can't find their backside with both hands. I say we give 'em some time and go in about midnight."

"That's my thinking, too. Let's find us a draw or something and rest up until midnight."

When the stars told them it was close to midnight, Chester and his men left one man with the horses and went forward on foot toward the small village. As they drew near they split into two groups. Chester led one group and Bud Cauthorn led the other. They approached from both sides of the small village.

The only light came from a large, flat-roofed building in the center of town. Judging from the drunken laughter coming from inside, Chester and Bud had guessed right. The outlaws apparently hadn't even bothered to post a guard.

Both carried sawed-off double-barreled shotguns as they

crept silently toward the open front door. Others were sent around back to cut off any escape attempt.

A woman's scream pierced the night accompanied by even louder drunken laughter. It was clear the outlaws were enjoying more than the drinking. When everyone was in place Chester and Bud stepped through the front door unnoticed with shotguns in their hands. Other Longhorn riders slipped in behind them and spread out on either side of the door, rifles in hand.

One table was piled high with stacks of money. Sitting in a chair beside the money was Clayton Dawson. His back was toward the door and his gaze locked on the activities taking place at the nearby table.

The drunken outlaws' attention focused upon a young woman one of the outlaws was chasing around a table.

"Go get her, Cat!" one of the outlaws yelled.

"Nobody move!" Chester shouted. "First man that even twitches gets blowed in half!"

Heads jerked around. Surprise washed across every face. Eyes walled white, clearly caught completely off guard. Obviously realizing they had no choice, the outlaws raised their hands.

"One at a time," Chester commanded. "Unbuckle those gun belts and let 'em drop to the floor."

One-by-one they complied with Chester's orders, all except two.

Neither the gunfighter they called Cat nor Clayton Dawson moved an inch. Cat stood defiantly, staring cold-eyed at Chester and Bud.

"You want my gun, you got to come and get it," the gunfighter snarled.

"Your move," Chester said evenly.

The drunken gunman hesitated for only a fraction of a second. His hand flashed toward the Colt tied to his right leg and barely touched the butt of his weapon when Chester feathered the trigger of his shotgun. The blast rocked the room. The heavy pellets tore into the outlaw, blowing him backwards across the table. He landed on his back. The only movement was his feet jerking in false life.

Clayton Dawson still sat in his chair. He hadn't moved. Bud Cauthorn walked across the room to stand in front of the outlaw. He looked down into the outlaw's defiant face. "I told you we'd meet again," Marshal Cauthorn said.

At the first sight of sunup, seventeen men sat on their horses. Their hands were tied behind their backs and nooses fitted tight around their necks. The ropes were looped around the protruding rafter beams of the cantina.

The entire village stood nearby, watching the spectacle. Behind each horse a Longhorn rider stood with a coiled rope in hand, waiting for the marshal's signal.

"Anything you boys want to say?" Marshal Cauthorn asked, looking squarely into Dawson's eyes.

Dawson returned Cauthorn's gaze. A thin smile lifted the corner of his mouth."We almost made it."

"Almost ain't good enough," the marshal told him, and nodded to the Longhorn men.

CHAPTER XXVI

Juliana had trouble keeping her gaze focused on the trail as she galloped through the night.

Her mind was a blur of tangled thoughts. *It's like I'm living a nightmare. First my brother, then Mother, and now my father is planning to burn a town and massacre everybody in it. Surely this is not real. Maybe I'll wake up and find this is all a terrible dream.*

Tears coursed down her cheeks, blurred her vision. She lifted a hand and scrubbed them away only to have tears return again and again. To determine her location her wet gaze swept the mountains towering on every side. Bitterness burned against her breastbone. She allowed her outrage to fuel the energy it took to keep going.

Snowflake was blowing hard. She needed to stop and rest her mount, but panic demanded she keep moving. *My friends are there. People I've known my whole life! I've got to warn them, got to stop this insanity.* She leaned forward in the saddle and patted Snowflake's sweaty neck, urging him onward.

It was the deepest part of the night when Juliana rode into Trinidad. Not a single light could be seen. She pulled Snowflake to a stop at the edge of town. Her breathing was sharp and heavy. Her chest pounded. She twisted a look around trying to decide where to go, whom to warn. Making up her mind, she reined her mount toward Miss Molly's boarding house.

She pulled Snowflake to a sliding stop and hit the ground running. The front door was unlocked and a lamp burned dimly in a hallway table. She ran to the door of the marshal's room and pounded upon it with a fisted hand.

"Who is it?" his sleepy voice called from inside.

"It's Juliana! I have to talk to you. Open the door."

The door swung open. Cody stood there in his long john bottoms with no top. Juliana was breathing so hard she could barely speak.

"It's…it's my father." she managed to get out between gasps of air. "He's hired a bunch of men from Denver. They're going to burn the town and kill everybody. You've got to stop him. I couldn't let this happen."

"Calm down," Cody told her. "Sit down here on the bed and catch your breath, then you can tell me what happened."

He took her arm and guided her to the bed. While she caught her breath, Cody lit the lamp and retrieved his britches, slipped them on, and sleeved into a shirt. He stomped into his boots and pulled a chair over near her and sat down.

"Now, take your time. Tell me exactly what you're talking about."

Before Juliana could explain, Miss Molly came hurrying into the room in her long-tailed gown and carrying another lamp.

"What on earth is going on?" the large woman said with concern in her voice.

"It's my father," Juliana began to explain. "Something's happened to him since my brother was killed. He's been acting crazy. Now he's hired a bunch of men from Denver to burn Trinidad and kill everybody in town."

"Land sakes alive!" Molly exclaimed. "What's got into him? He's always been a hard man, but nothing like this. Are you sure about this, Child? Maybe you misunderstood or something. He wouldn't burn our town."

"I'm afraid he would, Miss Molly. He's eaten up inside with hatred. He blames the town for my brother's death."

She turned her look toward Cody. Terror filled her eyes. "Can't you do something to stop him?"

Without stopping to think about it he reached open arms toward her. She filled them and buried her face in the hollow of his large shoulder. Wracking sobs erupted from deep within her and shook her body. A reservoir of tears surged from her eyes and wet his shirt. He held her for a good long time until her weeping ran its course.

"I'll go make some coffee," Molly said, turning and heading toward the kitchen. "This is liable to be a long night."

After Molly left the room, Cody released Juliana and sat back in his chair."Now, start at the beginning and just tell me everything you saw and heard. Don't leave nothing out. I need to hear it all."

She leaned her head back and stared at the ceiling for a time. She took a long breath and let it out in a long shuddering sigh, and began. Cody listened intently, leaning forward in his chair, sometimes shaking his head in disbelief that Higgins could do what he was doing, sometimes nodding he understood.

Miss Molly brought coffee and handed them both a cup before Juliana finished. Cody leaned back in his chair and bowed his shaking head over Juliana's story. "How many men did he hire?"

"I'm not sure, two dozen maybe, I wasn't close enough to see them all. I feel like a traitor," she said in a quivering voice. "I feel like I'm betraying my own father, but I couldn't let this happen. I had to try to stop it."

"You did the right thing," Cody tried to reassure her. "I've got to go talk with Mr. Hamilton and some of the others and decide what to do. How much time do we have? When are they planning to come?"

"Tonight, Father told them he would meet them at sundown."

"How long will it take them to get here?" Rising, he swung his gun belt around his waist.

"Two hours, maybe three."

"You stay here with me, Child," Molly told Juliana, wrapping her arm around the weeping young woman.

"I'll be back," Cody said over his shoulder, hurrying from the room.

A few minutes later Cody knocked on the front door of Ed Hamilton's, the town councilman's house. Somewhere a rooster crowed, welcoming a chilly morning. Suddenly it dawned on him. *It's Sunday. Why today of all days, why Sunday? Reckon if a man's gotta die, Sunday's as good a day as any. Better'n most.*

Ed Hamilton came to the door in a nightshirt and carried a lamp. His eyes appeared sleepy, but came suddenly awake when he saw the look on Cody's face. "What is it? What's wrong?"

"We need to talk, Mr. Hamilton. We've got trouble with a capital *T*."

"Come on in, Ellen's awake. We were just about to get up anyway. I'll have her make us some coffee. We can talk around the kitchen table."

They sipped coffee while Cody repeated the story Juliana told him. Cody watched the councilman's face. He saw something akin to terror, which grew more apparent during the telling. When Cody finished, Hamilton's eyes were as large as their coffee cups.

"What, what are we gonna do?" the man asked with panic in his voice. "What on earth *can* we do?"

"The way I see it we're down to two choices. We can sit around and let it happen or we can try to stop them. Is there any way we can get everybody together? We need to let them know what's going on."

"Well, today's Sunday. Most folks will be at the church anyway. Maybe we could tell them then."

"Reckon that'll have to do. In the meantime, spread the word and gather everybody there you can."

The small church looked packed. Every seat was full and more people stood along the walls. Word spread like wildfire. Folks who couldn't get inside the small building stood outside the doorway, craning their necks to see and hear what was going on.

Juliana and Miss Molly stood beside Cody. Ed Hamilton held up his hands trying to get people to quiet down.

"Folks, I expect most of you have already heard, but we wanted you to learn the straight of it. Arlis Higgins has been a friend and good neighbor for as long as most of us can remember. But since his boy got killed something bad has happened to his mind. He ain't thinking like the man we all know. Now he's gone and got himself a bunch of hired killers. He's got it in his mind to burn our town and kill everybody in it."

A chorus of gasps swept through the crowd. The councilman waited until it quieted down again before continuing.

"You sure about all this, Ed?" someone shouted above the noise. "This is too far-fetched to be real."

"It's real, all right. Higgins's own daughter is standing right here. She rode half the night to warn us. Now, I'm gonna turn it over to our new marshal. He's got some things to say."

Cody stepped up onto the platform and swept the room with a look. What he saw in the faces caused him to choose his words carefully. "Folks, I ain't been here in Trinidad long. I ain't even had a chance to meet some of you. From what I've seen you've got a nice little town here. I've only seen Arlis Higgins once, but from what I've been told he ain't in his right mind. "His daughter says there's no doubt, says he's gonna do what she says he's gonna do. Miss Juliana says her father's got two dozen hired killers, men who won't think more of shooting you and your family down in the street than they would think of stepping on a bug.

"Now, like I told Mr. Hamilton, the way I see it, you can turn tail and run and maybe save yourself and your family and let him burn your town, or we can stand up to him and try to stop it."

"How you think we can stop two dozen hired killers?" a man from the crowd shouted. "We ain't gunmen like you. Most of us never shot nothing 'cept a squirrel or deer."

"I ain't here to argue with you," Cody said. "It's your choice. The town hired me to keep order in Trinidad. I'm gonna do everything I can to do what you hired me to do, with or without your help."

With that said Cody stepped from the platform, pushed through the crowd and out the door, headed toward his office.

"Hondo!" Juliana called, running from the church after him. "Wait!"

He stopped, turned, and watched her running toward him. *Another time,* he thought. *Another place, maybe under different circumstances, there's a lady who would be easy to love.*

"Where're you going, Hondo?"

"I'm going to my office to get ready."

"Ready for what? To face my father and his killers alone? You can't do that. I won't let you. They'll kill you. You can't fight them all by yourself."

"A man's gotta do what a man's gotta do. I can't turn tail and run. I wouldn't be much of a man if I did. I ain't made that way. I couldn't live with myself."

"You're more man than anyone I've ever met. Please don't do this."

For a long moment their gazes met, but in that brief time something happened to Cody he had never experienced before. He saw something in her dark eyes he hadn't seen since the last time he looked into his mother's eyes. *Love.* He saw love in Juliana's eyes.

The realization shocked him. *Am I seeing what I think I'm seeing? No...there's no mistaking what I'm seeing.* He whispered,"Juliana."

She came to him. He wrapped her in his strong arms and held her close. There, in the middle of a dusty street in Trinidad, Colorado, a thing happened, something wonderful, something beautiful, something eternal.

It was as if they were the only two people in the whole world. Nothing else mattered. No one else could invade this moment in time. Their lips found one another's. They kissed and the world stood still.

The killers came in a thundering herd. Cody heard the pounding hooves a quarter-mile before they reached the edge of town. He crammed his front pocket full of shotgun shells and picked up the two sawed-off shotguns from his desk.

Beside him, Juliana levered a shell into her Henry rifle.

"I wish you would stay inside."

"No, Hondo. We've already talked about this. I'm going out there with you. Maybe seeing me will bring my father to his senses."

Maybe I ought to lock her in a jail cell until this is over. He considered this for a moment, but dismissed the idea when he saw determination in her eyes. He drew a shaky breath, touched her cheek, and opened the door. The rumble of the oncoming horses shook the ground as the two of them stepped to the middle of the street. Light from torches carried by the riders lit the night sky even before they entered town.

Cody was surprised to discover the street lit up almost as bright as day. All along it lighted lanterns hung from porch posts. *What's going on?*

His gaze searched the street, but not a single person was in sight.

"Looks like it's just you and me, Juliana."

Cody stood squarely in the middle of the street with Miss Higgins by his side. His hands made sweat on the stocks of his two shotguns. His mouth felt dry. It dawned on him that, of all the gunfights he was part of, this was the first time he felt fear. He thumbed back the four hammers, took a deep breath, and waited.

I figure I'll have time to get off four shots with my shotguns. After that I'll most likely run out of time. I just pray Juliana don't get hit. Surely her father won't allow that to happen.

The riders charged into town five wide and four deep in a cloud of churning dust. Arlis Higgins rode in front. Each man carried a lit torch in one hand and a rifle in the other. The street appeared as bright as noonday.

Cody tightened his grip on two shotguns and watched the horsemen bear down on them.

"That's him!" Higgins shouted at the top of his lungs. "That's the one who murdered my son. Ride him down!....That's Juliana! What's she doing here?"

His question was mostly lost in the shattering sound of shotgun fire. Lots of shotguns. Deafening noise sounded like the entire town exploded all at once. Cody flicked a look upward. Every rooftop on both sides of the street supported several men on them, each armed with a shotgun. *It's the townspeople. They decided to fight for their town....*

A hailstorm of buckshot rained down on the horsemen from above. Screams from both men and horses sounded above the steady barrage.

Riders dropped their torches and flung their arms skyward as the heavy buckshot tore into them, somersaulting them backwards out of their saddles. Two riders bore down on Cody and Juliana. Cody lifted a shotgun and feathered a trigger. The heavy shot lifted both men from their saddles. They tumbled along the street and came to rest at Cody's feet.

Cody saw Higgins spurring his mount madly to get to his daughter. Suddenly his horse swerved when its rider's weight shifted to one side. Slowly, as if in a dream, Higgens slid from his horse, his rifle flying from his hand. Arms and legs windmilled the air. He landed only a few feet in front of his daughter and didn't move.

"Father!" Juliana screamed, dropping her rifle and rushing to his side. She fell to both knees and lifted his head to place it in her lap.

Riderless horses galloped past them, trailing their reins. The street looked like a battlefield. Cody heard a galloping horse and swung a look. A bearded rider swung his rifle in Cody's direction. He triggered a hasty shot that tore the rider from his saddle, arms askew, and hands clawing empty air. A few riders wheeled their mounts around and raced back up the street bending low in their saddles, trying desperately to escape, only to be cut down by townspeople firing from windows and doorways.

As quickly as the battle began, it ended. Blue gun smoke billowed skyward. The acrid smell burned Cody's nose and eyes.

Through the smoky haze he saw Juliana leaning over her father. He went to her. Her body shook with heavy sobs. Slowly, gently and with a heavy sigh, he lifted Juliana to her feet and wrapped her tightly in his arms.

~The End~

A sneak preview Excerpt from LONGHORN BOOK III

The Saga Continues

The dead and dying littered the dusty street of Trinidad, Colorado. Blood pooled under and around twenty men—Arlis Higgins's hired killers. They came to burn the town and slaughter everyone in it. Instead they lay where they fell, cut down by a hailstorm of buckshot from angry townspeople.

One of the raiders, severely wounded with half his face blown away by the heavy pellets, clawed at the dirt, tying desperately to pull himself along on his stomach. A bloody trail followed his slow progress. In a last desperate gasp, his time ran out. Death won another victory.

One by one the townspeople began to emerge. Soon more and more ventured from their place of battle into the street. Ed Hamilton approached Cody and Juliana. He cradled a twelve-gauge shotgun in the crook of an arm. As he passed, he paused briefly and glanced down at Arlis Higgins.

"Real sorry about your pa, Juliana. I hope you can understand we couldn't let him burn the town and kill our families."

"I know. I just don't know what got into him. I would never have thought he would do something like this."

"Glad to see the town had a change of heart," Cody told the storekeeper.

"Yeah, well, after you said your piece and left the church we all agreed that if you was man enough to take on a bunch of killers single-handed we ought to be men enough to side you and fight for what's ours. Sorry we were a little slow in coming around."

"Well, the important thing is you did."

"Far as we can tell, only one got away. Last we saw of him he was riding hell bent for leather out of town. He's likely halfway to Denver by now."

O. J. Goodson, the judge/undertaker/doctor and Miss Molly strode up. He too, carried a shotgun over a shoulder. Molly carried a blanket that she spread over the body of Juliana's father.

"Looks like I've got a lot of work to do," Goodson said.

Molly wrapped an arm around Juliana's shoulder and pulled her close.

"Why don't you come on over to the house with me, child? Mr. Goodson and the men folk need some time to take care of things here. I've got a big pot of hot coffee already made. I reckon you've got lots of things all bottled up inside. Might be good to get it all out. We can talk woman to woman talk."

As they walked away Juliana glanced over her shoulder at Cody. Their gazes met. Juliana offered a weak smile. Cody smiled back sadly and nodded.

Working together, the men of Trinidad gathered all the bodies up and carried them over to Mr. Goodson's place in less than an hour. Several pitched in to help make wooden coffins. Others went to work digging graves in the *boot hill* section of the local graveyard. By sundown most of the hired killers were buried in unmarked graves.

Snow began falling by mid-afternoon. It fell like a pure-white blanket and the large flakes quickly covered the bloodstained street. It was as if the Gods were ashamed of what happened in Trinidad and wanted to hide the shame.

Arlis Higgins would be taken by wagon back to his ranch for burial.

It was still snowing heavily at dusk when Cody walked out the door of his office just as Ed Hamilton and a delegation of the town council hurried up.

"Got a minute, Marshal?"

"Reckon so," Cody said. "Just heading over to Miss Molly's for supper, step inside out of the weather. What of you men got on your mind?"

The councilmen stomped snow from their boots and stepped into the office. They gathered around the potbellied stove and held their hands out to the warmth.

"We just wanted to tell you what a fine job you're doing," Hamilton said. "We just had a little get together over at the store and decided you deserve a raise. As of now, you'll be making a hundred-fifty a month."

"I'm much obliged."

"The way you stood up to those killers was proof enough for all of us that you are the man for the job as marshal of Trinidad. We just wanted to show our appreciation."

"Well, to tell it like it is, I wouldn't have had a chance if you and the townspeople hadn't helped."

"We'll run along. We don't want to keep you from supper."

"Like I said, I'm obliged for the raise. I'll do the best job I know how."

The council members trooped out and Cody headed for Miss Molly's.

Juliana was helping Molly carry heaping bowls of food from

the kitchen when Cody walked in. Three other boarders sat already sipping coffee and waiting.

"Pull up a chair, kid," Molly said in her usual booming voice. "We'll have supper on the table before you can say scat. What with all that's been going on I'm running a tad late, but Juliana has been a lifesaver. She jumped in and helped me or it might have been breakfast time before you fellows got supper."

Juliana's eyes looked red to Cody like she had been crying. He supposed that would be natural seeing how she had just lost her father. As she placed a supper plate on the table in front of Cody he grasped her hand and squeezed it for a brief moment. He saw her lips quiver before she turned and hurried back into the kitchen.

She didn't return to the dining room until supper was over and the others had left. Cody sipped coffee and waited. She finally walked in slowly.

"Could we go for a walk?" she, her face sad. "I need to talk."

"Of course." He pushed up from his chair.

They walked through the falling snow along the street leading away from town. Neither spoke. Cody sensed she had things on her mind, but wasn't quite ready to talk about them.

The night was cold. Juliana pulled a white shawl she borrowed from Miss Molly tighter around her shoulders. Cody shoved both hands into the pockets and hunched deeper into his sheepskin coat.

"I'm so confused," she finally said, her voice breaking. "So heartbroken. I still can't believe my father would do such a thing."

Cody said nothing. He simply listened, his heart aching for her.

"First my brother, then Mother, and now my father. Seems

like my whole world has fallen apart, all within a few weeks. What am I going to do? Everyone I've ever loved is gone."

He reached a hand to brush snowflakes from her hair and encircled her shoulders with a strong arm. That simple touch seemed to open the floodgates of her pent-up emotions. She turned to him and buried her face in the hollow of his shoulder and wept. Her body shook with wracking sobs. He held her close until the weeping softened, which took a while.

The day was cold, gloomy for a funeral. Snow stopped sometime during the night, but several inches covered the ground. A coffin containing the body of Arlis Higgins was loaded into a wagon. O. J. Goodson drove and Juliana sat on the wagon seat beside him. A long line of wagons, buggies, and horsemen followed. Cody rode Cincinnati and led the procession.

They arrived at the Higgins ranch at noontime. All the hands of the ranch had heard of the events in town and were gathered with hats in hand when the wagon containing the coffin pulled to a stop at the little family graveyard.

Juliana felt like she was living a nightmare. She was aware of Cody being there. She felt his hand helping her from the wagon. Molly and Cody walked beside her. She moved on shaky legs to stand near an opening in the ground beside her mother's fresh grave.

The coffin was placed on two ropes held by four ranch hands. She became only vaguely aware of the minister from town speaking, but she didn't comprehend a word he said. Her mind lay a tangle of twisted emotions, of questions with no answers, of overwhelming guilt. *Is all this my fault? Maybe if I had been more understanding with father. Maybe if I had talked to him more. Maybe…*

Her thoughts were cut short by the preacher stepping up to her and extending a hand and soft whispers of comfort. She nodded. A seemingly endless line of folks approached, offering words of sympathy, most of which she didn't really hear.

As Miss Molly and Cody helped Juliana to the house she glanced back to see the ranch hands lift the coffin over the hole and slowly lower it. She tore her gaze away from the sight.

After the funeral, Cody and the townspeople from Trinidad headed back to town. Juliana went to her room where she stayed for the next three days. During that time alone she came to grips with her feelings of guilt. She decided there wasn't anything she did or didn't do to cause what happened.

She also came to the realization that the entire responsibility of the ranch now rested squarely on her shoulders. There had never been a need for her to be involved in the business dealings of the ranch since her father made all the business decisions. It dawned on her she didn't even know how large the ranch actually was or how many cattle and horses the ranch owned. *Surely father must have kept records. I'll see what I can find tomorrow,* she decided.

A typical Saturday night reigned in Trinidad. Cody broke up two fights and arrested a miner for drunk and disorderly conduct.

It was well after midnight. The drunk was sleeping it off in one of the two cells in back and the rowdies had all ridden back to wherever they called home. Cody decided it was time to call it a day.

I'd better make the rounds before I head to Miss Mollies. Pulling the door to his office closed behind him, he strode down the street.

The town was quiet, the street dark. Citizens of Trinidad had long since retreated to warm beds. The only light to be seen was the lamp at Miss Mollies at the edge of town. She always left the lamp on until Cody got home. Its yellow glow cast a splash of light across the snow-covered ground.

Traffic from horses and wagons had turned the single street into a quagmire, but elsewhere the recent snow still covered the ground and clung stubbornly to the rooftops and trees.

Cody pulled the collar of his coat up around his neck against a chilling wind coming down from the mountains. He trudged slowly along the narrow boardwalk, his gaze sweeping the street. He didn't expect anybody in their right mind would be out on a night like this, but it was his habit to always be on the alert anyway.

Pausing, he checked several doors to make sure they were locked. All seemed well, at least until he passed Hamilton's mercantile store. A small sound from inside the store reached his hearing. He stopped and listened, but heard nothing more. *Probably Ed's big black cat he let stay in the store to catch mice and rats.* Still, he decided he'd better check.

He stepped over to the large glass showcase widow where Hamilton always displayed the latest ladies dress and pressed his cupped hands against the frosted window, seeing nothing but darkness inside.

Turning, he stepped off the boardwalk into the snow-covered ground beside the store. When he rounded the corner and reached the back door he found it ajar. Somebody had pried the door open. He slipped his Colt from its belly holster and thumbed back the trigger.

Pressing his back against the side of the building, using his left hand, he slowly pushed the door open. Inside the store a gun exploded. The bullet splintered the doorframe only inches from Cody's face.

"Whoever you are inside," Cody called out. "Throw your gun out and come out with your hands up!"

He listened, but no sound or movement could be heard from inside the store. He waited, knowing whoever was inside wasn't going anywhere and the shot would most likely bring help.

Heavy footsteps running along the boardwalk told Cody help had arrived. Ed Hamilton rounded the corner of his store, cautiously followed by Blackie Bishop, the owner of the Silver Nugget, and Pete the blacksmith. All three carried shotguns.

"What's the shooting about?" Hamilton asked, hunkering down against the side of the building behind Cody.

"Somebody's inside the store. Whoever it is took a shot at me. Couple of you cover the front. Ed, stay here in case he gets by me. I'm going in."

"Be careful, marshal."

Cody swung a quick look around. A stack of firewood sat piled along the outside wall. He scooped up a piece, took a deep breath, and tossed it as far as he could through the door into the room.

It must have hit a glass display case because the sound of crashing glass was followed immediately by a shot. Cody dove through the open door and landed flat on his belly on the wooden floor.

The afterglow from the intruder's shot still lingered, outlining the shooter's silhouette clearly. The man crouched behind the wooden counter with only his head and shoulders showing.

Cody snapped off two quick shots aimed just below the

intruder's fading form. He heard his heavy .44 slugs tear through the thin wood of the counter and heard the familiar slapping sound when the slugs struck man.

A loud grunt, followed by the sound of a body hitting the floor told Cody his bullets found their mark. He cautiously climbed to his knees and then to his feet, all the time watching and listening for any movement from the direction of the counter.

"Come on in, Ed," he called. "I think I got him. Where's a lamp or lantern?"

"The lamp's right over here. I'll light it."

Cody kept his gaze fixed in the direction of the counter while Ed lit the lamp. Light filled the large room with a dull glow. Cody peered over the counter. A man lay on his stomach in a growing puddle of blood. He didn't move and appeared to be dead.

Ed Hamilton approached cautiously carrying the lamp. Cody walked around the end of the counter and turned the man over onto his back.

"It's Harvey Jessup," the storekeeper said. "He's the no-good husband of Juliana's childhood friend, Mary Ann. I ain't surprised. He's been a thief for years. Looks like his thieving days are over."

"I reckon I better go tell his wife what happened," Cody said

"I'll go with you."

As Cody and Hamilton were leaving the store the undertaker hurried up.

"Got another customer, O. J.," Hamilton told him. "He's inside. It's Harvey Jessup. Me and the marshal are on our way to tell his wife what happened."

"So Jessup finally got caught, eh? I doubt there'll be much grieving on his account."

"Reckon you're right about that," Ed said.

* * *

The Jessup place looked dark when Cody and Ed Hamilton rode up. They dismounted and walked through the cluttered yard to the front of the house. Ed knocked on the door. He repeated his knock twice before a lamp lit up the inside.

A young woman opened the door a crack with the lamp in her hand and peered out.

"Who is it?" she asked in a weak voice.

"It's Ed Hamilton from the store and the town marshal. We need to talk with you. Could we come in?"

"What's wrong?" she asked, opening the door wider and stepping aside.

Hamilton and Cody climbed the rickety steps and stepped inside. The place looked like a pigsty. What little furniture occupied the room was broken and looked like salvage from the town dump.

Cody took one look at the woman and cut a glance at Hamilton. The storekeeper shook his head sadly.

Mary Ann Jessup had been beaten to a pulp. Her lip was cut and swollen and one of her eyes was black and blue, swollen shut. The thin gown she wore barely covered her body. Dark bruises on her arm showed plainly even in the dim light.

"Did Harvey do that to you?" Hamilton asked.

"He didn't mean to. Is something wrong?" she asked, her voice taking on a frantic tone. "Has something happened to Harvey?"

"I'm afraid so, Mary Ann," the storekeeper told her. "He broke into my store tonight. The marshal caught him and Harvey tried to shoot him. Harvey is dead. I'm sorry."

Mary Ann's eyes went wide. She covered her mouth to stifle a scream. Tears burst from her eyes and her frail body shook with sobs. Ed gathered her in his arms and held her until the weeping subsided. She looked up at him through tear stained eyes.

"What will I do? Where will I go? How can I survive without Harvey?"

"Why don't you get the children up and let us take you to Miss Molly's until we can work something out?" Ed suggested.

The next day Juliana spent all morning poring over the books and records she found in her father's desk. She also found a short-barreled Colt in the desk drawer. Juliana was no stranger to weapons. According to Rafael, the aged Mexican who had taught her to shoot, she could outshoot half the hands on their ranch. She checked to see if the gun was loaded. It was. She replaced it in the middle desk drawer.

She soon discovered that the Higgins Ranch encompassed six thousand acres. According to the figures she found, their cattle herds added up to something over three thousand head.

In her searching she also found the combination to the large safe that set in the corner of the den. It took several tries, but the handle finally turned and the heavy door swung open. Inside she found a stack of official looking papers and a metal box. Inside the box lay two large bundles of money, lots of money.

Juliana sent one of the young Mexican boys who did odd jobs around the ranch to find Roy, the ranch foreman, and tell him she wanted to see him. Within minutes the foreman entered the den.

"You wanted to see me?" he asked, pausing at the door with hat in hand.

"Yes, come in and have a seat."

"I'm real sorry about your pa, Miss Juliana," he said as he folded into a chair in front of the desk.

"Thank you, Roy. How long have you been with us here on the ranch?"

"About fifteen years, I reckon. Went to work for your pa when I was still wet behind the ears. He took me in and gave me a job when I didn't know beans about ranching. The ranch has been my home most of my life. Never worked nowhere else. Never wanted to."

"Roy, I know my father sent you to Denver under the pretext of buying a breeding bull. But it's not really what you really went for, was it?"

He dropped his head and stared at his boots for a long moment before answering.

"No, ma'am, it wasn't."

"What was the real reason you went?"

Roy Stamps raised his face toward the ceiling and took a deep breath. He circled the hat in his hand between his thumb and fingers. He let his breath out in a long sigh. "He told me to hire twenty gun hands."

"Did he tell you why?"

"No, ma'am, not exactly, not until I got back."

"Did you ask him?"

"Yes, ma'am. But he got real upset and threatened to fire me and get somebody else to do what he wanted done. Like I tried to tell him, I'd worked for him fifteen years and never once questioned what he told me to do, but what I figured he had in mind wasn't right. I'd never seen him like that before."

Juliana nodded her head in agreement. "I know. I think losing Trace was more than he could deal with. He wasn't himself those last few weeks. One more question. Why didn't you go with them when they raided Trinidad?"

"I finally got enough sand in my craw to tell Mr. Higgins that what him and the others were fixin' to do was wrong and I didn't want no part in it. He got madder than a wet hen and told me he would deal with me when he got back. I've already got my gear packed. I figured it's why you wanted to see me. If you don't want me to stay I'll move on."

"Nonsense. I want you to stay. I can't run this ranch without you. What does my father pay you?"

"Seventy-five a month, but it ain't about money. This is my home. Has been more'n half my life."

"You'll always have a job here as long as I have anything to say about it. As of now you'll be drawing a hundred a month."

Roy's eyes saucered wide. "I'm much obliged, Miss Juliana."

"How many do we have working for us on the ranch?"

"We got twenty-four cowboys, not counting the Mexican workers who take care of the house and stuff like that. As you know, some of our hand's been with us a long time. We got a real good crew, Miss Juliana. I hope we can keep them on, too. A few of them's got families who live in the shacks down by the river."

"Yes, I know. I haven't been down there since I returned from Denver. I want to ride down tomorrow. What do we pay our ranch hands?"

"Same as always, forty a month and found."

"I'm raising their wages to fifty a month starting today. How many cattle does the ranch have?"

"In the neighborhood of three thousand, give or take a few. That number will go up when the spring calf crop comes in. Right now, they're spread out in valleys all over the ranch. We need to start gathering them in closer before hard winter sets in."

"How much land do we actually own?"

"Last I talked to Mr. Higgins about it he owned six thousand acres, but he's got a lease arrangement with the Mountain Ute Indians for grazing rights to almost twenty thousand acres. Him and their chief, an Indian named Tusabe, signed it a year or so ago."

"I see. Tell me, Roy, if this were your ranch, what would you do that we aren't doing?"

"Hmm, hard question. When I was in Denver I heard the market for beef was strong. The cattle brokers are paying forty-five dollars a head delivered in Denver. We've been selling our cattle mostly to the mining camps scattered all over this part of Colorado, but we don't get but twenty a head for 'em.

"I think you'd be smart to try to buy some cattle from some of the small outfits scattered around that don't want to winter them. We got more grazing land then we need for our herds. I figure we could get them pretty cheap. Then come spring, I'd drive a herd of the older ones to the Denver market."

"Could we do it with the hands we have now?"

"We could get by with hiring a few more."

Juliana thought on Roy's suggestion for a few minutes. "I'll let you know in a day or two. Would that be soon enough?"

"Yes, ma'am. I'm gonna have some of the boys start gathering our stock and moving them in closer so we can keep an eye on 'em during the winter."

"Good. Anything else?"

"Not that I can think of."

Juliana stood up and stuck out her hand. "Thank you for coming, Roy. If you ever need to talk to me about anything I'll always be willing to listen."

"Obliged, ma'am," the foreman said, standing and leaving the room.

Juliana pored over the records the rest of the day and far into the night. Lamps had been extinguished long ago and still Juliana worked, absorbing the many legal documents and endless columns of figures.

The big grandfather clock in the hallway just struck two o'clock when the sound of a door opening reached her hearing. *Who could that be?* She lookied up from the documents in front of her with curiosity. *Who would be up at this time of night?*

Her answer came when a complete stranger opened the door of the den and stepped inside. The side of his wool coat was blood-soaked and his left arm hung slack. He had been shot. He clutched a gun in his right fist.

"Who are you?" Juliana demanded. "What do you want?"

As he staggered toward the desk she suddenly recognized him as one of the men she had seen around the campfire the night before the raid on Trinidad. He was one of her father's hired killers. She remembered Ed Hamilton saying one had escaped. This had to be the one.

"I want my money. That's what I want. Higgins promised us five hundred apiece. I want it. All of it!"

"I don't know what you're talking about. Get out of my house!"

She saw the man's gaze cut toward the open door of the safe in the corner. "Maybe I'll just kill you and help myself," he slurred, starting toward the safe. His right hand with the gun in it clutched his left shoulder.

"One shot and every man on the ranch will be in here in half a minute," Juliana threatened.

The evil-eyed outlaw stopped in his tracks, obviously thinking about what she said and replaced his gun in the holster. He withdrew a long hunting knife from a belt scabbard and turned toward Juliana. Lamplight reflected from the wide blade and flashed across the room as he stalked toward her.

Suddenly it dawned on her. He was going to kill her. She gasped. Her heart pounded as she looked frantically around for a way to escape. Her mind raced, searching for an answer. *I have to do something, but what? Should I scream? Should I try to run?*

Don't miss Longhorn: Book III of the Cordell Dyasty, in the exciting Longhorn series. Coming soon.

About the Author

I was born and raised in eastern Oklahoma—formerly known as the Indian Territory. My home was only a half-day's ride by horseback from old historic Fort Smith, Arkansas, home of Judge Isaac C. Parker, who became famous as "The Hanging Judge."

As a young boy I rode the same trails once ridden by the likes of the James, Younger, and Dalton gangs. The infamous "Bandit Queen," Belle Starr's home and grave were only thirty miles from my own home. I grew up listening to stories of lawmen and outlaws.

For as long as I can remember I love to read, and the more I read the more I wanted to write. Hundreds of poems, songs, and short stories only partially satisfied my love of writing. Dozens of stories of the Old West gathered dust on the shelves of my mind. When I retired I began to take down those stories, dust them off, and do what I had dreamed of doing ever since I was a small boy—writing historical western novels.

Dusty Rhodes loves to hear from his many fans.